THE SKRAYLING TREE

MICHAEL MOORCOCK

THE SKRAYLING TREE

THE ALBINO IN AMERICA

ASPECT®

WARNER BOOKS

An AOL Time Warner Company

Aspect® name and logo are registered trademarks of Warner Books, Inc.

Warner Books, Inc., 1271 Avenue of the Americas, New York, NY 10020
Visit our Web site at www.twbookmark.com.

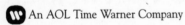 An AOL Time Warner Company

Printed in the United States of America
First Printing: February 2003
10 9 8 7 6 5 4 3 2 1

Library of Congress Cataloging-in-Publication Data
Moorcock, Michael.
    The skrayling tree / Michael Moorcock.
        p. cm.—(Eternal champion series)
    ISBN 0-446-53104-9
    1. Elric of Melnibonâ (Fictitious character)—Fiction. 2. Albinos and albinism—Fiction. 3. Swordsmen—Fiction. I. Title.

PR6063.O59 S58 2003
823'.914—dc21   2002027247

Book design by H. Roberts Design

For Jewell Hodges and them Gibsons
with great respect

Thanks, too, as always to Linda Steele for her
good taste and patience

Prologue

Nine by nine and three by three,
We shall seek the Skraeling Tree.

WHELDRAKE,
"A Border Tragedy"

The following statement was pinned to a later part of this manuscript. The editor thought it better placed here, since it purports to be at least a partial explanation of the motives of our mysterious dream travelers. Only the first part of this book is written in a different, rather idiosyncratic hand. The remaining parts of the story are mostly in the handwriting of Count Ulric von Bek. The note in his hand demanding that the manuscript not be published until after his death is authentic.

More than one school of magistic philosophy insists that our world is the creation of human yearning. By the power of our desires alone, we may bring into being whole universes, entire cosmologies, and supernatural pantheons. Many believe we dream ourselves into existence and then dream our own gods and demons, heroes and villains. Each dream, if powerful enough, can produce still another version of reality in the constantly growing organism that is the multiverse. They believe that just as we dream creatively, we also dream destructively. Some of us have the skills and courage to come and go in the dreams of others, even create our own dreams within the host dream. This was the accepted wisdom in Melniboné, where I was born.

In Melniboné we were trained to enter dreams in which we lived whole and very long lives, gaining the experience such realities brought. I had lived over two thousand years before I reached the age of twenty-

five. It was a form of longevity I would wish upon only a handful of enemies. We pay a price for a certain kind of wisdom which brings the power to manipulate the elements.

If you were lucky, as I was, you did not remember much of these dreams. You drove them from your mind with ruthless deliberation. But the experience of them remained in your blood, was never lost. It could be called upon in the creation of strong sorcery. Our nature dictates that we forget most of what we dream, but some of the adventures I experienced with my distant relative Count Ulric von Bek enabled me to record a certain history which intertwined with his. What you read now, I shall likely forget soon.

These dreams form a kind of apocrypha to my main myth. In one life I was unaware of my destiny, resisting it, hating it. In another I worked to fulfill that destiny, all too aware of my fate. But only in this dream am I wholly conscious of my destiny. And when I have left the dream, it will fade, becoming little more than a half-remembered whisper, a fleeting image. Only the power will stay with me, come what may.

Elric Sadric's son, last Emperor of Melniboné

Should you ask me, whence these stories?
Whence these legends and traditions,
With the odors of the forest,
With the dew and damp of meadows,
With the curling smoke of wigwams,
With the rushing of great rivers,
With their frequent repetitions
And their wild reverberations,
As of thunder in the mountains?
I should answer, I should tell you,
"From the forests and the prairies,
From the great lakes of the Northland,
From the land of the Ojibways
From the land of the Dacotahs,
From the mountains, moors, and fen-lands
Where the heron, the Shuh-shuh-gah,
Feeds among the reeds and rushes.
I repeat them as I heard them
From the lips of Nawadaha,
The musician, the sweet singer."

LONGFELLOW, "The Song of Hiawatha"

THE FIRST BRANCH
OONA'S STORY

Nine Black Giants guard the Skraelings' Tree,
Three to the South and to the East are Three,
Three more the Westward side will shield,
But the North to a White Serpent she will yield;
For he is the dragon who deeply sleeps
Yet wakes upon the hour to weep,
And when he weeps fierce tears of fire,
They form a fateful funeral pyre
And only a singer with lute or lyre,
Shall turn the tide of his dark desire.

WHELDRAKE, "The Skraeling Tree"

CHAPTER ONE

The House on the Island

Hearing I ask from the Holy Races,
From Heimdall's sons, both high and low;
Thou wilt know, Valfather, how well I relate
Old tales I remember of men long ago.

I remember yet the giants of yore,
Who gave me bread in the days gone by;
Nine worlds I knew, the nine in the tree
With mighty roots beneath the mold.

THE POETIC EDDA,
"The Wise Woman's Prophecy"

 am Oona, the shape-taker, Grafin von Bek, daughter of Oon the Dreamthief and Elric, Sorcerer Emperor of Melniboné. When my husband was kidnapped by Kakatanawa warriors, in pursuit of him I descended into the maelstrom and discovered an impossible America. This is that story.

With the Second World War over at last and peace of sorts returned to Europe, I closed our family cottage on the edge of the Grey Fees, and settled in Kensington, West London, with my husband Ulric, Count Bek. Although I am an expert archer and trained mistress of illusory arts, I had no wish to follow my mother's calling. For a year or two in the late 1940s I lacked a focus for my skills until I found a vocation in my husband's sphere. The unity of shared terror and grief following the Nazi defeat gave

7

us all the strength we needed to rebuild, to rediscover our ideal-
ism and try to ensure that we would never again slide into aggressive bigotry and authoritarianism.

Knowing that every action taken in one realm of the multiverse is echoed in the others, we devoted ourselves confidently to
the UN and the implementation of the Universal Declaration of
Human Rights which H. G. Wells had drafted, in direct reference
to Paine and the U.S. Founding Fathers, just before the War. The
U.S.A.'s own Eleanor Roosevelt had helped the momentum. Our
hope was that we could spread the values of liberal humanism and
popular government across a world yearning for peace. Needless
to say, our task was not proving an easy one. As the Greeks and
Iroquois, who fathered those ideas, discovered, there is always
more immediate profit to be gained from crisis than from tranquillity.

By September 1951, Ulric and I had both been working too
hard, and because I traveled so much in my job, we had chosen to
educate our children at boarding school in England. Michael Hall
in rural Sussex was a wonderful school, run on the Steiner Wal-
dorf system, but I still felt a certain guilt about being absent so
often. In previous months Ulric had been sleeping badly, his
dreams troubled by what he sometimes called "the intervention,"
when Elric's soul, permanently bonded to his, experienced some
appalling stress. For this reason, among others, we were enjoying
a long break at the Frank Lloyd Wright–designed summer house
of Nova Scotian friends currently working in Trinidad. They were
employed by the West Indies Independence Commission. When
they returned to Cap Breton we would then leave their airy home
to visit some of Ulric's relatives in New England before taking the
Queen Elizabeth back to Southampton.

We had the loveliest weather. There was already a strong hint
of autumn in the coastal breezes and a distinct chill to the water
we shared with the seals, who had established a small colony on
one of the many wooded islands of the Sound. These islands were
permanently fascinating. The comings and goings of the wildlife
provided just the right relaxation after a busy year. While Ulric

and I enjoyed our work, it involved a great deal of diplomacy, and sometimes our faces ached from smiling! Now we could laze, read, frown if we felt like it and stop to enjoy some of nature's most exquisite scenery.

We were thoroughly relaxed by the second Saturday after we arrived. Brought by the local taxi from Englishtown, we had become wonderfully isolated, with no car and no public transport. I must admit I was so used to activity that after a few days I was a trifle bored, but I refused to become busy. I continued to take a keen interest in the local wildlife and history.

That Saturday we were sitting on the widow's walk of our roof, looking out over Cabot Creek and its many small, wooded islands. One of these, little more than a rock, was submerged at high tide. There, it was said, the local Kakatanawa Indians had staked enemies to drown.

Our binoculars were Russian and of excellent quality, bought on our final visit to Ulric's ancestral estate in the days before the Berlin Wall went up. That afternoon I was able to spot clear details of the individual seals. They were always either there or about to appear, and I had fallen in love with their joyous souls. But, as I watched the tide wash over Drowning Rock, the water suddenly became agitated and erratic. I felt some vague alarm.

The swirl of the sea had a new quality I couldn't identify. There was even a different note to a light wind from the west. I mentioned it to Ulric. Half asleep, enjoying his brandy and soda, he smiled. It was the action of Auld Strom, the avenging hag, he said. Hadn't I read the guide? The Old Woman was the local English name for the unpredictable bore, a twisting, vicious current which ran between the dozens of little islands in the Sound and could sometimes turn into a dangerous whirlpool. The French called her Le Chaudron Noir, the black cauldron. Small whaling ships had been dragged down in the nineteenth century, and only a year or two before three vacationing schoolgirls in a canoe had disappeared into the maelstrom. Neither they nor their canoe had ever been recovered.

A harder gust of wind brushed against my left cheek. The

surrounding trees whispered and bustled like excited nuns. Then they were still again.

"It's probably unwise to take a dip tomorrow." Ulric cast thoughtful eyes over the water. He sometimes seemed, like so many survivors of those times, profoundly sad. His high-boned, tapering face was as thrillingly handsome as when I had first seen it, all those years ago in the grounds of his house during the early Nazi years. Knowing I had planned some activity for the next day he smiled at me. "Though sailing won't be a problem, if we go the other way. We'd have to be right out there, almost at the horizon, to be in real danger. See?" He pointed, and I focused on the distant water which was dark, veined like living marble and swirling rapidly. "The Old Woman is definitely back in full fury!" He put his arm around my shoulders. As always I was amused and comforted by this gesture.

I had already studied the Kakatanawa legend. Le Chaudron was for them the spirit of all the old women who had ever been murdered by their enemies. Most Kakatanawa had been driven from their original New York homeland by the Haudenosaunee, a people famous for their arrogance, puritanism and efficient organization, whose women not only determined which wars would be fought and who would lead them, but which prisoners would live and who would be tortured and eaten. So Auld Strom was a righteously angry creature, especially hard on females. The Kakatanawa called the conquering Haudenosaunee 'Erekoseh', their word for rattlesnake, and avoided the warriors as conscientiously as they did their namesakes, for the Erekoseh, or Iroquois as the French rendered their name, had been the Normans of North America, masters of a superb new idea, an effective social engine, as pious and self-demanding in spirit as they were savage in war. Like the vital Romans and Normans, they respected the law above their own immediate interests. Normans employed sophisticated feudalism as their engine; the Iroquois, a shade more egalitarian, employed the notion of mutuality and common law but were just as ruthless in establishing it. I felt very close to the past that day as I romantically scanned the shore, fancying I glimpsed one of those legendary warriors, with his shaven head, scalp lock, war paint and breechclout, but of course there was no one.

I was about to put the glasses away when I caught a movement and a spot of color on one of the near islands among the thick clusters of birch, oak and pine which found unlikely purchase in what soil there was. A little mist clung to the afternoon water, and for a moment my vision was obscured. Expecting to glimpse a deer or perhaps a fisherman, I brought the island into focus and was very surprised. In my lens was an oak-timbered wattle-and-daub manor house similar to those I had seen in Iceland, the design dating back to the eleventh century. Surely this house had to be the nostalgic folly of some very early settler? There were legends of Viking exploration here, but the many-windowed house was not quite that ancient! Wisteria and ivy showed how many years the two-storied house had stood with its black beams rooted among old trees and thick moss, yet the place had a well-kept but abandoned look, as if its owner rarely lived there. I asked Ulric his opinion. He frowned as he raised the binoculars. "I don't think it's in the guide." He adjusted the lens. "My God! You're right. An old manor! Great heavens!"

We were both intrigued. "I wonder if it was ever an inn or hotel?" Ulric, like me, was now more alert. His lean, muscular body sprang from its chair. I loved him in this mood, when he consciously jolted himself out of his natural reserve. "It's not too late yet for a quick preliminary exploration!" he said. "And it's close enough to be safe. Want to look at it? It'll only take an hour to go there and back in the canoe."

Exploring an old house was just enough adventure for my mood. I wanted to go now, while Ulric was in the same state of mind. Thus, we were soon paddling out from the little jetty, finding it surprisingly easy going against the fast-running tide. We both knew canoes and worked well in unison, driving rapidly towards the mysterious island. Of course, for the children's sake, we would take no risks if the pull of Le Chaudron became stronger.

Though it was very difficult to see from the shore through the

thick trees, I was surprised we had not noticed the house earlier.
Our friends had said nothing about an old building. In those days
the heritage industry was in its infancy, so it was possible the local
guides had failed to mention it, especially if the house was still pri-
vately owned. However, I did wonder if we might be trespassing.

To be safe we had to avoid the pull of the maelstrom at all
costs, so we paddled to the west before we headed directly for the
island, where the gentle tug actually aided our progress. Typically
rocky, the island offered no obvious place to land. We were both
still capable of getting under the earthy tree roots and hauling
ourselves and canoe up bodily, but it seemed an unnecessary ex-
ercise, especially when we rounded the island and found a perfect
sloping slab of rock rising out of the sea like a slipway. Beside it
was a few feet of shingle.

We beached easily enough on the weedy strip of pebbles, then
tramped up the slab. At last we saw the white sides and stained
black oak beams of the house through the autumn greenery. The
manor was equally well kept at the back, but we still saw no evidence of occupation. Something about the place reminded me of
Bek when I had first seen it, neatly maintained but organic.

This place had no whiff of preservation about it. This was a
warm, living building whose moss and ivy threatened the walls
themselves. The windows were not glass but woven willow lattice.
It could have been there for centuries. The only strange thing was
that the wild wood went almost up to its walls. There was no sign
of surrounding cultivation—no hedges, fences, lawns, herb gardens, no topiary or flower beds. The tangled old bracken stopped
less than an inch from the walls and windows and made it hard
going as our tweeds caught on brambles and dense shrubbery. For
all its substance, the house gave the impression of not quite be-
longing here. That, coupled with the age of the architecture,
began to alert me that we might be dealing with some supernatural agency. I put this to my husband, whose aquiline features
were unusually troubled.

As if realizing the impression he gave, Ulric's handsome
mouth curved in a broad, dismissive smile. Just as I took the mag-

ical as my norm, he took the natural as his. He could not imagine what I meant. In spite of all his experience he retained his skepticism of the supernatural. Admittedly, I was inclined to come up with explanations considered bizarre by most of our friends, so I dropped the subject.

As we advanced through the sweet, rooty mold and leafy undergrowth I had no sense that the place was sinister. Nonetheless, I tended to go a little more cautiously than Ulric. He pushed on until he had brought us to the green-painted back door under a slate porch. As he raised his fist to knock I noticed a movement in the open upper window. I was sure I glimpsed a human figure.

When I pointed to the window, we saw nothing.

"Probably a bird flying over," said Ulric. Getting no response from the house, we made our way around the walls until we reached the big double doors at the front. They were oak and heavy with iron. Ulric grinned at me. "Since we are, after all, neighbors"—he took a piece of ivory pasteboard from his waistcoat—"the least we can do is leave our card." He pulled the old-fashioned bell-cord. A perfectly normal bell sounded within. We waited, but there was no answer. Ulric scribbled a note, stuck the card into the bell-pull, and we stepped back. Then, behind the looser weaving of the downstairs window, a face appeared, staring into mine. The shock staggered me. For a moment I thought I looked into my own reflection! Was there glass behind the lattice?

But it was not me. It was a youth. A youth who mouthed urgently through the gaps in the weaving and gestured as if for help, flapping his arms against the window. I could only think of a trapped bird beating its wings against a cage.

I am no dreamthief. I can't equate the craft with my own conscience, though I judge none who fairly practice it. Consequently I have never had the doubtful pleasure of encountering myself in another's dream. This had some of that reported frisson. The youth glared not at me but at my husband, who gasped as one bright ruby eye met another. At that moment, I could tell, blood spoke to blood.

Then it was as if a hand had gripped my hair and pulled it.

Another hand slapped against my face. From nowhere the wind had begun to blow, cold and hard. Beginning as a deep soughing, its note now rose to an aggressive howl.

I thought the young albino said something in German. He was gesticulating to emphasize his words. But the wind kept taking them away. I could make out only one repeated sound. "Werner" was it? A name? The youth looked as if he had stepped from the European Dark Ages. His unstirring white hair fell in long braids. He wore a simple deerskin jacket, and his face was smeared with what might have been white clay. His eyes were desperate.

The wind yelped and danced around us, bending the trees, turning the ferns into angry goblins. Ulric instinctively put his arm around me, and we began to back towards the shore. His hand felt cold. He was genuinely frightened.

The wind appeared to be pursuing us. Everywhere the foliage bent and twisted, this way and that. It was as if we were somehow in the middle of a tornado. Branches opened and closed; leaves were torn into ragged clouds. But our attention remained on the face at the window.

"What is it?" I asked. "Do you recognize the boy?"

"I don't know." He spoke oddly, distantly. "I don't know. I thought my brother—but he's too young, and besides . . ."

All his brothers had died in the First War. Like me, he had noticed a strong family resemblance. I felt him shake. Then he took charge of his emotions. Although he had extraordinary self-control, he was terrified of something, perhaps even of himself. A cloud passed across the sinking sun.

"What is he saying, Ulric?"

" 'Foorna'? I don't know the word." He gasped out a few more sentences, a nonsensical rationale about the fading light playing tricks, and pulled me rather roughly into the bracken and back through the woods until we arrived at the shore where we had drawn up our canoe. The wild wind was bringing in clouds from all directions, funneling towards us in a black mass. I felt a spot of rain on my face. The wind whipped the turning tide already beginning to cover the tiny beach. We were lucky to have returned early. Ulric almost hurled me into the canoe as we pushed off and took up our paddles, forcing the canoe into the darkness. But Auld Strom had grown stronger and kept forcing us back towards the shore. The wind seemed sentient, deliberately making our work harder, seeming to blow first from one side then another. It was unnatural. Instinctively, I hated it.

What irresponsible idiots we had been! I could think of nothing but my children. The salt water splashed cold on my skin. My paddle struck weed, and there was a sudden stink. I looked over my shoulder. The woods seemed unaffected by the wind but were full of ghostly movement, shadows elongated by the setting sun and hazy air pursuing us like giants advancing through the trees. Were they hunting the young man who was even now running down the long slab of rock and into the water, his braided milky hair bouncing on his shoulders as he tried to reach us?

With a grunt and a heavy splash Ulric gouged his paddle into the water and broke the defenses of that erratic tide. The canoe moved forward at last. The wind lashed our faces and bodies like a cowman's whip, goading us back, but we persevered. Soaked by the spray we gained some distance. Yet still the youth waded towards us, his eyes fixed on Ulric, his hands grasping, as if he feared the pursuing shadows and sought our help. The waves grew wilder by the moment.

"Father!" The birdlike cry blended with the shrieking wind until both resonated to the same note.

"No!" Ulric cried almost in agony as we at last broke the current's grip on us and found deeper water. There was a high sound now, keening around us, and I didn't know if it was the wind, the sea or human pursuers.

I wished I knew what the youth wanted, but Ulric's only thought was to get us to safety. In spite of the wind, the mist was thicker than it had been! The young albino was soon lost in it. We heard a few garbled words, watched white shadows gathering on the shore as the setting sun vanished, and then all was grey. There was a heavy smell of ozone. The keening fell away until the water lapping against the canoe was the loudest sound. I heard Ulric's breath rasp as he drove the paddle into the water like an automaton, and I did what I could to help him. Events on the island had occurred too rapidly. I couldn't absorb them. What had we seen? Who was that albino boy who looked so much like me? He could not be my missing twin. He was younger than I. Why was my husband so frightened? For me or for himself?

The cold, ruthless wind continued to pursue us. I felt like taking my paddle and battering it back. Then the fog rose like a wall against the wind which roared and beat impotently upon this new impediment.

Though I felt safer, I lost my bearings in that sudden fog, but Ulric had a much better sense of the compass. With the wind down, we were soon back at our old mooring. The tide was almost full, so it was easy to step from the canoe to the house's little jetty. With some difficulty we climbed the wooden staircase to the first deck. I felt appallingly tired. I could not believe I was so exhausted from such relatively brief activity, but my husband's fear had impressed me.

"They can't follow us," I said. "They had no boats."

In the bright modern kitchen I began to feel a little better. I whipped up some hot chocolate, mixing the ingredients with obsessive care as I tried to take in what had just happened. Outside, in the darkness, there was nothing to be seen. Ulric still seemed dazed. He went around checking locks and windows, peering through closed curtains into the night, listening to the sound of the lapping tide. I asked him what he knew, and he said, "Nothing. I'm just nervous."

I forced him to sit down and drink his chocolate. "Of what?" I asked.

His sensitive, handsome face was troubled, uncertain. He hesitated, almost as if he were going to cry. I found myself taking him by the hand, sitting next to him, urging him to drink. There were tears in his eyes.

"What are you afraid of, Ulric?"

He attempted to shrug. "Of losing you. Of it all starting again, I suppose. I've had dreams recently. They seemed silly at the time.

But that scene on the island felt as if it had happened before. And there's something about this wind that's come up. I don't like it, Oona. I keep remembering Elric, those nightmarish adventures. I fear for you, fear that something will separate us."

"It would have to be something pretty monumental!" I laughed.

"I sometimes think that life with you has been an exquisite dream, my broken mind compensating for the pain of Nazi tortures. I fear I'll wake up and find myself back in Sachsenhausen. Since I met you I know how hard it is to tell the difference between the dream and the reality. Do you understand that, Oona?"

"Of course. But I know you're not dreaming. After all, I have the dreamthief's skills. If anyone could reassure you, it must surely be me."

He nodded, calming himself, giving my hand a grateful squeeze. He was flooded with adrenaline, I realized. What on earth had we witnessed?

Ulric couldn't tell me. He had not been alarmed until he saw what appeared to be his younger self at the window. Then he had sensed time writhing and slipping and dissipating and escaping from the few slender controls we had over it. "And to lose control of time—to let Chaos back into the world—means that I lose you, perhaps the children, everything I have here with you that I value."

I reminded him that I was still very much with him, and in the morning we could stroll the few miles down to Englishtown, call Michael Hall and speak to our beloved children, who were happily going about their schooling. "We can make sure they're well. If you still feel uneasy, we can leave for Rochester and stay with your cousin." Dick von Bek worked for the Eastman Company. We had his permanent invitation.

Again he made an effort to control his fear and was soon almost his old self.

I remarked on the distorted shadows we had seen, like elongated mist giants. Yet the youth's outline had remained perfectly clear at all times, as if only he were in full focus! "The effects of fog, like those of the desert, are often surprising."

"I'm not sure it was the fog . . ." He took another deep breath.

That distortion of perspective was one of the things that had disturbed him, he told me. It brought back all the worlds of dreams, of magic. He remembered the threat, which we must still fear, from his cousin Gaynor.

"But Gaynor's essence was dissipated," I said. "He was broken into a million different fragments, a million distant incarnations."

"No," said Ulric, "I do not think that is true any longer. The Gaynor we fought was somehow not the only Gaynor. My sense is that Gaynor is restored. He has altered his strategy. He no longer works directly. It is almost as if he is lurking in our distant past. It isn't a pleasant feeling. I dream constantly that he's sneaking up on us from behind." His weak laughter was uncharacteristically nervous.

"I have no such sense," I said, "and I am supposed to be the psychic. I promise you I would know if he were anywhere nearby."

"That's part of what I understand in the dream," said Ulric. "He no longer works directly, but through a medium. From some other place."

There was nothing more I could say to reassure him. I, too, knew that the Eternal Predator could hardly be conquered but must forever be held in check by those of us who recognized his disguises and methods. Still I had no smell of Gaynor here. The wind had grown stronger and louder as we talked and now banged around the house tugging at shutters and shrieking down chimneys.

At last I was able to get Ulric to bed and eventually to sleep. Exhausted, I, too, slept in spite of the wailing wind. In the night I was vaguely aware of the wind coming up again and Ulric rising, but I thought he was closing a window.

I awoke close to dawn. The wind was still soughing outside, but I had heard something else. Ulric was not in bed. I assumed that he was still obsessed and would be upstairs, waiting for the light, ready to train his glasses on that old house. But the next sound I heard was louder, more violent, and I was up before I knew it, running downstairs in my pajamas.

The big room was only recently empty.

There had been a struggle. The French doors to the deck were wide open, the stained glass cracked, and Ulric was nowhere to be seen. I dashed out onto the deck. I could see dim shapes down at the water's edge. The ghostly marble bodies were obviously Indians. Perhaps they had covered their bodies with chalk. I knew of such practices among the Lakota ancestor cults but had never witnessed anything of the kind in this region. Their origin, however, was not the most pressing question in my mind as I saw them bundling Ulric into a large birchbark canoe. I could not believe that in the second half of the twentieth century my husband was being kidnapped by Indians!

Calling for them to stop, I ran down to the grey water, but they were already pushing off, the spray causing odd distortions in the air. One of them had taken our canoe. His back rippled as he moved powerful arms. His body gleamed with oil, and the single lock of hair decorated with feathers flowed like a gash down his back. He wore unusual war paint. Could this be one of those old "mourning wars" on which the Indians embarked when too many of their warriors had been killed? But why steal a sedentary white man?

The mist was still thick, distorting their shapes as they disappeared. Once I glimpsed Ulric's eyes, wide with fear for me. They were paddling rapidly directly towards Auld Strom. The wind came up again, whipping the water and swirling the mist into bizarre images. Then they were gone. And the wind went with them, as if in pursuit.

My instincts took over my mind. In the sudden silence I began to quest automatically out and into the water, seeking the sisterly intelligence I could already sense in the depths far from the shore. She became alert as I found her and readily accepted my request to approach. She was interested in me, if not sympathetic. Water flowed into my entire consciousness, became my world as I continued to bargain, borrow, petition, offer all at the same time, and in the space of seconds. Grudgingly, I was allowed to take the shape of the stately old monarch who lay still and wise in the deep water below the tug of the current, receiving obeisance from every one of her tribe within a thousand miles.

The children of the legendary piscine first elemental *Spammer Gain*, the Lost Fishlings of folklore are a community of generous souls to whom altruism is natural, and this lady was one such. Her huge gills moved lazily as she considered my appeal.

It is not my duty to die, I heard her say, *but to remain alive.*

And one lives through action, I said. *Is one alive who does nothing but exist?*

You are impertinent. Come, your youth shall combine with my wisdom and my body. We shall seek this creature you love.

I had been accepted by Fwulette the Salmon Wife. And she knew the danger I meant to face.

Such ancient souls have survived the birth and death of planets. Courage is natural to them. She let me swim with extraordinary speed in pursuit of the canoes. As I had guessed, they were not heading back to the island but directly towards the whirlpool. While I could feel the current tugging me inwards, I was too experienced to fear it. I had gills. This was my element. I had followed thousands of currents for millions of years and knew that only if you fought them could they harm you.

I was soon ahead of the canoes, swimming strongly towards the surface with the intention of capsizing the larger one and rescuing Ulric. I was as long as their vessel and did not anticipate any hindrance as I prepared to leap upwards under them. To my dismay, my straining back met massive and unexpected resistance. The thing was far heavier than it had seemed. I was winded. Already, as I tried to recover from the self-inflicted blow, the canoe's prow began to dip as she was taken down by the pull of the maelstrom. The whole scale appeared to have altered, but I had no choice. I followed the canoe as it was sucked deep into the center of the vortex. My supple body withstood all the stresses and pressures I expected, but the canoe, which should have been breaking up, remained in one piece. The occupants, though gripping hard to the sides, were not flung out. I got one clear view of them. They had the fine, regular features of local forest Indians but were dead white, not albino. Their hair was black against oiled, shaven skulls, hanging in a single thick strand. Their black eyes glared into the heart of the maelstrom, and I realized they were deliberately following it to the core. I had to go with them.

Deeper and deeper we went into the wild rush of white and green while all around me great boulders and pillars of rock rose up, their scale shifting back and forth in the unstable water. This was no ordinary natural phenomenon. I knew at once that I had effectively left one world and entered another. It was becoming impossible to orient myself as the rocks changed size and shape before my eyes, but I did everything in my power to continue my pursuit. Then suddenly the thing was before me, the size of the *Titanic,* and I had been struck a blow directly to the head. I felt myself grow limp. I thrashed my tail to keep my bearings. Then another current was pushing me up towards the surface, even as I fought to dive deeper.

Unable to sustain the descent, I let the current take me back towards shore, exhausted. Fwulette knew we had failed. She seemed sad for me.

"Go with good luck, little sister," she said.

The Salmon Wife returned to her realm, her head slightly sore and, for reasons best known to herself, her humor thoroughly restored.

Fwulette thanked, I called for my own body and returned to the house as fast as I could. We had no telephone, of course. The nearest was miles away. I had no other means of pursuing my husband's abductors, not a single hope of ever seeing him again. I was not the only one whose life had changed totally in the last few hours, but this understanding made my loss no easier. I felt horribly ill as I began looking for my clothes.

Then I saw something I had not noticed in my haste to rescue my husband. Ulric's kidnappers had lost something in the struggle. Presumably I had not seen it earlier because it had fallen down the slats in the stairs and now stood upright against a wall:

a large round thing, with the dimensions of a small trampoline, made from decorated deerhide stretched on wicker and attached to its frame with thongs. It was too big for a shield, though the handles at the back suggested that purpose. I had seen the Indians carrying similar shields but in closer proportions to their bodies. I wondered if it was what was called a dreamcatcher, but it lacked any familiar images. It might even be a holy object or a kind of flag.

Made of white buckskin with eight turquoise stripes radiating from a central hub, at the boss was what appeared to be a thunderbird framed by a tree. The entire thing was painted in vivid blues and reds. Ornamented with scarlet beads around the rim, with more colored beads and porcupine quills throughout the design, it was of superb craftsmanship and had the feel of a treasured possession. Yet its purpose was mysterious.

I left it leaning against the wall while I went upstairs to bathe and get some clothes. When I returned to the main part of the house, the sun was everywhere. I could hardly believe I had not been dreaming. But there was the huge deerskin disk, the cracked glass, and other signs of the fight. Ulric must have heard them come in and delivered himself straight into their hands. There was no note. I had not expected one. This was not an attempt to get ransom.

I was now ready to walk to the filling station. I could do it in under an hour. But I was also reluctant to leave, fearing that if I did so I would miss some important sign or even Ulric's return. It was possible that he could have escaped from his captors after all and been dragged up to the surface as I had been. But I knew this was really a forlorn hope. As I prepared to go, I heard a sound like a car approaching, and then came a knock at the front door. Hoping in spite of all realism, I ran to open it.

The gaunt figure who raised his bowler hat to me was dressed in a neat black overcoat, with black polished shoes and a copy of the local newspaper under his arm. His hard black eyes shifted in the depths of their sockets. His thin, peculiar smile chilled the surrounding air. "Forgive me for coming so early, Countess. I have a message for your husband. Could I, do you think, see him for a moment?"

"Captain Klosterheim!" I was shocked. How had he known where to find me?

He bowed a modest head. "Merely *Herr* Klosterheim, these days, dear lady. I have returned to my civilian calling. I am with the church again, though in a lay capacity. It has taken some time to locate you. My business with your husband is urgent and in his interest, I think."

"You know nothing of the men who were here in the night?"

"I do not understand you, my lady."

I loathed the idea of being further involved with this villain-ous ex-Nazi who had allied himself with Ulric's cousin Gaynor. Was he the supernatural medium Ulric had sensed? I doubted it. His psychic presence was powerful, and I would have detected it before now. On the other hand he might be the only means I had of discovering where they had taken Ulric, so I drew on my pro-fessional courtesy and invited him in.

Entering the big main room he immediately went towards the huge artifact the Indians had left behind. "The Kakatanawa were here?"

"Last night. What do you know?"

Scarcely thinking, I took a double-barreled Purdy's from the cabinet and dropped in two shells. Then I leveled the gun at Klosterheim. He looked around at me in surprise.

"Oh, madam, I mean you no ill!" He clearly believed I was going to blow him apart on the spot.

"You recognize that thing?"

"It's a Kakatanawa medicine shield," he said. "Some of them think it helps protect them when they go into the spirit lands."

"The spirit lands? That's where they have gone?"

"Gone, madam? No, indeed. They mean here. These are their spirit lands. They hold us in considerable awe."

I motioned with the gun for him to sit in one of the deep leather armchairs. He seemed to spill across it. In certain lights he became almost two-dimensional, a black-and-white shadow against the dark hide. "Then where have they gone?"

He looked at the chair as if he had not known such comfort were possible. "Back to their own world, I would guess."

"Why have they taken him?"

"I am not sure. I knew you were in some kind of danger, and I hoped we could exchange information."

"Why should I help you, Herr Klosterheim? Or you help us? You are our enemy. You were Gaynor's creature. I understood you to be dead."

"Only a little, my lady. It is my fate. I have my loyalties, too."

"To whom?"

"To my master."

"Your master was torn apart by the Lords of the Higher Worlds on Morn. I watched it happen."

"Gaynor von Minct was not my master, lady. We were allies, but he was not my superior. That was mere convenience to explain our presence together." He might even have been a little offended by my presumption. "My master is the essence. Gaynor is merely the vapor. My master is the Prince of Darkness, Lord Lucifer."

I would have laughed if I were not in such bizarre circumstances. "So do you come here from Hell? Is that where my husband is to be found—the Underworld?"

"I do come from Hell, my lady, though not directly, and if your husband were already there, I would not be here."

"I am only interested in my husband's whereabouts, sir."

He shrugged and pointed at the Kakatanawa artifact. "That would no doubt help, but they would probably kill you, too."

"They mean to kill my husband?"

"Quite possibly. I was, however, referring to myself. The Kakatanawa have no liking for me or for Gaynor, but Gaynor's interests are no longer mine. Our paths parted. I went forward. He went back. Now I am something of a watcher on the sidelines." His cadaverous features showed a certain humor.

"I am certain you are not here through the promptings of a Christian heart, Herr Klosterheim."

"No, madam. I came to propose an alliance. Have you heard of a hero called Ayanawatta? Longfellow wrote about him. In English 'Hiawatha'? His name was used for a local poem, I believe."

I had, of course, read Longfellow's rather unfashionable but hypnotic work. However, I was scarcely in the mood to discuss creaking classics of American literature. I think I might have gestured with the gun. Klosterheim put up a bony hand.

"I assure you I am in no way being facetious. I see I must put it another way." He hesitated. I knew the dilemma of all prescient creatures, or all those who have been into a future and seen the consequence of some action. Even to speak of the future was to create another "brane," another branch of the great multiversal tree. And that creation in turn could confuse any plans one might have made for oneself to negotiate the worlds. So we were inclined to speak somewhat cryptically of what we knew. Most of our omens were as obscure as the *Guardian* crossword.

"Do you know where Gaynor is?"

"I believe I do, in relation to our present circumstances and his own." He spoke with habitual care.

"Where would that be?"

"He could be where your husband is." An awkward, significant pause.

"So those were Gaynor's men?"

"Far from it, my lady. At least, I assume so." He again fell silent. "I came to propose an alliance. It would be even more valuable to you, I suspect. I can guarantee nothing, of course . . ."

"You expect me to believe one who, by his own confession, serves the Master of Lies?"

"Madam, we have interests in common. You seek your husband and I, as always, seek the Grail."

"We do not own the Holy Grail, Herr Klosterheim. We no longer even own the house it is supposed to reside in. Haven't you noticed that the East is now under Stalin's benign protection? Perhaps that ex-priest has the magic cup?"

"I doubt it, madam. I do believe your husband and the Grail have a peculiar relationship and that if I find him I shall find what I seek. Is that not worth a truce between us?"

"Perhaps. Tell me how I may follow my husband and his abductors."

Klosterheim was reluctant to give away information. He brooded for a moment, then gestured towards the round frame. "That medicine shield should get you there. You can tell by its size it has no business being here. If you were to give it the opportunity to return to where it came from, it might take you with it."

"Why do you tell me that? Why do you not use the shield yourself?"

"Madam, I do not have your skills and talents." His voice was dry, almost mocking. "I am a mere mortal. Not even a demon, madam. Just a creature of the Devil, you know. An indentured soul. I go where I am bid."

"I seem to remember that you had turned against Satan. I gather you found him a disappointment?"

Klosterheim's face clouded. He rose from the chair. "My spiritual life is my own." He stared thoughtfully into the barrels of my shotgun and shrugged. "You have the power to go where I need to go."

"You require a guide? When I have no idea where they have taken Ulric? Less idea than you, apparently."

"I lack your grace." He spoke quietly, though his jaw tightened as if in anger. "Countess, it was your husband's help I sought." Something struggled in him. "But I think it is time for reconciliation."

"With Lucifer?"

"Possibly. I opposed my master as my master opposed his. I scarcely understand this mania for solipsism or how it came about. Once half our lives were spent contemplating God and the nature of evil. Now Satan's domain throughout the multiverse shrinks steadily." He did not sound optimistic.

I thought him completely mad with his weird, twisted pieties. I had made it my business to read old family histories long before I decided to marry Ulric. Half the von Beks, it seemed, had had dealings with the supernatural and denied it or were disbelieved. A manuscript had only recently been found which claimed to be some sort of ancestral record, written in an idiosyncratic hand in old German; but the East German authorities, unfortunately, had claimed it as a state archive, and we had not yet been able to read it. There was a suggestion that its contents were too dangerous to publish. We did know, however, that it had something to do with the Holy Grail and the Devil.

Again he gestured towards the medicine shield. "That will take you to your husband, if he still lives. I don't require a guide. I require a key. I do not travel so easily between the worlds as you. Few do. I have given you all the information I can to help you find Count Ulric. He does not possess what I want, but what I want is in his power to grant me. I hoped he would have the key."

I was losing interest in the conversation. I had decided to see what the Kakatanawa medicine shield could do for me. Perhaps I should have been more cautious, but I was desperate to follow Ulric, ready to believe almost anything in order to find him.

"Key?" I asked impatiently.

"There is another way to reach the world to which he's been taken. A door of some kind. Perhaps on the Isle of Morn."

"How did you think Ulric could help you?"

"I hoped the door through to that world is on Morn and the key to that door would be in your husband's keeping." He seemed deeply disappointed, as if this was the culmination of a long quest which had proven to be useless.

"I can assure you we have no mysterious keys."

"You have the sword," he said, without much hope. "You have the black sword."

"As far as I know," I told him, "that, too, is in the hands of the East German authorities."

He looked up in some dismay. "It's in the East?"

"Unless the Russians now have it."

He frowned. "Then I have bothered you unnecessarily."

"In which case . . ." I gestured with the shotgun.

He nodded agreeably and began walking towards the front door. "I'm obliged to you, madam. I wish you well."

I was still in an appalling daze as I watched him open the door and leave. I followed him and saw that he had come in a taxi. It was the same driver who had brought us from Englishtown. I had a sudden thought, asked him to wait, and went inside. I wrote a hasty note to the children, came out, and asked him to post it for me. As Klosterheim got into his cab, the driver waved cheerfully. He had no sense of the supernatural tensions in the air, nor of the heartbreaking tensions within me, the impossible decision I had to make.

After watching them drive off, I returned to the house and picked up the medicine shield. I had no interest in Klosterheim's ambitions or any conflict he was engaged in. All I cared about was the information he had given me. I was prepared to risk all to let the shield take me to my husband.

Almost in a trance, I carried the thing through a blustering wind that tugged and buffeted at it, down to the jetty. Then I stripped off my outer clothes, threw the shield into the water and gasped as I flung myself after it. Feeling it move under me, I climbed onto it, using it like a raft. The wind wailed and bit at my flesh, but now the shield had a life of its own. It felt as if muscles began to form in the skin as it moved rapidly across the water out towards the island we had visited. I expected it to follow its owner into the maelstrom.

Had the medicine shield come completely alive? Did it have intelligence? Or did it intend to fling me against the rocks? For now it seemed to protect me as the cold water heaved and the cold wind blew.

My fingers dug deep into the edges. Even my toes tried to grip parts of the frame as it bucked and kicked under me.

Then I felt it lift suddenly and move rapidly out to sea, as if it hoped to escape what threatened us. My fingers were in agony, but I would have clung on dead or alive. My will had molded me to that huge woven frame.

All at once it was diving. I had no time to catch my breath, and I no longer had gills. It was going to drown me!

I saw the high jagged pillars of rock coming up towards me, saw massive dark shapes moving in the swirling water. I cursed myself for an irresponsible fool as my lungs began to fail. I felt my grip on the shield weakening, my senses dimming, as I was dragged inexorably downward.

CHAPTER TWO

On the Shores of Gitche Gumee

Nine by nine and seven by seven,
We shall seek the roots of heaven.

WHELDRAKE,
"A Border Tragedy"

uddenly I had burst back out of the water into blinding light. I could see nothing and could hear only the wild keening of a wind. Something icy had me in its grasp. Frozen air wrapped itself around me and effortlessly ripped my hands from the shield. My willpower was useless in the face of such a force. I did all I could to get my grip back, but the wind was relentless. If I had not known it before, I certainly understood it now. This was a sentient wind, a powerful elemental, which clearly directed its wrath specifically at me. I could sense its hatred, its personality. I could almost see a face glaring into mine. I could not imagine how I had offended it or why it should pursue me, but pursue me it did.

There was absolutely no resisting that force. It snatched the shield away and threw me in the other direction. I believe it intended to kill me. I felt myself strike water, and then I had lost consciousness.

I had not expected to awake at all. When I did, I felt a surprising sense of well-being, of safety. I was lying on springy turf, tightly wrapped in some sort of blanket. I could smell the sweet grass and heather. I was warm. I was relaxed. Yet I remained calmly aware of the danger I had escaped and of the urgency of my mission. In contrast to my earlier experience, I now felt completely in control of my body, even though I could barely move a finger! Had I reached the realm where my husband had been taken? Was Ulric near? Was that why I felt safe?

I could see the grey, unstable sky. It was either dawn or twilight. I could not turn my head enough to see a horizon. I moved my eyes. Above me a man's face looked down at me with an expression of stern amusement.

He was a complete stranger, but instinctively I knew I had no reason to fear him. I had found my imagined warrior. The smooth-shaven face was well proportioned, even handsome, and decorated with elaborate tattoos etched across his forehead, cheeks, chin and scalp. His head was mostly shaven, the only piece of hair worn in a long, gleaming black lock interwoven with three bright eagle feathers, but his healthy copper skin told me that he was not one of those who had captured my husband. He wore earrings, and his nose and lower lip were pierced with small sapphires. On his temples, cheeks and chin was a deep scarlet smear of paint. Running down either side of his chest were long, white scars. Between these scars a design had been pricked into his skin. On his well-muscled upper arms were intricately worked bracelets of raw gold, and around his throat he wore a wide band of mother-of-pearl which seemed to be a kind of armor. His tattoos were in vivid reds, greens, blues and yellows and reminded me of those I had once seen displayed by powerful shamans in the South Seas. A nobleman of some sort, confident of his own ability to protect the wealth he displayed with such careless challenge.

He regarded me with equal frankness, his dark eyes full of ironic humor. "Sometimes an angler prays for a catch and gets more than he bargains for." He spoke a language I understood but could not identify. This was a common experience for moonbeam walkers.

"You *caught* me?"

"Apparently. I am rather proud of myself. It was less exhausting than I had expected. I enjoyed the dancing. With the appropriate incantations and trance, I laid out the robe with the head facing the moon and the tail facing the water. I did as I had learned. I invoked the spirits of the wind. I called to the water to give up her treasure. Sure enough there was an agitation in the air. A strong wind blew. Being in a trance, I heard it from a distance. When I at last opened my eyes I found you thus and wrapped you in the robe for your health, your modesty and because the incantation demanded it." He spoke with a sardonic, friendly, slightly self-mocking air.

"I was naked?" Now I recognized the special sensation of soft animal skin against my own. Whatever one's notions about taking a fellow creature's life, that touch is irresistible. While I'd accepted my adopted culture's ways, I had no special concern about being seen undressed. I had far more urgent questions. "But what of the medicine shield?"

He frowned. "The Kakatanawa war-shield? That was yours?"

"What happened to it? I was caught up in a violent wind which seemed to have intelligence. It deliberately separated me from the shield."

The warrior was apologetic. "I believe—you'll recall I was in a trance—I believe that is what I saw spinning away in that direction. A wind demon, perhaps?" He pointed to a thickly wooded hillside some distance away around the lake. "So it was a medicine shield and has been stolen by a demon. Or escaped you both and gone home to its owner?"

"Without me," I said bitterly. I was beginning to realize that this man had, through his magic, somehow saved my life. But had he or the elemental diverted me from following Ulric? "That shield was all that linked me with my husband. He could be anywhere in the multiverse."

"You are of the Kakatanawa? Forgive me; I knew they had adopted one of you in their number, but not two." He was obviously puzzled, but some sort of understanding was dawning, also.

"I am not a Kakatanawa." I was no longer quite so thoroughly in control of my emotions. A note of desperation must have come into my voice. "But I seek the shield's owner."

He responded like a gentleman. He seemed to understand the

supernatural conditions involved and lowered his head in thought.

"Where is its owner? Do you know?" I began to struggle in the soft robe. With a word of apology, that elegant woodsman knelt down and untied rawhide knots.

"No doubt with the other Kakatanawa," he said. "But that is where I am going, so it's reassuring for me. I do not know how they will receive me. It is my destiny to carry my wisdom to them. The fates begin the weaving long before we understand the design. We will go together as our mutual fate demands. We will be stronger together. We will achieve our different goals and thus bring all to resolution."

I didn't understand him. I stood up, wrapping myself in the robe. It was wonderfully supple, the skin of a white buffalo, decorated with various religious symbols. I looked around me. It was just after dawn, and the sun was making the wide, still water shine like a mirror. "If you told me your name, your calling and your purpose with me, I would be at less of a disadvantage."

He smiled apologetically and began busying himself with his camp. Behind him was the rising sun, now clearing the furthest peaks of a massive mountain range, its orange light pouring across forest and meadow, touching the small, undecorated lodge erected on the grassy lakeside. From the wigwam came a wisp of grey smoke. It was a hunter's economical kit. The lodge's coverings could be used as robes against the cold, and the poles could function as a travois to carry everything else. A hunting dog could also be used to pull the travois, but I saw no evidence of dogs. The shadows were dissipating, and the light was already growing less vivid as the sun climbed into a clearing sky.

My host seemed in very high spirits. He was a charming man. Nothing about him was threatening, though he radiated a powerful personality and physical strength. I wondered if his tattoos and piercings marked him as a shaman or sachem. He was clearly accustomed to authority.

I was obviously no longer on the Nova Scotian coast, but the surrounding world did not look very different from the landscapes

I had just left. Indeed, it was vaguely familiar. Perhaps it was Lake Superior?

Pulled up on the grassy bank of our natural meadow was a large, exquisitely fashioned canoe of glittering silver birchbark, its copper-wound edges finished in exquisite wooden inlays painted with spiritual symbols. There was no sign of another human being in the whole of creation. It was like the dawn of the world, a truly virgin America. The season was still early autumn with a hint of winter in the freshening breeze. The breeze did not overly alarm me. I asked him which lake this was.

"I was born not far from here. It is commonly called Gitche Gumee," he said. "You know the Longfellow poem?"

"I understood Longfellow mangled half a dozen languages in the process and got all the names wrong." I spoke, as one some-times does, in a kind of cultural apology, but I was also remembering something Klosterheim had said. I was fairly certain this man was not just a modern romantic adopting a favorite role in the wilderness. I doubted, if I looked further, I would find a station wagon nearby!

This man was wholly authentic. He smiled at my remark. "Oh, there's nothing wrong with what Longfellow included. The rituals remain in spite of the flourishes. Nobody ever asked the women their story, so their rituals remain secret, undistorted. There are many roads to the spirit's resolution with the flesh. It is with what old Longfellow excluded and what he added that I have my quarrel. But it is my destiny to bring light to my own story. And that is the destiny which I dreamed in that journey. I must restore the myth and address the great Matter of America." He seemed embarrassed by his own seriousness and smiled again. "As if I'd hand over the spiritual leadership of the Nations to a bunch of half-educated Catholic missionaries! There is no trinity without White Buffalo Woman. So it is a triptych missing a panel. That ludicrous stuff Longfellow put in at the end was a sop to drawing-room punctilio and worse than the sentimental ending Dickens tacked on to *Bleak House*. Or was it *Great Expectations*?"

"I've never been able to get into Dickens," I said.

"Well," he replied, "I don't have much opportunity myself." He frowned slightly and looked up at me. "I don't want to take credit for more than is right. While it is my destiny to unite the Nations, I might fail where an alter ego might have succeeded. One wrong step, and I change everything. You know how difficult it is." He fell into frowning thought.

"You had better introduce yourself, sir," I said, half anticipating his answer.

He apologized. "I am Ayanawatta, whom Longfellow preferred to call 'Hiawatha.' My mother was a Mohawk and my father was a Huron. I discovered my story in the poem when I made my dream journey into the future. Here. I have something for you . . ." He threw me a long doeskin shirt which was easily slipped on and fit me very well. Was he used to traveling with such things? He laughed aloud and explained that the last man who tried to kill him had been about my size.

He began expertly to dismantle the wigwam. To close down his fire he simply put a lid on the pot he carried it in and secured it with a bit of rawhide. The lodge's contents were folded in the hides and rolled into a tight bundle. The firepot was tied on top. I saw now that the poles were made of long, flint-tipped spears. He laid these along the bottom of the canoe and put the bundle in the middle. He had broken the entire encampment with little evident expenditure of energy.

"You seem very familiar with English literature," I said.

"I owe it a great deal. As I said, through Longfellow's poem I discovered my destiny. I had reached the time of my first true dream-quest. I dreamed a dream in which I saw four feathers. I decided that this meant I must seek four eagles in the places of the four winds. First I went into the wilderness and took the north path called The Eagle, for I thought that was the meaning of the dream. It took me into a land of mountains. It was not a true path. But in leaving that path, I found myself in Boston at the right time. I was looking to see if I had a myth. And if I had a myth I had to find out how to follow it and make it true. Well, you can work out that irony for yourself. I entered a time in the future long after I had died. I learned strange skills. I learned to read in the language of these new people, whose appearance at first astonished me. There were many amiable souls in those parts more than willing to help me, though the self-righteous voices of the bourgeoisie were often raised against my appearance. However, learning to read that way was part of my first real spirit journey. For once I had opened my spirit to the future, I received not just a vision of the founding of the Haudenosaunee, the People of the Same Roof, but I saw what was to follow them, unless I trod a certain path. In order to find the future I desire, I must maintain the immediate future as exactly as possible."

"You weren't offended by Longfellow's acquisition of various native mythologies?"

"Longfellow was genial, lively, kind. And hideously hairy. As a Mohawk I inherited a distaste for male body hair. The Romans were the same, apparently. Yet, for all that, the poet's good nature cut through any prejudice I felt about his appearance. He had an eccentric, springy gait and bounced when he walked. I remember thinking him a bit overdressed for the time of year, but he probably considered me underdressed. I hadn't acquired these." He fingered his tattoos with modest pride.

"I was originally interested in the transcendentalists. Emerson planned to introduce me to Thoreau, but Longfellow dropped into Parker House that day as well. It was by chance that we had occasion to talk. He was not entirely sure that I was real. He was so absorbed in his poem I think he suspected at first he had imagined me! When Emerson introduced us, he probably considered me some sort of noble savage." Ayanawatta laughed softly. "Thoreau, I suspect, found me a little coarse. But Longfellow was good-natured almost to a fault. It was a fated meeting and played an important part in his own journey. I understood his poem to be a prophecy of how I would make my mark in the world. The four feathers I had mistaken for eagle feathers in my dream were, of course, four quill pens. Four writers! I had made the wrong interpretation but taken the right action. That was where the luck really came in. I was a bit callow. It was the first time I had visited the astral realm in physical form. Sadly, that phase of the journey is over. I don't know when I'll see a book again."

Ayanawatta began to roll up his sleeping mat with the habitual neatness and speed of the outdoorsman. "Well, you know we use wampum in these parts, to remind us of our wisdom and our words." He indicated the intricately worked belt which supported his deerskin leggings. "And this stuff is as open to subtle and imaginative interpretation as the Bible, Joyce or the American Constitution. Sometimes our councils are like a gathering of French postmodernists!"

"Can you take me to my husband?" I was beginning to realize that Ayanawatta was one of those men who took pleasure in the abstract and whose monologues could run for hours if not interrupted.

"Is he with the Kakatanawa?"

"I believe so."

"Then I can lead you to them." His voice softened. "I have had no dream to the contrary, at least. Possibly your husband could be or will become the friend of my friend Dawandada, who is also called White Crow." He paused with an expression of apology. "I talk too much and speculate too wildly. One gets used to talking to oneself. I have not had a chance for ordinary human conversation with a reasonably well-educated entity for the last four years. And you, well—you are a blessing. The best dance I ever danced, I must say. I had expected some laconic demigoddess to complete our trio. I wasn't even sure you were going to be human. The dream told me what to do, not what to expect. There is an ill wind rising against us, and I do not know why. I have had confusing dreams."

"Do you always act according to your dreams?" I was intrigued. This was, after all, my own area of expertise.

"Only after due consideration. And if the appropriate dance and song bring the harmony of joined worlds. I was always of a spiritual disposition." He began carefully cleaning one of his beautifully fashioned hardwood paddles, curved in such a way that they were also war-axes. His bow and quiver of arrows were already secured in the canoe. He paused. "White Buffalo Woman, I am on a long spiritual journey which began many years ago in the forests of my adopted home in what you know as upper New York. I am bound to link my destiny with others to achieve a great deed, and I am bound not to speak of that part of my destiny. Yet when that deed is done I will at last possess the wisdom and the power I need to speak to the councils of the Nations and begin the final part of my destiny."

"What of the Kakatanawa? Do they join your councils?"

"They are not our brothers. They have their own councils." He had the air of a man trying to hide his dismay at extraordinary political naivete.

"Why do you call me White Buffalo Woman? And why would I go with you when I seek my husband?"

"Because of the myth. It has to be enacted. It is still not made reality. I think our two stories are now the same. They must be. Otherwise there would be dissonances. Your name was one of several offered in the prophecy. Would you prefer me to call you something else?"

"If I have a choice, you can call me the Countess of Bek," I said. In the language we were using this name came out longer than the one he had employed.

He smiled, accepting this as irony. "I trust, Countess, you will accompany me, if only because together we are most likely to find your husband. Can you use a canoe? We can be across the Shining Water and at the mouth of the Roaring River in a day." Again, he seemed to speak with a certain sardonic humor.

For the second time in twenty-four hours, I found myself afloat. Ayanawatta's canoe was a superb instrument of movement, with an almost sentient quality to its responses. It sometimes seemed hardly to touch the water. As we paddled I asked him how far it was to the Kakatanawa village.

"I would not call it a village exactly. Their longhouse lies some distance to the north and west."

"Why have they abducted my husband? Is there no police authority in their territory?"

"I know little about the Kakatanawa. Their customs are not our customs."

"Who are this mysterious tribe? Demons? Cannibals?"

He laughed with some embarrassment as his paddle rose and fell in the crystal water. It was impossible not to admire his extraordinarily well-modeled body. "I could be maligning them. You know how folktales exaggerate sometimes. They have no reputation for abducting mortals. Their intentions could easily be benign. I do not say that to reassure you, only to let you know that they have no history of meaning us harm."

I thought I might be assuming too much. "We are still in America?"

"I have another name for the continent. But if you lived after Longfellow, then your time is far in my future."

Such shifts of time were not unusual in the dream-worlds. "Then this is roughly 1550 in the Christian calendar."

He shook his head, and the breeze rippled in the eagle feathers. I realized I had never seen such brilliant colors before. Light sparkled and danced in them. Were the feathers themselves invested with magic?

He paused in his paddling. The canoe continued to skim across the bright water. The smell of pines and rich, damp undergrowth drifted from the distant bank. "Actually it's A.D. 1135, by that calendar. The Norman liberation of Britain began sixty-nine years ago. I think the settlers worked it out on the date of an eclipse. Well, they just picked a later eclipse. They were trying to prove we took the idea of a democratic federation from them."

He laughed and shook his head. "And before them was Leif Ericsson. When I was a boy I came across a Norseman whose colony had been established about a hundred years earlier. You could call him the Last of the Vikings. He was a poor, primitive creature, and most of his tribe had been hunted to death by the Algonquin. To be honest I'd mistaken him for some sort of scrawny bear at first.

"They called this place Wineland. He was bitter as his father and grandfather were bitter. The Ericssons had tricked his ancestors with stories of grapes and endless fields of wheat. What they actually got, of course, was foul weather, hard shrift and an angry native population which thoroughly outnumbered them. They called us 'the screamers' or 'skraelings.' I heard a few captive Norse women and children were adopted by some Cayugas who had survived an epidemic. But that was the last of them."

Though he was inclined to ramble on, he was full of interesting tales and explanations, making up for his years of silence. Now that I knew we sought the Kakatanawa, I devoted myself to finding Ulric as soon as possible. There was a remote possibility that we would arrive before he did, such was the nature of time. But somehow Ayanawatta's endless words had comforted me, and I no longer felt Ulric to be in danger of immediate harm; nor was I so convinced that Prince Gaynor was behind the kidnapping. The mystery, of course, remained, but at least I had an ally with some knowledge of this world.

I reflected on my peculiar luck, which again had brought me into another's dream. I had been attacked by that wind, I was certain. An aerial demon. An elemental. Ayanawatta was supremely confident. No doubt, since this was his final spirit journey and he was back in his familiar realm, he had defeated many obstacles. I had some idea of what the man had already endured. Yet he bore the burden of that experience lightly enough.

A current in the lake took our canoe gently towards the farther shore. Resting, Ayanawatta slid a slender bone flute from his pack. To my surprise he played a subtle, sophisticated melody, high and haunting, which was soon echoed by the surrounding hills and mountains until it seemed a whole orchestra took up the tune. Crowds of herons suddenly rose from the reeds as if to perform their aerial ballet in direct response to the music.

Pausing, Ayanawatta took the opportunity to address the birds with a relatively short laudatory speech. I was to become used to his rather egalitarian attitude towards animals, his way of speaking to them directly, as if they understood every nuance of his every sentence. Perhaps they did. In spite of my fears, I was delighted by this extraordinary experience. I was filled with a feeling of vibrant well-being. In spite of Ayanawatta's company, it had been ages since I knew such a sense of solitude, and I began to relish it, my confidence growing as I was infected by his joyous respect for the world.

By evening we had reached the reedy mouth of a river on the far side of a lake. After we drew the canoe ashore, Ayanawatta pulled some leggings and a robe from the pack. Gratefully I put the leggings on and wrapped myself in the blanket. The air was becoming chilly as the sun poured scarlet light over the mountain peaks and the shadowy reeds. The sachem carefully restarted his fire and cooked us a very tasty porridge, apologizing that he should have caught some fish but had been too busy recounting that disappointing meeting with Hawthorne. He promised fish in the morning.

Soon he was telling me about the corrupt spiritual orthodoxy of the Mayan peoples he had visited on an earlier stage of this journey. Their obscure heresies were a matter of some dismay to this extraordinary mixture of intellectual monk, warrior and storyteller. It all turned on certain Mayan priests' refusal to accept pluralism, I gathered. Any fears I had for Ulric were lulled away as I fell into a deep and dreamless sleep.

In the morning, as good as his word, the Mohawk nobleman had speared us two fat trout which, spiced from his store of herbs, made a tasty breakfast. He told me a little more of his dreamquests, of the stages of physical and supernatural testing he had endured to have reached this level of power. I was reminded of the philosophy of the Japanese samurai, who at their best were as capable of composing a haiku as of holding their own in a duel. Ayanawatta's dandified appearance in the wild suggested he cultivated more than taste. He was warning potential enemies of the power they faced. I had traveled alone and understood the dangers, the need to show a cool, careless exterior at all times or be killed and robbed in a trice. As it was, I envied Ayanawatta his bow and arrows, if not his twin war clubs.

After we had finished eating, I expected us to get on the move. Instead Ayanawatta sat down cross-legged and took out a beautiful redstone carved pipe bowl, which he packed with herbs from his pouch. Ceremoniously he put a hollow reed into a hole in the bottom of the bowl. Taking a dried grass taper from the fire he lit the pipe carefully and drew the smoke deeply into his lungs, then puffed smoke to the Earth's quarters, by way of thanks for the world's benevolence. An expression of contentment passed over his face as he handed me the pipe. I could only follow his example with some dread. I hated smoking. But the herbs of the pipe were sweet and gentle to the throat. I guessed they were a mixture containing some tobacco and a little hemp, also dried spearmint and willow bark. I was no smoker, but this beneficent mixture was a secret lost to Ulric's world. A peace pipe indeed. I was at once mentally sharpened and physically relaxed. This world remained intensely alive for me.

In a short while Ayanawatta stood up with stately dignity. He was clearly in a semi-trance. Slowly he began to sing, a rhythmic song that sounded like the wind, the whisper of distant water, the movement of distant thunder. As he sang he began a graceful dance, stamping hard on the ground while performing a complicated figure. Each nuance of movement had meaning. Although I had not been prepared for this display, I found it deeply moving. I knew that he was weaving his being into the fabric of the worlds. These rituals opened pathways for him. Unlike me, he had no natural gift for travel between the realms.

This particular ritual was, however, over swiftly. He made a somewhat shy apology and said that since we were traveling together, he hoped I would forgive him if he performed similar rituals from time to time. It was as important to his religion as my need to pray quietly to myself five times a day.

I had no objection. I knew of some cultures where people devoted their entire lives to learning ways of entering other worlds and usually died before they could accomplish anything. What I had been doing naturally since I was a young child had been inherited from my parents. Such movement was virtually impossible for most people and very difficult for everyone else. We moonbeam travelers have little in common but our talents. We learn the disciplines and responsibilities of such travel at the musram.

Even with my poor sense of direction it did not take me long to realize, as we set off downriver, that the current was not flowing from north to south and that judging by the position of the sun we were probably heading east. Ayanawatta agreed. "The road to Kakatanawa is a complicated one," he said, "and you're wise to approach with the appropriate charms and spells. That, at least, is clear from the prophecy. It isn't possible to go there directly, just as some moonbeam paths are more circuitous than others. And, as yet, I haven't worked out where to expect to find either the giants or the dragon. I intend to dream on the subject as soon as possible." He did not explain further.

With me settled in the front of the canoe, we were now paddling downstream at some speed, with huge stands of pines rising on both sides and the water beginning to dash at the rocks of the banks. The air was misty with white spray, and above us great grey clouds were beginning to build, threatening rain.

Before it finally started to rain, the river had turned a bend and widened and had become lazy, peaceful, almost a lake, with the tall mountains massed in the distance, the forest making swathes of red, gold, brown and green as the leaves turned. All this was reflected in the depths of the river. Heavy drops soon fell into the gentle waters and added to the sense of sudden peace as the narrow torrent was left behind. Our paddling became more vigorous, just to keep us moving at any reasonable speed.

While I understood that my journey could not take place with any special urgency, I remained nonetheless anxious to continue. I imagined a dozen different deaths for the man I loved as we actually headed away from the Kakatanawa territory. Yet I was a dreamthief's daughter. I understood certain disciplines. The direct path was almost never the best. I kept charge of my feelings most of the time, but it had never been harder.

Ayanawatta being unusually laconic, I remarked over my shoulder how much more peaceful the river had become. He nodded a little abstractedly. I realized that as he paddled he was listening carefully, his head cocked slightly to one side. What did he expect? Was he listening for danger? There could be no alligators in these cold waters.

I began to ask him, but he silenced me with a gesture. The wind was rising, and he was straining to hear above it. He leaned to his right a little, expectantly. Then, not hearing what he thought, he leaned forward to where I was now positioned and murmured, "I have powerful enemies who are now your enemies. But we have the medicine to defeat them all if we are courageous."

I shuddered with a sudden chill. It occurred to me to remind him that I was not here to help him in his spirit journey but to find my kidnapped husband. Before my mother vanished, presumably absorbed at last into a dream she had planned to steal, she would have been a more useful ally to him than I. Now, of course, it was unlikely she even knew her own name.

All too well, I understood the Game of Time. Mother had taught me most of what I knew, and the mukhamirim masters of Marrakech had taught me the rest. But it was sometimes difficult to remind myself. Time is a field with its own dimensions and varying properties. To think in terms of linear time is to be time's slave. Half of what one learns as a moonbeam walker involves understanding time for what it is, as far as we understand it at all. Our knowledge gives us freedom. It allows us some control of time. I do not know why, however, there are more women on the moonbeam roads than men, and most of the legendary figures of the roads are women. Women are said to be more able to accommodate Chaos and work with it. There are honorable exceptions, of course. Even the most intelligent man is inclined on occasion to hack a path through an obstacle. But he is also, in the main, somewhat better with a stone lance when it comes to dealing with large serpents.

This last thought came as I watched, virtually mesmerized, while a long, gleaming neck rose and rose and rose from the river until it blotted out the light. Vast sheets of water ran off its body and threatened to capsize the canoe as, with a shout to me to steady us, Ayanawatta took one of the spears from beneath his feet and threw it expertly into flesh I had assumed to be hugely dense. But the spear went deep into the creature, as if into a kind of heaving, wet sawdust, and the water bubbled with the thing's hissing breath. It groaned. I had not expected such a noise from it. The voice was almost human, baffled. It thrashed violently until the spear was flung free, and then it disappeared upstream, still groaning from time to time as its head broke the water, trailing a kind of thin, yellow ichor like smoke.

"I haven't seen anything close to that since I was in the Lower Devonian," I said. I was still shaking. The word *devour* had gained a fresh resonance for me. "Did it mean to attack us?"

"It probably hoped to eat us, but those are known along this river as the Cowardly Serpents. It takes little to drive them off as you saw, although if they capsize your canoe, you are in some danger, of course."

Much as I was trained not to think in linearities I was aware that in this realm gigantic water-serpents had long since become extinct. I put this to Ayanawatta as he paddled to where his spear floated, shaft up, in the reedy, eddying water. A strong smell of firs and the noise of feeding birds came from the bank, and I drank in the simplicity of it to steady myself. I knew the supernatural better than that which my husband insisted on calling "natural," but I felt resentful that I was being forced to take extra risks as I sought to save him. I said as much to Ayanawatta.

The Mohawk prince reassured me. He was simply obeying the demands of his dream-quest. This meant that my own dream-quest was in accordance with his, which meant that as long as we continued in the current pattern and made no serious mistakes our quests would be successful. We should both get what we desired.

The wind was still blustering and slapping at our clothes. I drew my blanket closer. Ayanawatta hardly noticed the drop in temperature. As for the "prehistoric" nature of our dangers, he regretted that some sort of crisis had occurred. Such anomalies were becoming increasingly common. He believed that the source of our own troubles was also causing the disruptions. The great prairies offered natural grazing and ample prey for predators. They were, he admitted, generally moving south these days, and the altering climate took increasing numbers of those that remained.

I said that I had noticed it growing colder.

Still apparently oblivious of the chill, Ayanawatta sighed. "Once," he said, "this was all unspoiled. Those serpents would never have come this far downriver. It means you lose all the river game, and before you know it the whole natural order is turned upside down. The consequences are disastrous. It becomes impossible to lead any kind of settled life. Do you see any villages on the banks these days? Of course not! It used to be wonderful here. Girls would wave at you. People would invite you in to hear your stories . . ."

Grumbling thus, he paddled mechanically for a while. The encounter with the river serpent had not so much frightened as irritated him. Even I had not been terrified of the beast. But Ayanawatta's sense of order and protocol was upset, and he was becoming concerned, he said, about the wind.

Again he surprised me. He had a habit of noticing everything while appearing to be entirely concerned with his own words. For such people, words were sometimes a kind of barrier, the eye of a storm, from which part of them could observe the world without the world ever guessing.

The wind was the king of the prairie, Ayanawatta continued. The most important force. He suspected that we had somehow engaged its anger.

He paused in his paddling and took out his flute. He blew a few experimental notes, then began a high, slow tune which made use of the echoes from the distant mountains and turned them back and forth so that once again it seemed the whole of the natural world was singing with him.

The wind dropped suddenly. And as it dropped, Ayanawatta's flute died away.

The extraordinary scenery seemed to go on forever, changing as the light changed, until it was close to twilight. The river ahead had begun to rumble and hiss. Ayanawatta said we would have to bypass the rapids tomorrow. Meanwhile we would make camp before sunset, and this time, he promised, he would catch whatever fish the serpent had left us.

In the morning when I awoke Ayanawatta was gone. The only movement was the lazy smoke from his fire, the only sound the distant lapping of water and the melancholy wail of a river bird. I felt the ground shiver under me. Was this the sound of the rapids he had spoken about?

I rose quickly, hardly able to believe I was not experiencing an earthquake. I heard the chirping of frogs and insects, steady, high. I smelled the smoke and the rich, earthy pines, the acrid oaks and sweet ash. I heard a bird flap and dive, and then I heard a disturbance in the water. I looked up and saw a hawk carrying a bird in its talons. I found myself wondering about the magical meaning of what I had seen.

The earth shuddered again, and wood snapped within the forest. I looked for Ayanawatta's bow and arrows, but they were gone. I found one of his lances, still in the bottom of the boat, and armed myself with it. As I turned, however, it became immediately obvious that a stone lance, even a magic one, might not be much use against this newcomer. Out of the thick woods, scattering branches and leaves in all directions, a fantastic apparition loomed over me.

While I was familiar with the Asian use of domestic elephants, I had never seen a man seated on the back of a black woolly mammoth with tusks at least nine feet long curving out over an area of at least twenty feet!

The rider approaching me was clearly a warrior of the region, but with subtle differences of dress, black face paint, shaven head, scalp lock worn long, a lance and a war-shield held in his left hand, his right hand gripping the decorated reins of his huge mount. It was impossible to judge the rider's size, but it was clear the mammoth was not young. The old tusks were splintered and bound but could still very easily kill almost anything which attacked their owner.

My heart thumped with sickening speed. I looked for some advantage. At the last moment the mammoth's trunk rose in a gesture of peace. At the same time the painted warrior raised his palm to reassure me.

The mammoth swung her weight forward and began to lower herself onto her knees as the newcomer slid blithely down her back and landed on the turf.

His tone was at odds with his ferocious black mask. "The prophecy told me I would meet my friend Ayanawatta here but only hinted at his companion. I am sorry if I alarmed you. Please forgive the death paint. I've been in a fairly intense dispute."

This thoroughly decorated man had a similar grace of manner to Ayanawatta, but something about his movements was familiar to me. His posture, however, was more brooding. His paint was a black, glowing mask in which two dark rubies burned. I held on to the spear and took a step back. I began to feel sicker still as I recognized him.

Silently, fascinated, I waited for him to approach.

CHAPTER THREE

A Prince of the Prairie

Do not ask me how I came here,
Do not ask my name or nation,
Do not ask my destination,
For I am Dawadana, the Far Sighted,
Dawadana, Seer and Singer,
Who bore the lance, the Justice Bringer,
Who brought the law out of the East,
Sworn to seek but never speak.

W. S. HARTE,
"The Maker of Laws"

 e was, of course, the same youth I had seen at the house. His face was so thickly painted I knew him only by his white hands and red eyes. He did not appear to recognize me at all and seemed a little disappointed. "Do you know where Ayanawatta is?"

I guessed he'd failed to find fish in the river and had gone hunting in the woods, since his bow and a lance were missing.

"Well, we have some big game to hunt now," the newcomer said. "I've found him at last. I would have reached him sooner if I had understood my pygmy dream better." This was offered as apology. He returned to his mount and led the great woolly black pachyderm down to the water to drink. I admired the saddle blanket and the beaded bridle. Attached to the intricately carved wooden saddle was a long, painted quiver from which the sharp metal tongues of several lances jutted. Beaver and otter fur covered the saddle and parts of his bridle. The mammoth herself was, as I had thought, not in her prime. There were grizzled marks around her mouth and trunk, and her ivory was stained and cracked, but she moved with surprising speed, turning her vast, tusked head once to look into my eyes, perhaps to convince herself that I was friendly. Reassured, she dipped her trunk delicately into the cold water, her hairy tail swinging back and forth, twitching with pleasure.

As his mount quenched her mighty thirst, the young man knelt beside the water and began rubbing the black paint from his face, hair and arms. When he stood up he was once again the youth I had seen at the house. His wet hair was still streaked with mud or whatever he had put in it, but it was as white as my own. He seemed about ten years younger than me. His face had none of the terror and pleading I had seen such a short time before. He was ebullient, clearly pleased with himself.

I chose to keep my own counsel. Before I offered too much, I would wait until I had a better idea of what all this meant. I would instead give him a hint.

"I am Oona, Elric's daughter," I said. This apparently was nothing to him, but he sensed I expected him to recognize me.

"That's a fairly common name," he said. "Have we met before?"

"I thought we had."

He frowned politely and then shook his head. "I should have remembered you. Here, I have never seen a woman of my own coloring and size." He was unsurprised.

"Were you expecting to see me?"

"You are White Buffalo Woman?"

"I believe so."

"Then I was expecting to see you. We play out our parts within the prophecy, eh?" He winked. "If we do not, the pathways tangle and strangle themselves. We should lose all we've gained. If you had not been here, at the time I foretold, then I should have been concerned. But it disturbs me that the third of our trio is missing."

I knew enough of travelers' etiquette not to ask him any more than he told me. Many supernatural travelers, using whatever means they choose, must work for years to reach a certain road, a particular destination. With a single wrong step or misplaced word, their destination is gone again! To know the future too well is to change it.

"What name will you give for yourself?" I asked.

"My spirit name is White Crow," said the youth, "and I am a student with the Kakatanawa, sent, as my family always sends its children, to learn from them. My quest joins with yours at this point. I have already completed my first three tasks. This will be my fourth and last great task. You will help me here as I will help you later. Everything becomes clear at the right time. We all work to save the Balance." He had undone the straps holding the surprisingly light saddle and supported it as it slid towards him, dumping it heavily to the ground, the spears rattling. "We walk the path of the Balance." He spoke almost offhandedly, filling a big skin of water and washing down the black mammoth's legs and belly. "And this old girl is called Bes. The word means 'queen' in her language. She, too, serves the Balance well." With a grunt and a great heave, Bes moved deeper into the water, then lifted her long, supple trunk and sprayed her own back, luxuriating in the absence of her saddle.

"The Cosmic Balance?"

"The Balance of the world," he said, clearly unfamiliar with my phrase. "Has Ayanawatta told you nothing? He grows more discreet." The young man grinned and pushed back his wet hair. "The Lord of Winds has gone mad and threatens to destroy our longhouse and all that it protects." He took bunches of grass and began to clean the long, curving tusks as his animal wallowed deeper into the stream, gazing at him with fierce affection. "My task was to seek the lost treasures of the Kakatanawa and bring them to our longhouse so that our home tree will not die. It is my duty and my privilege, for me to serve thus."

"And what are these treasures?" I asked.

"Together they comprise the Soul of the World. Once they are restored, they will be strong enough to withstand the Lord of the Winds. The power of all these elementals increases. They do not merely threaten our lives but our way of thinking. A generation ago we all understood the meaning and value of our ways. Now even the great Lords of the Higher Worlds forget."

I was already familiar with those insane Lords and Ladies of Law who had lost all sense of their original function. They had gone mad in defense of their own power, their own orthodoxy. Lords of the Wind normally served neither Law nor Chaos, but like all elementals had no special loyalties, except to blood and tradition. White Crow agreed.

"There's a madness in Chaos," he said, "just as there can be in Law. These forces take many forms and many names across the multiverse. To call them Good or Evil is never to know them, never to control them, for there are times when Chaos does good and Law does evil and vice versa. The tiniest action of any kind can have extreme and monumental consequences. Out of the greatest acts of evil can spring the greatest powers for good. Equally, from acts of great goodness, pure evil can spring. That is the first thing any adept learns. Only then can their education truly begin." He spoke almost like a schoolboy who had only re-cently learned these truths.

Clearly there was a connection with the events Ulric and I had experienced earlier, but it was a subtle one. This battle for the Balance never ended. For it to end would probably be a contra-diction in terms. Upon the Balance depended the central paradox of all existence. Without life there is no death. Without death there is no life. Without Law, no Chaos. Without Chaos, no Law. And the balance was maintained by the tensions between the two forces. Without those tensions, without the Balance, we should know only a moment's consciousness as we faced oblivion. Time would die. We would live that unimaginably terrible final moment for eternity. Those were the stakes in the Game of Time. Law or Chaos. Life or Death. Good and evil were secondary qualities, often reflecting the vast variety of values by which conscious crea-tures conduct their affairs across the multiverse. Yet a system which accepted so many differing values, such a wealth of altering realities, could not exist without morality, and it was the learning of those ethics and values which concerned an apprentice mukhamirim. Until it was possible to look beyond any system to the individual, the would-be adept remained blind to the supernatural and generally at its mercy.

I was also beginning to realize very rapidly that these events were all connected with the ongoing struggle we wanted to think finished when the war against Hitler was won.

"Do you journey back to your people?" I asked.

"I must not return empty-handed," he told me, and changed the subject, pointing and laughing with joy at a flight of geese settling in the shadowy shallows of the river. "Did you know you are being observed?" he asked almost absently as he admired the geese, graceful now in the water.

A whoop from the trees, and Ayanawatta, holding a couple of birds aloft in one hand and his bow in the other, called his pleasure. His friend could join us for breakfast.

The two men embraced. Again I was impressed by their magnetism. I congratulated myself that I was blessed with the best allies a woman could hope for. As long as their interests and mine were the same, I could do no better than go with them in what they were confident was their preordained destiny.

I waited impatiently in the hope that White Crow would again raise the subject of our being watched. Eventually, when the two had finished their manly exchanges, he pointed across the river to the north. "I myself have known you were on the river since I took the shortcut, yonder." He pointed back to where the river had meandered on its way to this spot. "They have made camp, so it is clear they follow you and no doubt wait to ambush you. It is their usual way with our people. A Pukawatchi war party. Seventeen of them. My enemies. They were chasing me, but I thought they had given up."

Ayanawatta shrugged. "We'll have a look at them later. They will not attack until they are certain of overwhelming us."

White Crow expertly plucked and cleaned the birds while I

drew up the fire. Ayanawatta washed himself thoroughly in the river, singing a song which I understood to be one of thanks for the game he had shot. He also sang a snatch or two of what was evidently a war-song. I could almost hear the drums beginning their distinctive warnings. I noticed that he kept a sideways eye on the northern horizon. Evidently the Pukawatchi were an enemy tribe.

I asked White Crow, as subtly I could, if he had ever been to an island house with two stories and had a vision there. I was trying to discover if he remembered me or Ulric. He regretted, he said, that he was completely ignorant of the events I described. Had they happened recently? He had been in the south for some while.

I told him that the events still felt very recent to me. Since there was no way of pursuing the subject, I determined to waste no more time on it. I hoped more would come clear as we traveled.

I had begun to enjoy Ayanawatta's songs and rituals. They were among the only constants in this strange world which seemed to hover at the edges of its own history. I became increasingly tolerant of his somewhat noisy habits, because I knew that in the forest he could be as quiet as a cat. As he was a naturally sociable and loquacious man, his celebratory mood was understandable.

My new friends added their share of herbs and berries to the slowly cooked meat, basting with a touch of wild honey, until it had all the subtle flavors of the best French kitchen. Like me, they knew that the secret of living in the wild was not to rough it, but to refine one's pleasures and find pleasure in the few discomforts. Ironically, if one wished to live such a life, one had to be able to kill. Ayanawatta and White Crow regarded the dealing of death as an art and a responsibility. A respected animal you killed quickly without pain. A respected enemy might suffer an altogether different fate.

I was glad to be back in the forest, even if my errand was a desperate one. A properly relaxed body needs warmth but no special softness to rest well, and cold river water is exquisite for drinking and washing, while the flavors and scents of the woods present an incredible sensory vocabulary. Already my own senses and body were adapting to a way of life I had learned to prefer as a girl, before I had become what dreamthieves call a mukhamirin, before going the way of the Great Game or making my vows of marriage and motherhood.

The multiverse depended upon chance and malleable realities. Those who explored it developed a means of manipulating those realities. They were natural gamblers, and many, in other lives, played games of skill and chance for their daily bread. I was a player in the Eternal Struggle fought between Law and Chaos and, as a "Knight of the Balance," was dedicated to maintaining the two forces in harmony.

All this I had explained as best I could to my now missing husband, whose love for me was unquestioning but whose ability to grasp the complexity and simplicity of the multiverse was limited. Because I loved him, I had chosen to accept his realities and took great pleasure from them. I added my strength to his and to that of an invisible army of individuals like us who worked throughout the multiverse to achieve the harmony which only the profoundly mad did not yearn for.

There was no doubt I felt once more in my natural element. Though fraught with anxiety for Ulric's well-being and my own ability to save him, at least for a time I knew a kind of freedom I had never dared hope to enjoy again.

Soon we were once more on the move, but this time Ayanawatta and I joined White Crow upon Bes the mammoth, with the canoe safely strapped across her broad back. There was more than enough room on her saddle, which was so full of tiny cupboards and niches that I began to realize this was almost a traveling house. As he rode, White Crow busied himself with rearranging his goods, reordering and storing. I, on the other hand, was lazily relishing the novelty of the ride. Bes's hair was like the knotted coat of a hardy hill-sheep, thick and black. Should you fall from her saddle, it would be easy to cling to her snarled coat, which gave off an acrid, wild smell, a little like the smell of the boars who had lived around the cottage of my youth.

White Crow dismounted, preferring, he said, to stretch his legs. He had been riding for too long. He and Ayanawatta did their best not to exclude me from their conversations, but they were forced to speak cryptically and do all they could, in their own eyes, not to disturb the destiny God had chosen for them. Their magical methods were not unlike different engineering systems designed to achieve the same end and had strict internal logic in order to work at all.

While White Crow ran to spy on whoever was following us, we continued to rest on the back of the rolling monster. Ayanawatta told me that the Kakatanawa prince had been adopted into the tribe but was playing out a traditional apprenticeship. His people and theirs had long practiced this custom. It was mutually advantageous. Because he was not of their blood, White Crow could do things which they could not and visit worlds forbidden or untraversable by them.

As we moved through those lush grasslands growing on the edge of the forest, Ayanawatta spoke at length of how he wanted to serve the needs of all people, since even the stupidest human creature sought harmony yet so rarely achieved it. His quick brain, however, soon understood that he might be tiring me, and he stopped abruptly, asking if I would like to hear his flute.

Of course, I told him, but first perhaps he would listen to me sing a song of my own. I suggested we enjoy the tranquil river and the forest's whispering music, let the sounds and smells engulf us, carry us on our fateful dream-quest, and like the gentle river's rushing, draw us to the distant mountains and beyond them to that longhouse, lost among the icy wastelands where the Kakatanawa ruled. And I sang a song known as the Song of the Undying, to which he responded, echoing my melody, letting me know his quest was noble, not for self, or tribe or nation, but for the very race of Man. In his dreams the tree of all creation was threatened by a venomous dragon, waiting in angry torment, his tears destroying every root. Too sick to move, the dying dragon had lost his skefla'a and thus lost his power to rise and fly.

He said the Kakatanawa protected some central mystery. He had only hints of what that mystery was and most of that from myth and song. He knew that they had sent their most valued warriors out to seek what they had lost and what they needed. Where they had failed, White Crow had succeeded.

Continuing in grim reflection, he told me how his story was already written, how important to his own quest it was that he return to Kakatanawa, seek their longhouse and their people, bring back the objects they called holy, perform the ritual of restoration, restore reality to the dream. In that final restoration he would at last unite the nations, at last be worthy of his name. His dream-name was Onatona. In his language that meant Peacemaker. The power of his dream, his vision of the future, informed everything he did. It was his duty to follow the story and resolve each thread with his own deeds. I was in some awe of him. I felt as if I had been allowed to witness the beginning of a powerful epic, one which would resonate around the world.

I agreed his task was mighty. "Unlike you I have no dream-story to live. If I have I'm unconscious of it. All I know is that I seek a husband and father I would like to return to his home and his children. I, too, work to unite the nations. I long to bring peace and stable justice to a world roaring and ranting and shouting as if to drown all sense. I'll help you willingly in your quest, but I expect you in turn to help me. Like you, I have a destiny."

I told Ayanawatta how in my training as a mukhamirim my mother had taught me all my secrets, how some of these secrets must be kept to myself, even from my own husband and children. But I did not need to remind him. "I am in no doubt of the power or destiny of White Buffalo Woman. I am glad you elected to act her story. You complete the circle of magic which will arm us against the greater enemies and monsters we are yet to face."

The line of thick forest moved back from the river, making our way easier. Ahead lay rolling meadows stretching into infinity. Gentle, grassy drumlins gave this landscape a deceptively peaceful air, like an English shire extended forever. I had enjoyed far more bizarre experiences, but nothing quite like holding a conversation about the socioeconomics of dream-visions on the rolling back of a gigantic pachyderm with a mythological hero who had enjoyed the privilege of seeing his own future epic and was now bound to live it.

"There are bargains one strikes," said Ayanawatta with a certain self-mockery, "whose terms only become clear later. It taught me why so few adepts venture into their own futures. There's a certain psychological problem, to say the least."

I began to take more than a casual interest in our conversation, which showed how close to my training Ayanawatta's was. Like the dreamthieves, I had a rather reckless attitude towards my own future and spawned fresh versions without a thought. A more puritanical moonbeam walker took such responsibilities seriously. We were disapproved of by many. They said too many of our futures died and came to nothing. We argued that to control too much was to control nothing. In our own community Law and Chaos both remained well represented.

A sharp, rapid cawing came from our right, where the forest was still dense and deep. Someone had disturbed a bird. We saw White Crow running out of the trees. I was again struck by his likeness to my father, my husband and myself. Every movement was familiar. I realized that I took almost a mother's pleasure in him. It was difficult to believe we were not in some way related.

White Crow's moccasins and leggings were thick with mud. He was carrying his longest spear with a shaft some five feet long and a dull metal blade at least three feet long. In the same hand was a straight stick. He had been running hard. Bes stopped the moment she saw him, her trunk affectionately curling around his waist and shoulders.

He grinned up at me as he rose into the air and patted his beast's forehead. "Here's your bow, my lady Buffalo!" He threw the staff to me and I caught it, admiring it. It was a strong piece of yew wood, ready-made for a new weapon. I was delighted and thanked him. He drew a slender cord from his side-bag and handed that up. I felt complete. I had a new bow. I had left my old bow, whose properties were not entirely natural, in my mother's cottage when I closed it up, thinking I would have no further need of it in twentieth-century Britain.

"They are following us without doubt," said White Crow, slipping down to the ground, his face just below my feet. He spoke softly. "About half a mile behind us. They hide easily in the long grasses."

"Are you certain they mean us harm?" Ayanawatta asked him.

White Crow was certain. "I know that they are armed and painted for war. Save for me, they have no other enemies in these parts. They are a thousand miles at least from their own hunting grounds. What magic helped them leave their normal boundaries? The little devils will probably try for us tonight. I don't believe they realize we know they are there, so they'll be expecting to surprise us. They fear Bes's tusks and feet more than they fear your arrows, Ayanawatta."

Ayanawatta wanted to maintain our speed. It was easier at this stage to continue overland, because the river curved back on itself at least twice.

We had left the forest behind us and rode towards the distant range. The great pachyderm had no trouble at all carrying her extra passengers, and I was surprised at our pace. Another day or two and we should be in the foothills of the mountains. White Crow knew where the pass was. He had already made this journey from the other direction, he said.

I could now make out the mountains in better detail. They were the high peaks of a range which was probably the Rockies. Their lower flanks were thick with pine, oak, ash, willow, birch and elm, while a touch of snow tipped some of the tallest. They climbed in red-gold majesty to dominate the rise and fall of the prairie. The clouds behind them glowed like beaten copper. These were spirit mountains. They possessed old, slow souls. They offered a promise of organic harmony, of permanence.

With Ayanawatta and White Crow I accepted the reality of the mountains' ancient life. In spite of my constant, underlying anxiety, I was glad to be back with people who understood themselves and their surroundings to be wholly alive, who measured their self-esteem in relation to the natural world as well as the lore they had acquired. Like me, they understood themselves to be a part of the sentient fabric, equal to all other beings, all of whom have a story to play out. Every beggar is a baron somewhere in the multiverse and vice versa.

We are all avatars in the eternal tale, the everlasting struggle between classical Law and romantic Chaos. The ideal multiverse arises from the harmony which comes when all avatars are playing the same role in the same way and achieving the same effect. We are like strings in a complex instrument. If some strings are out of tune, the melody can still be heard but is not harmonious. One's own harmony depends on being attuned to the other natural harmonies in the world. Every soul in the multiverse plays its part in sustaining the Balance which maintains existence. The action of every individual affects the whole.

These two men took all this for granted. There's a certain relaxing pleasure in not having to explain yourself in any way. I realized what a sacrifice I had made for the love of Ulric and his world, but I did not regret it. I merely relished these mountains and woods for what they were, getting the best, as always, from a miserable situation. Only the persistent wind disturbed me, forever tugging at me, as if to remind me what forces stood between me and my husband.

I took the first watch. For all my growing alertness as I strung my bow that night in camp, I heard only the usual sounds of small animals hunting. When White Crow relieved me, I had nothing to report. He murmured that he had heard seven warriors moving some twenty feet from our camp, and I became alarmed. I was not used to doubting my senses. He said perhaps they were only getting the lie of the land.

Before I went to sleep I asked him why people would come so far to try to kill us. "They are after the treasures," he said. He had recently outwitted the Pukawatchi, and they were angry. But all he was doing was taking back what they had stolen.

He said we must be alert for snakes. The Pukawatchi were expert snake-handlers and were known to use copperheads and rat-
tlesnakes as weapons. This did not enhance my sense of security.
Although not phobic, I have a strong distaste for snakes of any
size.

It was not until Ayanawatta's time of watch that I was awakened by thin shouts in the grey, dirty dawn. Our pasture was
heavy with dew, making the ground spongy and hard to walk on.
There was no sign of our erstwhile enemies, and I began to believe
they lacked stomach for their work.

Then I saw the huge copperhead writhing near the fire, moving slowly towards us. I snatched an arrow from Ayanawatta's
quiver, nocked and shot in a single fluid, habitual action. One's
body rarely forgets as much as one's mind. My arrow pinned the
copperhead to the ground. Its tongue scented in and out between
those long, deadly fangs, and I felt less conscience in killing it
than I had in eating the birds.

They decided to attack at dawn in the north wind's chill,
shrieking high-pitched, hideous war cries and swinging stone
clubs almost as big as themselves. They fell back well before they
reached us. These tactics were designed to put us on our feet and
make us more vulnerable to their next strategy, but White Crow
had journeyed among these people and anticipated most of their
tricks.

When their arrows came pouring into the camp, we were
ready for them. Instantly a fine mesh net was thrown up over us
all, including Bes. The net caught the arrows and bounced most
of them to the ground.

Two more snakes were hurled into our midst. I dispatched one
with the same arrow I had used on his fellow. Ayanawatta killed
the other with one of his twin war clubs.

White Crow was no longer interested in our attackers. He was
roaring his approval of my archery. I had the eye and arm of any
man, he said. He was making an observation, not offering a com-
pliment.

The snakes were abnormally large, especially for this climate, and it was easy to see how the Pukawatchi alarmed their enemies. It quickly became clear, however, why they were not in themselves very terrifying.

Not one of them was over three and a half feet high! The Pukawatchi were perfect pygmies.

I had not realized from the conversations I had overheard that the tallest Pukawatchi could scarcely reach my chest. They were conventionally formed little people. Their scrawny bodies were heavily muscled. They showed a tenacity of attack which made you admire them. I assumed they had evolved in similar circum- stances to the African bushmen. Unlike Ayanawatta, they were a square-headed, beetle-browed people, clearly from a different part of the world altogether, yet they dressed in deerskin, with breech- clouts, fur caps, decorated shirts and moccasins. But for their fea- tures and diminutive size, they might have been any tribe east of the Mississippi.

The trick with the net gave us a certain advantage over the pygmies.

It did not much surprise me that the man leading them was not dressed like a Pukawatchi. He hung back in the grass, point- ing this way and that with his sword, directing the attack. He wore a long black cloak, a tall black hat with black plumes, and his weapon was a slender saber. He looked more like a funeral horse than a man, but there was no mistaking that gloomy skull of a face.

I had seen him recently.

Klosterheim, of course. How long had it taken him to get here? I knew it could not have been an easy path. He seemed older and even more haggard than before. His clothes looked threadbare.

Their attack having failed, the Pukawatchi withdrew around their leader. Either the party had reduced itself since White Crow last saw it, or part of it was elsewhere planning to attack from an- other angle.

As one of the warriors ran up to him to receive orders I real- ized with a shock that, like the Pukawatchi who attacked us with such vigor, Klosterheim was scarcely any taller than a ten-year-old boy! He seemed to have paid a radical price for his obsession with the Grail. A moment later he hailed us, his voice unusually high, and suggested a truce.

At that exact moment Bes decided to utter her outrage. Her huge tusks lifted. She raised her head and pawed at the quivering ground. A noise struck our ears like the last trump, and a horrible stench filled the air. Klosterheim's speech was completely drowned. He could not control his fury. Equally, we could not control our amusement. Despite the gravity of our situation, the three of us found ourselves weeping with laughter.

The mammoth's answer to Klosterheim had been to utter a massive fart.

CHAPTER FOUR

Strange Dimensions

Have they told of the Pukawachee,
Fairy people of the forest?
Have they heard of Hiawatha,
Fate's favored son, the peaceful one?

SCHOOLCRAFT'S TR.,
"Hiawatha's Song"

losterheim thought we were merely mocking him for the failure of his attack. Laying down his sword, he signaled for the Pukawatchi to stay where they were while he approached us. His expression was one of gloomy distaste as he reached a small hillock a few yards from where we stood. Here, perhaps unconsciously seeking to be at eye level with us, he paused. He removed his black hat and wiped the inside band. "Whatever sorcerer has blown you up to such gigantic proportions, madam, I trust the spell is easily reversed."

I was able to remain grave now. "I thank you for your solicitousness, Herr Klosterheim. How long is it since we last met?"

He scowled. "You know that, madam, as well as I do." He expelled an irritated sigh, as if I offered just one more frustration for him to contend with in this world. "You'll recall that it was some four years ago, at that angular house of yours near Englishtown."

I said nothing. As anticipated, Klosterheim's route to this realm had been hard. I had a sense of his extraordinary age. How many centuries had he spent crossing from one realm to another in this bleak pursuit? His experiences had changed neither his de-

6 7

meanor nor, presumably, his ambition. I was still not sure exactly what he sought here, but my curiosity was high. Moreover, he was the only link I had to my husband, so I was relieved that we occupied the same realm, if on different scales.

For all his tiny stature, Klosterheim remained entirely solipsistic. His rigid confidence in his own perceptions and understanding was unshaken. He did not doubt himself for a second. He was irritated that I chose not to remember how four years had passed or acknowledge that I had decided to become a giant in the meantime!

I remembered Ulric saying, in the context of Nazi anti-Semitism, that he believed Klosterheim had served the Lutheran Church in some capacity until expelled. The German was clearly of that puritanical disposition uncomfortable with our complicated world's realities. It was a tribute to his great need that he had pursued this goal for centuries. Such minds seek to simplify an existence they cannot understand. All they can do is reduce it to what they believe are fundamentals. Their narrow reasoning demonstrates a complete absence of spiritual imagination. Klosterheim was the apotheosis of Law turned inward and gone sour. Was he aggressively determined to destroy Chaos at its roots and thus achieve absolute control, which is death? Chaos, unchecked, would stimulate all possibility until perception became nullified and intellect died. That was why some of us temperamentally disposed to serve Chaos sometimes worked for Law and vice versa.

Klosterheim knew all this but did not care. His own parochial obsession was with his master, the Satan he had served, rejected and longed to serve again.

White Crow stepped forward, scowling ritualistically. "How do you now lead my enemies? What do you promise these Little People that they follow you out of their ordained hunting grounds to their deaths?"

"They seek only what has been stolen from them." Klosterheim uttered the words with hollow irony.

White Crow folded his arms theatrically. His body language

was as formal and controlled as any diplomat's speech. "They stole and murdered to gather the treasures. The lance was never their property. They merely fashioned it. You have persuaded them of honor which they have not earned. The lance blade was made by the Nihrain. The Pukawatchi performed a task. They did not create the blade. You bring nothing but disaster to the Pukawatchi. We serve the Balance, and the lance belongs to the Balance."

"The lance was made by their ancestors and is rightfully theirs. Give them back their Black Lance. You are White Crow the trickster. They simply reclaimed their property. You are White Crow the truth-twister, who deceived them into giving up that property."

"It is not their treasure. I merely argued with that mad shaman of theirs on his own terms. It was my logic won me the blade, not my lies. The Pukawatchi are too intelligent for their own good. They can never resist a philosophical argument, and that is all I offered them in the end. But I won the treasures through clever thought, not cunning. Besides, I no longer have them all. I gave them away."

"I am not here to be a passive audience for your decadent psychological notions," said Klosterheim, only half understanding what had been said to him. "Trickery it was and nothing else."

"Which, as I recall, was the rationale you were using in Germany during the 1930s when we first met?" I pointed out.

"I tell you again, madam, that I never subscribed to that philistine paganism." Even at his reduced height he achieved a kind of dignity. "But one must ally oneself with the strongest power. Hitler was then the strongest power. A mistake. I admit it. I have always been inclined to underestimate women like yourself." He offered this last remark with some venom. Then he considered his response and looked up at me almost in apology. His personality seemed to be breaking up before my eyes. How difficult had it been for him to follow me here, and how stable was his dream self?

One of the Pukawatchi, smeared with brightly painted medicine symbols all over his body, presumably as protection against us, a strutting bantam of a fellow who clearly thought much of himself, came to stand behind Klosterheim, displaying offense and outrage. Upon his head was the skin of a large snake, the head still on it, the jaws open and threatening. Swaying from side to side to his own rhythms, he stretched his arms forward, making the signs of the horned deceiver. I could not tell if he described himself or his enemies. He sang a short song and stopped abruptly. Then he spoke:

"I am Ipkeptemi, the son of Ipkeptemi. You claim much, but your medicine curdles, your spirits wither, and your tongues turn black in your mouths. Give us what is ours, and we will return to our own lands."

"If you continue this war with us," said Ayanawatta reasonably, "you will all die."

The little medicine man made spitting sounds to show his contempt for these threats. He turned his back on us, daring us to strike.

Then he whirled to face us again, shaking his fingers at us. It was clear he feared the power of our medicine. While his was little more than a primitive memory of the reality, he might well have a natural talent. I did not underestimate him or any power he might have stumbled upon. I watched him warily as he continued.

"The Kakatanawa are banished from our land as we are from theirs, yet they came and took the lance our people made. You say we have no business here, but neither have you. You should be living under the gloomy skies of your own deep realm. Give us what is ours, then go back to the Land of the Black Panther."

Again White Crow drew himself into an oratorical stance. "You know nothing, but I know your name, small medicine. You are called Ipkeptemi the Two Tongues. You are Ukwidji, the Lie-Maker. You speak truth and you speak lies with the same breath. You know it is our destiny to make and guard the Silver Path. We must go where the Balance and the tree manifest themselves. You know that is true. Your treasures are gone. Your time is past."

White Crow threw his arms wide in a placatory sign of respect. "Your destiny is complete, and ours is not yet accomplished."

The Two Tongues scowled deeply at this and lowered his head as if considering a reply.

From behind me, an arrow flew past my ear. I ducked down. Another arrow fell short of Klosterheim, who, with eyes narrowing, began to stumble back to where his men awaited his orders. I saw him pick up his sword and begin directing the attack on us again. I whirled, my bowstring pulled, and took another sturdy little warrior in the shoulder. I had a habit of wounding rather than killing, although it was not always appropriate! What was strange, however, was how the arrow made a sound as if it had struck wood. The head was barely in the wound. The pygmy pulled it free and ran off. This strange density of physique was common to them all.

The Two Tongues had created a diversion, of course. I had been fascinated by his performance. So fascinated that I had not heard the other Pukawatchi creeping up from the river line. Ayanawatta turned in a single movement to hurl a lance into our nearest attacker. Bes swung her immense bulk around to face the newcomers and stood blaring her rage as a Pukawatchi arrow bounced off her chest. She seemed more upset by the archer's bad manners than by any pain he might have inflicted. He was in her trunk in seconds and flying across the prairie to land, a broken puppet, at Klosterheim's feet.

Grumbling, Ayanawatta stooped to pick up his twin war clubs from the bundle at his feet. Their wide, flat edges ended in serrations, like the teeth of a beast. He spun them around his head, making them sing their own wild war-song as he waded towards the pygmies, slaughtering with a kind of joy I had only seen once before in my father when he had faced Gaynor's men. This battle-rage was cultivated by many adepts who argued that if one had to kill to defend oneself, then the killing had better be done with due consideration, ceremony and efficiency.

White Crow had taken out one of his lances. He did not throw it, but used it like a halberd, keeping his opponents at a distance and then stabbing once, quickly. I had thought at first it was corroded or rusted like so much of the found metal these people used, but now I recognized it for what it was.

The metal was black through and through. As the youth wielded his lance with expert skill, it began to murmur and scream. Red inscriptions flickered angrily at its heart. I was oddly cheered. Surely where that blade sang, Ulric must be near!

I had found the black blade, though I had not sought it. I could see Klosterheim grinning in anticipated triumph. For him, the blade was not nearly as important as the cup his people called the *Gradel*. Klosterheim wanted the thing for his own ambitions. If he took it back to Satan, he was certain he would be restored in his master's eyes. The central irony was that Satan himself sought reconciliation with God. It was as if our danger were so great that the time had come for the two to bury their differences.

Yet it was impossible for Klosterheim to work for the common good. The gaining of the Grail must be by his achievement, I knew, or he would see no respect in his master's eyes. This complicated and contradictory relationship with the Prince of the Morning was, to be frank, somewhat beyond my powers of perception.

White Crow had not seen all the Pukawatchi. A third war party had swept up from a bend in the river. There must have been another forty of the pygmies, all armed with bows. They had walked across the river bottom, like beavers, and had emerged immediately behind us. Our only advantage was that the bows were not especially powerful, and the pygmies were not expert shots.

While we covered him, White Crow repacked Bes's saddle, adjusting straps and other harness until he was satisfied that all was secure. The canoe would now act to guard our backs.

I kept the new party at a distance with my bow. Their own arrows could be shot back, but not with any great power as they were too short. Ayanawatta's arrows, however, were perfect. Slender and long, they were a joy to use. They were so accurate that they might have been charmed. But there were not enough.

Fewer and fewer were being shot back by the Pukawatchi. Slowly they were closing the circle.

White Crow adjusted the copper mesh protecting Bes's front and head. She kneeled for us.

White Crow shouted for us to get onto the mammoth, and we scrambled into that massive saddle. We pushed the maddened pygmies back with our bowstaves. Ayanawatta was the last to come up, his twin war clubs cracking skulls and bones so rapidly that it sounded like the popping of a hot fire made with damp wood. He worked with astonishing skill and delicacy, knowing exactly which part of each club would land where. Those dense skulls were hard to crack, but he fought to kill. Each single blow economically took a life. When Bes moved away from the tumbled corpses towards the pygmy archers, they scattered back.

The remains of Klosterheim's band continued to stalk in our wake, but they, too, had few arrows left. They followed like coyotes tracking a cougar, as if they hoped we would lead them to fresh meat.

Their numbers were now badly reduced. They must have been debating the wisdom of continuing with this war party. Klosterheim had not delivered what he had promised them. The Two Tongues probably had some self-interest in leaguing himself with my husband's old enemy. If he had expected Klosterheim to know how to defeat us, he had been disappointed.

I was surprised when they began to drop back. They were soon far behind us. No doubt they were discussing fresh strategies. Klosterheim would, for his part, insist on the pursuit. I understood him well enough to know that.

The woodlands were sparser now, breaking into isolated thickets as the undulating grasslands opened up before us. Huge mountains dominated the distant landscape. The pygmies were among the grasses and wild corn. The smoke we saw behind us showed that at least some of them had made camp. White Crow remained suspicious. He said it was an old trick of theirs to leave one man making smoke while the rest continued in pursuit. After studying it for a while though, he decided most of the Pukawatchi were there preparing food. He could tell by the quality of the smoke that they had made a good kill. This would be the message any stragglers would see, and it would bring them into the camp.

Ayanawatta said the Pukawatchi were a civilized people and would feel shame if they ate their meat raw. The fire told of a beast serving the whole party. While this was not a deliberate message, the Pukawatchi would know how friend and enemy alike would read it. They had called off hunting us, at least for the moment.

"And a big deer will fill a lot of little stomachs!" Ayanawatta laughed.

I asked him if there were many people of Pukawatchi height, and he seemed surprised at my question. "In their own lands, all is to their stature. Even their monsters are smaller!"

"That is what made it both easy and hard for me," chimed in White Crow. "I was easy to see but hard to kill!"

The Pukawatchi were cliff dwellers from the southwest living in sophisticated cave-towns. Most of their civic life was conducted inside. When he had visited Ipkeptemi the Wise, their greatest medicine chief, White Crow had experienced some difficulty crawling through the city's smaller tunnels.

"And did you steal their treasures?" I asked. I had, of course, a specific interest in the black blade.

"I am charged to bring important medicine back to the Kakatanawa. Only I can handle the metal, since they lost their previous White Crow."

"Who was their previous White Crow man?" I asked almost hesitantly. I could not help fearing this road of inquiry would take me somewhere I did not want to go.

His answer was not the one I had anticipated.

"My father," he said.

"And his name?" I asked.

White Crow looked at me in some surprise. "That is still his own," he said.

I had offended some protocol and fell silent by way of apology. In this strange world where dream-logic must be followed or consign you forever to limbo I swam again in familiar supernatural waters, ready for all experience. Old disciplines returned. I was prepared to make the most of what I could. Even the most dedicated adventurers accepted how form and ritual were essential to this life. A game of cards depends upon chance, but can only be played if strict rules are followed.

We played the ball game that evening after we had made early camp. It was a form of backgammon but required more memory and skill. Such games were cultivated by Ayanawatta's people, he said. Those who played them well had special status and a name. They were called *wabenosee* or, more humorously, *sheshebuwak*, which meant 'ducks' and was also the nickname for the balls used in their game.

"Presumably we are at the mercy of fate, like the rattling balls," I said. "Do we control anything? Do we not merely maintain the status quo as best we can?"

Ayanawatta was not sure. "I envy you your skills, Countess Oona. I still yearn to walk the white path between the realms, but until now my dream-journeys, dangerous and enlightening as they have been, have been accomplished by other means."

He did not know if I was any more or less at the mercy of fate than himself. He longed to make just one such walk, he said, before his spirit passed into its next state.

I laughed and made an easy promise. "If I ever can, I'll take you," I said. "Every sentient creature should look once upon the constantly weaving and separating moonbeam roads." The women of my kind, of course, constantly crossed and recrossed them. And in our actions, in the stories we played out, we wove the web and woof of the multiverse, the fabric of time and space. From the original matter, acted upon by our dreams and desires, by our stories, came the substance and structure of the whole.

"Divine simplicity," I said. With it came the full understanding of one's value as an individual, the understanding that every action taken in the common cause is an action taken for oneself and vice versa. "The moonbeam roads are at once the subtlest and easiest of routes. Sometimes I feel almost guilty at the ease with which I move between the realms." All other adepts hoped to achieve the ability, natural to dreamthieves and free dream-travelers, of walking between the worlds. Our unconscious skills made us powerful, and they made us dangerous but also highly en-dangered, especially when the likes of Gaynor chose to challenge the very core of belief upon which all our other realities de-pended.

"The path is not always easy and not always straight," I told him. "Sometimes it takes the whole of one's life to walk quite a short distance. Sometimes all you do is return to where you began."

"Circumstances determine action? Context defines?" Grin-ning, White Crow made several quick movements with his fin-gers. Balls rattled and danced like planets for a moment and then were still. He had won the game. "Is that what you learned at your *musram?*" And he darted me a quick, sardonic look, to show me that he could use more than one vocabulary if he wished. Most of us know several symbolic languages, which affords us few prob-lems with the logic and sound of spoken language. We are equally alert to the language of street and forest. We are often scarcely aware which language we use, and it never takes us long to learn a new one. These skills are primitive compared to our monstrous talent for manipulating the natural world, which makes shape-taking almost second nature. Quietly, however, White Crow was reminding me that he, too, was an adept.

"To wander the paths between the worlds at will," he said, "is not the destiny of a Kakatanawa White Crow man."

Ayanawatta lit a pipe. White Crow refused it, making an ex-cuse. "We need have no great fear of the Pukawatchi now, but it would be wise to keep guard. I go forward to seek an old friend and hope to be with you in the morning. If I am not, continue as we are going, towards the mountains. You will find me."

And then, swiftly, he disappeared into the night.

We smoked and talked for a little longer. Ayanawatta had had dealings with the pygmies. They had skills and knowledge denied to most and were fair traders, if hard bargainers. When I told him that Klosterheim had been the same size as me when I last saw him, Ayanawatta smiled and nodded as if this were familiar enough. "I told you," he said, "we are living in that kind of time."

Did he know why Klosterheim was now the size of a Pukawatchi? He shook his head. White Crow might know. The dwarves and the giants were leaving their ordained realms. But he and others like him had begun the process, by exploring into those realms. He, after all, had broken the rules, as had White Crow, long before the Pukawatchi began to move north. The dwarves had always lived at peace with those from the other two realms, each with its own hunting grounds. All he knew now was that the closer to the sacred oak one came, the closer the realms conjoined.

I had been taught that the multiverse had no center, just as an animal or a tree had no center. Yet if the multiverse had a soul, that was what Ayanawatta seemed to be describing. If the multiplicity of everything was symbolized in a living metaphor, there was no reason the multiverse should not possess a soul. I went to unroll my buffalo robe and wrap myself against the cold.

Ayanawatta was enjoying his pipe more than usual. He lay on his side, staring up at a three-quarter moon over which thin, white clouds floated on a steady breeze from the south. He wore his soft buckskin shirt against the cold. It was of very fine workmanship, decorated with semiprecious beads and dyed porcupine quills, like the leggings and the fur-trimmed cap he also pulled on against the night's chill. Again I had the impression of a well-to-do Victorian gentleman adventurer making the best of the wilderness.

He had already removed and stored his eagle feathers in a hollow tube he carried for the purpose, but he still wore his long earrings and studs. His elaborate tattoos did nothing but enhance his refined, sensitive features. He took a deep pull from the pipe before handing me the bowl into which I placed my own reed to draw up the smoke. "What if that tree-soul which the Kakatanawa guard were the sum of all our souls?"

I agreed that this was a philosophical possibility.

"What if the sum of all our souls was the price we paid should that tree die?" he continued significantly.

I drew the mixture into my lungs. I tasted mint, rosemary, willow, sage. I inhaled a herb garden and forest combined! Unlike tobacco, this spread lightness and well-being through my whole body. "Is that what we are fighting for?" I asked, handing him back the bowl.

He sighed. "I think it is. When Law goes mad and Chaos is the Balance's only defense, some believe we are already conquered."

"You do not agree?"

"Of course not. I have made my spirit-quest into my future. I understand how I must play my part in restoring the Balance. I studied for four years and in four realms. I learned how to dream of my own future and summon for myself both flesh and form. I have read my own story in the books of the horse-people. I have heard my story called a false one. But if I give it life, I will redeem it. I will respect the people it sought to celebrate. I will bring respect to both the singer and the song."

He took another long, delicious pull on the pipe. He was gravely determined. "I know what I must do to fulfill my spiritual destiny. I must live my story as it is written. Our rituals are the rituals of order. I am working to give credible power back to Law and to fight those forces which would disrupt the Balance forever. Like you, I serve neither Law nor Chaos. I am, in the eyes of a mukhamirim, a Knight of the Balance." He let the smoke from his lungs pour out to join that of our small fire, curling gracefully towards the moon. "I have that lust for harmony, unity and justice which consumes so many of us."

The firelight caught his gold and copper, reflected in his glowing skin, drew contrasting shadows. I was, in spite of myself, enormously attracted to him, but I did not fear the attraction. Both of us had been well schooled in self-control.

"It is sometimes hard to know," I said, "where to place one's loyalty . . ."

He experienced no such ambiguities. He had taken his dream

journey. "My story is already written. I have read it, after all. Now I must follow it. That is the price you pay for such a vision. I know what I must do to make sure the story comes true in every possible realm of the multiverse. Thus I'll achieve that ultimate harmony we all desire more than life or death!"

Feeling overwhelmed by my own thoughts, I again took the first watch, listening with an attention which had once been habitual. But I was certain Klosterheim and his pygmies were not out there.

I was ready for sleep when I woke Ayanawatta to take his watch. He settled himself comfortably against Bes's gently rising and falling chest and filled another pipe. For all his appearance of indolence, I knew that every sense was alert. He had the air of all true outdoors folk, of being as securely comfortable in that vast wilderness under the moon and stars as another might be in the luxury of an urban living room.

The last thing I saw before I went to sleep was that broad, reassuring face, its tattoos telling the tale of his life journey, staring contentedly at the sky, confident of his ability to live up to everything his dream demanded of him.

In the morning Bes was restless. We washed and ate rapidly and were soon mounted again. We let the mammoth take her own course, since she evidently had a better idea than we where to find her master.

The only weapon White Crow had taken was his black-bladed lance.

I feared for him. "He might have been overwhelmed by the pygmies."

Ayanawatta was unworried. "With those senses of his, he can hear anything coming. But there is always the chance he's met with an accident. If so, he is not far from here. Bes can find him if we cannot."

By noon we had yet to see a sign of White Crow. Bes kept moving steadily towards the mountains, following the gentle curves of the landscape. Sometimes we could see for miles across the rolling drumlins. At other times we traveled through shallow valleys. Occasionally Bes paused, lifting her wide, curving tusks against the sky, her relatively small ears moving to follow a sound. Satisfied, she would then move on.

It was close to evening before Bes slowly brought her massive body to a halt and began to scent at the air with her trunk. Made long and dark by the sun, our shadows followed us like gigantic ghosts.

Once more Bes's ears waved back and forth. She seemed to hear something she had been hoping for and strained towards the source of the sound. We, of course, let her have her head. She began to move gradually to the east, to our right, slowly picking up speed until she was striding across the prairie at what amounted to a canter.

In the distance now I heard a strange mixture of noises. Something between the honking of geese and the hissing of snakes, mixed with a gurgling rumble which sounded like the first eruptions of a volcano.

All of a sudden White Crow appeared before us, waving his lance in triumph, grinning and shouting.

"I've found him again! Quickly, let's not lose him." He began running beside the mammoth, keeping easy pace with her.

I heard the noise again, but louder. I caught a sweet, familiar smell as we crested a broad, sweeping hill. Setting behind the mountains, the sun turned the whole scene blood red. And there we saw White Crow's intended prey.

The size of a three-story building, its brilliant feathered ruff was flaming with a thousand hues in that deepening light. I had never seen so much color on one animal. Dazzling peacock feathers blazed purple, scarlet and gold, emerald and ruby and sapphire. Such beautiful plumage was the finery of a creature whose nightmare features should have disappeared from the Earth countless millions of years before. Its brown-black beak looked as if it had been carved from a gigantic block of mahogany. Above the beak two terrible brilliant yellow eyes glared, each the size of a dressing mirror. The mouth snapped and clacked, streaming with pale green saliva. As we watched, the thing lifted a yelping

prairie fox in its right front claw and stuffed it into its maw, gag-
ging as it swallowed.

The creature had a hungry, half-crazed look to it. It stretched
its long neck down to the ground and sniffed, as if hoping to find
food it had overlooked. It then stood upright on massive back feet
which had a somewhat birdlike appearance, though its forepaws
more closely resembled lizard claws.

Any one of the reptile's neck feathers, erect now as he sensed
our presence, was the height of a tall man and layered in rich reds,
yellows, purples and greens. Ulric would have called it a dinosaur,
but to me it was a cross between a huge bird and a giant lizard, its
feathered tail train being by far its longest part. Clearly it was a
link with the dinosaur ancestors of our modern birds.

As we watched, the tail slashed back and forth like a scythe,
cutting and trampling great swathes in the wild corn. I sniffed and
realized it was the sweet scent I had smelled earlier. Suddenly
awash with totally inappropriate emotions, I longed for the corn-
fields of the farm where I grew up during the period of my
mother's attempted retirement.

"I think," said White Crow regretfully, climbing up into the
saddle to sit with us, "I am going to have to kill him."

CHAPTER FIVE

Feathers and Scales

Do you live the tale,
Or does the tale live you?

WHELDRAKE,
"The Teller or the Tale"

hy kill him?" I asked. "He is offering us no harm."

"He is an invader here," said White Crow. "But that is the business of those who hunt this land. He has moved north with the warming. That is not why he will die." He added almost as an aside, "Many years ago, he ate my father."

The shock which came with this news was horrible. The first time I saw this youth, he had called Ulric "Father."

There was nothing to do or say. My reaction was entirely subjective. For all their resemblance it was obvious there was no close connection between Ulric and White Crow.

"But that is not why we hunt him," Ayanawatta reminded him gently. "We hunt him for what your father carried when he was eaten."

"What was that?" I asked before I thought better of it.

But White Crow answered with apparent easiness, staring at the thing which rattled its huge ruff in frustration and screamed its hunger. "Oh, some medicine he had with him when the *kenabik* took him."

His tone was so inappropriate that I glanced hard at his face. It was a mask.

The feathered dinosaur had our scent, but the blustering breeze was varying and dropping. He kept losing it, turning this way and that and grunting to himself, drooling. He hardly knew what he was smelling. He seemed an inexpert hunter. His nostrils were heavy with ill health. His breathing was a rasp.

The last of the sun now poured over the mountains and drenched the plain with deep light. Big clouds came in behind us with a stronger wind, bringing more rain. Eventually the creature began to lumber away from us, then turned and came back for a few paces. He was still not sure what he scented. He might have been shortsighted, like rhinos. Clearly past his prime, he was scarcely able to fend for himself.

When I mentioned this to Ayanawatta he nodded. "This is not their place," he said. "The *kenabik* do not breed. His tribe have all died. Something as beautiful replaces them, we hope."

He spoke distractedly as he studied the beaked dragon, who was still casting bewildered yellow eyes back and forth. "And of a more appropriate size," he added with a slight smile.

White Crow pulled in our mount. Bes stood still as a rock while her master studied the *kenabik*. The beaked dragon's feathers were layered, pale blue on green, on gold, on silver, on scarlet. There were subtle shades of brown-yellow and dark red, of glittering emerald and sapphire. When that black maw opened it revealed a crimson tongue, broken molars, cracked incisors. There seemed something wrong with that mouth, but I was not sure what.

Then the sun disappeared. It was suddenly pitch black. From somewhere in that darkness, the *kenabik* began to keen.

That keening was one of the most mournful sounds I had ever heard. The note was absolutely desolate as the monster cried for itself and for its lost kind.

I looked at White Crow again.

His face was still totally immobile, but I saw the silver trail of tears running to his lips. It was hard to know whether he wept for the pain of this creature, the thought of having to destroy it or the loss of his father.

Again, that awful, agonized call. But it grew fainter as the thing moved off.

"We will kill it in the morning," White Crow said. He seemed glad to put off the unsavory moment for a little longer.

How three humans armed with bows and spears were to set about killing the *kenabik* had not yet been explained to me!

Neither was it to happen as White Crow had said.

The monster determined our agenda.

I was awake when the *kenabik* became famished enough to attack. I heard it running towards us over the low hills. It went through the camp in one terrible, violent moment, even as I tried to wake my friends.

Ayanawatta found his bow and arrows while White Crow hefted his spears.

"They never hunt at night." White Crow sounded offended.

Bes had stumbled to her feet, still bleary with sleep, her trunk questing about for White Crow. She could not see him, and the feathered dinosaur was coming in rapidly on her left.

Bes was ready. In time to take the *kenabik*'s second attack, she swung her huge tusks in the direction of the noise. The beast came thudding into the camp screaming its own terror at our fire and grabbing about for something, anything, to eat.

Bes stepped forward. A sweep of her great head, and a long, deep gouge appeared along the beast's left side. He shrieked as those ivory sabers began to sweep back the other way.

The old mammoth staggered and was momentarily knocked off balance, but she held her ground, the *kenabik*'s blood streaming from her massive tusk. Her eyes narrowed, her trunk curling, she displayed her pleasure at her own achievement. She was almost skittish as she turned to trumpet after her fleeing foe.

"Why would it behave so uncharacteristically?" I was panting, trying to gather up my few possessions while the others retrieved the rest of our scattered goods.

"It is mad," said White Crow sadly. "It has nothing to eat."

"There must be plenty of prey on the prairie?"

"Oh, yes," he said. "There is. And as you saw, every so often

he devours some. What we probably will not see is the *kenabik* dis-
gorging most of what he eats. Unfortunately he was not born a
meat eater. What he misses is the rich foliage and lush grass of his
native south. The transition from herbivore to carnivore is impossible. The meat he eats is killing him. What vegetation grows
here is too sparse and too hard for him to harvest. Even if we did
not kill him, he would be dead soon, and it would be a bad, ignoble death. His shame would be great. It would weight his spirit
and keep him bound to this realm. He would have long to brood
on the ignobility he has brought to himself and his tribe. We can
offer him better. We can offer him the respect of our arms. You
could say it was his own fault for leaving his grazing grounds, but
predators were moving up behind his kind, picking them off as
they weakened. He was chased from his homeland. I wish to try
to kill him mercifully."

"You show much forgiveness for the beast that ate your father."

"I understand that it was an accident. The *kenabik* probably
didn't even know he was eating him. There was no malice involved. My father took a risk and failed." Two red stones shone in
White Crow's rigid face.

I turned away.

Ayanawatta had recovered his bow and quiver while White
Crow collected all the fire he could find back into the pot. The
little lean-to we had put up against the rainy breeze was totally
trampled, so again Bes gave us her massive bulk for shelter. The
two of us slept warily as White Crow elected to keep watch until
dawn.

I woke once to see his profile set against the grey strip of light
on the horizon, and it seemed to me he had not moved. When I
woke again, his face and head were set exactly as I had seen them
hours earlier. He resembled one of those extraordinary, infinitely
beautiful marbles of the Moldavian Captives Michelangelo had
carved for the French pope. Infinitely sad, infinitely aware of the
cold truth of their coming fate.

Once again I felt an urgent wish to take him in my arms and

comfort him. An unexpected desire to bring warmth to a lonely, uncomplaining soul.

He turned at that moment, and his puzzled gaze met mine. Then, with a small sigh, he gave his attention back to the distant mountains. He recognized what was in my eyes. He had seen it before. He had a cause. A dream to live out. His destiny was the only comfort he allowed himself.

When we woke it was drizzling hard. White Crow had pulled a robe over his shoulders as he struggled to settle the great saddle on his mammoth's back. Ayanawatta moved to help him. Everything smelled of rain. The whole sky was dark grey. It was impossible to see more than twenty yards ahead. The mountains, of course, had vanished.

I wrapped myself tightly against the cold and wet. The mammoth rose to her feet, groaning and muttering at the winter wind stiffening her joints. We had not tried to make a fresh fire the night before, and our firepot was low, so we ate cold jerky as we rode.

We followed the *kenabik*'s bloodstained trail. Bes had injured him enough at least to slow him down.

We were warier than usual, because we knew the *kenabik* might be waiting in cover to attack. The steady rain finally stopped. The wind dropped.

The world was strangely silent. What sounds there were became amplified and isolated as the going became harder through the soaking grasslands. Occasionally the sky cleared and thin sunbeams banded the distant tundra. The mountains, however, remained hidden. We heard the splash of frogs and small animals in the nearby water. We smelled the strong, acrid aroma of rotting grass from an old nest, and then once again came the sudden hissing wind bringing rain. We heard the steady sound of Bes's feet as she carried us stolidly on after our prey.

We reached a kind of wallow, a muddy bayou filled with weed. It was clear the monster had rested, attempting to eat some of the weed. We also found the half-digested remains of various smaller mammals and reptiles. White Crow had been right. This creature was too specialized to survive here. Also the wound was clearly more serious than we had originally guessed. There were signs that he had made a crude attempt to stanch a flow of blood with some of the grass. How intelligent was this creature?

I asked Ayanawatta his opinion. He was not sure. He had learned, he said, not to measure intelligence by his own standards. He preferred to assume that every creature was as conscious as himself but in different ways. It was as well, he said, to give every creature the respect you would give yourself.

I could not entirely accept this view. I told him that I could not believe, however conscious they might be, that animals possess a moral sensibility. And the most unstable of rocks are poor conversationalists.

Almost immediately, I found myself smiling, amused by my own presumption. Not long before, I had been accusing my husband of being insufficiently imaginative.

Ayanawatta was silent for a moment, raising his eyebrows. "I may be mistaken," he said, "but I seem to recall an adventure I once had among the rock giants. They are, indeed, extremely laconic."

The sideways glance he threw in my direction was humorous.

White Crow slipped suddenly down Bes's flank without stopping her progress and began to pad beside her, studying the muddy creek. It reminded me of what Ulric must have seen in the trenches at the end of the first war. The *kenabik* had clearly been in agony, rolling over and over in an effort to stop the pain.

Our hunt took on a peculiar gravity. It had something of the air of a funeral procession.

The rain came down harder until we could scarcely see for the sweeping sheets of water. As we descended a long hill, we confronted a stand of tough, green grass that reached almost to Bes's shoulder. She found it difficult to walk on through. White Crow told her to turn and move back to a better place. Slowly she crushed her way out of the confining growth and made for the high ground again.

Then through the pounding rain we heard the *kenabik*. No

longer did it squawk and scream and moan as it had done. No longer did its voice have the fading note of pain and self-pity. The sound had the fullness of a baritone, rhythmic and slow, the noise of a bull-roarer, booming from that massive diaphragm.

White Crow took a slender spear from the long quiver. The edges were tipped with silver, the shaft bound with ivory and copper. With this, he again dismounted and was quickly lost in the rain and deep grass.

Bes came to a stop, turning her head as if she feared for him.

"What is the *kenabik* doing now?" I asked Ayanawatta.

"I am not sure," said the warrior, frowning, "but I think he is singing his death song."

The beast's voice grew deeper still, and something connected with me. I could feel his bewildered mind reaching into mine, questing for something. Not me. Not me. There was a mutual repulsion. Curiosity. An almost grateful quality as the monster tasted tentatively at my identity.

All the time that song went on. Somehow I believed he was telling the story of his people, of their glory, of their virtue and their destruction. A psychologist would consider this transference, would argue that the beast could not feel such complicated emotions and ideas. Yet, as Ayanawatta said, who are we to measure the value or quality of another's perceptions?

I could not bring myself to bond with the *kenabik*'s brain. It was too unlike anything I understood. It dreamed of tall fields of cane and thick, nourishing ferns, and its song began to reflect this dream more and more. A harmony grew between the strange view of Paradise and the thrumming voice. Whatever it is in sentient creatures that needs to communicate, that is what I heard. It was a confused, frightened mixture of half-understood images and feelings. Who else could the dying creature reach out to? Another voice entered the song, taking the melody until it was impossible to tell which was which.

In response to this, the monster abruptly shifted its attention elsewhere. I was, I must admit, deeply relieved. While it could not be the first time I had attended a dying spirit, this strange, anachronistic being found little comfort from me.

The clouds parted for a moment or two, and the rain passed. We saw that we stood in waist-high grass. Some distance off, with his back to us, was White Crow. From his stance and the position of his head I understood the *kenabik* to be somewhere below him. Then, out of the misty foliage, I saw a beaked head rise. Huge yellow eyes sought the source of the other song. The eyes were filled with baffled gratitude. As it died, the monster received grace.

The clouds rolled in again. I saw White Crow lift his silvertipped spear.

Both songs ended.

We waited for a long time. The rain lashed down, and the wind blew the grass into glistening waves. We had become used to these blustering elemental attacks. At last Ayanawatta and I made a decision. We dismounted, telling Bes to remain where she was unless she needed to escape danger, and pressed on through the fleshy stalks surrounding us, our moccasins sinking into the thick, glutinous mud. Ayanawatta paused, cautioning me to silence, and he listened. Slowly I became aware of soft footfalls.

White Crow came crashing out of the grass. Over his shoulder he carried his lance and two huge feathers, gorgeous against that grey light. He was covered from head to foot in blood.

"I had to go inside it," he said. "To find the medicine of my father."

We followed him to where Bes waited. The mammoth was visibly pleased at his return. He took the two gigantic brilliant feathers and stuck them into the wool near her head. Her hair was so thick that they did not fall, but White Crow assured her he would attach them more securely later. Bes looked oddly proud of her new finery. White Crow was acknowledging her victory. Then he went back to the creek and washed the blood off his body, and again he sang. He sang of Bes and her hero-spirit. She would find her ancestors in the eternal dance and celebrate her deeds forever. He sang of the great heart of his finished enemy. And it felt to me as if that monster's spirit were at peace leaving the world to join its brothers in some eternal grazing grounds.

White Crow spent the rest of that day and part of the night washing himself and his clothing. When he came back to the camp he seemed grateful for the fire we had made. He sat down, took a pipe, and smoked for a while without speaking. Then he reached to where he had placed his pouch on top of his freshly washed clothes and slid his hand inside. His fist closed on something, and he withdrew it, opening the palm to show us what he had retrieved.

The firelight threw wild shadows. It was hard for me to see.

"I had no choice but to go into his guts," said White Crow. "It was difficult. It took some time. The *kenabik* had three bellies, all of them diseased. I had hoped to find more. But this was what there was. Perhaps it is all we need."

The fire flared, lighting the night, and I saw the tiny object clearly. Turquoise, ivory, scarlet. Round. It was horribly familiar . . .

I recognized it.

I had an immediate physical reaction. My head swam. I gasped. My mind refused what my eyes saw!

I looked at an exact miniature of the huge medicine shield on which I had made my way into this world. I had no real doubt that it was the same. Every detail was identical, save for the size.

"It was my father's," said White Crow, "when he was White Crow Man. I am truly White Crow Man now." This statement was made flatly. His voice was bleak. He closed his fingers tightly around the talisman before putting it away in his bag.

I looked at Ayanawatta, as if for confirmation that I was right in recognizing the tiny medicine shield, but he had never properly seen it as I had. He had merely glimpsed it in his summoning dream. Every detail was the same, I was sure. Yet how had it become so tiny? Was it some process in the animal's belly? Some supernatural element I had not perceived?

Was Klosterheim a dwarf? Or was I the giant? What had gone

wrong with the scale of things? The workings of Chaos? Or had Law, in its crazed wisdom, wished this condition upon the world?

"What is that you hold?" I asked at last.

White Crow frowned. "It is my father's medicine shield," he said.

"But the size . . ."

"My father was not a large man," said White Crow.

CHAPTER SIX

The Snows of Yesteryear

Northward to the northern waters,
Northward to the farthest shore . . .

W. S. HARTE,
"The Maker of Laws"

nd so, having reached that particular stage in the dream-quest of my two companions, we continued our journey north. All obstacles seemed to be behind us. The weather, though cooler, was bright and clear. I felt instinctively confident that Ulric still lived and that we should soon be reunited. Only the constant, thrusting, whispering, insistent wind reminded me that I still had mysterious antagonists, those who would stop me seeing my husband again.

Game became increasingly plentiful, and I was able to feed us on antelope, hare, grouse and geese. Now there was wild alfalfa, maize and potato. Both my companions carried bags of dried herbs which they used for cooking and smoking. I was by far the best shot, and the men were content to let me hunt. We became used to eating very well, usually around sunset, while Bes, the mammoth, grazed happily on the rich grasses and shrubs. We enjoyed exquisite light saturating gorgeous scenery, the tall peaks of the horizon, the varied greens and yellows of the prairie. The evening sky was deep yellow, flooded with scarlet and ocher.

We ate heartily, as if to keep our strength against the coming winter.

The wind grew steadily fresher and more invigorating. For a

while it was almost playful. There was a sharpness to the air which brought clearer details and keener scents. Beavers worked in the creeks. Prairie dogs were hunted by huge, cruising eagles. We startled a kangaroo rat in a swathe of wild roses whose petals sailed through the twilight as he leaped to avoid us. Families of badgers came squinting into the last of the sun. The occasional possum would play dead when we scared him inspecting our camp at night. Most of the animals were not unusually nervous of us. They had no reason to be. Ayanawatta, lacking a human listener, was perfectly happy to address an audience of thoughtful toads.

More than once we saw herds of bison grazing their way south, but they were not food for us. We had no time to preserve the meat or cure the hide. Buffalo tastes delicious when one has eaten little else, but the tough, gamey meat is not to everyone's favor. Neither were we tempted by the coats of the splendid bulls who guarded their cows and calves. We shared a notion that to kill a buffalo only for its hide was offensive. My companions had been trained as children to kill swiftly and without cruelty and practiced all the disciplines of a halal slaughterman. They could not imagine a civilized human being behaving in any other manner. There are few willing vegans on the prairie.

I fell in love with the great, placid bison. I found myself drawn to them. I would leave my weapons behind and stroll among them, touching them and talking to them. They were not in any way afraid of me, though sometimes they seemed a little irritated. I learned not to put my hands on the young. There was a wonderful sense of security at the center of the herd. Increasingly I understood the deep pleasures of herd life. Our strength was in the herd, in the alertness of the males, in the wisdom of the cows. And we were eternal.

Eventually our ways parted. The huge mass of buffalo—a great, restless sea of black, brown and white—made its way towards the blue horizon. From a hill, I watched it moving slowly across the prairie under the rising sun. Briefly I had an urge to follow it. Then I ran to rejoin my companions.

The mountains, which had seemed so easily reached, were

separated from us by scrub, woodland, rivers and swamps, but even these were more easily negotiated than before. Where there was water and shelter, we saw stands of old trees, the remains of a great forest. The ground became firmer as the air grew colder. For her age Bes the mammoth had extraordinary stamina. White Crow said she had not long since walked for five days and nights, pausing only three times to drink.

While White Crow shared my enjoyment of solitude, of listening to the subtle music of the prairie, Ayanawatta remained as talkative as ever. I must admit my own mind was rather narrowly focused.

The wind returned forcefully and erratically. This world had increasing inconsistencies. Klosterheim had become a dwarf. The medicine shield was now small enough to fit on the palm of a hand. Size in this realm was alarmingly unstable. Was this the work of Chaos? Was this changing but persistent wind actually sentient? Dread rose inside me and threatened to consume me. It was some time before I could regain complete control of myself.

Ayanawatta drew his robe around him. "The weather grows chillier with the passing of the hours. This wind never ceases." We wrapped ourselves in the great folds of his wigwam hides and at night built a larger fire. The canoe now acted as a canopy over the saddle, held there by four staves, and protected us against rain. At night two of us could sleep under it and give the other the benefit of the fire.

I remained mystified by the size of the medicine shield and where it had been found. White Crow now wore it around his neck on a beautiful beaded thong. He said nothing else about his father. Etiquette did not allow me to ask. I could only hope coming events would illuminate me.

I was bound to discover more. This careful living of the details of a dreamed future or a granted vision was characteristic of Ayanawatta's people. I understood loyalty to a visionary destiny. I understood the grueling discipline of his chosen way. Every step was a figure in a formal dance. A masque which must be performed perfectly. By dancing the exact step, the achieved ambition was reached. It was not quite creativity. It was an act of reproduction or interpretation, a strengthening. Following this discipline took the most extraordinary qualities of character. Virtues which I did not possess. Crude folk renderings of this discipline had been discussed during my training in Marrakech, where we had also looked at the Egyptian and Mayan Books of the Dead.

That strict path had no appeal for me. The musram teaches that time is a field and that space could be a property of time, one of many dimensions. By subtle repetition we weave our common threads and give longevity to our particular story. I suppose it was my training to find new patterns. In this sense we represented a balance of the opposite forces of Law and Chaos. Certainly the animism and cosmology of White Crow and Ayanawatta were far more in harmony with the eternal realities than Klosterheim's grim disciplines. If their Law was modified by my Chaos, equally my Chaos was modified and strengthened by their Law.

Klosterheim, in rejecting Chaos completely, rejected any prospect of ever achieving his own particular dream of reconciliation and harmony. In some ways I found the ex-priest a more interesting and complex figure than our defeated enemy Gaynor. Ulric's cousin had been that rare thing, an adept entirely without loyalty to anything but himself. Such creatures achieved their power through means which by definition denied them the harmony of the Balance. Gaynor, or those avatars who played his role throughout the multiverse, tended to come to a sticky end not because they were overwhelmed by the forces of virtue, but because their own flawed characters ultimately betrayed them. Had he, as Klosterheim suggested, drawn all his scattered bodies back into a single self?

I had been unprepared for this adventure. It was occasionally difficult to believe that it was happening at all. At any moment I might take control of my own dream and return to normality.

I found myself missing the advice of my old mentor, Prince Lobkowitz. A tower of strength, a fixed point in my emotional ocean, he understood more of the structure of the multiverse than anyone. He had helped me harness a little of the genetic talent which enabled me to roam the moonbeam roads at will.

Some called the myriad worlds of the multiverse the Shadow Realm or the Dream Worlds. Some understood them to be real.

Others believed them an illusion, a symbol, a mere version of something too intense for our ordinary senses. Many believed them to be a little of both. Some suggested we were the vermin of the multiverse, living in the cracks and crannies of divine reality and mistaking a crumb of cheese for a banquet. Many cosmologies recognized only a small group of realms. Whatever the ultimate truth, some of us were able to wander between such worlds more or less at will, as I did, while others endured extraordinary training to be able to take a simple step between one version of their reality and another. The interconnection of human dreams formed its own nexus of reality, its own realm, where travelers wandered or searched for some specific goal. It was in this vast realm of realms, worlds of the soul's dread and the heart's desire, that the dreamthieves earned their dangerous living.

Each slight variance of one realm from another is marked by a change in scale so great that one is undetectable to another. For those of us who walk the moonbeam ways every step takes us through a further scale. Or perhaps we travel beyond scale, as over a rippling pond? Many say this could mean that the matter of our beings is forever forming and re-forming. Instantly re-created by an act of will? Dreaming dust? That said, the reality is almost impossible to describe in mere words. Some achieve their travel through what they call sorcery, others through dreams or some form of creativity. Whatever it is called, it involves a monstrous act of will.

One learns temperance with one's travels. One also learns to live and invite experience. Each twist of a moonbeam branch on the great, eternal tree takes one to fresh knowledge and self-revelation. It is a fascinating and endless life. However, for the likes of myself, who will not steal others' dreams as my mother did, it can become unsatisfying. What Ulric had given me back was a moral focus and a sense of purpose. I had learned to tackle the problems of one small sphere rather than engage in the great, eternal conflict between Chaos and Law.

I no longer felt a particular longing for the moonbeam roads. Sometimes I did yearn for the silver-and-scarlet light warping and sliding in the air around my cottage, that particular music which came when certain spheres intersected and produced their glorious harmonies. But chiefly I hoped my old life, with my husband and my children, would soon be restored.

The days grew shorter and still colder, but they brought some sort of promise. We must soon enter Kakatanawa lands. There, I knew, I would find Ulric. But how would I rescue him or bargain for his release?

The first sign that again we were being followed came during a flurry of sleet, when sheets of grey misery stretched across the plains and hid even the foothills. The curtain parted for a few seconds and revealed a hillock covered in spiky prairie grass and clover, glinting in the thin light. It was just behind us and to our right. Looking over my shoulder at it as we rode along, I thought I saw a figure standing there, its grey robes rising in the wind, its grey face the very personification of winter death.

Klosterheim!

The man was relentless.

Had he returned to his normal size? I had not seen him long enough to be able to tell. I continued to peer back over my shoulder as Bes strode stoically on through the icy rain but did not see Klosterheim again.

No doubt he had his pygmies with him and his ally, the Two Tongues. I warned the others of what I had seen. We agreed it would be wise to mount a guard again when we camped.

We rested Bes regularly. White Crow said normally she would have been put to pasture years before. Then he had talked about this dream, this destined scenario, with her. She had wanted to go, he said. "She believes this journey is good for her and prepares her for the afterlife."

We were lucky. That evening the rain disappeared and left us with a watery sunset brightening a stand of heavy, old oaks. Of the groves we had passed, these were the thickest and most ancient we had seen. The boles and branches were so dense they offered excellent cover. The smell of the ancient glade was intoxicating!

"Good," said Ayanawatta, striding around in what was virtually a cave of woven branches into which a single shaft of sunlight fell upon a slender sapling at the center. "This is the place to make our medicine. It is a world within the world, with a roof and four corners and the tree at the center. It will amplify our medicine and make it work as it has to do."

Although he talked more around the subject, he added no further information. We built a small fire in our pot, as you might in someone's home. It felt somehow wrong to disturb the floor of this ancient grove. Many branches were thicker than most trunks. They could be thousands of years old. Perhaps an earlier culture had left a few stands of uncleared woodland? Maybe some natural disaster had destroyed all but a patch or two of these timeless trees?

Ayanawatta burned a little of our food as an offering to the grove for its security. There is a special consciousness which trees have. They respond well to respect. I had the distinct sense that night that I slept in a holy retreat, in a temple.

Strangely for me I dreamed. The tree under which I slept became my multiverse in which I wandered. I dreamed of relatives. I dreamed of the world where my name was Ilian of Garathorm. She was a powerful warrior, an avatar of the Eternal Champion, a soul-cousin to my father. Her world was nothing but ancient trees. To the northwest were the great redwoods, to the northeast the giant oaks and birches. In the south were mangroves and more exotic trees. All were united in one vast world of tangled roots and branches. The entire planet was an organic nest of growing flora, with massive, fleshy blossoms. Magnolias and rhododendrons, vast chrysanthemums and roses bloomed to make a world in which Ilian coexisted with all manner of huge insects and birds. She rode the branches of her world as I strode the moonbeams of mine.

In my dream Ilian was troubled. She saw the end of her world. The death of everything. The withering of her home tree and therefore her own end. She called to her ancestors and the spirits of her world. She summoned them together to aid her in her final fight. She spoke to creatures she knew as silverskins, and as she woke she recalled the story of Piel d'Argent, of Le Courbousier Blanc, the silver man, the Prince of Faery, whom the Kakatanawa called White Crow.

Upon waking, my dream fled away from me. I held what I could of it, for there was now a nagging idea somewhere in the back of my mind, something which linked White Crow to some-one or something else, some faint memory, perhaps of childhood. I became increasingly certain that we were related.

I looked at the sleeping face of the albino youth. He was com-pletely at rest, yet I knew he could come alert in seconds. I hardly liked to breathe for fear he would mistake any sound I made for an alarm. What had I been dreaming which concerned him? What were these tiny patches of memory he had left me with? I moved a little closer to the fire. My steaming breath was pale on the air. I drew my buffalo robe closer around me and was soon warm.

At last I slept again. In the morning I saw that it had snowed. The thickness of the oaks had protected us. We now inhabited a many-chambered palace of icy greens and golds. We looked out over a prairie purified by the first snowfall of winter. Sitting near our merry little fire and contemplating that immensity of snow, White Crow pulled rather cheerfully on his pipe and, as soon as he knew we were awake, took up a small drum and began to sing a song.

In a lifetime of moving between the realms I had heard few voices as beautiful as White Crow's. The song wove among the branches and glittering icicles. Its echoes turned into harmonies until the entire grove sang with him. Together they sang of ancient ways, of bitter truths and golden imaginings. They sang an elegy for all that had ever been lost. They sang of the morning and of the hours of the day, of the months and the passing of the seasons. As they sang I could barely stop myself from weeping with the beauty of it. Ayanawatta stood straight, with his arms folded, listening with absolute intensity. He wore only his tattoos, his paint, his jew-elry and a breechclout of fine beaded vellum. His copper skin glowed in the wonderful light, his chest swelling, his muscles clenching, as he gave his whole being to the music.

Wearing her hero feathers, Bes, too, stirred to this song as if with a sense of security. Yet as well as comfort, the song had power. It had purpose.

Through the surrounding lens of ice, I saw something moving

on the horizon. Gradually I made out more detail. It trotted quite rapidly towards us and stopped abruptly about ten yards from where Ayanawatta and White Crow still sang.

Again, I was unsure of the scale, but the beast they had summoned seemed huge. Regarding us with solemn, curious eyes as a fresh curtain of snow began to fall stood a massive white bison, a living totem, the manifestation of a Kakatanawa goddess. Her red-rimmed eyes glaring with proud authority, she stared deeply into mine. I recognized a confirmation. She pawed the snow, her breath steaming.

Bes lifted her trunk and uttered a great bellow which shook the forest and set ice cracking and falling. The white buffalo tossed her head as if in alarm, turned and was gone, trotting rapidly into the deep snow.

Ayanawatta was delighted. He, too, had seen the buffalo. He was full of excitement. Everything, he said, was unfolding as it should. Bes had warned the buffalo of our danger, and she had responded. Powerful medicine protected the land of the Kakatanawa, which in turn protected their city, which in turn protected the eternal tree. Once we crossed the mountains, we would enter the great valley of the Kakatanawa. Then we would almost certainly be safe, ready to begin the last crucial stage of our journey.

I had no reason to doubt him. I kept my own counsel, congratulating him on the beauty, rather than the power, of his voice. I knew, of course, that I was in the presence of skilled summoners. My father was one who could call upon bargains his family had made with the Lords of the Higher Worlds, with powerful elementals. He could invoke spirits of air, earth, fire and water as easily as another might plow a furrow. I could not be sure who had summoned the white buffalo, or whether she had heard both men singing and come to inspect us. If she was as strict with us as she was with her own herd, and indeed with herself, she would soon give us an order. I wondered why I should feel such sisterly feelings towards the animal. Was it simply because Ayanawatta had given me the Indian name of White Buffalo Woman?

The drum continued its steady beating. White Crow rose

gracefully to his feet. Swaying from side to side he began to dance. It was only then that I realized what Ayanawatta had meant.

White Crow was opening the gateway for us. We were attempting to pass between the realms. The land of the Kakatanawa lay not in the looming mountains, but in the world beyond them, where this strange tribe guarded their treasures and their secrets in mysterious ways.

As he danced I soon became aware of another presence, something drawn not by his summoning, but by the *smell* of his magic. And then at last I confirmed the identity of my particular enemy. An elemental but also a powerful Lord of the Higher Worlds, Shoashooan, the Turning Wind, who was native to this realm and therefore more dangerous.

I heard rumbling. A distant storm gathered and moved in our direction. Purples, crimsons and dark greens flooded the sky. They drew themselves across the horizon like a veil, but almost immediately they began to join again, shrieking and threatening and forming into that familiar leering, shifty, destructive fellow: Shoashooan, the Demon Wind, the Son Stealer, the Lord of the Tornadoes, the undisputed ruler of the prairie, before whom all spirits and creatures of the plains were powerless. Lord Shoashooan in all his writhing, twisting, shouting forms, his bestial features glaring out of his swirling body.

Standing on the right side of the Bringer of Ruins stood the Two Tongues, his body burning as his own life stuff was fed to the summoned spirit. Ipkeptemi would not last long. On the other side of the furious spirit, his ragged buffalo cape flapping and cracking in the blustering force from his new ally, was the ghastly, half-frozen figure of Klosterheim.

He might have been dead, turned to ice where he stood.

His lips were drawn back from his teeth.

For a moment I thought he was smiling.

Then I realized he was profoundly terrified.

CHAPTER SEVEN

The White Path

Tread the path that shines like silver,
To the city made of gold,
Where the world-snake slowly dies.
Where a lance moans like a woman,
And the pipe denies all lies.

W. S. HARTE,
"Onowega's Death Song"

losterheim's face was the last human thing I saw before the whirling Elemental Lord screeched and rose into the air. His limbs and organs proliferated so rapidly that he now had a hundred hands, a thousand legs, all writhing and spinning. And every limb held a shivering, slicing blade. The terrible, beastly face glowering and raging, he roared and railed as if something were pulling him back where he had come from.

Still the Two Tongues burned, and still his life stuff fed the Chaos Lord, giving him the substance he needed to remain in this realm. Yet it was an inexpert summons and therefore perhaps only a partial manifestation. The shaman burned for nothing.

Something *was* driving Lord Shoashooan back.

White Crow was singing. His voice covered two octaves easily and rose and fell almost like the movement of the oceans. His song was taken up by the mountains. Notes rippled from peak to peak, achieving their own strange, extended melody. Raising his arms from where he stood beside that great black pachyderm, he flung back his head and sang again. His handsome, ivory face shone with ecstasy. The red hawk feathers in his white hair were garish against his delicate coloring, emphasizing the gemlike redness of his eyes. Behind him, in its quiver, the Black Lance began to vibrate to the same notes. It joined in the song.

Lord Shoashooan growled and feinted and turned and keened, came closer and retreated. Then, with an angry howl, he vanished, taking the two men with him.

"Those fools," said White Crow. "They have neither the skills nor the powers to control such an entity. My grandfather banished him. No human can destroy him once he has established himself in our world. We can only hope he failed to find true substance and could not make a full manifestation." He looked around, frowning. "Though here, it would be easy enough."

I asked about the two men. He shook his head. He was sure they had not gone willingly.

"They summoned a monster, and it devoured them," said Ayanawatta. "Perhaps that is the end of it. If Lord Shoashooan had been able to secure his manifestation, he would be free to feast however and wherever he chose. We can only hope that two amateur sorcerers were enough for him. Lord Shoashooan is infamous for his lethal whimsicalities, his horrible jokes, his relish for flesh."

Glancing to my left I saw the strain on White Crow's face. Here was proof that Lord Shoashooan's disappearance had not been voluntary. I was impressed. Few had the strength and skill to oppose a Lord of the Higher Worlds. Had White Crow's magic driven the creature back to his own plane, taking with him as trophies those who hoped to evoke his aid?

A light wind danced around us.

White Crow lifted his head and began to sing and drum again, and again Ayanawatta joined with him in the music. I found that wordlessly I, too, was singing in harmony with my comrades. Through our song we sought to find our accord again, to set ourselves back on our path, to be true to our stories.

White Crow's small hand-drum began to pound more rapidly,

like the noise of a sudden downpour. Faster and faster he moved his stick back and forth, back and forth, around and around, down the side, against the bottom, back up the side to finish in a pulsating rhythm which would strengthen our medicine. Slowly the beats grew further apart.

The wind began to flutter and die away. The sun came out again in a single silver band slanting through billowing clouds and cut a wide swathe across the prairie.

White Crow continued to beat his drum. Very slowly he beat it. And his new song was deep and deliberate.

The shining path of cold sunlight fell until it lay before us, stretching out from our strange ice temple and disappearing towards those wild, high mountains. This silvery trail surely led to a pass through the mountains. A pass which would take us to the land of the Kakatanawa. A pass which began to reveal itself like a long crack in the granite of the mountains.

The clouds boiled in, and the sun was lost again.

But that gleaming, single, silvery beam remained. A magic path through the mountains.

White Crow stopped drumming. Then he stopped singing. The light of day dimmed beneath the heavy snow clouds. But the silver road remained.

White Crow was clearly satisfied. This was his work. Ayanawatta congratulated him enthusiastically, and while it was not good manners to show emotional response to such praise, White Crow was quietly pleased with himself.

He had sung and drummed a pathway into the next realm. He and Ayanawatta had woven it from the gossamer stuff of the Grey Fees, creating the harmonies and resonances necessary to walk safely perhaps only a short distance between two worlds.

Ironically I reflected on their envy of my skills. I could walk at will across the moonbeam roads, while they had immense difficulty. But I was not a creator as they were. I could not fashion the roads themselves. The only danger now was that Shoashooan would follow us through the gateway we had made.

With light steps we restored the saddle to Bes's back and adjusted our canoe canopy. White Crow then urged his old friend to move on.

I watched her set those massive feet on the pathway we could now see through the snow. She was confident and cheerful as she carried us forward. When I looked back, I saw that the road had not faded behind us as we progressed over it. Did that mean Klosterheim or one of his allies could now easily follow us?

Bes trod the crystal trail with an air of optimistic familiarity. Indeed there was something jaunty about the mighty mammoth as she carried us along, her own brilliant feathers now held securely in a sort of topknot. I wondered if there were any other mammoths to whom she could tell her stories, or would she be remembered only in our own tales?

The prairie lay under thick snow. There was nothing supernatural about it. You could taste the sharp snowflakes, see the hawks and eagles turning in the currents high overhead. In a sudden flurry a small herd of antelope sprang from cover nearby and fled over the snow, leaving a dark trail behind them. There were tracks of hares and raccoons.

We had plenty of provisions, and there was no need to leave the tentlike interior of the makeshift howdah. While the mammoth plodded through deep snow, for us this journey was sheer luxury.

Once in the distance we saw a bear walking ahead of us along the trail, but he soon blundered off into the brush near a creek, and we lost sight of him. For some time Ayanawatta and White Crow discussed the possibility that this was a sign. They eventually decided that the bear had no special symbolic meaning. For several hours Ayanawatta expounded on the nature of bear-spirits and bear-dreams while White Crow nodded agreeably, occasionally confirming an anecdote, always preferring to be the audience.

Slowly the mountains grew larger and larger until we were looking up at their tree-covered lower slopes. The silver trail led through the foothills and into the pass. The two men became quietly excited. Neither had been sure the magic would work, and even now they were unsure of the consequences. Would there be a price to pay? I was in awe of their power, and so were they!

The snow started to fall steadily. Bes seemed to enjoy it. Perhaps her great woolly coat was designed for such weather. Snow soon banked itself on both sides of us, as the trail grew rockier. We entered the deep, dark fissure which would lead us to the land of the Kakatanawa. Here little snow had settled, and it was still possible to see the trail ahead.

I had not expected further attack, certainly not from above. But in an instant the air was thick with ravens. The huge, black birds swarmed around us, cawing and clacking at us as if we invaded their territory. I could not bring myself to shoot at them, and neither could my companions. White Crow said the black ravens were his cousins. They all served the same queen.

The noise of the attack was distracting, however, and disturbing to Bes. After some twenty minutes of enduring this, White Crow stood up in the saddle and let out a tremendous cackle of angry song which silenced the ravens.

Seconds later the big birds had settled on outcrops of rock. They sat waiting, heads to one side, black eyes shining, listening as White Crow continued his irritable address. It was clear how he had come by his name and no doubt his totem. He spoke their language fluently, with nuances which even these rowdy aggressors could appreciate. I was amused that he spoke so little in human language and could be so eloquent in the tongue of a bird. When I asked him about it, he said that the language of dragons was not dissimilar, and both came easily to him.

Whatever he said to the ravens, he did not drive them away. But at least it stopped the noise. Now they sat along both sides of our path, occasionally croaking out a complaint or chittering among themselves. Then with a snap and shuffle of their wings, the ravens took to the air, flooding upwards in a long, ragged line towards the distant sky, cawing back at us after they had gained a certain distance. Birds usually felt benign towards humans, but these were clearly the exception.

As we continued down the great cleft in the rock, surprisingly

I began to feel a claustrophobia I had never known on the moon-beam roads. The day became so overcast and the cliffs so steep that we could not easily see the sky. The pathway shone no brighter, and we might not have known it was there, save for the banked snowdrifts.

Night fell, and still we followed the glistening path until we came to a place where the trail widened. Here we camped, listening to the strange sounds in the cliffs, where unfamiliar animals scuttled and foraged. Bes was eager to continue. She had not wanted to rest, but we thought it best to catch our breath while we could.

In the morning I awoke to discover that we had again been camping in an ancient holy place. Our shelter was the neglected entrance to a huge stone temple whose roof had long since fallen in. Its walls were carved with dozens of regular pictograms in an obscure language. The elements had worn them to an even more mysterious smoothness. Two vast nonhuman figures on either side of the pass were obviously male and female. The natural rock overhead had been carved into an arch to represent their hands touching, symbolizing the Unity of Life.

Ayanawatta asked if we might pause while he studied these massive pillars. He smiled as he ran his hands over the figures. He seemed to be reading the glyphs, for his lips were moving. Then I thought that he might be praying.

He rejoined us in a good mood and climbed up to find some of his herbs and smoking mixture in his stowed bundle. These he held in one hand while he dismounted again from Bes and ran quickly to both pillars, sprinkling a little of the mixture at the base of each statue.

He sighed his contentment. "They say these two are the first male and the first female, turned to stone by the Four Great Manitoos. It was their punishment for telling the Stone Giants the secret path to the tree which the Kakatanawa now guard. We call them the Grandsires. They gave birth to our world's four tribes. They are monuments to our past and our future."

He frowned at the carvings as we rode past them. He seemed

surprised they were so inanimate. "When I was last here, they had more life. They were happier."

He looked up into the dark crags and sighed. "There is great trouble now, I think. There's no certainty we shall save anything from the struggle."

After we passed under the arch, the quality of light subtly changed. Even the echoes were of a different nature. If we were not already in the land of the Kakatanawa, we were beginning to enter their jurisdiction. I thought I saw shadows above us, heard the skip of a stone, a muffled exclamation. But perhaps it was only the clatter of our own progress.

I wondered if the tree the Kakatanawa said they guarded was really a tree or perhaps merely a symbol, a contradictory core lying at the heart of their beliefs.

For long periods in that dark crevasse, I thought we were never going to be free of a universe of rock. The sheer sides threatened to narrow so much as to become impassable, yet somehow we squeezed through even the tightest gap.

The path went relentlessly forward, and relentlessly we followed it until it widened and we saw before us a huge lake of ice which the mountains encircled. Spectacular and vast under the clearing pewter sky, the pale, frozen lake was not, however, what captured our attention.

Ayanawatta let out a high, long whistle, but I could not speak for wonder.

Only White Crow knew the place. He gave a grunt of recognition. Nothing I had heard could have prepared me for my first sight of the Kakatanawa "longhouse."

While it was easy to see how the phrase fitted the conception, the reality was utterly unlikely. Their longhouse was not only the size of a mountain, it appeared to be made of solid gold!

Standing about a mile from the shore, this mighty, glittering pyramid rose at the center of the frozen lake. The Kakatanawa longhouse dominated even the brooding peaks which completely surrounded it.

Under a paling blue sky reflected in the great plain of ice,

Kakatanawa gleamed. An immense ziggurat, as high as a sky-scraper, it was an entire city in a single structure. The base was at least a mile wide, and the tiers marched up, step by enormous step, to a crown where what might be a temple blazed.

The city was alive with activity. I could see ranks of people moving back and forth between the levels, the gardens which draped startling greenery over balconies and terraces. I saw transports and dray animals. It was an entire country in a single immense building! While it sat on an island, I guessed that it also extended below the ice. Was there never a time when the ice melted, or were we now so far north that the lake remained forever frozen?

I could not contain myself.

"A city of gold! I never believed such a legend!"

Ayanawatta began to laugh, and White Crow smiled at my astonishment. "All that glistens is not gold," he said ironically. "The plaster contains iron pyrites and copper powder, perhaps a little gold and silver, but not much. The reflective mixture produces a more durable material. And it suits their other purposes to make Kakatanawa shine like gold. I do not know whether the city or the myth came first. There is a legend among the Mayans about this city, but they think it is further south and east. No Kakatanawa can ever reveal the location of his home to strangers."

"Are we not strangers?" I asked.

He began to laugh. "Not exactly," he said.

"The name of the city is the same as that of your tribe?"

"The Kakatanawa are the People of the Circle, the People of the Great Belt, so called because they have traveled the entire circle of the world and returned to their ancestral home. Everywhere they went they left their mark and their memory. They are the only people to do this thing and understand what they have done. Even the Norsemen have not done that. This is Odan-a-Kakatanawa, if you prefer. The Longhouse of the People of the Circle. It is this people's destiny to guard the great belt, the story of the world's heart."

"And is that where I will find my husband?" My own heart had

begun to beat rapidly. I controlled my breathing to bring it back
to normal. I longed to see Ulric, safe and well and in my arms
again.

"You will find him." White Crow for some reason avoided my
eye.

There was no doubt in my mind that the Kakatanawa had
kidnapped Ulric and brought him here. Now perhaps all I had to
do was storm a city-sized pyramid! I hoped that my association
with White Crow would make that unnecessary.

I believed I was approaching a people whose motives were
mysterious and possibly thoughtless, but who were not malevo-
lent. Of course, my feelings were subjective. I could not help liking the youth, who might have been a son, and there was no
doubt I felt a daughter's security in the company of the older
sachem, Ayanawatta, so talkative and humorous, so full of ideal-
ism and common sense. There was a fitting unity about our trinity. But it was Ulric who remained my chief concern. While
certain I would find him here, I still did not know why he had
been brought here or, indeed, how White Crow had known where
to find the medicine shield.

A sharp wind was beginning to blow from the east, and we
sank deeper into our furs. I could smell every kind of sorcery on
that wind. I remained confused, uncertain of its source or its
purpose.

The faint path of silver continued to cross the ice. It ended at
the great golden pillars which supported what could only be the
main gate with heavy doors of bronze and copper. The city's architecture was covered in complicated carvings and paintings of
the most exquisite workmanship. I remembered the Sinhalese temples of Anuradhapura. Scarcely an inch was undecorated. From
this distance it was impossible to make out anything but the largest
details. Each tier of the ziggurat's extraordinary structure
abounded with doors and windows. The population of a small
town must live on each of the lower levels. Other levels were
clearly cultivated, so that Kakatanawa was entirely self-supporting.
She could resist any siege.

I asked a stupid question. "Will the ice bear Bes's weight?"

White Crow turned his head, smiling. "Bes is home," he said. "Can't you tell?"

It was true that the amiable mammoth looked more alert, excited. Did she still have a family in Kakatanawa? I imagined stables full of these massive, good-natured beasts.

White Crow added, "This ice is thicker than the world. It goes down forever."

Then, as we continued to move forward, the mountains shook and grumbled. Dark clouds swirled around their peaks. The sky became alive with racing shafts of yellow, dark green and deep blue, all crackling and roaring, rumbling and shrieking. A wild screeching.

I reached for my bow, but I felt sick. I knew very well what that noise heralded.

Lord Shoashooan, the Demon of the Whirlwind, appeared before us.

His dark, conical shape was more stable. The wide top whirled, and the tip twisted into the ice, sending out a blur of chips. I could see his flickering, bestial features, his cruel, excited eyes. It was as if Klosterheim and the Two Tongues had released him from some prison, where he had been frustrated in his work of destruction. We had not driven him away. We had merely made him retreat to reconsider his strategy.

There again on one side of him stood Klosterheim, shivering in his agitated cloak, while all that was left of the Two Tongues lay dying, breath hissing in the corner of his horrible, toothy mouth. Klosterheim had the air of a man who believed his odds of survival small.

White Crow flung up his arm, waving his great black-bladed spear. "Ho! Would a mere breath of air stop me from returning to Kakatanawa with the Black Lance? Do you know what you challenge, Lord Shoashooan?"

Klosterheim spoke through cracked lips over the shriek. "He knows. And he knows how to stop you. Time will freeze, as this lake is frozen. It will allow me to do everything I must do. Your medicine is weak now, White Crow. Soon the Pukawatchi will come and destroy you and take back the things which are their own."

White Crow frowned at this. Was it true? Had he expended all his power in conjuring the Shining Path?

Behind the great Lord of All Winds the golden city sparked and shifted so that sometimes it seemed only a vision, a projection, an illusion. Not a real place at all. Beyond us, nothing moved. Time did indeed seem to have stopped.

White Crow bowed his head. "I am their last White Crow man," he said. "If I do not bring them back the Black Lance, it will not only be the last of the Kakatanawa, it will be the last we shall ever know of the multiverse, save that final, eternal second before oblivion. He has seen that my medicine is now weak. I have no charms or rituals strong enough to defend us against the anger of Shoashooan."

He looked desperately to Ayanawatta, who replied gravely. "You must fly to the Isle of Morn and find help. You know this is what we planned."

White Crow said, "I will use the last of my magic. Bes will stay here with you. I will send you the help you need. But know how dangerous this will be for all of us."

"I understand." Ayanawatta turned to me. "It is for you to help us now, my friend."

Then without another word, White Crow was leaving us. I watched in astonishment as he ran swiftly away. He ran through the foothills and was soon lost from sight. I almost wept at his deserting us. I would never have anticipated it.

Klosterheim cackled. "So the heroes show their real characters. You are not fit enough for these tasks, my friends. You challenge forces far too great."

I took my bow and stepped forward. Perhaps in my right mind I would have shot Klosterheim. I knew a kind of cold anger. I longed to be reunited with my husband, and I was determined not to be stopped. I do not know what instinct informed me, but I forced myself to walk closer and closer to the shrieking madness that was Lord Shoashooan, fitting an arrow to my bow. I could see a face in the center of the tornado. That same fierce, white-hot anger remained. I knew nothing of fear as I loosed my first arrow into Lord Shoashooan's forehead.

Without thought, I nocked and loosed again. My second arrow took him in the right eye. The third arrow took him in the left eye.

He began to squeal and bellow in outrage. Bizarre limbs clutched at his head. I knew Lord Shoashooan could not be killed so easily. My idea was to try to stay out of his reach and, like a bull terrier, worry at him until he was weak enough to be overcome.

It was no doubt a stupid idea, but I did not have a better one!

I had been too confident. I had only blinded the monster for a few seconds. Before I knew it, he seized me in his icy tendrils and drew me closer and closer to his chuckling maw. I could reach no more arrows. All I had was my bow. I flung the staff into that horrible mouth.

Lord Shoashooan's many eyes glared. He gagged. I had caused some sort of convulsion. He scraped at his mouth and clutched his throat, and suddenly the sentient tornado flung me away.

I saw gleaming white all around me as I fell heavily to the ice. I was dazed and barely conscious. I forced myself to gather my strength.

I knew I had no other choice.

For a moment I refused the inevitable, but it was a pointless rebellion. I knew it as I made it. I could still hear the terrible howling and clawing of Lord Shoashooan as he wrestled with the bow-stave I had flung into his maw.

I, too, had a preordained story in this world. A story which I must follow in spite of myself.

I was reconciled to what was expected of me. I had no other choice, even though I risked a terrible death. In one moment of recovered memory, I knew exactly what had led to this moment. I knew why I was here. I knew what I must now do. I understood it in my bones, in my soul.

I knew what I had to become.

I readied myself for the transformation.

THE SECOND BRANCH
ELRIC'S STORY

I, Elric, called the White, son of Sadric,
Am the bearer of the black rune-sword.
Long ran the blood rivers ere the reavers came.
Great was the grieving in the widows' songs.
Souls were stolen by the score
When skraelings sent a thousand to be slain.

THE THIRD EDDA, "Elrik's Saga"
(TR. WHELDRAKE)

This was my dream of a thousand years
Each moment liv'd, all joys and every fear.
Through turning time and space gone mad,
I sought my magic and my weird.
For a millennium I trailed what I had lost.
My unholy charge, which e'en my soul had cost.

AUSTIN, "A Knight of the Balance"

CHAPTER EIGHT

Conversation in Satan's Garden

*From Loki's Yard came Elrik Silverskin
Speaking with old stones he carried wisdom with him
To that fateful, thrice-doomed Diocletian's hall
And sought for one whom the Norns held thrall.*

THE THIRD EDDA,
"Elrik's Saga" (TR. WHELDRAKE)

his is my Dream of a Thousand Years. In reality it lasted a single night, but I lived every moment of the dream, risked every kind of death in one last attempt to save myself. I describe it here, through Ulric's agency, because of its relevance to his tale. It was a dream I dreamed as I hung crucified on the yardarm of Jagreen Lern's triumphant flagship, the banner of my own defeat. I had lost my much-needed burden, the demon-blade Stormbringer. I was racking my memory for some means of recovering the sword to save myself and Moonglum and if possible stop the tide of Chaos which threatened the Cosmic Balance and would turn the whole of creation inchoate.

In this dream I was searching for the Nihrainian smith who had forged the original black blade. I had heard of one called Volnir. He lived close to the world's northern edge in what some called Cimmeria but which you know better as North America. If I found him, I should then be able to find Stormbringer. By such means I might save myself, my friend and even my world. I knew the price to be paid for following this dream path.

It would be the second time I had undertaken the Dream of a Thousand Years. To a youth of my genesis it is integral training. It must be done several times. You go alone into the wilderness. You fast. You meditate and seek the path to the world of long dreams. These are the worlds which determine and reveal the future. They offer the secrets of your past. In such worlds one serves more than one rules. Certain knowledge is gained by extended experience as well as study. The Dream of a Thousand Years provides that experience. The memory of those lifetimes fades, leaving the instinctive wisdom, the occasional nightmare.

One does not learn how to rule the Bright Empire of Melniboné without such service. Only in the extreme could I use my skills. I knew the danger involved, but I had no choice. The fate of my world depended upon my regaining, for a few moments, control of the black sword.

To attempt this desperate and unlikely magic, I had summoned all my remaining powers of sorcery. I had allowed myself to sink into a familiar trance. Jagreen Lern had already provided me with more than sufficient fasting and physical privations. I sought a supernatural gateway to the dream-worlds, some link to my own youthful past, where our many destinies are already recorded. And it brought me to your world in the year A.D. 900. I would leave it in the year 2001 upon the death of a relative.

Riding from Vienna, having but recently returned from a conquered Jerusalem, by October I found myself in the rocky Balkan mountains, where a tradition of banditry lived side by side with a tradition of hill farming to break the hearts and backs of most other peasants.

While wolf's-heads might covet my fine black steel helmet and armor, they had the sense not to test the great claymore I carried at my side. She was called Ravenbrand, sister to my own Stormbringer. How I came by Ravenbrand in that place is a tale yet to be told.

Until finding temporary peace with my wife, Zarozinia, I had been a mercenary outlaw in the Young Kingdoms. I had no difficulty making a good living here. Both the blade and I had repu-

tations few were ready to challenge. Already I had served in
Byzantium, in Egypt, fought Danes in England and Christians in
Cadiz. In Jerusalem through a bizarre sequence of events, covet-
ing a particular horse, I had helped create an order of the Knights
Templar, founded by Christians, to ensure that no temporal master should ever claim the Holy Sepulchre. My interest was not in
their religions, which are primitive, but in their politics, which are
complicated. Their prophets constantly make false claims for
themselves and their people.

Because their maps put Jerusalem at the heart of the world, I
had hoped to find signs of my smith there, but I was following a
fading song. The only smiths I found were shoeing crusader horses
or repairing crusader arms. In Vienna I heard at last of a Norseman who had explored the farther reaches of the world's edge and
might know where to find the Nihrainian smith.

My journey through the Balkans was rarely eventful. I was
soon in the Dalmatian hinterland, where the blood feud was the
only real law, and neither Roman, Greek nor Ottoman had much
influence. The mountains continued to shelter tribes whose only
concession to the Iron Age was to steal whatever they could from
those who carried any kind of metal. They used old warped cross-
bows and spears chiefly and were inaccurate with both. But I had
no trouble from them. Only one band of hunters attempted to
take my sword from me. Their corpses served to enlighten the
others.

I found warm and welcoming lodging at the famous Priory of
the Sacred Egg in Dalmatia. Their matronly prioress told me how
Gunnar the Norseman had anchored a month since to make
minor repairs at the safe harbor of Isprit on the protected western
coast. She had heard it from one of his homebound sailors. Gunnar, tired of slim pickings in the civilized ports, was determined to
sail north to the colonies Ericsson and his followers had established there. He was obsessed with an idea about a city made entirely of gold. The sailor, a hardened sea-robber, swore never again
to sail under a captain as evil as Gunnar. The man spent an un-

likely amount of the time with the confessor and then left, saying he thought he would try his luck in the Holy Land.

The Wendish prioress was an educated woman. She said Isprit had known greater glory. The real center of power had shifted to Venice. The Norseman had made a good choice. Using the local name for the place, the prioress told me the old imperial port was little more than three days' ride on a good horse. Two, the buxom Wend offered with a hearty laugh, if I wished to risk trespassing in Satan's backyard. She hugged my shoulders in an embrace which might have snapped a less battle-hardened invalid. I relaxed in her uncomplicated warmth.

The sailor had said the Norseman was anxious to leave port as soon as possible. He feared they should be trapped there. The Vikings had already angered the Venetians with a raid on Pag, which was successful, and another on Rab, which was not. Those dreaming old Adriatic ports now relied upon Venice for their prosperity and security and were glad to be off the main crusader routes. The knights and their armies brought little benefit and much destruction. The pope had called the Crusade in 1148. He had infected the whole of Europe and Arabia with his own dementia, which he then proceeded to die of. He had invented the jihad. The Arabs learned his lesson well.

I had no quarrel with any of the warring sects, who all claimed to serve an identical God! Human madness was ever banal. Jerusalem commanded no more of my interest. I had all I needed from the city. I had my horse, some gold and the odd ring on my finger. I found myself dragged briefly into the civic business of the city, but it was of no interest to me now whether or not order had been restored. Jerusalem was the turbulent heart of all their sects and would no doubt remain so.

Meanwhile Venice expanded her influence wherever the Turk's attention was distracted. Venice had most reason to see a nuisance in the Norseman. Her navy had already tried to trap him at Nin, but he had escaped, damaging *The Swan* in the attempt. The Viking would not take the risk of his beloved *Swan* being captured. They said she was the last of her kind, as Gunnar was the last of his. The other Vikings had made themselves kings and indulged in imperial expansion, missionaries of their Prince of Peace.

While the Crusades drew the world's attention, the man I sought was raiding through the winter months, taking the rather impoverished towns of the Adriatic, careful never to attract the wrath of Venice. Until recently neither Byzantines, Turks nor any other of the various local powers had will or men to send ships after a sea-raider. His skills and ferocity were infamous, his vessel so fast and lithe in the water many thought her possessed. *The Swan* was as lucky as she was beautiful. But previously neutral or disputed ports now came under the protection of Venice. Venice was rapidly expanding her trade. The Doge coveted Gunnar's legendary ship.

Gunnar, I was told, was not even a Viking by birth. He was a Rus. Outlawed from Kiev he'd returned to the reiving trade of his forefathers more from necessity than romance. Otherwise he was something of a mystery. Evidently neither Christian, Jew nor Moslem, he had never revealed his face, even to his women. Night and day he wore a reflective steel mask.

"Sounds a devilish wicked creature, eh?" the prioress said. "Not plague or leprosy, so I gather."

This matronly prioress, a woman of the world, had, until her retirement, run a brothel in Athens. She had a strong interest in the doings of the region. It was useful, pleasurable and politic to succumb to her charms, even if she found mine a little more supernatural than she bargained for. Before retiring, however, we were joined by another intelligent person of some experience, who was, by coincidence, lodging there for the night.

This guest had arrived a few hours ahead of me. A cheerful, wide-mouthed redheaded little man, he might have been a relative of my old friend Moonglum. My memory, as always in these dreams, was a little dim regarding any other life. This friar was a soldier-priest, with a mail shirt under his heavy homespun cassock, a useful-looking sword of Eastern pattern in an elaborate sheath and boots of fine quality that had seen better days.

He introduced himself in Greek, still the common tongue of the region. Friar Tristelunne had been a Heironymite hermit until his own natural garrulousness took him back, he said, to society. He now made ends meet as best he could, from marriages, deaths, funerals, letter writing, and selling the occasional small relic. Sadly there was often more work for his sword than his prayer book. The Crusade had been a disappointment to him. It no doubt satisfied the Christian appetites of the city's liberators, he said, but it wasn't man's work. He drew the line at skewering old Jewish women and babies in the name of the Lord of Light.

Friar Tristelunne knew the Norseman. "Some call him Earl Gunnar the Ill-famed, but he has a dozen worse names. A captain so cruel only the most desperate and depraved will sail with him."

A pagan, Gunnar's attempt to join and profit from the Crusade had been thwarted.

"Even the realistic, pious and opportunistic Saint Clair could not excuse the recruitment of an unreformed worshipper of Woden."

Gunnar was famous for his treachery, and there was no guarantee that once he reached the Holy Land he would not discover a better master in Saladin. The only good reason anyone would have to strike an alliance with Gunnar the Doomed was if they needed a good navigator. "His skills are greater than the Ericssons'. He uses magic lodestones. He takes wild risks and survives them, even if all his comrades do not. Not only has he reached the rim of the world, he has sailed completely around it."

Friar Tristelunne had met Earl Gunnar, he said, when the captain was a mercenary in Byzantine employ. The monk had been fascinated by his mixture of intelligence and rapacity. Indeed, Gunnar had tried to get him involved in a scheme for robbing a wealthy Irish abbey said to be the home of the *gradal sante*. But his methods ultimately disgusted the Byzantines, who outlawed him. He had worked for the Turkish sultan for a while but was once again sailing on his own behalf, getting a new expedition ready. He was busy promising every man who would sail with him that even their fleas' shares would be worth a caliph's ransom.

Friar Tristelunne had considered joining the adventure, but he knew Gunnar to be notoriously treacherous. "The chances of returning alive to the civilized world would be slim indeed." He had a passage on a ship leaving Omis for the Peninsula in a few days' time. He had decided to strike out for Cordova, where he could get plenty of translation work and study to his heart's content at their great library, assuming the caliph was still well disposed towards unbelievers.

The friar, like so many in that region, knew me as Il Pielle d'Argent or 'the Silverskin', and my sword was called Dentanoir. Many avoided me for my sickly looks, but Friar Tristelunne seemed untroubled. He spoke to me with the easiness of an old, affectionate friend. "If, against the good prioress's advice, you choose the short route to the coast, it might be to your advantage to pause when you meet the Grandparents. They might have something to tell you. They speak briefly but very slowly. There is a trick to hearing them. Each deep note contains the wisdom of a book."

"The Grandparents? Your relatives?"

"They are the relatives of us all," said the redheaded monk. "They knew the world before God created it. They are the oldest and most intelligent stones in this part of the world. You will recognize them when you see them."

While I respected his beliefs and judgment, I did not pay a great deal of attention to his words. I was determined to take the shortest route I could through the mountains and down to the port, so was already prepared to ignore the nun's warning.

I thanked the warrior-monk and would have spent longer talking to him if he had not made an excuse and headed for his bed. He could stay here, he said, for only a short time. He had a dream of his own to follow. And I was already engaged for the evening.

In the morning, the prioress told me he had left before dawn, reminding me to pay attention to old stones. Again she warned me not to cross the Devil's Garden. "It's a place of ancient evil," she said. "Unnatural landscapes, touched by Chaos. Nothing grows there. This is God's sign to us not to go there. It is where the old pagan gods still lurk." She had stirred her own imagination; I could tell from her eyes. "Where Pan and his siblings still mock the message of Christ." She squeezed my hand almost conspiratorially.

I assured her that I was comfortable enough with most excesses of Chaos. I would, however, watch for treachery and cunning aggression along the way. She kissed me heartily on the lips. Pressing a bag of provisions and sustaining herbs into my hands, she wished me God's company in my madness. She also insisted on presenting me with a precious text, something from their holy books, which made some mention of the Valley of Death. With this reassuring parchment tucked into my shirt below my chain mail—which I had donned more as a means of quieting the prioress than of guarding against attack in the Devil's Garden—I kissed her farewell and told her that I was now invulnerable. She answered in Wendish, which I hardly understood. Then in Greek she said, "Fear the Crisis Maker." It was what she had told me last night when she had laid out the cards for us both to read.

The other nuns and novices had gathered on the walls of the priory to see me leave. They had, it seemed, all heard tales of the Silverskin. Had their prioress committed the saintly act of sharing her bed with a leper? I suspected those who believed it, believed she must have her place in their Heaven already reserved.

With respectful irony, I saluted them, bowed and then spurred my massive black stallion, Solomon, along a rocky road populated in those days by deer, bears, goats and boar, all of them hunted by local farmers and bandits, who were frequently one and the same. The road would take me through the Devil's Garden and down to the western coast.

The local Slavs were in the main a coarse, rather pale people. They had wiped out most of their best bloodstock through complicated and extended family feuding. When they had that romantic touch of Mongolian blood, Dalmatians achieved a stunning beauty.

Elsewhere powerful cultures had arisen and influenced the

world, but these rocks offered solace only to the troubled visionary. Along the coasts were a few pockets of civilization, but most
of that was in decay, exhausted by tributes to a dozen powers.

Isprit itself had been the retirement palace of the Emperor
Diocletian, who had famously divided the Roman Empire into
three, then left its running to a triumvirate who quarreled and
killed one another, as well as Diocletian's daughter. His confusing
stamp on the politics of the region would last for millennia. The
hapless ex-emperor, who had hoped to balance power between
the various warring factions, was the last real inheritor of Caesar's
authority. Now the old Empire was sustained chiefly by those who
had rallied to Charlemagne after he had been crowned Holy
Roman Emperor by the pope. Their translation of their greed for
booty into a chivalric ideal created an extraordinary expansion
whose conquests, frequently under the banner of religious reform,
would not stop until they owned the Earth. Already the Normans
had imposed their haughty and efficient feudalism onto much of
France and England. They in turn would carry these methods
across the world. Opinion in Rome agreed that the unruly Saxons
and Angles needed the strong hand of the Dukes of Normandy to
form them into a nation which might one day balance the power
of the Holy Roman Emperor.

At the abbey, in exchange for their hospitality, I had retailed
the gossip of the day. Of course, I had only so much curiosity
about their world, and most of that related to my search. But
much small talk is picked up in the taverns, which a wanderer like
myself, largely shunned by all, is frequently forced to use. I had little interest in the details of these peoples' history. It was raw and
unsophisticated compared to that of mine, and I was still Melnibonéan enough to feel a superiority to mortals of most persuasions.

Through my senses Count Ulric had the opportunity to witness the genesis of his clan into a nation, and in his dreams he experienced my dreams as if they were his own. He dreamed my
dream as I dreamed his. But he did not live my dream as I did, and

I suspect he remembers even less. How much he chooses to remember is his own affair.

The late summer sun was surprisingly hot on my overarmored head when I became aware of the nature of the landscape changing. The crags were sharper, the cliffs more terraced, and little streams echoed through deep valleys, giving the place an unearthly music. Clearly I had entered the Devil's Garden. The shale became much harder for my horse to negotiate.

The stark landscape was astonishingly beautiful. Little grew here. The smell of the occasional fir invigorated me. The great limestone crags sparkled in the summer sunshine. All the trails were treacherous. Narrow rivers dancing with vivid life poured in falls from level to level among strangely shaped rocks.

The sun cast dense shadows, contrasting extremes of black and white, on the massive glittering cliffs which rose into the sky. Sudden lakes, icy blue beneath the sun, were turned by passing clouds into blinding sheets of reflective steel. Rock pools shone like coral in their delicacy of color. Groves of dark blue pines and fleshy oaks grew in the few spots of soil. Frequently I heard the rattle of loose rocks as a goat leaped for cover. Crumbling earth on worn stone. Ferns and willowherb growing in crevices. These were the familiar landscapes of a childhood when, as von Bek, I had holidayed here with my family, who kept a villa on the coast. It was also reminiscent of the hinterland of Melniboné, where the Phoorn, our dragon allies, had built their first magnificent city from fire and rock and little else.

As the day grew hotter still, the steady blue sky threw extremes of color everywhere. I began to feel an unlikely nostalgia. The experience was not entirely pleasant. All I understood was a sense of invasion, as if other intelligences attacked my own. Not merely my dream self intruded, but something older and heavier, something which reminded me again of Mu Ooria and invoked images, memories of events which perhaps had not yet even occurred in the history of this particular world.

Used to controlling myself in such circumstances, I was still very uneasy. My horse, Solomon, too, was growing nervous, perhaps reflecting my own mood. I wanted to get out of the place as soon as possible. Doggedly, we continued westward, the horse holding with uncanny ease to the path. Loose grey shale skittered and bounced steeply away from us. Sometimes it seemed we clung to the walls of the rock like lizards, staring down at the radically angled slopes, the glittering, weirdly colored waters far below.

That night I camped in a natural cave, having first made sure it was not the castle of an incumbent bear. It had not seen any kind of human settlement. Nothing in this landscape could sustain human life.

I rose early in the morning, watered, fed and saddled Solomon, set my war-gear about me, changed my helmet for a hood, and again was struck by the supernatural quality of the valley. At the far end in the distance was a wide, shimmering lake.

As I urged Solomon forward, I sensed other presences. I knew the smell of them, the weight of them. I had instinctive respect for them even though I was not really conscious of their identity. They were nearby and they were many. That was all I could be sure about. Beings seemingly older than the Off-Moo, who had seen every stage of the Earth's history. They remembered the moment when they had been expelled from the Sun's gassy Eden to begin the forming of this planet.

Even the stars of this world's firmament were subtly different from mine. I knew it would be better to learn what the Devil's Garden had to tell me rather than impose my own Melnibonéan speculation on the place. I sensed that this had once been a great battlefield. Here Law and Chaos had warred as they had never warred until now. It was one of the oldest supernaturally inhabited regions in this realm. It was one of the most remote. It was one of the most enduring. I was at last recognizing it for what it was. Its denizens were unaffected by the major movements of human history. They were philosophical beings who had witnessed so much more than any others, and they had seen all human ideals brought low by human folly. Yet they were incapable of cynicism. I knew them, just as I knew their young cousins, still hiding goat-footed in the rocks, still sliding in and out of trees and streams, still asking favors of Nature rather than making demands on her, the old godlings whom the Greeks had known, half-mortals who sensed their own extinction. These ancient creatures had such old, slow thought processes they were all but undetectable, yet they were the Earth's memory.

Their name for themselves took several mortal lifetimes to pronounce. Adepts gave them considerable attention. Few consulted them, though more knew how. Their answers were usually slowly considered, and the one who had asked could be dead before they reached a conclusion. When they slept it was for millions of years. When they awoke it might be for a few seconds. And they never wasted words. I was beginning to understand what Friar Tristelunne had hinted at.

I had passed part of my apprenticeship among such ancients, but I was still uneasy. If Moonglum had been with me, he would have expressed reasonable fear and I should have mocked him for it, but now I was alone. I had survived a hundred great fights with less fear than now.

As I dismounted and led Solomon down to one of the deep valley streams to drink, I looked around me and saw that the sides had widened. I was effectively in a steep, white amphitheater, scarcely touched by vegetation. A few hardy wildflowers grew here and there, but otherwise the great glade was empty save for the carpet of soft green itself. It had that cultivated atmosphere about its lawns which I had noticed in other places where sheep and goats habitually grazed. Here the limestone crags had split away. Much of the rock stood like tall independent heads or figures. Fancifully I thought I detected expressions. Emotions, life of various kinds, stirred in those huge natural pillars. It was easy to see how the region was rife with tales of ogres.

Old maps referred to the place as Trollheim. Half the legendary giants of Europe were believed to originate here. Remembering the redheaded priest's words, I sought for inscriptions on the stones. I could read Greek, Latin, Arabic easily but had far more trouble with some other languages.

I found no inscriptions. As I ran my hands over the surface of the rock, however, I felt a distinct but very deep vibration, a kind of grumbling, as if I had awakened a sluggish hive. I dropped my hand and stepped back, seeing faces everywhere in the high cliffs, feeling a certain panic. Should these rocks prove sentient and antagonistic, I knew I could not cut myself clear with my sword.

Though my senses were sharper than most mortals', the horse heard the sound before I did. Solomon snorted and whinnied. Then I detected it. A deep, even rumbling, as if from far underground. It rose rapidly to a heavy hum, and the whole valley swayed to it. All the hillsides shimmered with movement. The stones were dancing. They were singing. Then the note deepened again, and I felt a shock as tremendous vitality flooded up to fill the canyon, as if Mother Earth herself were coming awake.

Solomon, who had been unusually quiet, now voiced a huge snort. I could see that his huge back legs were trembling, and his eyes had begun to dilate badly. My brave beast was actually too terrified to move. His enemy seemed everywhere.

My own emotions were quieter. I still found it difficult to coordinate my actions. Then, quite suddenly, the whole vale became suffused with an extraordinary sense of benign good will.

A single enormous throb! The great slow heart of the world had given a beat. The vibrations filled my body with joy and meaning. My hand fell away from my sword, where it had remained from habit. Now with wizard's eyes I saw their faces. I was an actor on a stage. These stones were my audience. Rank upon rank of them, rising up the flanks of the vale, their eyes hidden in deep shadow, their mouths showing a kind of eternal irony that was not judgmental of humanity yet spoke of a wisdom born of their age. As gases they had been conscious. As molten lava they had been wise. As the still-animate crust of the planet they had been moral. And as mountains they were contemplative. That consciousness, old and slow as it was, carried their experience. Their lives had been devoted, down the millions of millennia, to observation and understanding.

Something of great importance to the fate of the multiverse, to their world and my own, had stirred them to speak. Little of their words could be heard by any mortal ear.

They spoke four words, and those words took four days to utter; but that was not our only communication. The mighty heads looked down at me. They studied me and compared me and no doubt recalled all the many others who, seeking their wisdom, had come this way. My horse grew calm and cropped at the grass. I sat and listened to these Grandfathers and Grandmothers, the very spirits of our origin, who in their roaring youth had fled away from the parent Sun to form the planets.

Their love of life had slowed, but it had not faded. Their thoughts were as substantially concentrated as their physical forms. Each word translated became several lines in even the most laconic of languages. In comparison old Melnibonéan was baroque and clumsy. Only a trained ear could detect the slight differences of tone. I was forced to recall an old spell and slow down my own perception of time. It was the only way to understand them.

With what they communicated supernaturally, I began to understand a little of what they told me. Why these first stone men and women of the world had chosen to speak to me I did not know. I understood, however, that this was an important part of my dream. I sat, and I immersed myself in a strange, but not unpleasant, communication. In those four days, heedless now of Gunnar's imminent leaving, I listened to the stones.

The first word the Grandparents spoke was:

WHERE THE WINDS MEET
A WOMAN'S HORNS DEFY
THE DESTROYER OF DESTINY
AND MAKE HER YOUR BEST ALLY

I had an image of a white beast, a lake, a glittering building, the whole lying in another natural amphitheater. I knew this must be my destination, where I would discover the meaning of my dream.

The second word the Grandparents spoke was:

THE BLADE PIVOTS THE BALANCE
THE BOWL SUSTAINS IT
THE DRAGON IS YOUR FRIEND

I had the impression of a sword blade without a hilt, its tip immersed in some kind of basin while in the shadows a great, yellow eye opened to regard me.

The third word the Grandparents spoke was:

ROOT AND BRANCH THE TREE SUSTAINS
BALANCE AND ALL LIFE MAINTAINS

I saw an enormous tree, a spreading oak, whose branches seemed to shelter the world. Its roots went deep into the core of the Earth. Its branches covered another image, which was the same thing in a different form. I knew it was the Cosmic Balance.

And the fourth word the Grandparents spoke was:

GO MAKE TRUE

For a fleeting moment I received a glorious image: a great green oak tree against a sky of burnished silver. Then that special vibrancy faded, leaving only the natural grandeur of the stark cliffs and the soft grass below. The Grandparents were silent. Already they returned to sleep. With a sense of added burden rather than revelation I paid them my respects. I assured them I would think upon their words. I admitted to myself that they made little sense. Had the rocks reached a state of senility?

Suddenly I was struck by the stupidity of my excursion. I had crossed the Devil's Garden to save time. I had then lost a day rather than gained one. The Norseman might already be leaving Isprit. From the slowest of mortals, I became one of the fastest. I needed my stallion to do his best.

Solomon had carried me all the way from Acre. I had acquired him from a Lombardian knight who, like so many of my crusader comrades, had joined the expedition entirely for the land it

promised. Finding the promised land a little barren, he had joined
the Templars, turned to disappointed drinking and gambling and
from there to the inevitable duel. I had let him pick it. I had long
coveted his horse. Being of a weakly disposition, I also needed a
soul or two for my sustenance and preferred my food ripe.

The religious posturings of these brutes were as corruptly self-
deceiving as anything I had witnessed. Religions so at odds with
mankind's nature and its place in the natural order only produce a
kind of madness, where the victims are constantly attempting to
force reality to confirm their fantasies. The ultimate result must be
the ultimate destruction of the realm itself. In their histories, wherever the banner of pious Law was raised, Chaos quickly followed.

Though their people were said to have visited Cimmeria,
there was still every possibility that the Norseman would not be
able to help me. I would soon know.

I had been to Isprit before, but from the sea. The mountains
became greener and more forested and the ride to the port pleasant, if hurried. I arrived above the city just before sunset. The
Adriatic stretched, tranquil pewter, beneath a golden sun. Protected by a huge promontory, the port had been chosen by Diocletian for its views and air. Parts of walls and columns along the
harbor were clearly from Roman times. But where imperial sails
had blossomed on bulky triremes, the ships were now traders, fish-
ing craft. There was only one reefed sail on a tall, slender mast,
her crow's nest decorated with vivid dragons curling around the
tip, where a black flag flew. The sail was recognizable to anyone
but an inlander. It was the typical scarlet-and-azure stripes on a
white field of the old Norseman. Gunnar was still in port.

From this height the town looked unplanned and ramshackle,
a sprawl of huts and badly thatched houses standing among the
marble ruins of a vast Roman compound. As you drew closer, the
real wonder of the place made itself evident, as did the rather
pungent smell of the dust heaps and sewage dumps inland of the
harbor. None of this was noticeable, however, when you looked
out over a dark blue sea turning to a pool of blood in the dying

sunlight. I rode down the old trade trail from the mountains into that extraordinary port.

Several hundred years before, the emperor had built himself a palace here overlooking his private moorings and the Adriatic. An extensive complex of buildings, its entire purpose was to comfort the abdicated emperor and help him forget the troubles of the world, many of which were his own creation. The walls were high. There were cloisters and fountains; pleasant walks and groves; benches and tables of basalt, marble and agate; temples and chapels. The baths were exquisitely luxurious. When I had last been here the decay was less extensive.

When Rome's power faded, the barbarians' power over Isprit had grown. Byzantium lacked the resources to claim much in the way of sovereignty, so the port had filled with free fishermen, scrap-metal shippers, slavers, timbermen, traders, pirates, furriers and all the other honest and outlaw callings known to men. It was not an important port, strategically, but it was a lively one. The ostentatious palace was now the core of an entire community. They occupied its rooms and galleries, used its gardens for growing food, its halls for trading and meeting, its baths—those still in working order—for supplies of running water. Even to me this infestation of brawling, squabbling, embracing, praying, shrieking, giggling uninhibited human life had a certain charm.

The fountains had long since dried up. Some had been turned into the hubs of dwellings, their fanciful masonry in contrast to the simplicity of the people. Pigs, sheep and goats were kept in pens on the outskirts, so the stench increased as you approached but lessened as you reached the streets.

I rode through shacks and shanties of driftwood and stones which looked like the debris of a dozen sea-raids in which everything of wealth had been taken. Yet there was probably more life here now than when the emperor came. In those imperial ruins the fallen mighty had given way to the vital mob. This was one of the lessons I had tried to teach my countrymen. Their final lesson came when I demonstrated their weaknesses and the strength of the new, human folk who challenged them.

I had led those human reavers. I had destroyed the Dreamer's City. It was no wonder that I preferred this dream. Here I was merely a leprous wizard with a talent for warfare. There I was the prince who had betrayed his own people and left them scattered, homeless, dying from their world's memory. My actions had allowed Jagreen Lern, who always sought to emulate Melnibonéan power, to raise the Lords of the Higher Worlds, to threaten the Cosmic Balance in the name of the Gods of Entropy.

The forces of Law and Chaos were not themselves good or evil. It was by their actions that I judged such Higher Lords. Some were more trustworthy than others. My own patron Lord of Chaos, Duke Arioch, was a consistent if ferocious being, but he had little power in this world.

The only lighting in the warren of cobbled streets and apartments came from the taverns and dwellings themselves. Behind the oiled vellum of windows, the candles and lamps gave the twilit town a sepia look. I searched for a seamen's hostelry Friar Tristelunne had told me of. The smell of ozone was strong in my nostrils, as was the smell of fish. I was hungry for some fresh octopi, which Melnibonéans had always eaten with great respect. The creatures possess intelligences greater than most mortals. Certainly their flavor is considered subtler.

My own Melnibonéan appetites and impulses were forever at odds with the ideas I had inherited from my human companions. Cymoril, while she was alive, never knew that cannibalism disgusted me. She had taken her place at the ritual tables without a thought. I derived very little pleasure in the arts of torture cultivated by Melnibonéans for thousands of years. For us there were formal methods of dying as well as of killing.

As a youth I began to doubt the wisdom of these pursuits. Cruelty was scarcely a trade, much less an art. My fears for Melniboné had been practical. I had lived and traveled in the lands of the Young Kingdoms. I understood how soon they must overwhelm us. Had that been the reason that I had joined the ranks of my enemies? I dismissed this guilt. I had no time for it now.

I found the tumbledown, straw-roofed shingle building with a dim fish-oil lamp illuminating a sign that read in old Cyrillic *Odysseus's*, which was either the name of the owner or of the hero with whom he wished to be associated. The tavern had declined a little since the Golden Age.

Not trusting the Dalmatians, I dismounted from Solomon to lead him into the tavern. It stank of stale wine and sour cheese. The straw on the floors had not been replaced in months. There was a dead dog in one corner. The dog offered the advantage of attracting most of the flies and covering up the worst of the smells. The majority of the other customers were collected at a bench playing backgammon. A couple of men who sat talking quietly in the corner farthest from the dog attracted me. They had the filthy fair hair of the typical Danish pirate, arranged in two greasy plaits which had enjoyed as much of their meat gravy as they had. But they seemed in good humor and spoke enough kitchen Greek to make themselves understood. Clearly they were not disliked, for the landlord's girl was relaxed with them and told a joke which had them all laughing until they saw me a little more clearly.

"Nice horse," said the taller, his eyes narrowing a little, though he tried to disguise his expression. I was familiar with the response. He had recognized me as the Silverskin. He was wondering if he was going to find out what it was like to contract leprosy. Or have his immortal soul turned to roughage.

"I'm looking for a boy to keep an eye on him," I said. "He might even be for sale." I held up a silver Constantine. Shadow rats appeared from everywhere. I selected one and told him the Constantine was his as long as the horse was safe and well groomed. If he knew of a likely customer he would get a commission. Then I stared into the unhappy faces of the Vikings and told them I was looking for a man named Gunnar the Luckless. The men understood this subtle snub. "He's called Earl Gunnar the Wald, and he has a liking for good manners," said the younger, clearly wishing he had not been put in this position. They were Leif the Shorter and Leif the Larger.

As the boy took away my horse to the ostler's, I turned to one of the serving women and ordered a skin of their best yellow wine.

I, too, I said, appreciated good manners and would feel snubbed if they did not join me. The group with the backgammon board, hearing us speaking Norse, displayed only a passing interest in me, having identified me as an outlander. I heard one of them refer to me as Auberoni and was amused. I was no king of the fairies. The men were Venetian fishermen who had settled here recently and clearly had never heard of Il Pielle d'Argent or his sword, which was still known in Venice as Il Corvo Noir after its legendary maker, who had not actually forged the sword but had made the fanciful hilt. A large body of opinion believed the sword had taken its first soul from Corvo.

I dusted off the crusader's surcoat I still wore and joined the wary lads, Leif and Leif, who typically had hands as carefully groomed as their hair was greasy. I supposed if they ate mostly with their fingers, there was a point to keeping them clean. Needing neither to shave nor, in the conventional sense, pass feces, few Melnibonéans were familiar with beards or urinals. Many human habits remain deeply mysterious to us.

The Vikings probably thought me some effete Byzantine affecting Oriental manners. They had enough respect for my reputation, however, and showed me perfect courtesy. Renowned for their love of poetry and music and fine workmanship, Vikings enjoyed cultured living and hospitality. These two sea-robbers, though they served under one of the most evil captains known, were well informed and told me they had discussed deserting Gunnar for crusading or working as mercenaries in Byzantium. But they had no real choice. Their fate was to sail with Gunnar until the Valkyries came to carry them to Valhalla. They found a boy to run to Gunnar.

By the time we finished the skin, there came a stirring and a chorus of greetings. Earl Gunnar had arrived.

He hated to show his face. They said his wounds were so hideous he could not bear to look on his own features. I was surprised at the baroque workmanship of his mask, fashioned like a gryphon's head with an open, threatening mouth, but where the gullet would be was a face of silvered steel. Of Eastern origin, the helmet's crest had been cleverly crafted in silver and pewter: gryphon ascendant. But it was my own face I saw when I first looked at him. He was coming towards me, striding with dangerous inelegance.

Gunnar the Doomed was a bear. He was twice my width and slightly taller. I could imagine this terrifying figure on the bridge of his ship. He wore fine-woven plaids and linens and, like all his kind, his hands were girlishly tended. Hanging down over his shoulders his hair showed a little grey. With his well-trimmed, flowing locks, his rich clothing and knee-high doeskin boots, he could have been a Danish noble of the previous century. There was a generally archaic air about the man. It had been a hundred years since the last Vikings had gone on raiding expeditions.

The Norse sailors most reminded me of my old friend, the bluff, direct and solidly realistic Smiorgan Baldhead of the Purple Towns. As an individual Gunnar struck me as Smiorgan's opposite. There was something unwholesome about him. He affected the rough manners of a nobleman too long in the company of brutes. Yet he was a real diplomat. He knew enough not to threaten me. Instead he preferred to charm me. He ordered another skin of Bulgar wine and had it brought to the table where I still sat with his men. I could, of course, read nothing from the face, completely covered by the mirrored steel of the helmet. There were dark cavities in the mask. Through two of these he stared at me. Through another he fed himself tiny scraps of some kind of meat he carried in his hand. Otherwise he had the familiar manner of those who do not know me. He kept a little distance between us on the chance that I was actually a leper. Courteously I refused his wine. I had drunk my fill, I said. "I have some business with you, Earl Gunnar."

Gunnar shrugged. "I'm not a merchant, and my ship is not for hire."

"You are an adventurer, like myself, and your ship is your own. I'm not here to hire you, Earl Gunnar. A man like yourself does not strike me as one who would sing to another's tune no matter how sweet the melody."

"You've come overland, have you? Where from? Constantinople? Did you ride through the Devil's Garden?"

I told him that I had. He nodded. He sat back in his chair, that more-than-enigmatic mask regarding me with some interest. "So you saw all those massive heads. You'd think they were alive, eh? I saw something like them when I sailed with the Rose on her twin-hulled ship *The Either/Or*. We passed an island which marked the boundaries of that people's empire. Huge eyes staring from these stone faces. An island of giants. We did not go closer."

Gunnar had a certain witch-sight. No ordinary mortal would have seen those stones for what they were. I held my own counsel and let Gunnar continue.

"So you know me by my reputation, as I know thee, Sir Silverskin. And it pleases you to flatter my pride. Yet you know I do indeed work for hire on occasions. So, while I appreciate your courtesy, I'd be as happy to get down to business, if we have any, as not. I sail on the morning tide, and my crew is already aboard, save for these two, whom I came to find." He paused. Taking a reed from within his jerkin he placed one end in his wine cup and the other in the aperture in his mask. He sipped delicately. "My destination's already determined."

"I understand that also." I dropped my voice. "North and west to the World's Rim?"

He was too canny a captain to respond immediately. "You know more than I do, Sir Silverskin. We are merely setting sail for Las Cascadas to find fresh crewmen. Winter approaches, and at this time we normally go down to Zanzibar, where we take an interest in the slave trade. It's a poor business, but there are few other ways for an independent captain to make a living in these oversettled times."

I opened my palm and showed him what was there. "Give me a berth on your ship, Earl Gunnar, and I'll tell you more about this."

It was not in his nature to hesitate.

"The berth is yours," he said. "We sail on the first tide."

CHAPTER NINE

Pielle d'Argent

Darkling dragon, reiver's pride,
Rides high upon the turquoise tide.
His weird-drenched wave
Shall bear him to a rich retreat.
Darkling dragon, reiver's pride,
Lord of the Last, destined to die.
In Woden's waves he'll find no grave
His death's pre-written on his own black blade.

LONGFELLOW,
"Lord of the Lost"

 little before dawn I was down at the harbor looking over the long, slender ship lying against the dock. Solomon had been sold for a fair price to a Greek merchant who had some fancy to show himself off as a knight. I threw in the surcoat for good measure. At least he could pretend to fellow Christians to have been a crusader. Solomon would be making his way home to Lombardy shortly after we sailed. If he was lucky, the merchant would not be on the stallion's broad and cunning back.

Narrow, seemingly delicate, yet full of sinewy power even at anchor, *The Swan* pulled eagerly at her traces, haughty and confident as her namesake. I heard Gunnar had bought her from the impoverished Greenlanders who had made her but lacked the skills to sail her.

I admired the lines of the ship. Her fine, beaky figurehead

139

might deliberately have been a cross between a swan and a wyvern. She had the swan's calm stateliness, but also an air of menace, which had something to do with the rake of her deck, the set of her mast.

In the old Viking manner there were shields strapped to the rail above the board which ran between the rowing benches and the shutbeds where men could store their goods and get sleep when utterly worn out. I knew that many Vikings preferred to sleep at their oars and had developed ways of hanging over the great, golden sweeps to find the total rest of the thoroughly exhausted. But half the shield spaces were empty. I suspected they were not filled by born Norsemen.

I waited patiently near the gangplank as the sea-raiders arrived. They represented most nations, from Iceland to Mongolia. "By Ishtar," murmured a Persian, seeing me, "Gunnar's more desperate for men than we knew." Some of the races I did not recognize at all, but there were tall, thin East Africans, a couple of burly Moors, three Mongols and a mixture of Greeks, Albanians and Arabs. All of them had the grim look of men who knew violence more thoroughly than peace. Settling in to the ship, some of them took places by shields they had clearly acquired from the dead. The two Ashanti had brought their own long shields. Others had no shields at all. There was a miscellaneous mixture of weaponry. If ever a crew was born to sail a ship into the realms of Chaos, it was *The Swan's*.

Out on the far horizon something moved. I glanced up. Melnibonéans were also a seafaring people, and I had their way of scanning the ocean out of the corner of my eye. One of the Mongols ran up the mast like a rat to yell out his urgent fear.

"Venetian war galleys. Making good speed."

Gunnar came brawling down to the dock, half a dozen whores and hounds forming a living train behind him, shouting orders which were followed like thoughts by his obedient men. He took a moment to turn his faceless head to me and yell "We sail for Las Cascadas. We'll be safe there. Come aboard. If we can't strike a bargain, I'll set you off on the island." He swung his heavily cloaked body up over his rail and headed for the stern.

Las Cascadas was a notorious rock in the western Mediterranean with a single port. It was still some days' sail away, and we had the Venetians, possibly the Turks, perhaps the Byzantines, the Italians and the Caliphates to deal with, all of whom claimed authority over these seas. Gibr al Tairat itself was not so thoroughly untakable, but Las Cascadas's harbor was so well protected no enemy fleet could hope to enter. Any attempt to attack by land was thwarted by the steep, volcanic cliffs which rose sheer from the water. As a result the place had become a refuge for every corsair on the Red Coast and beyond and had its own queen, the infamous pirate known across the seafaring world as the Barbary Rose, whom Gunnar boasted of sailing with. Her strangely named twin-prowed ship was unmistakable and had been built apparently by shipwrights the Rose had brought with her from the South Sea Empire, which few European navigators even believed existed. Only the two tattooed giants, who still served the she-captain, knew the secret of making such vessels.

The black-and-gold sails of Venice were slightly larger on the horizon now. The tide was beginning to run our way, and I squeezed into a space between the mast and the deckhouse, marveling at the efficiency of these seamen. With a single woollen sail, they could get a ship into battle order in moments.

The oars bit the water as Gunnar roared the beat. We leaped out of the harbor, oblivious of everything but escape. Dhows and wherries scattered as we shot through the outer walls and into open sea, oars and sail combining to bring the ship about as Gunnar himself stood at the steering sweep, making adjustments with the touch of his hand, the balance was so beautiful. The unshipped oars moved in amazing uniform, like a neatly choreographed dance, and The Swan darted like a live thing under our feet, thrusting out into the deep water long before the Venetians saw us. We were already running for the Mediterranean, and unless they had laid a real trap for us there, we might even leave them behind completely. Once we were seen to reach the safety of Las Cascadas, any other pursuers would give up. Earl Gunnar had always made a point of staying on good terms with the Caliphates.

Two-masted, slave-rowed, heavy in the water and clumsy fore and aft, built more for endurance and protection than attack, the Venetian ships needed good weather and great luck even to keep pace with us. We quickly saluted farewell as our glorious pursuers fell below the horizon. Then we ran down the Illyrian coast and, with oars at full speed, sail bellying with a powerful southwester, rounded the Italian peninsula with a strong wind for Sicilia and the Tyrrhenian Sea, where we ran into a small flotilla of black-sailed ships expectantly lying in wait for us. Two brigantines and a brig.

Gunnar stood on his own bridge holding his sides and jeering with laughter as we sped by the lumbering vessels. "Three!" he shouted. "Three ships! Only three to catch *The Swan*! Your wealth makes you stupid!" He then turned to me. "They insult us, eh, Sir Silverskin?"

It was clear he felt a bond with me which I did not share.

I was exhilarated by the ship's performance. Gunnar, however, continued to act as if being overtaken by the Venetians were imminent. Like me he had learned not to relax too soon.

Later that night he finally gave the order to slow oars. His men slept instantly over their sweeps. Almost at her own volition *The Swan* continued to glide through the water. Gunnar planned to hug the Numidian shore all the way to the Magreb. In the west, only a few miles of sea separated the coast from Las Cascadas.

Gunnar joined me in the prow, where I had found a little solitude and was looking up at the great splash of the Milky Way, staring at stars which were at once familiar and unfamiliar. I had wrapped myself in my deep indigo oilskin cloak. Golden autumn touched the ocean. I remembered the story told to Melnibonéan children of the dead souls who walk the star-roads of the Milky Way, which we called the Land of the Dead. I was, for some reason, thinking of my father, the disappointed widower who blamed me for my mother's death.

Gunnar made no apology for interrupting me. He was in good spirits. "Those fat merchant bastards are still wallowing their way around Otranto!"

He clapped me on the back, almost as if feeling for a weakness. "So are you going to tell me how you think you know my plans? Or am I going to throw you overboard and put you out of my mind?"

"That would be ill-advised," I said. "But also impossible. You know I am effectively immortal and invulnerable."

"I won't know that until I put it to the test," he said. "But I do not believe you are any less mortal than myself."

"Indeed?" I saw no point in quarreling with him. He recognized the token I showed him. The ring which seemed freshminted.

"Aye, Elric Sadricsson, I know you from King Ethelred's time, when he paid you with that ring for your aid against the Danes. But the ring's far more ancient, eh. I thought the Templars had it now."

"Ethelred ruled a century and a half ago," I said. "Do I seem so old? I am, as you know, not a well man."

"I think you are much older than that, Sir Templar," Gunnar said. "I think you are ageless." There was a sinister note to his voice, a mocking quality which irritated me. "But not invulnerable."

"I think you mistake me for Luerabas, the Wandering Albanian, whom Jesus cursed from the tomb."

"I know for a fact that story's nonsense. Prince Elric of Melniboné, your story is far from being finished. And far from judgment."

He was trying to disturb me. I did not show him he had succeeded. "You know much for a mortal," I said.

"Oh, far too much for a *mortal*. It is my doom, Prince Elric, to remember everything of my past, my present and my future. I know, for instance, that I shall die in the full knowledge of the hopelessness and folly of existence. So dying will be a relief for me. And if I take a universe with me, so much the better. Oblivion is my destiny but also my craving. You, on the other hand, are doomed to remember too little and so die still hoping, still loving life . . ."

"I do not plan to die, but if I do, I doubt if it will be hoping," I said. "The reason I am in this world is because I search for life, even now."

"I search for death. Yet our quest takes us to the same place. We have common interests, Prince Elric, if not desires."

I could not answer him directly. "You have a place, no doubt, in this dream," I said. "You are some sort of dream-traveler. A dreamthief, perhaps?"

"You seem determined to insult me."

I would not rise to this. I was beginning to get the man's measure. He did know a great deal more about me than anyone else in this world. True, when I first entered this realm I served King Ethelred, known as the Unready. I traveled with a woman I called my sister, and we were both betrayed in the end.

But my apparent longevity was only the stuff of dreams, not my own reality. Gunnar was enjoying my supposed bafflement. I had shown him the ring because I had thought it might have meaning for him. It clearly bore more significance for him than I had guessed. I had acquired the thing in Jerusalem, off the same knight from whom I had taken Solomon.

"Come," Gunnar said. "I've something to show you. It will be interesting to know if you recognize it." He led me amidships into the little deckhouse. Inside was a chest which he opened without hesitation, swinging the bronze oil lamp over it so that I could see inside. There was a sword, some armor, some gauntlets, but on top of these was a round shield whose painted design was elegantly finished in blues, whites and reds, the pattern suggesting an eight-rayed sun. Was it of African origin? Had he found it in that famous expedition to the South Seas with the Rose? It was not metal, but hide covering wood, and when Gunnar put it into my hands it was surprisingly light, though about the same size and proportions as a Viking shield. "Do you know this plate?" he asked, using the Norse meaning.

"I had a toy like it once perhaps. Something to do with my childhood? What is it?" I balanced it in my hands. It seemed vibrant, alive. I had a momentary image of a nonhuman friend, a dragon perhaps. But the workmanship was in no way Melnibonéan. "Some sort of talisman. Were you sold it as a magic shield? That could be the sign of Chaos as easily as it could be the points of the compass. I think you have placed too high a value on this thing, Earl Gunnar. Was it meant to enchant me? To persuade me to your cause?"

Gunnar frowned. He simply did not believe me. "I envy you your self-control. You know the nature of that ring! Or is it self-deception? Lack of memory?"

"I seem to have little else but memory. Far too much memory. Self-deception? I remember the price I pay for slaying my own betrothed . . ."

"Ah, well," said Gunnar, "at least I am not burdened by such depressing and useless emotions. You and I are each going to die. We both understand the inevitable. It is merely my ambition to achieve that fate for the whole of creation at the same time. For if Fate thinks she jokes with us, I must teach her the consequences of her delusion. Everything in the multiverse will die when I die. I cannot bear the idea of life continuing when I know only oblivion."

I thought he was joking. I laughed. "Kill all of us?" I said. "A hard task."

"Hard," he agreed, "but not impossible." He took the bright "plate" from my hands and placed it back on top of his war hoard. He was disgruntled, as if he had expected more from me. I almost apologized.

"You'll have a great desire for that shield one day," he said. "Perhaps not in this manifestation. But we can hope."

He expected no real response from me. It seemed he sought only to pull me down to his level of misery. My own was of a different order. I had no "memory" of the future, and it was true my memory of the past was often a little dim. My concern was with my own world and an ambitious theocrat who had summoned forces of Chaos he could not now control. I needed to be free of him. I needed to be able to kill him slowly. I was still Melnibonéan enough to need the satisfaction of a long and subtle revenge. To achieve this end I must find the Nihrainian smith who forged the archetype of the black blade. Why it should be here, in a world given over to brutality and hypocrisy, I did not know.

Having baffled me when he hoped to intrigue me, the faceless captain let an edge creep into his voice. I was reminded of his essential malevolence.

"I have always envied you your ability to forget," he said. "And it irks me not to know how you came by it."

I had never met the man before. His words seemed like the merest nonsense. Eventually I made an excuse, settled myself in the forward part of the boat and was soon asleep.

The next day, with a heavy sea mist at last beginning to burn off, we came in sight of the Tripolitanian coast. Gunnar sent a man up the mast to look for ships and obstacles. Few others would sail in such weather, but most of the ships in the region were coast-luggers, transporting trade goods from one part of the Moorish Confederacy to another. The richest and most cultured power in the region, the Arabs had brought unprecedented enlightenment. The Moors despised the Romans as uncouth and provincial and admired the Greeks as scholars and poets. It was to those oddly opposed forces that this world owed most of its creativity. The Romans were engineers, but the Moors were Chaos's thinkers. Romans had no real notion of balance, only of control. A pattern so at odds with the rhythms and pulses of the natural and supernatural worlds seemed destined to produce disaster.

Las Cascadas, called by the Moors Hara al Wadim, was a haven in a region too full of ships to be safe for us. I prayed that the Venetians or Turks had not taken their place in the meantime and were lying in wait for us. It was highly unlikely. Though nominally under the authority of the Caliphates, the strongest power in the region, Las Cascadas was a law unto herself, with one easily defended harbor. While the Mussulman Fatimids and their rivals continued to quarrel over stewardship of Mecca, as the

Byzantines quarreled over the stewardship of Rome, and so long as the Matter of Jerusalem was the focus of the world's attention, the island remained safe.

The Barbary Rose was prudent. She confined her activities to those waters not claimed by the Caliphates or Empire. First fortified by Carthage, Las Cascadas was considered safe, too, because she was ruled by a woman. I had sailed with that woman in my time. Gunnar told me her twin-hulled ship I greatly admired, *The Either/Or*, was wintering in North Africa, probably in Mirador with an old ally of hers and mine, the Welsh sea-robber and semi-mortal, Ap Kwelch, who had also been hired by King Ethelred. Ap Kwelch was known in English waters for a cunning foe but an awkward ally.

I was relieved I would not have to encounter Kwelch. We had an unresolved argument not best settled at Las Cascadas where all weaponry was collected and put under lock and key at the dock.

Before we ever saw the island, Gunnar ran up his flags, as if they would not recognize *The Swan* for who she was. Perhaps he had a code to let the defenders know he was still captain.

We sighted Las Cascadas at midday, approaching her from the harbor side. At first the island fortress was like a mirage, a series of silver veins twinkling in the sunlight. Then it became clear those veins ran down the sides of cliffs formed by the crater of an enormous volcano. There were no evident signs of a harbor entrance, only the still lagoon within. It seemed to me that this mysterious island could only be occupied from the air or from below, and such supernatural forces were no longer summonable.

I had seen the fate of those forces of nature and supernature, exiled to bleak parts of the world like the Devil's Garden and slowly dying. When all such souls died, it was thought by our folk, the Earth died also. This war had been going on for centuries between Law and Chaos. Soon Arabia might be the only region not conquered by thin-lipped puritans.

Gunnar again took the steering sweep. He wrapped his huge arm around one of the sail ropes, guiding his ship as if it were a skiff. Beyond the rocks which guarded the harbor, I saw a great

cluster of houses, churches, mosques, synagogues, public buildings, markets and all the dense richness of a thriving, almost ver-
tical city. It was built up the sides of the harbor. The rivers and
waterfalls which gave Las Cascadas its name sparkled and gushed
between buildings and rocks. The whole island glinted like a raw
silver ingot. Pastel-colored houses were dense with greenery and
late-summer flowers. From their roofs and balconies, their gardens and vineyards, people raised up to look at us as we came
about before the sea-gates of Las Cascadas. Two enormous doors
of brass and steel could be drawn over a narrow gap between the
rocks, just wide enough for a single ship to come or go. I was reminded vividly of Melniboné, though this place lacked the soar-
ing towers of the Dreamers' City.

I heard shouted greetings. Figures moved about the
stonework which housed the doors, levers turned, slaves hauled
huge chains and the sea-gate opened.

Gunnar grunted and touched his steering sweep a little to
port, then a little to starboard. Delicately he guided us through
the narrow gaps, swift and smooth as an eel. The gates groaned
closed again behind us. We rowed in slowly beneath the gaze of
Las Cascadas's citizens. Everyone here lived off the proceeds of
piracy. They were all devoted subjects of the pirate queen. The
beautiful Barbary Rose had diplomatic skills which made her the
equal of Cleopatra.

A great variety of ships already stood at anchor in the harbor.
I recognized a Chinese junk, several large dhows, a round-hulled
Egyptian ship, and the more sophisticated fighting galleys, most of
modified Greek pattern, which were the favorite vessels of corsair
captains. I had a feeling I might meet old friends here, but not recent acquaintances. Then, as I hauled my gear to the dock, I
heard a name being called. "Pielle d'Argent, is it you?" I turned.

Laughing, the little redheaded Friar Tristelunne came bustling
along a quayside already crowded with the riffraff of Las Cascadas
turning out in hope of casual employment. But whatever booty
Gunnar brought to Las Cascadas to pay for his security, it was not
cargo. For a while Tristelunne disappeared in the crowd, then

bobbed up again nearby, still smiling. "So you took my advice," he said. "You spoke to the old ladies and gentlemen?"

"They spoke to me," I said. "I thought you headed for Cordova."

"I was about to disembark. Then I heard Christians and Jews were again out of favor with the caliph. He believes there has been a fresh conspiracy with the Empire. He's considering expelling all Franks. Indeed, he is wondering if expelling might not be too good for them. I thought it wise to wait out the winter here, administering to what faithful I can find. I'll see how the weather feels in spring. My alternative, at present, is the Lionheart's England, and quite honestly, it's no place for a gentleman. The forests are full of outlaws, the monasteries full of Benedictines and worse. Their divinely appointed king remains a prisoner in Austria, as I understand it, because his people have no particular interest in paying his ransom. John is an intellectual and therefore not trusted by anyone, especially the Church." Gossiping continually, Tristelunne guided me up steep, cobbled streets to the inn, which he insisted was the best on the island.

Behind me Gunnar roared a question. I told him I would see him at the inn.

I sensed his unease with my independence. He was used to control. It was second nature to him. He was baffled, I suspected, rather than angry.

Amused by all this, Friar Tristelunne led me into the inn's sunny garden. He sat me down at a bench and went inside, returning with two large shants of ale. I did my best with this hearty stuff, but yellow wine was the only drink that suited my perhaps overrefined palate. The fighting friar was not upset by this. He fetched me a cup of good wine and finished the ale himself. "You got advice, I hope, from the Grandparents?"

"They seemed more in a prophetic mood," I said. "Some mysterious visions."

"Follow them," he said firmly. "They'll bring you the thing you desire. You know already, in your heart, what the thing you desire will bring you." And he sighed.

"I have no interest in foreknowledge," I said. "My fate is my fate. That I understand. And understanding it releases me to drift wherever the tides of fate take me, for I trust in my own fortune, good or bad."

"A true gambler," he said. "A veritable mukhamir!"

"I'd heard all that before," I told him. "I belong to no society nor guild. I practice no formal arts, save when necessary, and I believe in nothing but myself, my sword and my unchangeable destiny."

"Yet you struggle against it."

"I am an optimist."

"We have that in common." He spoke without irony. He sat back against a post and stared around him at the flowers which flooded the entire courtyard. These blossoms vied with the bright colors worn by the customers, none of whom paid us much attention. I knew the people of Las Cascadas thought it ill mannered to show excessive attention to strangers.

On my first visit to Las Cascadas I had had status. The Rose and I were lovers then. On my second visit I had been a captive and something of her dupe. My ultimate turning of the tables had not made her any less aggrieved. But it was unlikely she had left any instructions about my fate, since she would hardly expect me to visit her stronghold again.

The friar confirmed that she was away until spring. She had sailed south again, he said. She always returned with exotic spices and jewels, and the occasional string of exquisite slaves. Ap Kwelch had gone with her. "That twin-prowed ship can sail faster and further than anything afloat," said Tristelunne. "She can sail to China and back in a single season. While we winter against the Atlantic, she's enjoying the sunshine and spoils of the Indies!"

"I thought Gunnar had taken *The Swan* there?"

"They both went in *The Swan*. She returned in *The Either/Or* after some dispute between them." He stopped suddenly and looked up. I knew Gunnar had come into the courtyard. The friar began to laugh, as if at his own joke. "And then the other dog said, 'No I only came in to get my claws trimmed.'"

Gunnar's hand fell on my shoulder. "We still have business to discuss," he said. "You, Sir Priest, have no business with me, I understand."

Pulling his worn cassock about him Friar Tristelunne got up. "I will never be desperate enough, sir, to seek the devil's employment."

"Then I was right," said Gunnar. "Is there no service in here?" He went inside. The friar seemed completely amused. He shrugged, winked at me, told me that our paths were bound to cross again and slipped out of the gate as Gunnar came back holding a boy by his ear. "All the girls are elsewhere, is it?"

"It is, sir," said the boy, dropped back to the paving of the yard. "I'm all that is left."

Gunnar cursed the urgency of his own men's drives and bellowed at the boy to bring ale. I told the lad to bring one more shant, tossed him a coin and got up. Gunnar's glittering mask looked at me in evident astonishment.

"You have the advantage of me, sir, and I cannot judge you for that," I said, "but it's clear you've no experience of partnership. I do not wish to hire your ship. I think you have some misunderstanding about me. You already told me that you know my blood and position. While I expect little from these kulaks and other rabble, I expect far more from one who claims to know my rank."

A sardonic bow. "Well, I apologize if that suits you. A breath of air and all is settled between us."

"Actions impress me more than words." I made to leave. I was, of course, playing a game, but I was playing it by following my own natural inclinations.

Gunnar, too, knew what was going on. He began to laugh. "Very well, Sir Silverskin. Let's talk as equals. It's true I'm used to bullying my way through this world, but you see the kind of company I'm forced to keep these days. I, too, was a Prince of the Balance. Now you find me a wretched corsair, clutching at legends for booty when once I crushed famous cities."

I sat down again. "While I am certain you have no intention of telling me your whole story, I suggest you let me know when you intend to sail for Vinland. Only the god-touched would venture into those seas in winter."

"Or the damned. Sir Silverskin, the course I propose to sail is directly through the realms of Hel. The entrance is on the other side of Greenland. Through the Underworld, through the moving rocks and the sucking whirlpools, through the monstrous darkness, to a land of eternal summer where riches are for the taking. The land is lush, growing wild what we cultivate with the sweat of our brows. And for wealth, there is legendary gold. A great ziggurat made entirely of gold and mysteriously abandoned by her people. So since we venture into the supernatural world, I suspect it makes little difference whether the season be summer or winter. We sail to Nifelheim itself."

"You sail to the north and the west," I told him. "I have useful experience and something you value."

He sucked thoughtfully through one of his straws. "And what would you gain from this voyage?"

"I seek a certain famous immortal smith. A Norseman maybe."

The noise from within the helm might have been laughter. "Is his name Volund? For Volund and his brothers guard that city called Illa Paglia della Oro by the Venetians. It stands in the center of a lake at the place where the edge of the world meets Polaris. That is where I am bound."

Gunnar was not telling me the whole truth. He wanted me to think a city of gold his goal. I guessed he sought something else at the World's Rim. Something he could destroy.

For the moment, however, I was content. *The Swan* was going where I wished to go. Whether the realm of Hel was supernatural or natural scarcely mattered if we sailed the North Sea in December or January. "You trust your boat completely," I observed.

"I have to," he said. "Our fates are intertwined now. The ship will survive as long as I survive. I have magic, as I promised, and not the mere alchemical nonsense you hear in Nürnberg. I follow a vision."

"I suspect I do, also," I said.

CHAPTER TEN

The Mouth of Hel

Norn-curs'd Norsemen, nature-driven to explore Earth's End,
Followed their weird to Fimbulwinter's icey land.
Longswords lay unblooded in lifeless hands
When warriors went the way of Gaynor, call'd the Damn'd.

LONGFELLOW,
"Lord of the Lost"

hen we left port a few days later, the seas were still calm. Gunnar hoped to make headway through a good autumn. We might even reach Greenland before the ice settled in.

I asked him if, beyond Nifelheim, he did not expect to find empires and soldiers as powerful as any in this sphere. He looked at me as if I were mad. "I've heard the story from a dozen sources. It's virgin land, free for the taking. The only defenders are wretched savages whose ancestors built the city before they offended the gods. It's all written down."

I was amused. "So that makes it true?"

We were in his tiny deckhouse. Stooping, he opened a small chest and took out a parchment. "If not, we'll make it true!" The parchment was written in Latin, but there was runic scattered through the text. I glanced over it. The account of some Irish monk who had been the secretary of a Danish king, it told the story, in bare details, of a certain Eric the White. He had gone with five ships to Vinland and there established a colony, building a fortified town against those whom they called variously *skredlinj,*

153

skraelings or *skrayling*. This was the Viking name for the local people. As far as I could tell it meant 'whiner' or 'moaner', and the Vikings considered them wretches and outlaws.

On this evidence Gunnar was prepared to sail through Nifelheim. I had heard similar stories from every Norseman I had known. Moorish philosophers proposed that the world was the shape of an elongated egg with the barbarian, godless races somehow clinging to the underside in perpetual darkness. In all such matters, as one is taught to do in the Dream of a Thousand Years, I remained silent. This was a dream I could not afford to have truncated. This was the last possible dream I could occupy before Jagreen Lern destroyed our fleet and then destroyed Moonglum and myself.

"So we will have only a land full of savages to conquer," I said sardonically. "And, say, thirty of us?"

"Exactly," said Gunnar. "With your sword and mine, it will take us a couple of months at most."

"Your sword?"

"You have Ravenbrand"—the faceless man tapped the swaddled blade at his side—"and I have Angurvadel."

He pulled away some of the covering to reveal a red-gold hilt hammered with the most intricate designs. "You'll take my word that the blade has runes embedded in it which flame red in war and that if it be drawn it must be blooded . . ."

I was, of course, curious. Did Gunnar carry a faux-glaive? Or did his sword have genuine magic? Was Angurvadel just another cursed sword of which the Norse folktales abounded? I had heard the name, of course, but it was an archetype I sought. Even if it were not false, Angurvadel was only one of the black sword's many brothers.

As Gunnar had hoped, the sailing was fair into the Atlantic. We stopped to take in provisions at a British settlement far from the protection of Norman law. There were only a few villagers left alive after Gunnar's men had finished their slaughter. These were forced to help kill their own animals and haul their own grain to our ship before they were in turn disposed of. Gunnar had an old-fashioned efficiency and attention to detail in his work. Like mine, his own sword was not drawn during this time.

We sailed on, knowing it would be some while before anyone considered pursuing us. Gunnar had a lodestone compass and various other Moorish instruments, which was probably what his men considered his magic. This made it far easier to risk quicker routes. As it happens, the sea was extraordinarily calm and the pale blue skies almost cloudless. Gunnar's men ascribed the weather to a damned man's luck. Gunnar himself had the air of a man thoroughly satisfied with his own good judgment.

During the few hours we had, I talked to some of the crew. They were friendly enough in a generally uncouth manner. Few of these reavers had much in the way of imagination, which was perhaps why they were prepared to follow Gunnar's standard.

One of the Ashanti, whom we called Asolingas, was by now wrapped in thick wool. He spoke good Moorish and told me how he and ten others had been captured after a battle and taken down the coast to be sold. Bought to row a Syrian trader, they had overwhelmed the rest of the ship within an hour of being at sea and, with the few other slaves who had joined them, managed to get themselves to Las Cascadas where, he said, they had been cheated out of the boat. The others had all been killed in later raiding expeditions.

Asolingas said he was homesick for Africa. Since his soul had already died and returned there, he supposed it would not be long before he followed it. He knew he would be killed sometime after we made our final landfall.

"Then why do you go?" I asked.

"Because I believe that my soul awaits me on the other side," he said.

A sigh came from starboard as the wind rose. I heard a gull. It would not be long before we made landfall.

In Greenland the colonists were so poor that the best we could get for ourselves was their water, a little sour beer and a weary goat that seemed glad to be slaughtered. Greenland settlements were notoriously impoverished, the settlers inbred and in-

sular, forever at odds with the native tribes over their small resources. I said to Gunnar how I hoped that the entrance into
Nifelheim was close. We had provisions for two weeks at most. He
reassured me. "Where we're going, there won't be time for eating
and drinking."

When we put out from Greenland, heading west, the weather
was already growling. A sea which had been slightly more than
choppy began sending massive waves against the bleak beaches.
We had considerable trouble getting into open water. We left behind perhaps the last European colony, struggling no more in that
harsh world. Gunnar often joked that he was God's kindest angel.
"Do you know what they call this blade in Lombardy? Saint
Michael's Justice." He began telling me a story which rambled off
into nothing. He seemed to absorb himself psychically in the
mountainous waves. There was a massive, slow repetition to the
sea, even as it howled and thrashed and tossed us a hundred feet
into the air, even as the wind and rain whistled in the rigging, and
we dived another hundred feet into a white-tipped, swirling valley of water.

I grew used to the larger rhythm to which the ship moved. I
sensed the security and strength which lay beneath all that unruly ocean. Now I knew what Gunnar and his men knew, why
the ship was thought to be a magic one. She slipped through all
that weather like a barracuda, virtually oblivious and scarcely
touched by it. She was so beautifully constructed that she never
held water between waves and almost always rose up as another
wave came down. The exhilaration of sailing on such an astonishingly well-made vessel, trusting her more than one trusted
oneself, was something I had never experienced before. The
nearest experience I knew was flying on a Phoorn dragon. I
began to understand Gunnar's reckless confidence. As I stood
wrapped in my blue sea-cloak and stared into the face of the
gale, I looked at the ship's figurehead in a new light. Was this
some memory of flight?

Gunnar began swinging his way along the running ropes, a
great bellow of glee issuing from within his faceless helm. Clearly

he was almost drunk on the experience. His head flung back, his laughter did not stop. At length he turned to me and gripped my arm. "By God, Prince Elric, we are going to be heroes, you and I."

Any pleasure I had felt up to that moment immediately dissipated. I could think of nothing worse than being remembered for my association with Gunnar the Doomed.

The Viking moved his head, like a scenting beast. "She is there," he said. "I know she is there. And you and I will find her. But only one of us will keep her. Whoever it is shall be the final martyr."

His hand fell on my back. Then he returned to the stern and his tiller.

I was, for a moment, reminded of my mother's death, of my father's hatred. I recalled my cousin's bloody end, weeping as the soul was sucked from her. Who was "she"? Who did he mean?

The waves crashed down again, and up we rose on the next, constantly moving ahead of the turbulence so that sometimes it really did seem we flew over the water. The ship's half-reefed sail would catch the wind and act like a wing, allowing Gunnar to touch the tiller this way and that rapidly, and swing her with the water. I have never seen a captain before or since who could handle his ship with his fingertips, who could issue a command and have it instantly followed in any weather. Gunnar boasted that however many he lost on land, he almost never lost a man at sea.

Foam drenched the decks, settled on the shoulders and thighs of the oarsmen. Foam flecked the troubled air. Black, red, brown and yellow backs bent and straightened like so many identical cogs, water and sweat pouring over them. Above, the sky was torn with wet, ragged clouds, boiling and black. I shivered in my cloak. I longed to be able to call Mishashaaa or any of the other elementals, to calm this storm by magic means. But I was already using my magic to inhabit this dream! The power of Ravenbrand was potent only in battle. To attempt anything else might result in uncontrollable consequences.

All day and all night we plunged on through the wild Atlantic waters. We used oars, tiller and sails to answer every change of the wind and, with the help of Gunnar's Moorish lodestone, now ran like an arrow due north until Gunnar called me into his deckhouse and showed me the instrument. "There's sorcery here," he insisted. "Some bastard's bewitched the thing!"

The stone was spinning in its glass, completely erratic.

"There's no other explanation," Gunnar said. "The place has a protector. Some Lord of the Higher Worlds . . ."

A howl came from the deck, and we both burst out of the deerskin deckhouse to see Leif the Larger, his face a frozen mask, staring at a vast head erupting from the wild water, glaring with apparent malevolence at our vulnerable little ship. It was human, and it filled the horizon. Gunnar grasped the Norseman by the shoulder and slapped him viciously. "Fool! It's a score of miles away. It's stone! It's on the shore!" But at the same time Gunnar was lifting his head to look upward . . . and then upward again. There was no question that what we saw was a gigantic face, the eyes staring sightlessly down from under the cloud which covered its forehead. We were too small for it to see. We were specks of dust in comparison. What Gunnar had noted was true. The thing did not seem to be alive. Presumably, therefore, we had nothing to fear from it. It was not a sentient human or god, rather an extraordinarily detailed sculpture in textured and delicately colored granite.

Leif the Larger drew in a breath and mumbled something into his golden beard. Then he went to the side and threw up. The ship was still tossing about in the ocean, was still on top of the waves. She continued the course we had set before our lodestar was enchanted. A course which took us directly towards that gigantic head.

When I pointed this out to Gunnar he shrugged. "Perhaps it's your giant who lives at the North Pole? We must trust the fates," he said. "You must have faith, Elric, to tread your path, to follow your myth."

And then, in an instant, the head opened its vast, black

mouth and the sea poured down into it, taking us relentlessly towards a horizon which was dark, glistening and thoroughly organic.

Gunnar roared his frustration and his despair. He made every effort to turn the ship. His men back-rowed heroically. But we were being drawn down into that fleshy pit.

Gunnar shook his fist against the fates. He seemed more affronted than terrified. "Damn you!" Then he began laughing. "Can't you see what's happening to us, Elric? We're being *swallowed!*"

It was true. We might have been the contents of a cup of water with which some monstrous ogre refreshed himself. I found that I, too, was laughing. The situation seemed irredeemably comical to me. And yet there was every chance I was about to perish. If I did so, I would perish in both realities.

All at once we were totally engulfed. The boat banged and buffeted, as if against the banks of a river. From somewhere amidships rose the sound of a deep, chanting song, its melody older than the world. Asolingas, the Ashanti, clearly believed his own particular moment had come.

Then he, too, fell silent.

I gasped and coughed at the foulness of the air. It was as if a street cur had breathed in my face. A whole series of fables I had heard about men being swallowed by gigantic fish came to mind. I could not recall a story about a ship being swallowed by a giant. Or was it a giant? Had we simply let ourselves see a configuration of rocks and made it into a face? Or was this some ancient sea-monster, large enough to swallow ships and drink seas?

The stink grew worse, but since it was the only air to breathe, we breathed it. With every breath, I filled my lungs with the dust of death.

And then we were in Nifelheim.

Leif the Shorter, from somewhere in the middle of the ship, cried out in frustration. "I should not be here. I have done nothing wrong. I killed my share. Is it my fault that I should be punished simply because I did not die in battle?"

I wrapped my sea-cloak more closely about me. It had become profoundly cold. The icy air was hard against my skin, threatening to strip it off. Breathing became painful. I felt I inhaled a thousand shards of glass.

There was no wind—just cold, pitch darkness, utter silence. I heard the sound of our oars dipping and rising, dipping and rising with almost unnatural regularity. A brand flared suddenly. I saw Gunnar's glittering mask, illuminated by the rush torch. I caught a faint impression of the rowers as he came back up the central board. "Where are we, Prince Elric? Do you know? Is this Nifelheim?"

"It might as well be," I said. The deck then slanted again, and we ran downwards for a short while before righting ourselves.

As soon as we were back into still water, the oars began to dip and rise, dip and rise. All around us was the sound of running water, like glaciers melting—a thousand rivers running from both sides of the narrow watercourse on which we now rowed.

Gunnar was jubilant. "Hel's rivers!"

The rest of us did not respond to his joy. We became aware of deep, despairing groans which were not quite human, of bubbling noises which might have been the last moments of drowning children. There was clashing and sibilant shushing, which could have been the sound of whispering voices. We concentrated on the dip and rise, dip and rise of our oars. This familiar slap was our only hold on logic as our senses screamed to escape.

Leif the Shorter's rasp came again. He was raving. "Elivagar, the Leipter and the Slid," he shouted. "Can you all hear them? They are the rivers of Nifelheim. The river of glaciers, the river of oaths, the river of naked swords. Can't you hear them? We are abandoned in the Underworld. That is the sound of Hvergelmir, the great cauldron, boiling eternally, dragging ships whole into her maw." He began to mumble something about wishing he had been braver and more reckless in his youth and how he hoped this death counted as a violent one. How he had never been a religious man but had done his best to follow the rules. Again he wailed that it was scarcely his fault he had not been killed in battle. Leif the Larger economically silenced his cousin. Yet even Leif the Shorter's wailings had not interrupted the steady rise and fall of our oars. Every man aboard clung to this effortful repetition, hoping it would somehow redeem him in the eyes of Fate and allow him entry into Paradise.

Now imploring voices called out to us. We heard the sound of hands on the sides of the ship, attempts to grasp our oars. Yet still the men rowed on at the same pace, Gunnar's voice rising over all the other sounds as he called out the rhythm. His voice was aggressive and bold and commanded absolute obedience.

Down dipped the oars and up again they rose. Gunnar cursed the darkness and defied the Queen of the Dead. "Know this, Lady Hel, that I am already dead. I live neither in Nifelheim nor in Valhalla. I die again and again, for I am Gunnar the Doomed. I have already been to the brink of oblivion and know my fate. You cannot frighten me, Hel, for I have more to fear than thee! When I die, life and death die with me!" His defiant laughter echoed through those bleak halls. And if, somewhere, there was a pale goddess whose knife was called Greed and whose dish was named Hunger, she heard that laughter and would think Ragnarok had come, that the Horn of Fate had blown and summoned the end of the world. It would not occur to her that a mere man voiced that laughter. Courage of Gunnar's order was rewarded in Valhalla, not Nifelheim.

Gunnar's defiance further heartened his men. We heard no more of Leif the Shorter's discovery of religion.

The sound of clashing metal grew louder, as if in response to Gunnar. The human voices became more coherent. They formed words, but in a language none of us knew. From out of that chilled darkness there emerged other, less easily identified sounds, including a gasping, bubbling, sucking noise like an old woman's death rattle. Yet still *The Swan* rowed on, straight and steady, to Gunnar's beating fist and rhythmic song.

Then he stopped singing.

A great silence fell again, save for the steady thrust of the oars. We felt a tug at the ship as if a great hand had seized it from below and was lifting it upward. A howling voice. A whirlwind. Yet we were being dragged into rather than out of the water.

I gasped as salt filled my mouth. I clung to whatever rigging I could find in the darkness while behind me Gunnar's laughter roared. He began to sing again as it seemed that he steered us directly into the drowning current. The ship creaked and complained as I had never heard before. She tilted violently, and at last the rhythm of her oars no longer matched the rhythm of Gunnar's song.

There was a tearing sound. I was convinced we were breaking up. Then came a great thrumming chord, as if the strings of an instrument had been struck. The chord consumed me, set every nerve singing to its tune and lifted me, as it lifted the entire ship, until we were driving upwards as rapidly as we had gone down. A white, blinding light dominated the horizon. My lungs filled entirely with water. I knew that I had failed in my quest, that in a few moments my only grasp on life was what was left to me as I hung in Jagreen Lern's rigging.

The ship began to yaw and spin in the water until I lost what little sense of direction I had. Suddenly the light faded to a pale grey. The noise became a steady shout, and again I heard Gunnar's laughter as he bawled to his men to return to their oars. "Row, lads. Hel's not far behind!"

And row they did, with the same extraordinary precision, their muscles bulging to bursting from the effort of it, while Gunnar lifted his gleaming helm towards heaven and pointed. Here was proof that we had left the supernatural world.

The bright light faded. Above us was a grey, darkening sky. Behind us some kind of maelstrom danced and sucked, but we had escaped it and were even now rowing steadily away from it.

Ahead of us lay a high, wooded coastline with a number of small islands standing off it. The cloud cover was heavy, but from the nature of the light sunset was not far off.

The sounds of the maelstrom fell away. I wondered at the extraordinary sorcery it had taken to achieve such a strange transition. Gunnar presented the coast to me with a proprietorial hand.

"Behold," he said with sardonic triumph, "the lost continent of Vinland!" He leaned forward, drinking it in. "The Greeks called it Atlantis and the Romans called it Thule. All races have their own name for it. Many have died seeking it. Few ever made the pacts I made to get here . . ."

A mist was rising. The coast vanished into it, as if the gods had grown tired of Gunnar's posturings. As we slowed oars and came in on a long, cold surf, we began to make out the darkening outlines of a fir-crowded coast edged by dark rock and small, unwelcoming beaches. Gunnar steered us between rocky, fir-clad islands as if he knew where he wanted to go. By the nature of the waves we had entered a bay and must be nearing a mooring of some sort, but there were still many small islands to negotiate.

I began to smell the land. It was rich with pine and ferny undergrowth, verdant with life. Gunnar's sense of that had been right, at least.

Asolingas saw the house first. He pointed and yelled to get Gunnar's attention.

Gunnar cursed loudly. "I'll swear to you, Elric—and I paid heavily in gold and souls for this information—I was told Vinland held nothing but savages."

"Who says they are not?" After all these years I was still confused by the fine distinctions.

"That manor could have been built in Norway last week! These aren't like the wretches we dealt with in Greenland." Gunnar was furious. "Leif's damned colonies were supposed to have perished! And now we're sailing into a port that probably has a dozen Viking ships in it and knows exactly what we're here for!"

He gave the order to back water and up oars. We drifted close in to the island and the house. The lower windows were already lit against the twilight and cast a mottled pattern on the surrounding shrubs. These windows were typically of lightly woven branches which admitted light and afforded privacy during the day but could be covered against the night. I wondered if the place was some sort of inn. There was thin smoke rising from its chimneys. It looked a good solid place, of big oak beams and white daub, such as any rich peasant might build from Normandy to Norway. If it was a little taller, perhaps a little more circular in shape than average, that was probably explained by local materials and conditions.

The manor's existence, of course, suggested exactly what Gunnar feared—that the Ericsson colonies had not only survived but prospered and produced an independent culture as typically Scandinavian as Iceland's. A house of these proportions and materials meant something else to Gunnar. It meant there were stone fortifications and sophisticated defenses. It meant fierce men who were conditioned to fighting the native skraylings and had a code of honor which demanded they die in battle. It meant that one ship, even ours, could not take the harbor, let alone the continent.

I was not, of course, disappointed. I had no quarrel with this folk and no eye on their possessions. Gunnar, however, had been promised a kingdom only to discover that apparently it already had a king.

As we passed the house we looked in vain for the city which we now expected to see. The shoreline was virgin woodland or harsh, pebble beach, with occasional slabs of rock rising up directly from the water. When night at last fell it was very clear there was no thriving harbor nearby. Gunnar was careful. He did not relax his guard. There were a dozen headlands which could be hiding a fair-sized fortified town. His position as a leader was threatened. He had promised an abandoned city of gold, not a city of stone crammed with warriors. The politics of our ship were beginning to shift radically.

The only light gleaming through all that watery, pine-drenched darkness was from the house on the island. At least we were not immediately threatened. If challenged, Gunnar would greet the Vikings as a brother, I knew. He would bide his time, search for their weaknesses, while he praised and flattered and told exotic stories.

Gunnar sighed with relief. He gave the order to row towards the island. I found myself hoping that the inhabitants were capable of defending themselves. Just as we began to look for an anchoring place, the lights in the house went out.

I looked up at the stars. They were far more familiar in their configuration than those I had most recently left behind. Had I somehow returned to the world of Melniboné? Instinctively I felt that my dreams and my realities had never been closer.

CHAPTER ELEVEN

Klosterheim

Famous in fierce foam the reivers raged,
Swords bared against their barren fortune.

LONGFELLOW,
"Lord of the Lost"

part from the lamp which burned in the front windows, there was no evidence that the house was occupied at all. Our men were by now totally exhausted. Gunnar knew this and told them to stop rowing. The Persian was sent forward with the plumb line. The water seemed shallow enough, but when we dropped anchor it would not hold. We were touching rock. The big millstone we used was slipping. Eventually we were able to get some sort of purchase in what was probably organic tangle. The ship drifted about before settling slowly with her dragon bird prow staring imperiously inward at the mysterious continent. Had Gunnar really thought it could be taken by thirty men commanded by a faceless madman?

I had no need of sleep the way the others had. I told them I would take first watch. I spent it in the little buckskin shelter we had made in the prow, which gave me a view of the water ahead. I heard what I thought were seals and checked the ship for swimmers. By the time my watch was up the night had been uneventful.

When I awoke just after dawn I heard birdsong, smelled wood smoke and forest and was filled with a sense of quite inappropriate well-being. From within the house, some sort of animal croaked, and I heard a human voice that was faintly familiar to me.

We drew anchor and rowed slowly around the island looking for a better landing place. Eventually we found a slab of rock jutting directly into the sea. A lightly clad man could stand on the rock and wade up easily to get a rope positioned for the rest of us. We would drown in our war-gear if we slipped.

At length, having left a small guard, we stood on the bank of the island. Out to sea, gulls and gannets fished on grey, white-flecked water. They flew low against a sky of windswept iron, with tall firs and mixed woodlands rising inland as far as we could see. Nowhere, save from the house, was there any smoke.

With a habitual curse, Gunnar began to march forward through the undergrowth leading his men. We were approaching the back of the house. There was no sign we had been detected until, as we came close, a bird inside began to screech in the most urgent and agitated manner. Then there was silence.

Gunnar stopped.

The Viking led us in a wide circle until we could see the front of the house with its solid oaken door, heavy iron hinges and locks, the bars at the windows in front of the lattice. A well-maintained and defendable manor house.

Again the bird made a noise.

Were they hoping we would go away?

Were they expecting us to attack?

Gunnar next told half the party to stay with me at the front while he circled the house. He was looking for something in particular now, I could tell. He murmured under his breath and counted something off on his fingers. He had recognized the place and feared it.

Certainly his manner changed radically. He yelled for us to get back, to get down to the ship immediately.

His men were used to obeying him. Their own superstition did the rest. Within seconds they were all stumbling back through the undergrowth, catching their hasty feet and cursing, using their swords to hack their way clear, thoroughly infected by their master's panic.

And panic it was! Gunnar was clearly terrified.

I would have followed had not the door opened and a rather gaunt, black-clad individual whom I did not recall greeted me with cold familiarity.

"Good morning, Prince Elric. Perhaps you'd take a little breakfast with me?"

He spoke High Melnibonéan, though he was a human. His face was almost fleshless, a cadaverous skull. His eyes were set so deep in their sockets it seemed a vacuum regarded you. His thin, pale lips forced a partial smile as he saw my surprise.

"I think my former master, Lord Gunnar, knows the nature of this place, but do not fear, my lord. It cannot do you harm. You do not recall me? I understand. You lead so many and such varied lives. You meet people far more remarkable than myself. You don't remember Johannes Klosterheim? I have been waiting here for Earl Gunnar to arrive some fifty years. We were once partners in sorcery. My own satanic powers are used elsewhere. But here I am."

"This house was brought here by sorcery?" I asked.

"No, sir. The house was built by my own and others' honest sweat. Only the stone posts were already in place. We erected the beams, the walls and floors. Each corner of the house is stone, as are many of the interior supports. We found the circle already here when I arrived."

"We? You and your pet?"

"I must apologize for the bird, sir. My only protection against the savages. But I was not referring to him. No, sir, I am lucky enough to be chief of a small tribe of native skraylings. Travelers like myself. We found this land already settled. It was the settlers helped me build my house."

"We saw no other lights, sir. Where would those settlers be?"

"Sadly, sir, they are all dead. Of old age. We fell out, I fear, myself and the Norsemen. My tribe triumphed. Apart from the women and children adopted to make up our numbers, the rest are now enjoying the rewards of Valhalla." He uttered a barking caw. "All mongrels now, eh, sir?"

"So settlers built this place for you?"

"They did most of the necessary work, yes. It's essentially circular, like their own houses. The island itself was a holy place locally. The natives were frightened of it when we arrived. I knew it would be a long while before you got here, so I needed somewhere comfortable to wait. But my tribesmen will not live here. A few remain with me but make their own camp in the mountains over on the other side of that ridge." He pointed inland at a distant, pine-covered terrace. "They bring me my food and my fuel. I am, these days, a kind of household god. Not very important, but worth placating. They've waited years, I suspect, for a more suitable Easterner. Gunnar could well be what they want, if he does not kill them before they have a chance to talk. You had better take me to him. I place myself under your protection, Prince Elric."

Without locking the house, Johannes Klosterheim closed his front door, left his jabbering bird inside and followed me. Some Vikings had already reached the gang-rope. *The Swan* rocked and bobbed under the weight as they pulled on the rope, hauling themselves through the water and up the side.

"Earl Gunnar," I called. "The master of the house is with me. He says he means us no harm. He can explain these paradoxes."

Gunnar was still half-panicked, raving. "Paradoxes? What paradoxes? There are no paradoxes here, merely dark danger. I will not risk my men's lives against it."

His men paused. They were not as impressed or terrified as he was. Gunnar gathered himself. He spoke with a slightly forced authority. He could not afford to show any further failures of judgment, or he would not last long.

"The master of the house is captured?"

"He comes as a friend. He says he awaits us. He is glad we have arrived."

Gunnar wanted no more of this in public. He grunted and

shrugged. "He can come aboard with us, if he likes. We need fresh water, and there's none I can see here."

Smiling faintly to himself Klosterheim held his own counsel. He bowed. "I am much obliged, Earl Gunnar."

Gunnar pushed back through his men to take a better look at the newcomer. "Do you know this realm?"

Klosterheim changed his language to Greek. "As well as anyone," he said. "I would imagine you are hoping for a guide."

Gunnar snorted. "As if I'd trust you!"

"I know why you fear this place, Gunnar the Doomed, and I know you have reason to fear it." Klosterheim spoke in a low, cold voice. "But I have no particular cause to fear it, and neither has any other man here, save you."

"You know my dream?" said Gunnar.

"I can guess what it must be, for I know what happened at that place. But you have nothing to fear in the house now."

"Aye," said Gunnar. "Call me a cautious old man, but I see no reason to trust my fortunes to you or that place."

"You had best trust me, Gunnar the Doomed, since we have goals in common."

"How can you know so much living at the World's Rim? Do vessels come and go every week from here to the Middle Sea?"

"Not as many as there used to be," said Klosterheim. "The Phoenician trade at its height was thriving on other shores than these. I have been to a country far from here where the folk speak Breton and are Christians. Slowly the land will change them. They will become as the others here. Men change not as they would, but as nature demands. The Norse and Roman trade was minimal. The Phoenicians and their Celtic allies fled here after the fall of Carthage. This continent has always absorbed its settlers. And made them its own."

Gunnar had lost interest. "So you say there's no big Norse settlement here? No major defenses? No fleet?"

"Just myself and the Pukawatchi now," said Klosterheim, almost humorously. "Patiently expecting your coming. I know what you carry with you here. How came you so swiftly to Vinland?" He spoke knowingly.

Gunnar saw the last of his men into the ship, then came back to talk further. "You mean that war plate?" he asked. "That skrayling shield?"

"It was more than luck brought you here before the winter snows," said Klosterheim. "It was more than one thing allowed you to take a shortcut through Hell!" He spoke with unusual force. "You need me, Earl Gunnar the Doomed, just as you do Prince Elric, if you are ever to see the Golden City and look upon the wonder of the Skrayling Tree."

"Do you know what I seek?" Gunnar demanded.

"Might it have something to do with the ring worn by our pale friend?"

"That's enough," said Gunnar.

He lapsed into uncharacteristic, brooding silence.

"And why am I here?" I asked. I held up the ring.

"You are not here, as you well know," said Johannes Klosterheim with narrowed eyes. "You are in peril in some other realm. Only desperation brings your dream self here."

"And you know what I seek?"

"I know what you would do. I cannot see how it can be done whether you serve Law or Chaos." He interrupted himself, looking to Gunnar. "Come back with me to the house. Leave your men to guard the ship. You can sleep, and we can talk further. I need your strength as you need my wisdom."

But Gunnar shook his head again. "Instinct tells me to avoid that house at all costs. It is associated with my doom. If you have warriors and would join forces, we'll improve our security. So I'll agree provisionally to an alliance. Until I see the mettle of your men. Should you reveal to me tomorrow that your tribe's no more visible than the average elf or dwarf, you'll have waited fifty years just to lose your head. Do you too claim to be a demi-mortal like our leprous friend here? The world is filling up with us. The best of these die bloodily at forty or so. Few live to sixty, let alone two hundred."

"I was born out of my time," Klosterheim offered by way of ex-planation. "I am an adventurer, like yourself, who seeks a certain revenge and recompense. I cannot die until Time herself dies. A young dreamthief's apprentice has tried to steal something from me and has paid a price for it. Now I travel as you do, with the help of sorcery. Why Time should accommodate us so thoroughly, I cannot tell, but we might learn one day."

"You're of a scientific disposition?" I asked.

"I have been acquainted with natural scientists and students of the Khemir and the Gibra for many years. All grope for wisdom as greedily as their lords and kings grope for power. To protect their wisdom from abuse by the temporal forces of this world, var-ious brotherhoods have been formed down the centuries. The most recent is the Brotherhood of the Holy Sepulcher. All under-stand that the sum of human wisdom, the secret of human peace, resides in a certain magical object. It can take the form of a cup, a staff or a stone. It is known by the Franks as the Gray Dale, which is a name they give to a ceremonial bowl used to greet and feast visitors. Some say it is a bowl of blood. Some say the heads of enemies swim in that bowl and speak of secret, unnatural things. Or it is a staff, such as Holy Roman Emperors carry to sym-bolize that they rule justly and with balance under the law. The Gauls and Moors are convinced it is a stone, and not a small one. Yet all agree the Gray Dale could take any of these forms and still be what it is, for sight of it is hidden from all but the most heroic and virtuous."

Again Gunnar was laughing. "Then that is why I am the Doomed. I am doomed to seek the cup but never see it, for I can-not claim to be a virtuous man. Yet only that cup could avert my fate. Since I'll never see it, I intend to ensure that no others shall ever set eyes on it . . ."

"Then let us hope," Klosterheim interrupted dryly, "that we are able to help you avert your fate."

"And you, Master Klosterheim," I said. "Do you, too, seek this staff, stone or cup?"

"To be honest," said Johannes Klosterheim with thin, terrifying piety, "I seek only one thing, and that is the cure for the World's Pain. I have one ambition. To bring harmony back to the world. I seek to serve my master, the Prince—"

"—of Peace?" Gunnar was feeling confident again now, and as usual this came out in a form of aggression. "I mistook you for a soldier or a merchant, sir, not a priest."

"My master inspires in me the greatest devotion."

"Aye. That devotion evaporates when you are forced to eat your own private parts," said Gunnar with a reminiscent chuckle.

He had regained whatever he had momentarily lost in his terror to get away from the house. Such weaknesses in one who was usually as courageous as he was ruthless! It made me curious. No doubt this curiosity was shared by his men, who trusted him only while his judgment remained impeccable. He knew, as well as anyone, that if he began to falter, there were thirty souls ready to challenge him for the captaincy of *The Swan*.

He had fired them with dreams of kingdoms. Now Klosterheim promised to take them to the Golden City. But Gunnar had by now seen the sense of that. He was no longer disputing our need for the skullface and others.

"And I must admit," added Klosterheim, "to have had some real trouble from the one who calls himself White Crow. One of your people, Prince Elric?"

"It is not a familiar name in Melniboné," I said. These humans believed anyone who was "fey" to be of Faery or some other imagined supernatural elfland.

I looked across at the shore with its great, wooded hills, its deep, ancient forest rolling like green waves back into the interior. Was this truly Atlantis, and did the continent surround the World's Pole? If so, would I find what I sought at the center, as I predicted?

"Tomorrow," Klosterheim continued, "we shall meet with my tribe, and together we shall find the Shining Path to the Golden City. Now we have allies, and all the prophecies combine to say the same thing. White Crow will give us no more trouble now.

He'll soon vanish from this realm forever. That which he stole shall be mine. This is what the oracle says."

"Aye, well," grumbled the faceless earl, "I have a habit of mistrusting oracles as well as gods."

Again Klosterheim offered us the hospitality of his home, and again Gunnar declined it. He repeated that Klosterheim should accept a place in the ship. Klosterheim hesitated before refusing. He had matters he must settle before joining us in the morning. He stated that his hall was our hall, and he had good venison and a full vegetable cellar if we cared to join him. My own appetite not being hearty and it being politic to keep my alliance with Gunnar in place, I refused. Accepting this with a baffled shrug, Klosterheim turned and made his way through the tangled undergrowth. There were no well-trodden paths to his house. From within came the agitated cackling of a bird.

It was now noon. The sun blazed through the gold and green of the late-autumn trees from a sky the color of rust and tarnished silver. I followed Klosterheim with my eyes as far as I could, but he was soon hidden in the brushy shadows.

Who was the young skrayling? A local leader, no doubt. Clearly Klosterheim hated the man. Yet what had he meant? White Crow was of my people? Was this land occupied by descendants of Melnibonéans?

The place being no longer occupied by Norse settlements, Gunnar was reassured. Once we were back aboard he gave the order to row towards the shore. He saw a good, low-rising beach with easy anchorage. We could easily wade from the boat to the shingle now. Soon Gunnar had men cutting down branches and setting up camp while the ship was secured and the guard determined.

At supper he asked me what I thought of Klosterheim. Was he a magician? I shook my head. Klosterheim was not himself a sorcerer but was employing sorcery. I did not know where he got this power or if he had other powers. "He's waited as long as he has and built that house for himself knowing he might have to wait for us even longer. Such patience must be respected. His need for an alliance might be of mutual benefit. He won't, of course, keep any bargain he might make with us."

Gunnar chuckled at this. The sound echoed in his helm and ended suddenly. "We'll keep no bargain we make with him. Who wins has the quickest wits and anticipates the others' moves best. This is the kind of game I like to play, Elric. With life and death to win as the only stake." Having escaped the terrors of that house, he was in unnaturally good spirits. I suspected an element of hysteria under his repeated reassurances that the future looked better than ever. With a larger fighting force, our chances of taking the City of Gold were immeasurably improved.

His ambitions were beyond me. I was prepared to bide my time and see what transpired. I, too, had my own ambitions and goals and did not intend to let either these or some mysterious dreamthief's apprentice stand in my way.

Next morning we roasted and ate a doe Asolingas and his friend killed. A little canoe rounded the island and slid rapidly towards us. The black-clad Klosterheim paddled it. I went down to the beach to greet him. Not a natural oarsman, he was out of breath. He let me help him beach the craft, gasping that the Pukawatchi were now assembled and awaiting us above the ridge, where they had built a peace camp. He pointed. Smoke puffed into the dawn sky.

The Pukawatchi, he explained, were not from these forests. Originally they had come with him from the south in search of their sacred treasures stolen by White Crow the trickster. The tribe had linked its destiny with his. Now they felt ready to ally with us and attack their ancient enemies.

We dragged *The Swan* ashore and disguised her deep in the forest. We removed all our war-gear, which included the great blue, red and white shield Gunnar had shown me that first night. As I had no shield, he loaned me that one. But there was a strict condition. Before we left the deckhouse, Gunnar flung me a cover. He helped me tie it over the outside of the shield. We would need that shield later, he said, and he did not want the Pukawatchi to see it. If I showed it, under any circumstances, it could be the end of us. I suspect Gunnar also thought the shield stolen. If it were discovered, he would rather I be thought the thief. It made no difference to me. Even with its cover, the thing was light, useful if attacked by spears and arrows, and practical if I needed something to throw at a horse to bring it down. Not that Klosterheim had said anything about horses when I asked him how long we had to go. He described everything in terms of marches. As one who hated to walk, who had ridden the wild dragons of Melniboné, I was not used to marching. Nor did I enjoy the prospect.

Following what appeared to be deer trails, we lumbered through the forest in our war-shirts and our iron helmets like so many ancient reptiles. I was impressed by the Viking hardiness. They had scarcely rested before they were again on the move, their legs doing the same kind of work their arms had done earlier. Gunnar knew the Norseman's secret of the loping march, which they had learned from the Romans.

We went uphill and down, through the heavy, loose soil, the root-tangled undergrowth of an endless green-gold forest. Hawks circled above us. Unfamiliar birds called from the trees. Our rhythmic tramping was relieved by what we saw. Rivers dammed by beaver, curious raccoons, the nests of squirrels and crows, the spoor of deer, bear and geese.

Then Klosterheim slowed us, lifting both hands in reassurance. We came out of the trees into a deep autumn meadow beside a narrow, silver stream where some forty lodges had been erected, their cooking smoke moving lazily in the air. The people reminded me very much of the Lapps I had encountered in the service of the Swedish king. They had much the same features, being rather short, stocky and square. They had dogs with them and all the other signs of an established camp. Yet something was slightly awry about the scene. They had posted no guards and so were surprised when we came into their village, Klosterheim leading the way.

There was an immediate cacophony when they saw me. It was something I was used to, but these people seemed to have some special animosity towards me. I remembered Klosterheim's reference. I could see he was trying to reassure them that I was neither their enemy nor one of their enemy's tribe.

He said something else I did not hear which cheered them. They began to sing, to raise their spears and bows in greeting. All were fairly short, though one or two of them were almost as tall as Klosterheim. They had certainly not gone soft during their wait. Displaying the physiques of men who lived by hunting, they wore jerkins and leggings of buckskin, softened and tightly sewn and decorated with all kinds of pictograms. The shoulders and sleeves of the jackets, the back and bottom edges of the leggings, were sewn with fringes of buckskin, handsome costumes on a somewhat unlovely people. The clothing all looked as if it had been cut down to fit. I asked Klosterheim how his tribe had learned to make such fine cold-weather garments.

The gaunt man smiled. "They discovered in the usual way. These lodges and most of these tools and weapons are what were left after the Pukawatchi came upon the original owners. The Pukawatchi have a policy of taking no long-term prisoners unless they need to replace their own dead. In this case the attack thoroughly surprised the tribe, whom my people wiped out to a child. So there are no more Minkipipsee, as I believe the indigenous folk termed themselves. You have no cause to feel insecure. Nobody cares to avenge them, even for the sport of it."

We entered the camp proper, a large public area encircled by the lodges. The tribe sent up a great wail of greeting. They seemed to be waiting for something or someone, and meanwhile they were painting for the war trail, Klosterheim told me. Something about their square, stern faces reminded me of Dalmatia. Daubed with white, scarlet and blue clay on their bodies, they smeared yellow clay on their hands and foreheads. Some wore eagle feathers. The men's weapons were elaborate, carved lances tipped with bone, obsidian and found metal. Both men and women raised their voices in this strange ululation, which sounded to my unpracticed ear more like a funeral lament. We responded as best we could and were made welcome.

These woods were not lacking in game. There were patches of vegetables where the Pukawatchi had made gardens. Again our party ate well. The men relaxed. They asked the skraylings if perhaps they could spare a little beer or wine, as they did not know what to make of the proffered pipes. They had the sense, however, to note that none of our hosts was drinking anything but water and a rather unpleasant tea made from spearmint and yarrow. Eventually, after trying the pipe, they resorted to explaining in some detail how beer was brewed.

With due ceremony we were introduced to the rather sourfaced individual whom Klosterheim called Young Two Tongues or Ipkaptam. With a scar across his cheek and lip, as if from a sword cut, his was a handsome, ungiving face. He had become the sachem, or speaker, of these people on his father's death. "Not because heredity demanded it," said Klosterheim in Greek, "but because he was known to have medicine sight and be lucky."

The local language was largely impossible for the Vikings to understand. The Pukawatchi thus tended to focus their attention on Gunnar and myself. We must have seemed demigods or, more likely, demons to them. They had a name for us which was impossible to translate.

But there was plenty to eat. The women and girls brought us dish after dish to enjoy, and soon a convivial atmosphere developed.

Klosterheim quelled the uncertainties of the still grim Ipkaptam, who had added more paint to his face. When Klosterheim suggested we retire to the speaking lodge to discuss our expedition, Ipkaptam shook his head and pointed first at my sword and then at my face, uttered the word "Kakatanawa" more than once and was adamant that I not be allowed into their councils. Klosterheim reasoned with him, but Ipkaptam stood up and walked away, throwing down an elaborate bag, which had been attached to his belt. I took this to mean he did not intend to share his wisdom with us.

Kakatanawa! The same word, spat as an oath and directed at me. Klosterheim spoke to him, brutally, urgently, no doubt encouraging some sort of common sense, for gradually Young Two Tongues glowered and listened. Then he glowered and nodded. Then he glowered and came back, fingering his scars. He picked up his bag and pointed to a large tepee set aside from the others near a stand of trees and a tumble of rocks. He spoke seriously and at some length, gesticulating, pointing, emphatic.

He grumbled something again and called to some women standing nearby. He gave orders to a group of warriors. Then he signaled that we should follow him as, still sour-faced, he walked grudgingly towards the big lodge.

"The talking lodge," said Klosterheim, and with a crooked grimace, "their town hall."

Gunnar and I followed Klosterheim and his friend towards the talking lodge. I gathered we were to prepare our assault on the City of Gold. Our weapons were left in the safekeeping of our men. Their own war-tools were so superior, they had little to fear from any "skraylings."

Nonetheless I entered the shaman's lodge with a rather uneasy sense of privilege.

CHAPTER TWELVE

The Vision in the Lodge

Ask me not my name or nation,
Ask me not my past or station,
But stay and listen to my story
Listen to my mystic calling
How I saw my path unrolling,
How I dreamed my dream of patience,
Dreamed how all might work together
Make their laws and peace together
Make their lodges one great cover,
And a mighty people fashion
Who will walk and seek with passion
Seek the justice of the mountains
Seek the wisdom of the forests
Seek the vision of the deserts
Then bring all this learning home.

Then we light the redstone peace pipe,
Pass the pipe that makes the peace talk,
Lets us speak of valorous virtue.
Pass the red bowled, smoking spirit
Declaim our noble deeds and dreams.
Let speakers see themselves in others,
Let listeners listen to their brothers,
Listen to sisters and their mothers,
To the dwellers in the forest
And the spirits of the sky.
Our tales are strong and live forever
Tales of luck and skill and cunning
When the White Hare she came running,
When the cackling Crow was flying,

When the Great Black Bear was charging,
When in War we faced our foes.
Speak to all, for all are brothers,
Speak of deeds and dreams of valor,
Breathe the smoke that soothes the soul.

W. S. HARTE,
"The Hobowakan"

t was already very hot inside the large lodge, and it took a while for my somewhat weak eyes to clear. Slowly I made out a central charcoal fire around which were arranged rich piles of animal hides. On the far side of the fire was a larger heap of furs. Those had a white skin thrown over them. I guessed this to be Ipkaptam's seat. Willow branches had been woven around it to make a kind of throne. I did not recognize several of the pelts used. Some must come from indigenous beasts. The air was thick with various herbal scents. A smoldering fire in which several round rocks were heated gave off heavy smoke, sluggishly rising to the top of the tepee. A strong smell of curing hides, of animal fat and what might have been wet fur permeated the room. I was also reminded of the smell of worked iron.

I asked Klosterheim the purpose of this discomfort. He assured me that I would find the experience engrossing and illuminating. Gunnar complained that if he had known it was going to be this sort of thing he would have hacked cooperation out of the bastards. Recognizing his tone, Ipkaptam smiled secretly. For a moment his knowing eyes met mine.

Once inside, the flaps of the lodge were tied tight, and the heat began to rise considerably. Knowing my tendency to lose my senses in such temperatures, I did my best to keep control, but I was already feeling a little dizzy.

Klosterheim was on my left, Gunnar on my right and the

Pukawatchi shaman directly ahead of me. We made a very strange gathering in that buffalo-hide wigwam. The lodgepoles were strung with all kinds of dried vermin and evil-smelling herbs. While I had known far worse ways of seeking wisdom in the dream-worlds, I have known better-scented ones. Yet I was struck by a strong sense of familiarity. My brain would not or could not recall where I had experienced a similar conference. Decorated as he now was with a white feather crown, turquoise and malachite necklaces and copper armbands, together with his medicine bag and its contents, Ipkaptam looked even more striking. He reminded me vaguely of the old Grandparents, the gods who had talked to me in Satan's Garden. I tried desperately to remember what they had told me. Would it be of use here?

The shaman produced a big, shallow drum. He beat on it with long, slow, regular strokes. From deep within his chest, a song grew. The song was not for us to hear but for the spirits who would help him in performing this séance. Half its words and cadences were outside the range of even my own rather sensitive ears.

Klosterheim leaned forward over the fire to splash water on the heated stones. They hissed and steamed, and Ipkaptam's chanting grew louder. I struggled to keep my breathing deep and regular. The scar on his face, which I had seen as an irregular wound, now took on shape. Another face lurked beneath the first, something baleful and insectlike. I tried to remember what I knew. I felt nauseated and dizzy. Were the Pukawatchi human? Or did their race merely take on human characteristics? According to Klosterheim such ambiguous creatures were quite common here.

As I came close to losing consciousness, I was alerted by Klosterheim's changing voice. He sounded like a monk. He was chanting in Greek, telling the tale of the Pukawatchi and their treasures. He threw fuel on the fire, blowing until the stones were red-hot and then splashing on more water. The fire danced up again, casting shadows, increasing the heat until it was impossible to think clearly. All my energies were largely devoted to remaining conscious.

The beating drum, the rhythmic chanting, the strange words,

all began to take me over. I was losing control of my own will. It was not pleasant to feel that somewhere I had experienced all this before, yet I was also somewhat heartened by the thought. I hoped a higher purpose was being served by my discomfort.

During my youthful training I had been absorbed into many such rituals. I, therefore, made no particular effort to hold on to individual identity but let myself be drawn into the dark security of the heat and the shadows, the chanting and the drumming. I say security because it is like a kind of death. All worldly and material cares begin to disappear. One is confronted with one's own cruelties and appetites, experienced as a victim might experience them. There is remorse and self-forgiveness, an incisive glance into the reality of one's own soul, as if we stand in judgment on ourselves. This creates a peculiar psychic spiral in which one is redeemed or reborn into a kind of purity of being, a state which enables one to be open to the visions or revelations which are almost always the result of such formalities.

Apologizing to us that he no longer possessed the tribe's traditional redstone pipe bowl, Ipkaptam produced a large ceremonial pipe and lit it with a taper from the fire. He turned to the four points of the compass, beginning in the east, chanting something I could not understand, puffing the smoke as he did so. He held the pipe aloft. Again he chanted and puffed. Then he passed the pipe to Klosterheim, who knew what to do with it.

Now Ipkaptam began to speak of the tribe's great past. In rolling tones he described the Great Spirit's creation of his people deep below the ground. The very first people had been made of stone, and they were slow and sleepy. They had in turn made men to run their errands for them, and then made giants to protect them against rebellion. The men ran away from the giants to another land, which was the land of the Pukawatchi.

The smaller Pukawatchi were too weak to fight so many; thus they fled underground. The giants had not pursued the men. The tall men had not pursued the Pukawatchi, and soon they were at one with men and giants.

All had been equal, and all had gifts the others could use.

Warmed in the womb of Mother Earth herself, they had no need of fire. Food was plentiful. They were at peace. Every year the great Eternal Pipe, the redstone smoking bowl of the Pukawatchi, which they had won in war against the green people, was produced and presented to the Spirit. The pipe was smoked by every tribe and every people in creation. It was always full of the finest herbs and aromatic bark, and it never needed to be lit. Even the bear people and the badger people and the eagle people and all the other peoples of the plains and forests and mountains were invited to the great powwow, to confirm their bond. All lived in mutual harmony and respect. Only in the world of spirits was there conflict, and their wars did not touch on the lands of the Pukawatchi, nor of the tall men, nor of the giants.

I realized I was no longer hearing Klosterheim's Greek but Ipkaptam's own language in his own voice. Ipkaptam easily made the mental links necessary for me to understand their language. At last the words had found their way directly to my mind.

With the words came pictures and narratives, crowding one upon the other. All were sufficiently familiar. I absorbed and understood them quickly. I was learning the whole history of a people, its rise and fall and rise again. I was hearing its own legends. Would I learn about a lost sword with a habit of escaping or killing those who possessed it?

More water was poured on the stones. The pipe was passed again and again. As I learned to inhale its strange smoke, my sense of reality grew even dimmer.

Ipkaptam's insectoid features seemed those of a great ant and his crown of feathers antennae. I refused to lose either my life or my sanity. I pretended his disguise was all that was visible to me. I remembered the teachings of a people I had lived among briefly, who spoke of a god they called the Original Insect. He was supposed to be the first created being. A locust. The story was told how the locust could not eat, so the spirits made it a forest where it might graze. But the locust was so hungry he ate the whole forest, and now he cannot do anything else. Unless stopped, he will attempt to eat the whole world and then eat himself.

I found nothing sinister in the tale the shaman told of his people's history. Perhaps there *was* nothing sinister in the tale itself, only in the teller. What Two Tongues had learned might not have been from his fathers. Nonetheless, I listened.

The steam and the smoke continued to make me very faint. My heart sank when the great red sandstone peace pipe was passed again. Once more it was offered to the spirits of the four winds. Klosterheim took a small, mean puff and passed it to me. I inhaled the fragrant barks and leaves and came suddenly alive. It was as if the smoke curled through every vein and bone in my body, inhabiting all of me and filling me with a sense of well-being, leaving none of the effects of my usual desperate drug-supported state. Those drugs fed off my spirit as I fed off their energy. These were natural plants, dried but not cured. I felt as if I inhaled all nature's benefits in one long pull on the pipe. I was hugely invigorated.

Ipkaptam took back the pipe with reverence. Again he offered it to the sky, then to the earth, then to the four winds, and only then replaced it on the stone before him. His widening lizard eyes glowed huge in the firelight.

"Many times," he said, "the spirits tried to involve us in their wars. We would fight neither for one side nor the other. These were not our wars. We did not even have the means to fight them. We did not have the will to kill our fellows." He seemed to grow in stature as he spoke with reminiscent pride. "Once all peoples, giants and men, came peacefully to trade with the Pukawatchi in their underground realm. We traded the metal we chipped from the rocks. With this metal the whole world tipped its arrows and lances and made fine ornaments." Iron was more highly prized than gold, said Ipkaptam, for with iron a man might win himself gold, but with gold he was always vulnerable to the man with iron. Metal was even more highly prized than agate and quartz for the edge it would take.

Men were cunning, had fire, but they did not know where to look for the metals and stones. Their tools and ornaments, their weapons, were made of flint and bone, so they traded furs and

cooked meat for the Pukawatchi iron. Giants had sorcerous powers and ancient wisdom, for they were the folk of the rock. They
had the secret of fire, and they knew how to burn metal and twist
it into shapes. All had to come to the Pukawatchi for their metal,
and the most prized of all the metals was the sentient iron mined
at the heart of the world.

The Pukawatchi were small and clever. They could find the
crevices where the metals and the precious stones lay and prize
them out. They had the patience to mine them and the patience
to work them. They made hammers and other tools strong
enough to flatten the iron, the copper, the gold. Striking them
over and over again, they made beautiful objects and impressive
weapons.

They lived in their great, dark realm for untold eons until
massive upheavals occurred below the ground and all around
them people went to war. The Pukawatchi were forced to the surface. Terrified of the sun, they became night dwellers, hiding from
all other peoples and keeping their own council. Sometimes they
were forced to steal food from villages they found. At other times
the villages left food for them, and they in turn repaired pots and
the like.

So the Pukawatchi wandered until they came to a place far
from the lands of other men. Here they built their first great city.
Now they were no longer brothers with their fellows. Now all
were at war. Yet the Pukawatchi brought their skills with them
when they fled, and they still had knowledge of the earth and
what was to be found there. After a while they built a great city
deep into the rock face of the land they had reached. The city was
fashioned like the dark tunnels and chambers they had known
below the ground. Now it was above the ground, but inside it was
as it had always been. And the people were safe and the people
prospered, living in their cool, dark cities. At last, against all sane
instinct, against the very will of the spirits, they began to work
with fire.

Soon the giants heard that the Pukawatchi had survived and
could be traded with. The Pukawatchi learned the secret of fire

and began to deal again with everyone except the spirits, who remained mindlessly at war. The war spread to men. The
Pukawatchi made weapons for all peoples and grew rich as a result. The men were exhausted by war. The Pukawatchi cities had
prospered and proliferated until the whole of the south and west
became their empire.

The Pukawatchi grew rich with all things men valued. They
had extended their rule further and further across the surface—
the Realm of Light, as they called it. They conquered other tribes
and made them subject to the Pukawatchi, and in the conquering
they won great treasures, among them the famous Four Treasures
of the Pukawatchi.

Each treasure had been won by a different hero, then lost in a
series of complicated epics, then won again. All these stories were
told to us in such a way that we absorbed them as we sat smoking
and sweating in the lodge, our ordinary human senses completely
lost to us.

The Four Treasures of the Pukawatchi were the Shield of
Flight, the Lance of Invulnerability, the Perpetual Peace Pipe
which never required filling, and the Flute of Reason, which, if
the right three notes were played upon it, could restore a mortally
wounded creature to life.

These treasures they kept in their city, deep within the complex of caves, in chambers they had hewn and elaborately decorated from the living rock. Pukawatchi cities could be defended
easily against attack by abandoning the lower levels and defending the upper. No other tribe had ever defeated the Pukawatchi,
who had gloried in their treasures, celebrating them each year
with the stories of how they came to be won by the heroes of the
tribe in deeds of extraordinary warfare.

Ipkaptam began to draw in the air. He painted pictures there
for us to see. He showed us the perpetually filled redstone pipe,
which had belonged to the green people who lived along the lakes
in stilt huts and who refused to pay the Pukawatchi a tribute of
fish. So the Pukawatchi hero Nagtani went against the green

people and destroyed their villages and took their pipe as a trophy. The green people were driven from the land.

Next the Kakatanawa, far in the north, asked the Pukawatchi to fashion a great lance of magical iron which the Kakatanawa had cut from the mother metal. This was the first great treasure of the Pukawatchi, for they had made it themselves. The Kakatanawa sent the magic metal to be made into a lance, but they refused to pay the higher price the Pukawatchi asked. The blade was more valuable, so the Pukawatchi kept it.

He showed us a vision of the lance, its shaft carved and decorated, its black blade running with scarlet letters. I was shocked. It was my sword, but turned into a spear! Then he showed us the Flute of Reason, and it seemed to me that Klosterheim responded with surprised recognition. I, too, experienced a flash of memory. And then Two Tongues showed us the Shield of Flight, the shield which allowed its owner to travel through the air. It was identical to the one I carried. I knew that the stolen artifact was only a few hundred yards from us at most, in the safekeeping of Asolingas.

Ipkaptam continued. "All these were our treasures and our history. Then White Crow came, and he was smiling. White Crow came, and he told us he was our friend. White Crow promised to teach us all his secrets and because he did not seem a Kakatanawa and therefore not our enemy, we accepted him. His medicine was brought to us, and he was our good luck. Because he was not of our people, he could not take a wife among us, but he had many friends in the great men of our tribe, and their daughters admired him. Our people welcomed him, for he said he came only to learn our wisdom. We understood that he followed his dream-journey, and we wished him well.

"And White Crow went away. We said: It is true. White Crow desires nothing from us. He is a good man. He is a noble man. He is a man who follows his way. He runs his own path. And we said that some great man was lucky indeed to have such a son.

"Then the next year and the year after that, White Crow returned. And still he was a model guest. He helped with the hunting, and he lived among us. What was difficult for us to do was easy for him. His strength and his height and his cleverness were such that we were glad of his company.

"Then the fourth spring White Crow came again and was welcome among us and shared our food and lived in our city and told tales of all the places he had visited. But this time he asked to see our sacred treasures, the Black Lance of Manawata, the only spear which can kill spirits; the Shield of the Alkonka, the only defense against the spirits; the Cherooki Pipe, the great redstone pipe which brings peace wherever it is smoked, even with the spirits. And the Flute of Ayanawatta, which, if the right notes are blown on it, will confer on the owner the power to change his ordained spirit path, even from death to life. It will heal the sick and bring harmony where there is strife.

"And White Crow tricked us and stole our treasures and took them away with him. An evil spirit seized him. He journeyed to the great wilderness, where there are no trees. There, at the foot of the mountains, White Crow called a great gathering of the Winds. He planned to make the Winds his friends. So he called to the South Wind. And the South Wind came. He called to the West Wind. And the West Wind came to his calling. And to each spirit of the wind he gave a gift to take back to their people. Even before we knew he had stolen them, he had given the Perpetual Pipe to the People of the South; the Shield of Flight he gave to the People of the West. He himself took the Flute of Reason to the People of the East. And each of them gave him a gift in return.

"Now he has set violent events in motion. There are prophecies, omens, portents. It is the end or the beginning for the Pukawatchi. So much is confused. But there is hope that we can recover our treasures. To the Kakatanawa themselves in the north, White Crow planned to carry the Black Lance. They are his most powerful friends, and his folk have always been allies of their folk, since the beginning of things. His people also made their great obscene pact with the Phoorn and so began the rule of ten thousand years. But if White Crow fails to take the Black Lance back to the Kakatanawa, then all our destinies can be changed. Thus we do everything we can to stop him and his allies. Already they stand on the final part of the path to the city of the Kakatanawa . . ."

"Where," Klosterheim told us, in more normal tones, "our magic defeats them. White Crow is prisoner, but his brother and sister carry the lance. We must stop them! They are held captive on the Shining Path by a great ally of mine, who makes it impossible for them to continue on the last part of the Shining Path. Time does not pass there. They are unaware of it, but they have remained under that spell for half a century, allowing us to grow strong again. They have tried all their sorcery against my ally, but he is too powerful for them. Only White Crow escaped, but *I* was too clever for him. Yet even my pact with Lord Shoashooan is finite, and that busy elemental will soon grow hungry. He must have his promised reward. So we must reach Kakatanawa as soon as possible. Alone we might not defeat White Crow and his talented friends, but together we will make their end inevitable."

"What of your other lost treasures?" I said. "How will you get those back?"

"It will be easier once we have the Black Lance," said Klosterheim. He added softly to me in Greek, "The treasures of the Pukawatchi are as nothing to the prize to be found in the city of the Kakatanawa."

"I am only interested in one damned treasure," said Gunnar, to Ipkaptam's disapproval. "And that's a jeweled cup I've been seeking for some centuries. Failing that, I have some business with Death."

I had sudden insight. "You call it the Holy Grail! The Templars were obsessed with it. Supposed to contain some god's blood or head? The Welsh also have a magic bowl. My erstwhile comrade Ap Kwelch told me he once discovered it. There are too many of these magic objects loose in a world so ambivalent towards sorcery! Your learned priests say it's a myth, a will-o'-the-wisp?"

"I know that it is not, sir," said Klosterheim disapprovingly.

"There are many legends but only one Grail. And that is what I expect to find in Kakatanawa."

Again the shaman was singing. He sang to apologize for our behavior to whatever spirits he had summoned. As we became quiet he spoke of his own destiny, the dream he had dreamed in his youth: to revenge his grandfather, who had died in the summoning of Lord Shoashooan. In that dream he had sought his people's treasures and he had led his people home.

"That is my destiny," he said. "To redeem my father's house. To reclaim our treasures and our honor. For too long we have followed a false dream."

CHAPTER THIRTEEN

The Trail of Honor

I am the God Thor,
I am the War God,
I am the Thunderer!
Here in my Northland,
My fastness and fortress,
Reign I forever!

Here amid icebergs
Rule I the nations.
This is my hammer,
Mjolner the mighty.
Giants and sorcerers
Cannot withstand it!

LONGFELLOW,
"The Saga of King Olaf"

Behold, this pipe. Verily a man!
Within it I have placed my being.
Place within it your own being, also,
Then free shall you be from all that brings death.

OSAGE PIPE CHANT
(LA FLESCHE'S TR.)

unnar the Doomed was in good spirits as we stumbled from the heat of the lodge out into the cold slap of a northern autumn evening. "By Odin," he said, "we are lucky men this day!" But I hardly heard him. I was still stupefied by the smoke and the heat of the lodge. I felt I was on the verge of understanding some great truth.

I looked up and almost reeled at the sight which met us. It took me a moment to realize that the Pukawatchi were decorated for battle. They looked like a hive of human-sized insects. They buzzed faintly. In all my travels I had never seen a people quite like this.

A sudden wilder buzzing—an ululation went up from the gathered warriors. Layers of different-colored paint in this light gave their faces the same quality I had noticed in that of their sachem, Ipkaptam the Two Tongues, as we sat in the lodge. Their eerie, insectlike quality was given further substance by a translucent black sheen which spread over the surface of the other colors. They had the dark iridescence of a beetle's wing. Some wore insectlike headdresses. The black overlay was symbolic. It meant they were prepared to fight to the death. The red-rimmed eyes announced they would show no mercy. Ipkaptam told me with some pride that they had named their path the Trail of Honor and would return with the nation's treasures or die nobly in the attempt.

Again something nagged at the million memories which shadowed those of my immediate incarnation. Who did these people remind me of? Was there a Melnibonéan folktale I had read? About machines become fish who became insects who became human? Who had followed a Trail of Honor to establish a city in the south? I was unsure of all I could recall. With somewhat sentimental notions of intelligence, sensibility and virtue, the story did not feel like a Melnibonéan tale. Perhaps I had heard it in the

Young Kingdoms or in another dream of baroque life and rococo death spent in a realm far less familiar to me than this?

In my youth I performed the five journeys and dreamed the Dream of Twenty Years, then the Dream of Fifty Years and then the Dream of a Hundred Years. Each of those dreams I had to dream at least three times. I had dreamed some several more times than that. But this was only the second time I had dreamed the Dream of a Thousand Years, and this was no longer the quest of an education but the hope of saving my own life, and that of most of surviving humanity, from unchecked Chaos.

Perhaps this moment was what one trained for? It seemed I was born and reborn for crisis. It was what the nun had told me at the Priory of the Sacred Egg in the Dalmatian highlands. She had read my fortune that night in the light of a tallow candle while we sat naked in the bed. Fetching the cards had been her response, as passion was satisfied, to her first real sight of my physique, of its scars and marks. She asked in some seriousness if she had shared herself with a demon. I told her that I had been a mercenary for some time. "Then perhaps you yourself have slept with a demon," she joked.

Fear the Crisis Maker, she had warned, by which I had decided she meant that I should fear myself. What was worse in a fully sentient universe than one who refused thought, who feared it, who was sickened by it? Who inevitably chose violence and the way of the sword, though he yearned for peace and tranquillity?

Fear the child, she had said. Again, the child was myself—jealous, greedy, demanding, selfish. Why should her God choose such a man for his service?

I had asked the matronly prioress this question, and she had laughed at me. All soldiers she met seemed to be soul-searching in one way or another. She supposed it was inevitable. "In some eras," she said, "the sword and the intellect must be as one. Those are our Silver Ages. That is how we create those periods we call Golden Ages, when the sword can be forgotten. But until the sword is fully forgotten, no longer part of the cycle, and men no longer speak in its language of gods and heroes and battles, every

Golden Age will inevitably be followed by an age of Iron and Blood." She had spoken of the Prince of Peace as if he might actually exist. I asked her about this. "He is my soul's salvation," she had said. I told her without irony that I envied her. But it was hard for me to understand the kind of man who was prepared to die on the chance that it might save others. In my experience, such sacrifices were rarely worth making. She had laughed aloud at this.

Her kind of Christianity, of course, was almost the apotheosis of what we Melnibonéans see as weakness. Yet I had also seen ideas growing from the common soil which, when examined, actually had the hope of becoming reality. It was not for me to denigrate their softness and their tolerance. My father frequently argued that where you exalted the weak above the strong, thus you turned your nation from predator into prey. However much the thinking of the Young Kingdoms influenced me, it had never occurred to me to choose to become a victim!

A Melnibonéan of my caste is expected to put himself through at least most of the tortures he will in the course of a long life bestow on others. This produces a taste, an intimacy, a conspiracy of cruelty which can give a culture its own special piquancy but in the end brings it to collapse. Imagination rather than inventive sensation will always be a nation's ultimate salvation. I had tried to convince my own people of this. And now the Pukawatchi faced a similar dilemma.

Indeed, as I came to know them, I discovered I had more in common with the Pukawatchi than with some of the crew of *The Swan*.

Preparations made, routes discussed, plans laid, we helped the Pukawatchi strike camp. Our somewhat ragged army slowly made ready for its long trek north. More pipes were smoked. More talks talked. The Vikings and the skraylings, as they still called their new allies, developed a reasonable camaraderie—good enough for the expedition, at least. Morally they shared much. The Pukawatchi understood the need to make a good death, just as the Vikings did. The warriors prayed for the right circumstances and the courage to display their virtues while they died.

These ideas were far closer to those of my immediate ancestors. Among the rest of what I still considered the Young Kingdoms, there had been developing a tradition which was as mysterious and as attractive to me as my own was familiar and repellent. It was that culture, not my own, I fought to save. It was those people whose fate would be decided by my success or failure in this long dream. I had no love for the millennia-old culture which had borne me. I rejected it more than once in preference to the simpler ways of the human mercenary. There was a certain comfort in taking this path. It demanded little thought from me.

There was some urgency to my situation, of course, as I hung in Jagreen Lern's rigging waiting to die. But there are no significant correspondences between the passage of time in one realm and another. I had elected, after all, to dream of a thousand years, and now the full thousand must be endured even if my object were achieved sooner. It is why I am able to tell you this story in this way. What I achieved in this dream would reflect through all the other worlds of the multiverse, including my own. How I conducted myself in this dream was of deep importance. A certain path had to be followed. When the trail was left it had to be left knowingly.

The path had already taken on a certain relentless momentum. From being a group of raiders or explorers, we were now an army on the march. Egyptians and Norsemen tramped side by side with the same extraordinary stamina they showed at the oars. Asolingas and the Bomendando jogged ahead with the Pukawatchi scouts.

Ipkaptam, Gunnar, Klosterheim and I marched at the center of the main group. The Pukawatchi went to war in finger-bone armor, with lances, bows and shields. They had jackets of bone and helmets fashioned from huge mammoth tusks decorated with eagle feathers and beads. The bone armor was decorated with turquoise and other semiprecious stones and was lighter than the chain mail most of our crew favored. Some warriors wore the carapaces of huge turtles and helmets made from massive conch shells. Braids were protected by beads and otter fur.

Just as I had noted the size of some of the huge pelts within the wigwam, I wondered at the size of the sea-life which supplied the Pukawatchi with so much. Klosterheim said somewhat dismissively that sizes were unstable in these parts, something to do with the conjunction of various scales. We were too close to "the tree," he said.

None of this made much sense to me. But as long as our journey took us forward to where I hoped to find the original of the black sword, I scarcely cared what rationales he presented.

We were now an army of about a hundred and fifty experienced warriors. Some of the women and youths and old people were also armed. At the far end of this mixed force of pirates and Pukawatchi came the unarmed women, the infirm, children and animals who would follow us until we began to fight. From what I had seen thus far, I expected the city to be a primitive affair, probably a stockade of some kind surrounding a dozen or so long-houses.

The Pukawatchi had no real beasts of burden, unless you counted their coyote dogs that pulled the travois on which they carried their folded lodges. Women and children did most of the work. The warriors rarely did anything except, like the rest of us, march at a steady, dogged pace. Those women who had what they called "men's medicine" dressed and armed themselves like the men and marched with the men, just as one or two of the men with "women's medicine" walked with the group at the back. Klosterheim told me such practices were common among many of the peoples of this vast land. But not all tribes shared values and ideas.

Ipkaptam, joining in, spoke of certain tribes who were beneath contempt, who ate insects or who tortured animals, but even those peoples they had exterminated he spoke well of, as people of honor. We Melnibonéans had never experienced noble feelings for people we sent to oblivion. Melnibonéans never questioned their own ruthless law, which they imposed on all they conquered. Other cultures were not of interest to us. If the people refused to accept our scheme of things, we simply slaughtered

them. But we had become too soft, my father complained, looking always at me, and allowed the Young Kingdoms to grow arro-
gant. There had been a time when the world never dared question
Melniboné. What we defined as the truth *was* the truth! But because it suited us to have fat cattle at our disposal, we allowed the
people of the Young Kingdoms to proliferate and gain power.

Not so, the Pukawatchi! They believed in the law of the blood
feud, so gave their enemies no chance to retaliate. Every member
of the rival tribe had to be eliminated or the babies taken to sub-
stitute for any Pukawatchi killed. Once they had been so few they
had stolen infants from stronger tribes. Now they needed no for-
eign babies.

Yesterday the Pukawatchi had been despised, said Ipkaptam,
both for their stature and their intelligence. Today all took them
seriously. Their story would survive. And when the Kakatanawa
were conquered, the Pukawatchi would dominate all worlds.
They had grown strong, he said, until they were the strongest of
all.

They were certainly sturdy. When walking and water were the
only two means of traveling long distances, the calves and the
arms became capable of enormous endurance and power. Their
means of transport ensured them success in battle.

The Pukawatchi would have preferred the greater speed of
water, but we were moving north and upstream of a small river
which was too narrow to take any kind of craft. Klosterheim said
there was a mooring rendezvous about two days ahead of us where
we would acquire canoes so that the war party could make better
progress. He seemed to have a greater sense of urgency than the
rest of us. Of course, it was his magic, his energy, which was holding our rivals at bay. He suggested that soon the army should
move on at a trot to the rendezvous, leaving the armed women
and children with a small guard of warriors. I elected to command
this guard. The idea of trotting did not appeal to me.

For the time being, we all continued at our regular pace.

Again I was impressed by the size to which everything in the
region grew. Plants were far larger than anything I had seen be-

fore. I should have liked to have stopped and examined more. The terrain we were crossing was wooded and mountainous, and we traveled through a series of valleys, still following the winding course of the river, as we drove deeper and deeper into country nobody was familiar with. It had been deserted of people, Ipkaptam told me, since a great disaster had struck here. He believed that the whole country around the Kakatanawa land was dead, like this. As you got closer, even the game began to disappear. But he had only heard this.

Before the beginnings of this war, no Pukawatchi had ever been allowed to cross the human lands, let alone visit the land of the Kakatanawa. They had come east in his grandfather's time. Equally, the Kakatanawa were forbidden to leave their own land. Until recently they, too, had kept to their pact. But others, such as the Phoorn, had done their work for them. Some of these Phoorn adopted human form and bore a resemblance to me, though my physique was different. Others were monstrous reptiles. Now that he knew me, said the sachem, he realized I was more like a Pukawatchi, yet it was still difficult, he said, to trust me. His instinct was to kill me. He could not be sure this was my natural form.

The Pukawatchi had never been this far north, and Ipkaptam worried that he did wrong. But wrongdoing had become the order of the day. Once the people of the south, north, west and east had respected one another's laws and hunting grounds. They had a saying: The West Wind does not fight the East Wind. But since White Crow had come to the world, Chaos threatened on all sides. In their fighting the Lords of the Air produced the hawk-winds which destroyed whole peoples and created demons who ruled in their place. These demons were called Sho-ah Sho-an and could only be defeated by the lost Pukawatchi treasures.

Ipkaptam also admitted that he was nervous of being sucked off the back of the world. At some point you must tumble into the bottomless void, fall forever, eternally living the sharp, despairing moment when you realize your death is inevitable. Far better to die the warrior's death. The clean death, as some called it. To

Pukawatchi and Viking alike a noble death remained more important than longevity. Those who died bravely and with their death songs on their lips could live the simple, joyous warrior's life for eternity.

My own responses to these notions were rather more complex. I shared their idea that it was better to make a noble death than lead an ignoble life. There was not one among us, save Klosterheim, who did not think that. The Ashanti, the Mongols, the Norsemen knew the indignities and humiliations of old age and preferred to avoid them, just as a promise of inevitable defeat made them anxious to take as many of their enemies with them as they could.

The Pukawatchi, so provincially self-important and so certain of their imperial rights, had a shared sense of afterlife which favored those who had died bloody deaths and sent as many others as possible to equally bloody deaths. The fate of women and children in these cosmologies was vague, but I suspect the women had their own more favorable versions which they told among themselves. For all their domestic power, they were more frequently the unwilling victims of the warrior code. Certain warriors prided themselves on their skill at dispatching women and children as painlessly as possible.

As we began to speak the same language I learned more about the skraylings, as Gunnar still insisted on calling them. The supernatural understanding of these natives was sophisticated, though their powers of sorcery were limited and usually restricted to needs of planting and hunting. Only the great line of shamans, of whom Ipkaptam was the latest, understood and explored the world of the spirits. This was where he drew his power.

Ipkaptam's was not an especially popular family. They had often abused their privileges. But the Pukawatchi believed in the family's famous luck. When that luck failed, I suspected, Ipkaptam would no longer be revered, tolerated or perhaps even alive.

Gunnar walked by himself much of the way. Few sought him out. The Pukawatchi suspected him to be some kind of minor demon. They displayed an instinctive dislike of me as well. Some were still convinced I was a renegade Kakatanawa.

Our alliance could break down at any moment. Gunnar and Klosterheim had common goals, but there would come a day when they would be at odds. Equally, no doubt, Gunnar was scheming how he would dispatch me when I had served my turn. Like my late cousin Yyrkoon, Gunnar spent a great deal of time planning how to gain the upper hand. Those of us who did not think competitively were always surprised by those who did. For my own part I responded with appropriate cunning or ferocity to whatever situation I found myself in. When one has had the training of a Melnibonéan adept, one rarely needs to anticipate another's actions. Or so I thought. Such thinking might well have led to our extinction as a people.

Yet Gunnar's weakness was also typical, as he believed me to be scheming as hard as he was. This might have been true of Klosterheim and Ipkaptam, but it was certainly not true of me. I was still prepared to believe that I could easily be following a chimera. The black blade's maker was my only interest.

The Vikings remained fairly cheerful. They had seen enough to know that there might be a city somewhere which could be looted, even if it was not made of gold. They knew the superiority of their iron weapons and had a fair idea of the way back to the sea and their ship. They probably believed a longer sailing would avoid the more terrifying aspects of the journey here. So most of them saw this as a standard inland expedition from which they might emerge with wealth and knowledge. They knew the value of the Pukawatchi furs and quickly understood how the Pukawatchi valued iron. The only iron the Pukawatchi worked was moon metal or ingots chipped from the rock. Somehow they had lost their legendary power to mine and smelt metal. As a result, a small iron dagger would buy a lot of valuable furs.

In my company, at least, the Vikings also had the sense that they carried secret power. I was surprised that my shield, the Pukawatchi stolen Shield of Flight tight under its cover, had not been sensed by their shaman, seemingly so sensitive to the supernatural. It remained to be seen whether it would give the gift of flight to anyone who carried it or whether spells and chants were involved to invoke the spirits associated with the shield.

Experience shows most magic objects depend far more upon the gullibility of the purchaser than on any blessing by the spirits. The shield could have no particular properties at all, except those of superstition and antiquity. How Gunnar found it in Europe, he refused to explain, but I had the impression he had come by it in trade some while ago, perhaps from one of the People of the West to whom, Ipkaptam said, it had been given. But here the People of the West would live far away from the sea, unless we were on a large island. If we were on an island, then it was possible the People of the West had somehow sailed around the rim of the world, as Gunnar would have it, from the China Seas, as he himself had done with the Rose. Or was this a treasure Gunnar had brought back from the expedition they made, when he had returned in *The Swan* while the Barbary Rose captained her own twin-prowed ship, *The Either/Or?*

There was some dispute among us as to whether we should make the quick march at all or keep to our present pace, so that we remained together. Klosterheim spoke of the gathering winter. It was becoming noticeably colder by the day. We were marching north. Normally, both Pukawatchi and Vikings reserved raiding expeditions for the spring. Winter made movement almost impossible. Ice would form on the rivers soon, and they would not be able to use the canoes.

So we called a further conference. Eventually it was decided that the two Ashanti, Asolingas and the Bomendando, who were our fastest runners, together with a Pukawatchi called Nagatche, would go ahead for a few miles to get the lie of the land. Then we could make a better-informed decision.

The three runners set off as the evening sky grew black overhead. An east wind began to blow steadily, biting through layers of clothing. I felt the lash of sleet against my cheeks.

Night fell. Ipkaptam, Klosterheim, Earl Gunnar and I again conferred around an uncertain fire in a small temporary lodge.

Ipkaptam believed that the season was coming unusually early. He would have expected another month before the snows arrived. Again he spoke anxiously about offending the winds. It would be best to reach the water as soon as possible. With snow, our journey to Kakatanawa would be far more difficult. With ice it might be impossible, and we would have to wait until the next year. He turned to Klosterheim for suggestions. Were there any other magical allies he could summon? Was there some way to placate the wind so that it blew the snow away from them? What if he were to offer the Snow Wind his most valuable possessions? His children's lives?

Klosterheim pointed out in Greek that most of his powers were already being used to sustain his supernatural ally Lord Shoashooan threatening our enemies. He had only been able to summon the demon in the first place because of the strange nature of this realm's semisentient winds, which Ipkaptam had already remarked on. It was even possible that Lord Shoashooan was drawing the bad weather to them. But if White Crow was allowed to take the Black Lance back to Kakatanawa, then the Pukawatchi would never defeat their ancient enemies, never redeem their honor. As for summoning powerful spirits, that was now entirely beyond him. With all his experience of the supernatural, he had never been able to control two such forces. Gunnar mumbled something about having made too many bargains already and said he was thinking on the problem. I—whose powers were virtually nonexistent here, but needed fewer drugs and sorcery to survive—was equally helpless.

"Then we must do our best with our natural brains," said Klosterheim with some humor.

The next morning one of the Ashanti returned. The Bomendando was glad of the camp. He stood by the fire shivering, his lanky body wrapped in a buffalo robe. He was uneasy and seemed frightened. He said he had left the other two guarding their find while he came to tell us what it was. They also would return if it became too dangerous. They had remained in case they should catch a glimpse of what they guessed was occupying the hills.

I had never seen such a disturbed look on the Bomendando's face. Clearly, he thought he might not be believed.

"Come on, man," demanded Gunnar, reaching a threatening hand toward him. "What have you seen out there?"

"It's a footprint," said the Bomendando. "A footprint."

"So there are other men here. How many?"

"This was not a man's footprint." The Bomendando shivered. "It was fresh, and we found others, fainter, when we looked. It is the footprint of a giant. We are in the realm of the giants, Earl Gunnar. This was not part of our agreement. You told us nothing of giants, nothing of the Stone Men. You spoke only of a poorly defended city. You said how the giants had been driven from this land by men and half-lings. You said giants were forbidden to go outside their city. Why did you not tell us of these other giants? These roaming giants?"

"Giants!" Gunnar was contemptuous. "A trick of the eye. The track had spread, that was all. I've heard tales of giants all my life and have yet to see one."

But the Bomendando shook his head. He held out his spear. With his hand he measured off another half-length again. "It was that wide and more than twice as long. A giant."

Ipkaptam became agitated. "They are not supposed to leave their city. They cannot leave it. They are forbidden. The giants have always guarded what they are sworn to guard. If they left, the world would end. It must have been a human you saw."

The Ashanti was adamant, tired of talk. "There is a giant out there, in those hills," he said. "And where there is one giant, there are often others."

There came a shout from the margins of the camp. Warriors ran towards us, pointing over their shoulders.

In the slanting sleet I saw a figure emerging. He was indeed very tall and broad. My head would scarcely have reached his chest, but he was a third the size of any giants I had previously en-countered.

He was dressed in a heavy black coat, covered by a fur-lined cloak. On his head was an oddly shaped hat, its brim turned up at three corners, sporting a couple of plumes. His white hair was tied back with a loose, black bow.

I heard Klosterheim curse behind me.

"Is that our giant?" I asked.

Ipkaptam was shaking his head. "That's no giant," he said. "That's a human."

The newcomer took off his hat by way of a peace sign. "Good evening, gentlemen," he said, "my name is Lobkowitz. I was traveling in these parts and seem to have lost my way. Is there any chance, do you think, that I could warm my bones a little at your fire?"

He loomed over us, almost as tall as our tepees. I felt like a ten-year-old boy in the presence of a very burly man.

Klosterheim came forward and bowed. "Good evening, Prince Lobkowitz," he said. "I had not expected to see you here."

"It's a turning multiverse, my dear captain." The broad-faced, genial nobleman peered hard at Klosterheim. He frowned in apparent surprise. "Forgive me if I seem rude," he said, "but is it my impression, sir, or have you shrunk a foot or two since last we met?"

CHAPTER FOURTEEN

The Gentleman at Large

But the mischievous Puk-Wudjies,
They the envious Little People,
They the fairies and the pygmies,
Plotted and conspired against him.
"If this hateful Kwasind," said they,
"If this great, outrageous fellow
Goes on thus a little longer,
Tearing everything he touches,
Rending everything to pieces,
Filling all the world with wonder,
What becomes of the Puk-Wudjies?
Who will care for the Puk-Wudjies,
He will tread us down like mushrooms,
Drive us all into the water,
Give our bodies to be eaten,
By the wicked Nee-ba-naw-baigs,
By the Spirits of the Water!"

LONGFELLOW,
"The Song of Hiawatha"

losterheim and Lobkowitz had been acquainted in Christendom. They were not friends. Klosterheim was deeply suspicious of every word the newcomer uttered. Lobkowitz, while more affable, seemed equally wary of Klosterheim. Gunnar said something about two peoples forever at odds. He believed the races must be natural enemies.

As Prince Lobkowitz stood with his back to our fire, Gunnar asked him what brought him to the region.

"Very little, sir. My business was with another party, but you know how it is, this close to a node on the great tree of time. Although it makes travel between the worlds a little easier, it also makes it confusing. Variances of scale, which would be so vast as to be unnoticed elsewhere, are not so great here. The closer to where worlds connect, the less we are, as it were, divided. We do our best, sir; but the Balance must be served, and the Balance determines everything in the end, eh?" The huge fellow had a rather quiet manner. It seemed odd to find delicacy in one of his size.

His apparent diffidence put a swagger into Gunnar the Doomed. He was the only one of us to be amused. "My men described your footprint. To hear them talk you were at least ten feet tall, though I must admit you're the biggest human being I've ever met. You're even bigger than Angris the Frank, and he is still a legend. Are they all your size where you come from?"

"Pretty much," said Prince Lobkowitz. Gunnar did not miss the sardonic tone. His faceless helm turned to regard the huge man with some curiosity. I, too, felt I was missing what might have been a joke.

The sleet continued to fall. It was not settling as snow. Ipkaptam decided it was too warm for bad snow, that what we had was no more than an autumn squall. In a couple of days it might even seem like summer again. He had experienced the phenomenon many times.

Now that we thought Lobkowitz was our giant, Ipkaptam was far more at ease. It was decided we would indeed send the main warriors ahead at a rapid trot while I would bring up the rear. Prince Lobkowitz, who knew the terrain no better than I did, elected to stay behind with us. "At least until it becomes possible to rejoin my party!"

While the prince went off to relieve himself, I was warned secretly by Gunnar to keep an eye on Lobkowitz and to kill him if he acted at all suspiciously. Klosterheim was especially uneasy. He said that the man was not necessarily malign but that his presence suggested there were other, possibly dangerous, elements involved in this adventure.

I asked him to be more specific. What did he know about Lobkowitz? Had the newcomer followed us here? Was he in league with the Kakatanawa?

"He has no more right to enter the Kakatanawa stronghold than I," said Klosterheim. "But he has friends who also seek what I seek and what Gunnar seeks. I believe he shares a mutual interest. It will do no harm to make an ally of him now. It's best he's kept in the rear, at least until we know what we are facing. He might be a spy, for instance, sent to learn our secrets. If not, we could use someone of his size."

Gunnar was unhappy. "There are too many unknown elements in this. My idea was to come here, take what I needed, and leave. I had not expected Klosterheim, the Pukawatchi—nor giants . . ."

"That man is not a giant," insisted Ipkaptam. "He is human. You would know if he was a giant."

With a scowl, Klosterheim agreed. "This is a strange area of the multiverse," he confirmed. "It is, as Lobkowitz says, a node. Where the branch joins the tree, eh? Usually we are too far away from a node to experience this phenomenon, but here I would guess it is common."

I accepted this oddness was familiar to them and trusted their judgment. Only Gunnar continued to be ill at ease. He kept muttering about superstition and repeating what was clearly a simplification if not a lie—that he was here for one reason only, and he had promised his fighters the loot of the City of Gold.

Ipkaptam signaled for Gunnar, Klosterheim and the others to follow and set off at a lope. The main war party fell in behind him, and all were soon lost in the mists of the deep valleys. I was glad to keep a slower pace. It gave me a chance to speak to the gigantic man, to ask him how he had found himself here. He said he was traveling with a friend and they had become separated. The next thing he knew, he said, he spotted our camp. His friend was clearly nowhere in the area.

"And is this friend similar in size to you?" I asked.

Prince Lobkowitz sighed. "These are not my natural surroundings, Prince Elric, any more than they are yours."

I agreed with some feeling that they were not mine. If I discovered I was on a wild-goose chase, then Gunnar should pay with interest for all my wasted hours. While I had once sought the seclusion and isolation of the countryside, nowadays I again preferred the alleys, the noisy streets and crowded public places of urban life. Nonetheless, events had curious resonances, I said. It made me think that perhaps this adventure had parallels with a life I could not quite remember.

As Ipkaptam predicted, the snow held off and the sleet continued to fall. The Pukawatchi boys and women were not loquacious. Lobkowitz and I were thrown together as a result. He was oddly closemouthed on some subjects, and when I accused him, half joking, of talking like an oracle, he laughed loudly. "I think that's because I am talking like an oracle," he said.

He explained that this age was not his own. He was something of an interloper. But this realm, or one like it, was similar to his own past. As he was sure I understood, he did not dare inadvertently reveal anything of the future, yet he was constantly tempted to use his knowledge.

It was the reason, he said, for prophecies and omens to be so obscure. A directly related account of coming events automatically changed those events. Knowledge of them meant that some could act to avoid what they disliked. This not only made prophecy dangerous, it added to the multiplicity of the worlds. A few ill-judged words could create branch after branch of additional alternatives. It served no general purpose, he said. Few such branches survived for long.

I remembered the Stone Giants and their meaningless prophecies, but I said nothing to Lobkowitz, even though we were together, tending to walk behind the main party, following tracks the Pukawatchi and Vikings had made.

Then as we began to approach the foothills of the mountains, the sleet changed to snow. By the following morning it had settled and the sky had cleared. It was a blue day. Snow lay before us all the way to the mountains, and tracks were rare. Where a buffalo had passed, you could see immediately. Also hare and birds had used the land ahead, but of the Pukawatchi trail there was nothing.

Prince Lobkowitz seemed both amused by and sympathetic to this turn of events. He suggested that with his extra height he could go on ahead and see if he could find the Pukawatchi camp. Not entirely trusting him I said that we could travel together. That way I could stand on his shoulders, perhaps, and get a longer view. Thus we could make the best use of each other's relative size.

This seemed to amuse him even further. I said I thought my suggestion perfectly reasonable. He was recalling another event, he said, which had nothing to do with me directly, and he apologized.

He agreed; so we increased our pace. When the going became difficult for me, I was able to ride his mighty shoulder or otherwise make use of his unusual size and strength. It was the strangest riding I have ever done and was something of a change for me, though again I was troubled by vague memories of distant incarnations. Yet as far as I know I have always been Elric of Melniboné, for all that various seers and sorcerers insist otherwise. Some people relish the numinous the way others value the practical. I have had enough experience of the numinous to place great value on what is familiar and substantial.

When Lobkowitz raised the subject, I told him what I knew for certain. While I hung in some distant realm facing the death of everything I loved, I also dreamed the Dream of a Thousand Years, which had brought me here. He would probably think I was mad.

He did not. He said that he was familiar with such phenomena. Many he knew took them for granted. He had traveled widely, and there was little that was especially novel to him.

As it happened, we did not go far before the snow began to melt, revealing enough of a trail for our trackers to follow again.

But a certain valuable camaraderie had developed between Prince Lobkowitz and myself. I had the impression he, too, had more in common with me than with the others, even Klosterheim. I asked him about that gaunt-faced individual.

"He is an eternal," Lobkowitz said, "but he is not reincarnated, simply reborn over and over again at the point of his death. This is a gift he received from his master. It is a terrible gift. His master is called in these realms 'Lucifer.' As I understand it, this Lord of the Lower Worlds has charged Klosterheim with finding the Holy Grail. This was the pivot, the regulator of the Great Balance itself. But Klosterheim also seeks some sort of alliance with the Grail's traditional guardian."

I asked who that was. He said that I was distantly related to the family who would become its guardians. The Grail had disappeared more than once, however, and when that happened, it must be sought wherever the path leads. The stolen artifact had a habit of disguising itself even from its protectors. He had never been directly involved in this Grail-quest, he said—not, at any rate, as far as he could recall—but the quest continued through a multiplicity of pasts, presents and futures. He envied me, he said, my lack of memory. He was the second to make that remark. I told him with some feeling that if my condition was what he called a lack of memory, I was more than glad to have nothing else to remember. He made an apology of sorts.

Soon we reached the rendezvous with the rest of our party. They had little to report. The original owners of the canoes had fled, leaving most of their camp intact, so we spent a good night. In the morning we began to load the canoes when the blizzard hit us. It howled through the camp for hours, heaping up snow in huge banks. A wild east wind. By the time we were able to go out again, we found three feet of snow and ice already forming on the river. Up ahead the snow was bound to be thicker. We would either have to winter here or go on by foot. Ipkaptam said we could load the canoes and use them as sleds. That would keep the tribe together, as it would be foolish to leave the women and children. And so we set off, first carrying the canoes and then, as it became possible to drag them, pulling them behind us until we had reached the mountains proper. The sharp crags rose darkly above us, threatening the evening sky.

"They're evil-looking peaks," said Gunnar the Doomed, bending to pick up a handful of snow and rub it with relish into his neck. "But at least the weather's improving." I had forgotten how much Norsemen love snow. They yearn for it the way Moors yearn for rain.

Klosterheim pointed out the pass through the mountains. A dark gash ran between peaks glinting like black ice, probably basalt. Already the mountainsides were heavy with snow, and more snow weighed down the pines and firs of the flanks. There was no moving water. Game was rarely seen. Occasionally I glimpsed a winter hare running across the snow, leaving black tracks in a white flurry. Hawks hung high in the sky, seeing no prey below. I do not think I had ever seen such a winter wasteland. In its own grandeur, its uncompromising bleakness, it was impressive. But unless some magical paradise lay within those mountains, protected from the weather, we were none of us likely to survive. All common sense told us to turn back while we could and spend the winter in more agreeable conditions.

Klosterheim and Gunnar were for going on. Ipkaptam pointed out that it would be stupid to continue. We would lose all our men and be no closer to what we sought. Prince Lobkowitz also advised prudence. I, who had the better part of a thousand years still to dream, said that I had no special thoughts, one way or another, but if Vikings could not survive a little cold weather, I would be surprised.

This spurred a general growling and posturing and, of course, we were on our way, leaving the weaker members of our band to keep camp if they could. If they could not, they were advised to rejoin the others and wait until we returned.

I do not know what happened to those Pukawatchi. It was the last I ever saw of them, the boys and the girls with their bows and lances, the women and old people giving us the sign of good journeying. Yet even as we left them behind, they still had something of the look of insects. I would never understand it.

I voiced my disquiet to Lobkowitz. He took me seriously. He said he believed they were in some kind of transition, and this was what gave them their insectlike appearance. Further generations might develop different characteristics. It would be interesting to see what they became. My guess was that most of these would soon be meat for the coyotes and bears. For all my aversion to their appearance, I felt a twinge of sympathy for them.

Ipkaptam's own wives and daughters were among those we left behind. He said that he had now given everything he valued most to the spirits, to use or treat as they wished. The spirits could be generous, but they always required payment.

My own instinctive belief, of course, was that the situation had driven him mad. All he could do now was go forward until he died or was killed. Or did Klosterheim have a special use for him?

I had a sense that the journey itself would require more sacrifice. Both Gunnar and Klosterheim swore that Kakatanawa was on the far side of the range. Once it was reached, the city was theirs for the taking. Klosterheim asked Prince Lobkowitz directly, "Do you want a share of the loot? You'd be useful to us because of your size. And we'd give you a full warrior's portion."

Lobkowitz said he would think over the proposition. Meanwhile he would march with us in the hope of catching a glimpse of his missing friend.

I asked him about the friend, whom I had gathered was of his size. Had they traveled here together?

Yes, he said. The situation demanded it. He added mysteriously that this was not what he had chosen. He had become disoriented. He would not forgive himself if he had to leave without his friend. He hoped they would find some sign of him in the mountains.

At last our mixed force of well-wrapped Pukawatchi and Vikings reached the opening of the pass. The sides, high and narrow, had the effect of keeping the worst of the weather out, and little snow had fallen here. We were even able to find easily melted water, but there was still no game. We relied on dried meat and grains to sustain ourselves. But then, one afternoon, as we set about making camp, a Pukawatchi scout came running down the canyon towards us. He was trembling with news, the horror still on his face.

An avalanche had come down on them. Many Pukawatchi and two Vikings who had lagged behind were buried. It was unlikely they would survive.

Even as the man told his story, there came a rumbling sound from above. The earth quaked and trembled, and a huge rush of snow began to course down the flanks of the canyon. In the aurora of this second avalanche I could have sworn that I saw a great, shadowy figure step from one mountain flank to another. The avalanche had been directed at us, and it seemed, indeed, to have been started by a giant. Then I saw that Prince Lobkowitz had begun to run in the opposite direction to everyone else.

Without thinking, I followed him.

I was running upwards through deep snow. In order to keep up I stepped in his tracks where I could. I heard him calling a name, but the whipping wind took it away. Then the clouds opened, and blue sky filled the horizon and broke over me like a wave. Suddenly everything was in stark contrast to the white of the snow, the deep blue of the sky and the red globe of the falling sun sending golden shadows everywhere. The avalanche was behind us, and I heard nothing of my companions, though every so often the voice of Lobkowitz came back to me as he stumbled on through the snow, sometimes falling, sometimes sliding, in pursuit of the giant.

It was almost sunset by the time I caught up with him. He had stopped on a ridge and was looking down, presumably into a valley, when I joined him.

I saw that the mountains surrounded a vast lake. The ice was turning a pale pink in the light. From the shore a glinting silvery road ran to the center of the lake, to what might have been an island in summertime, and there stood one of the most magnificent buildings I had ever seen. It rivaled the slender towers of Melniboné, the strange pinnacles of the Off-Moo. It rivaled all the other wonders I have ever seen.

A single mighty ziggurat rose tier upon tier into the evening sky, blazing like gold against the setting sun. With walls and walkways and steps, busy with the daily life of any great city. With men, women and children clearly visible as they continued their habitual lives. They were apparently unaware that a black whirlwind shivered and shrieked at the beginning of the silver road to the city. Perhaps it protected the city.

There was a sudden crack, a flap of white wings, and suddenly a large winter crow sat on Lobkowitz's shoulder. He smiled slightly in acknowledgment, but he did not speak.

I turned to ask Prince Lobkowitz a question. His huge hand reached to point out the warrior armed with a bow, who sat upon the back of a black mammoth seemingly frozen in midstride. Was this the enemy Klosterheim kept in check? He was too far away for me to see in any detail. The threatening whirlwind, however, was an old acquaintance, the demon spirit Lord Shoashooan.

Then from behind them I caught another movement and saw something emerging out of the snow. A magnificent white buffalo with huge, curving horns and glaring, red-rimmed blue eyes, which I could see even from here, shook snow from her flanks and trotted past the mammoth and its riders. I could see how big the buffalo was in relation to the mammoth. Her hump almost reached the mammoth's shoulder.

The white buffalo's speed increased to a gallop. Head down, the creature thundered full tilt at the roaring black tornado. From behind me Prince Lobkowitz began to laugh in spontaneous admiration. It was impossible not to applaud the sheer audacity of an animal with the courage to challenge a tornado, the undisputed tyrant of the prairie.

"She is magnificent," he said proudly. "She is everything I ever hoped she would become! How proud you must be, Prince Elric!"

The Third Branch
Branch
Ulric's Story

Thraw weet croon tak' the hero path.
Thraw ta give and thraw ta reave.
Thraw ta live and thraw ta laugh.
Thraw ta dee and thraw ta grieve.

"Thraw Croon /Three Crows," TRAD.
(WHELDRAKE'S VERSION)

Three for the staff, the cup and the ring,
Six for the swords which the lance shall bring;
Nine for the bier, the shield, the talisman,
Twelve for the flute, the horn, the pale man,
Nine by nine and three by three,
You shall seek the Skraeling Tree.
Three by seven and seven by three,
Who will find the Skraeling Tree?

WHELDRAKE, **"The Skraeling Tree"**

CHAPTER FIFTEEN

The Chasm of Nihrain

Let me tell you how I tarried,
Tarried in the starry yonder,
Tarried where the skies are silver,
Tarried in the tracks of time.

W. S. HARTE,
"Winnebago's Vision"

y struggle with the pale giants was brief. They were armed with spears and round shields, obsidian clubs and long flint knives, but they did not threaten me with their weapons. Indeed, they were careful not to harm me. They used their full strength only to pin my arms and collapse my legs. I did not give up readily and grabbed at their weapons, getting my hands first on a tomahawk, then on a war-shield. I was lucky not to be cut, for I had difficulty gripping them.

My attackers were very powerful. Though I am almost as fit as I was twenty years ago, I was no match for them. When I resisted them, my limbs seemed to sink into theirs. They were certainly not insubstantial, but their substance was of a different quality, protecting them and giving them added strength. Whatever their peculiar power, they soon bundled me into my own canoe and struck off towards the Old Woman as my beautiful wife, wide-eyed with fear, ran down to the jetty in pursuit. A wild wind was beginning to rise. It blew her fine, silvery hair about her face. I tried to call out to her, to reassure her, but it snatched away my words. Somehow I was not afraid of these creatures. I did not

219

think they meant me harm. But she could not hear me. I prayed she would not risk her own life in an effort to rescue me.

You can imagine the array of emotions I was experiencing. Every fear I had dismissed a few hours earlier threatened to become reality. I was being drawn from a dream of happiness and achievement back to some parallel existence of despair and threatened failure. But I sensed this was not a desperate fantasy of escape created by my tortured brain and body in a Nazi concentration camp. In spite of all my terrors and anxieties, it was Oona I feared for most. I knew her well. I knew what her instincts would tell her to do. I could only hope that common sense would prevail.

With extraordinary speed this bizarre raiding party neared the Old Woman, whose voice lifted in a strange, pensive wail. And from somewhere another wind rose and shrieked as if in frustrated anger. At one point it seemed that it extended fingers of ice, gripping my head and pulling me clear of my captors. It was not trying to rescue me. I was certain that it meant me ill.

I was relieved to escape it when suddenly the canoe dipped downwards, and we were beneath the surface. Everywhere was swirling water. I was not breathing, yet I was not drowning. Great eddies of emerald green and white-veined blue rose like smoke from below. I felt something bump the bottom of the canoe. On impulse I sought the source of the collision, but it was already too late.

Like an arrow, the canoe drove down through the agitated currents, down towards a flickering ruby light, tipped with orange and yellow. I thought at first we had begun to ascend and I was looking at the sun, but the flames were too unstable. Down here, deep at the core of the maelstrom, a great fire burned. What could this mean? We were heading for the very core of the earth! Where else could fire burn in water? Could these gigantic Indians be messengers of the Off-Moo, that strange subterranean people whom Gaynor had driven from their old cities? Were these their new, less-hospitable territories? The flames licked through the water, and I was sure we would be consumed. Then the canoe twisted slightly in the current, and immediately we were above an unfathomable abyss lit by dark blue-and-scarlet volcanic fires.

All sound fell behind us.

A great column of white flame stabbed upwards erratically from the depths and dissipated into roiling smoke. We drifted in neither air nor water, descending slowly through the foaming fumes into the chasm itself.

My captors had not uttered a word. Now I struggled in the strips of leather which bound me and demanded they tell me what they were doing and why. Could my words be heard? I was not sure. While they acknowledged me with some gravity, they did not reply.

The blackness of the chasm grew more intense in contrast to the vivid tongues of fire, which licked out every few seconds and illuminated my immediate surroundings before vanishing. Everywhere brooded a sense of massive stillness behind which was frenetic activity. I felt as if something had been bottled up in this chasm, and I could not guess if it was a physical or some crude supernatural force.

The glinting obsidian of the vast sides was veined with brilliant streams of fire. The mouths of caves, many of them clearly man-made, often glowed scarlet, like the open maws of hungry animals. Sounds were loud, then quickly muffled and echoing. My nostrils filled with the stink of sulphur. I choked on the thick air, almost drowning in it. The canoe continued to sink between the mighty black walls. I could see no surface, no bottom. Only the red-and-indigo flames gave us light, and what that light revealed was alien, ancient, unwholesome. I am not given to fanciful imaginings, especially at such times, but I felt as if I was descending into the bowels of Hell!

After a very long time the canoe began to rock gently under me, and I realized with a shock that we were floating on a great, slow-moving river. For a moment I wondered if it was the source of the river which both fed and lit the world of the Off-Moo. But this was almost the opposite of phosphorescent. This river seemed to *absorb* the light. I could now see that we drifted on water dark as blood which reflected the flashes of flame from above. By the weird, intermittent light my captors paddled into the entrance of a wide old harbor, its bizarre architecture built on a huge scale.

Every piece of stone was fluid and organic, but seemingly frozen at the moment of its greatest vitality. The sculptors had found the natural lines of the rock and turned these forms into exquisite but chilling imagery. Great eyes glared from agonized heads. Hands twisted into their own petrified flesh, as if trying to escape some frightful terror or seeking to tear their own organs from their bodies. I had half an idea that the statues had once been living beings, but the thought was too terrible. I forced the idea from my mind. Desperately my eyes darted everywhere, hoping to see some living creature among all this inanimate horror, while at the same time fearing what I might be forced to confront. What kind of life chose to inhabit such a hellish landscape? In spite of my situation, I began to speculate on the kind of minds which had found this place good and built their city here.

I was soon rewarded. My abductors carried me bodily to the slippery quayside whose cobbles were made dangerous by disuse. There was a musty smell of age in that rank air. A smell of resisted death. But death nonetheless. This place had passed its time and refused to die. It spoke of an age and an intelligence which had lived long before the rise of my own kind. Might it even be the natural enemy of my kind? Or perhaps just of myself? A wild proliferation of half-memories swam just below my consciousness but refused to come to the surface.

I fought confusion. I knew I must keep my head as clear as possible. Nothing here offered me immediate harm. That strange seventh sense I had developed since my encounters with Elric of Melniboné drew upon almost infinite memory. To say that I knew the peculiar feeling of repeating an experience, which the French call déjà vu, would give some idea of what I felt if multiplied many times over. I had somehow lived these moments many, many times before. It was impossible to rid myself of a sense of significance as I was carried away from the quayside. I looked towards an avenue which ran between the statues. I had heard a sound.

From out of the ranks of twisted sculpture there stepped a group of tall, graceful shadows. I at first mistook them for Off-Moo, since the steamy atmosphere gave them that same etiolated appearance. Like my captors, they were very tall. My eyes hardly reached the level of their chests. Unlike the Off-Moo, however, these people had refined, handsome human features and superb physiques, reminding me of the Masai and other East African peoples. Their bodies were half-naked, their exposed flesh glinting ebony, its depth emphasized by their silky yellow robes, not unlike those of Buddhist priests. These men, however, were armed. They carried heavy quartz-tipped spears and oblong shields. Their heads were as closely shaved as my captors', but bore no decoration. They were warriors, perhaps? They moved towards the pale giants with gestures of congratulation. Clearly they were compatriots. The newcomers stood and looked gravely down on me. Gently I was helped to my feet. I am a tall man and not used to being overlooked. It was a strangely irritating feeling. My instinct was to take a step or two back, but they were in the process of removing my bonds.

As I was freed, an even taller and more heavily muscled man stepped through the ranks. He carried a tangible charisma, an air of complete authority, and it was evident that the other handsome warriors deferred to him. There was nothing sinister about their leader. He had an air of peculiar gentleness as he reached forward and took my hand in his. The raven-black palm and fingers were massive, engulfing mine. The gesture was evidently one of pleasure. He again congratulated his friends in that wordless way I somehow understood. His strange eyes shone with triumph, and he turned to his companions as if to display me as proof of some argument. These people were not mutes; they simply did not need sound to communicate. He was clearly pleased to see me. I felt like a boy in his presence, and I knew immediately that he was not my enemy. I trusted him, if a little warily. These were, after all, the people who had presumably built this dark city.

I was at a disadvantage. They all seemed to have some idea of my identity, but I still knew nothing of theirs.

"I am the Lord Sepiriz," the black giant told me, almost apologetically. "My brothers and I are called the Nihrain, and this is our city. Welcome. You might not forgive us this uncivilized way of bringing you here, but I hope you will let me explain so that you will at least understand why we need you and why we had to claim you when the opportunity presented itself to us. It was not you the Kakatanawa sought, but a lost friend. Their friend was freed, but they brought you here with them in the hope you will elect to serve our cause."

"It only disturbs me further to think you had not planned to kidnap me," I said. "What possible purpose could you have in such reckless action?" I told him that my first concern was for my wife. Had he no idea what trauma my abduction had created?

The black giant lowered his eyes in shame. "It is our business sometimes to cause pain," he said. "For we are the servants of Fate, and Fate is not always kind. She has a way of presenting her opportunities abruptly. It is up to us to take advantage of them. Her service sometimes brings us disquiet as well as pride."

"Fate?" I all but laughed in his face. "You serve an abstraction?"

This seemed to amuse and please him. "You will have little trouble understanding what I must tell you. You are by instinct a servant of Law rather than Chaos. Yet you are married to Chaos, eh?"

"Apparently." I understood him to mean my strange relationship with Elric of Melniboné, with whom I had had a conscious but inexplicable connection since he had come to my aid in the concentration camp all those many years before. "But have you any conception of my family's anxiety?"

"Some," said Sepiriz gravely. "And all I can promise you is that if you follow your destiny, you will almost certainly see them again. If you refuse, they are lost to you—and to one another—forever."

Now my pent-up fears burst out in anger. I walked towards the giant, glaring up into his troubled eyes. "I demand that you return me to my wife at once. By what right do you bring me here? I have already done my duty in the fight against Gaynor. Leave me in peace. Take me home."

"That, I fear, is now impossible. This was ordained."

"Ordained? What on earth are you talking about? I am a Christian, sir, and believe in free will—not some sort of predestined fate! Explain yourself!" I was deeply frustrated, feeling like a midget surrounded by all these extraordinary, gigantic men.

A fleeting smile crossed Sepiriz's lips, as if he sympathized. "Believe me in this then—I possess knowledge of your future. That is, I possess knowledge of what your best future can be. But unless you work with me to help this future come about, not only will your wife and children perish in terrible circumstances, you, too, will be consigned to oblivion, erased from your world's memory."

As we spoke Sepiriz began to move with his men back into the shadows. I had little choice but to move with them. From one shadow to another, each deeper. We entered a great building whose roof was carved with only the most exquisite human faces all looking down on us with expressions of great tranquillity and good will. These faces were caught by the dancing flames of brands stuck into brackets on walls inscribed with hieroglyphs and symbols, all of which were meaningless to me. Couches of carved obsidian; dark, leathery draperies; constantly moving light and shadow. Sepiriz's own face resembled the ones looking down from the roof. For an instant I thought, This man is all those people. But I did not know how such an idea had come into my head.

While the giants arranged themselves on the couches and conversed quietly, Lord Sepiriz took me aside into a small antechamber. He spoke softly and reasonably and succeeded in calming my temper somewhat. But I was still outraged. He seemed determined to convince me that he had no choice in the matter.

"I told you that we serve Fate. What we actually serve is the Cosmic Balance. The Balance is maintained by natural forces, by the sum of human dreams and actions. It is the regulator of the multiverse, and without it all creation would become inchoate, a limbo. Should Law or Chaos gain supremacy and tip the scales too far, we face death—the end of consciousness. While linear time is a paradox, it is a necessary one for our survival. I can tell you that unless you play out this story—that is, 'fulfill your destiny'—you will begin an entirely new brane of the multiverse, a branch which can only ultimately wither and die, for not all the branches of the multiverse grow strong and proliferate, just as some wood always dies on the tree. But in this case it is the tree itself which is threatened. The very roots of the multiverse are being poisoned."

"An enemy more powerful than Gaynor and his allies? I had not thought it possible." I was a little mocking, I suppose. "And a tree which can only be an abstraction!"

"Perhaps an abstraction to begin with," said Sepiriz softly, "but mortals have a habit of imagining something before they make it real. I can tell you that we are threatened by a visionary intelligence both reckless and deaf to reason. It dismisses as nonsense the wisdom of the multiverse's guardians. It mocks Law as thoroughly as it mocks Chaos, though it acts in the name of both. These warring forces are now insane. Only certain mortals, such as yourself, have any hope of overcoming them and halting the multiverse in its relentless rush towards oblivion."

"I thought I had put supernatural melodrama behind me. I weary of this, I can tell you. And where are your own loyalties, sir? With Law or Chaos?"

"Only with the Balance. We serve whichever side needs us more. On some planes Chaos dominates; on others Law is in the ascendancy. We work to keep the Balance as even as possible. That is all we do. And we do anything necessary to ensure that the Balance thrives, for without it we are neither human nor beast, but whispering gases, insensate and soulless."

"How is it that I feel we have met before?" I asked the black giant. I stared at my surroundings, the strangely decorated ceiling, the resting figures of my captors.

"We have a close association, Count Ulric, in another life. I am acquainted with your ancestor."

"I have many ancestors, Lord Sepiriz."

"Indeed you have, Count Ulric. But I refer to your alter ego. You recall, I hope, Elric of Melniboné . . ."

"I want no more to do with that poor, tortured creature."

"You have no choice, I fear. There is only one path you can follow, as I explained. If you follow any other, it will take you and yours to certain oblivion."

My emotions were in turmoil. How did I know that this strange giant was not deceiving me? Yet, of course, I could not risk destroying my beloved family. All I could do was keep my own peace, wait and learn. If I discovered Sepiriz was lying to me, I vowed to take vengeance on him come what may. These were not typical thoughts for me. I wondered at the depths of my rage.

"What do you want me to do?" I asked at last.

"I want you to carry a sword to a certain city."

"And what must I do there?"

"You will know what to do when you get to the city."

I recalled the bleak chasm beyond these walls. "And how will I get there?"

"By horseback. Soon, I shall take you to the stables to meet your steed. Our horses are famous. They have unusual qualities."

I was hardly listening to him. "What is your interest in this?"

"Believe me, Count Ulric, our self-interest is also the common interest. We have given up much to serve the Balance. We have chosen a moral principle over our own comfort. You may wonder, as we sometimes do, if that choice was mere hubris, but it scarcely matters now. We live to serve the Balance, and we serve the Balance to live. Our existence is dependent upon it, as, of course, ultimately is everyone's. Believe me, my friend; what we do, we do because we have no other choice. And while you have choice, there is only one which will enable you and yours to live and thrive. We tend the tree that is the multiverse, we guard the sword that is at the heart of the tree, and we serve the Cosmic Balance, which pivots upon that tree."

"You are telling me the universe is a tree?"

"No. I am offering a useful way of formalizing the multiverse. And in formalizing something, you control it to a degree. The multiverse is organic. It is made up of circulating atoms but does not itself circulate in prefigured order. It is our chosen work to tend that tree, to ensure that the roots and branches are healthy. If something threatens them, we must take whatever drastic steps are necessary for their rescue."

"Including kidnapping law-abiding citizens while they are on holiday!"

Sepiriz permitted himself another quiet smile. "If necessary," he said.

"You are barking mad, sir!"

"Very likely," replied the black giant. "It is madness, I think, to choose to serve a moral principle over one's own immediate interests, eh?"

"I rather think it is, sir." Again, I had no way of challenging Sepiriz.

I turned to the pale giants Sepiriz had called "Kakatanawa." I could not think of them in relation to the normal-sized native population. These warriors rested in the attitudes of tired men who had worked well. One or two of them were already stretched out on the stone benches and were close to sleep. I felt physically as if I had been pummeled all over, but my mind was alert. If nothing else, adrenaline and anger were keeping me awake.

"Come," said Sepiriz. "I will show you your weapon and your steed." Clearly I had no real choice. Controlling my fury I strode after him as he led the way deeper into that strange, hewn city.

I asked where the rest of the inhabitants were. He shook his head. "Either dead or in limbo," he said. "I am still hoping to find them. This war has been going on for a long time."

I mentioned my past encounters with the Off-Moo,* whose own way of life had been savagely disrupted by the coming of Gaynor and Klosterheim to their world. Lord Sepiriz nodded with a certain sympathy and seemed merely to add that to a list that was already larger than any sentient creature could absorb. Somehow, without his saying a word, I had the impression of battles

---

*The Dreamthief's Daughter

being fought across a multitude of cosmic planes. And in all those conflicts, Sepiriz and his people had involved themselves. A race which lived to serve the Balance? It did not seem strange.

"What is your relationship with the men who seized me?" I asked him. "Are they your servants?"

"We are allies in the same cause." Sepiriz let out a massive sigh. "Just as you are, Count Ulric."

"It is not a cause I volunteered for."

Sepiriz turned, and again I thought he seemed strangely amused. "Few of us volunteered, Sir Champion. The war is endless. The best we can hope for are periods of tranquillity."

We reached a great slab of rock decorated with elaborate scenes carved in miniature from top to bottom. The whole formed a half-familiar shape which hinted at something in my memory.

Lord Sepiriz turned, opened his arms and began to chant. The sound found an echo somewhere, like a string resonating to its perfect pitch.

The great slab quivered. The scenes on it writhed and for a second were alive. I saw great battles being fought. I saw bucolic harvesters. I saw horror and joy. Then the song was over and the slab was motionless—

Except that it had moved closer to us, revealing a dark aperture behind. A door! Sepiriz had evidently opened it with the power of his voice alone! Again this struck a distant chord in me, but I could attach no specific memory, only the same sense of déjà vu. No doubt that peculiar duality I had with my half-human alter ego, Elric of Melniboné, caused these sensations. It was no comfort to know that I searched for the memory of another man, a man with whom I had shared a mind and a soul and from whom I knew now I would never be entirely free.

Taking a flickering brand from the bracket on the wall, the black giant signaled me to follow him.

Crimson light splashed over the stones, revealing a multitude of realistic carvings. The entire history of the multiverse might be depicted here. I asked Sepiriz if this was the work of his ancestors, and he inclined his head. "There was a time," he said, "when we had more leisure."

From being uncomfortably warm, the air now turned very cold. I shivered in spite of myself. I half expected to find this was a tomb full of preserved corpses. The figures looming over me, however, were of the same carved obsidian as the others I had seen. We seemed to spend hours beneath them until we came to an archway only just high enough to permit Lord Sepiriz to pass under it. Here he raised the brand in the air, making the faces writhe and change their expressions from serenity to twisted mockery. I could not rid myself of the idea that they were watching me. I remembered how the Off-Moo were capable of suspending their life functions so successfully that they effectively became stone. Was this quality shared with Lord Sepiriz and his people?

But my attention was quickly drawn from the carved faces to the far wall and what appeared to be a background of rippling copper. Framed against it was a familiar object. It was our old family sword, which I thought in the hands of the Communists.

It hung against the living copper which reflected the erratic light of the torch. That black iron, so full of an alien vitality, was caught as if by a magnet. Within the blade I was sure I detected moving runes. Then I thought they might have been mere reflected light from the brand. I shuddered again, this time not from cold but from memory. Ravenbrand was a family heirloom, but I knew little of its history, save that it was somehow the same sword as Elric's Stormbringer. In my own realm of the multiverse the blade had supernatural qualities, but in its own realm I knew it was infinitely more powerful.

Some deep strain within me yearned to hold that blade the moment I saw it. I remembered the wild bloodletting, the exhilarating horror of battle, the joy of testing your mettle against all the terrors of natural and supernatural worlds. I could almost taste the pleasure. I reached for the hilt before I had formed a single, conscious thought to do so. Then I reminded myself of my manners, if nothing else, and withdrew my hand.

Lord Sepiriz looked down on me with that same half-humorous expression, and this time there was a distinct sorrow in his voice when he spoke. "You will take it. It is your destiny to carry Stormbringer."

"My destiny! You confuse me with Elric. Why does he not claim this sword?"

"He believes he seeks it."

"And will he find it?"

"When you find him . . ."

I was sure that he was deliberately mystifying me. "I never entertained ambitions to act as your courier . . ."

"Of course not. That is why I have your horse ready. Nihrainian horses are famous. Come, leave the sword for the moment, and we will hurry to the stables. If we are in luck, someone is waiting there to meet you."

CHAPTER SIXTEEN

Fate's Fool

If you tell me what my name is,
Should you tell me what my station,
I will speak of the Pukwatchis,
I will lead you to their nation.
I will show you what to steal.

W. S. HARTE,
"The Starry Trail"

hough I grew familiar with this city's grotesque and fantastic sights, I was unprepared for the Nihrainian stables. Little of that intricately hewn city lay outside the great caverns into which it was carved. We made our way through miles of impossibly complicated corridors and tunnels, every inch of which was etched with the same disturbing scenes.

The muggy air tasted heavily of sulphur, and I had difficulty breathing. Lord Sepiriz did not slacken his steady gait and was hard to pace. Gradually the roofs grew higher and the galleries wider. I had the impression we were entering the core of the original city. What we had passed through up to now was a kind of suburb. Here the carvings seemed older. There was greater decay in the rock, some of which seemed almost rotten. Everywhere volcanic fires flared through windows and doorways and fissures in the ground, illuminating what seemed to me an astonishing desolation. Here was not the tranquillity of the Off-Moo chambers, but the stink of death so violent that its ancient memory permeated this living rock. I could almost hear the screams and shouts of those who had died terrible deaths, almost see their reflections trapped in the obsidian and basalt of the walls, writhing in perpetual torment. Once again I wondered if I was in Hell.

Lord Sepiriz touched his brand to another. This in turn lit the next until in a flash of light I saw we stood at the entrance of a huge amphitheater, like a massive Spanish bullring with tiers of empty stone benches stretching up into a darkness, heavy and threatening. Yellow flames lit the scene from without while from within came an unstable scarlet glow. I felt I stood on the threshold of some strange necropolis. Our very life seemed an insult to the place, as if we intruded on every kind of agony. Even Lord Sepiriz seemed borne down by the sadness and horror. We could have been in the killing fields of the universe.

"What happened here?" I asked.

"Ah." The black giant lowered his head. He was lost for words, so I did not press the question.

My foot stirred dark dust. It eddied like water. I imagined the blood which had been spilled in this arena, yet could not easily imagine how it had happened. There was no sense it had ever been used for gladiatorial fights or displays of wild beasts.

"What was this place?" I spoke with some hesitation, perhaps not wishing to hear the answer.

"At the end, it was a kind of court," said Lord Sepiriz. He drew in a deep, melancholy breath, like the soughing of a distant wind. "A court where all the judges were mad and all the accused were innocent . . ." He began to walk across the arena, towards an archway. "A place of judgment which sentenced both court and defendants to a terrible death. This is why there are only ten of us now. Our fate was as preordained as yours as soon as we forged the swords."

"You made them? You mined the metal here . . . ?

"We took the original metal from a master blade. War raged as always between Law and Chaos. We thought to make a powerful agent against one of them. The swords were forged to fight against whichever power threatened to tilt the Balance. Law against Chaos or Chaos against Law. We drew on all our many powers to make them, and when they were finished we knew we had found the means to save worlds and perhaps destroy them at the same time. A mysterious power entered one of the blades. While they were otherwise identical and could feed great vitality to those who wielded them, Stormbringer was subtly different. Those who made that particular blade and summoned the magic required to enliven it knew they had created something that was oddly, independently evil. Somehow, though Mournblade, the sister sword, had little such power, those who handled Stormbringer developed a craving for killing. Honest blacksmiths became mass murderers. Women killed their own children with the blade. Ultimately it was decided to put both the handlers and Stormbringer on trial . . ."

"Here?"

Sepiriz lowered his head in assent. "Here, in the stables. This is where the horses were exercised and exhibited. We loved our beautiful horses. But it seemed the only suitable place. Originally this ring was used for equestrian displays. Our Nihrainian horses are very unusual in that while they exist on this plane, they simultaneously exist on another. This gives them some useful qualities. And some entertaining ones." Sepiriz smiled as a happy memory intruded on the sadness.

Then, pulling himself together, he straightened his shoulders and clapped his enormous hands.

The sound was like a shot in the huge, silent arena. It brought an almost instant reaction.

From within came a whinny, a snort. Something pounded the hard surface. Another great whinny, and out of the archway, mane flaring as if in the wind, sprang a horse of supernatural proportions. A monstrous black stallion, big enough to carry Sepiriz. He reared, flailing bright jet hooves and glaring from raging ocher eyes. The beast's mane and tail became a wild mass of black fire. He was muscular, nervous. This gigantic beast expressed impatience rather than anger. But at a word from Sepiriz, the horse cocked his ears forward and immediately settled. I had never seen a creature respond so swiftly to human command.

Although there was no doubting the animal's physical presence, I quickly noticed that for all his activity, he scarcely stirred the dust of the arena floor and left no hoofprints of any kind.

Noting my curiosity, Sepiriz laid a hand gently on my shoulder. "The horse, as I told you, exists on two planes at once. The ground he gallops on is unseen by us."

He led me up to the horse, who nuzzled at him, seeking a familiar treat. The beast already wore a saddle and bridle and seemed equipped for war as well as travel.

I reached a hand towards the mighty head and rubbed the animal's velvet nose. I noted the bright, white teeth and red tongue, the hot, sweet breath.

"What is his name?" I asked.

"He has no name in your terms." Sepiriz did not elaborate. He looked towards the walls, searching for something he had expected to find there. "But he will carry you through all danger and serve you to the death. Once you are in his saddle, he will respond as any horse, but you will find him, I think, unusually intelligent and capable."

"He knows where I am to go?"

"He is not prescient!"

"No?" For a moment the ground beneath my feet shifted like liquid, then as quickly resettled. Again Sepiriz refused to answer my unspoken question. He was still searching. His eyes scanned the long, empty stone benches stretching into the gloom. I noticed that the darkness seemed to have absorbed some of the upper tiers. Smoke or mist swirled and gave carved figures expressions of gloating glee, then of wild, innocent joy.

Sepiriz noted this at the same time I did. I was certain I saw a flash of alarm in his eyes. Then he smiled with pleasure and turned as another horse emerged from the archway into the stadium. This horse had a rider. A familiar rider. A man I had met more than once. Our families had been related for centuries. His was a branch which had supported Mozart and been famous for its taste and intelligence.

This rider had first introduced himself to me in the 1930s as a representative of an anti-Nazi group. His handsome, heavy features were enhanced now by an eighteenth-century wig, a tricorn hat and military greatcoat. He looked like one of the famous portraits of Frederick the Great. Of course it was my old acquaintance, the Austrian prince Lobkowitz. His clothing was bulky, completely unsuitable for this volcanic cavern. His face was already beaded with sweat, and he dabbed at himself with a vast handkerchief of patterned Persian silk.

"Good morning, sir." His voice a little hoarse, he reined in and lifted his hat, for all the world as if we met on a country bridle path near Bek. "I'm mightily glad to see you. We have a destiny to pursue. Sentient life depends upon it. Have you brought the sword?"

Lobkowitz dismounted as Lord Sepiriz came towards him, towering over the Austrian, who was not a short man. Sepiriz kneeled to embrace him. "We were unsure you could perform so complicated a figure. We had other means ready, but they were even more fragile. You must have succeeded thus far, or you would not have joined us."

Prince Lobkowitz put his hand on Lord Sepiriz's arm and came to shake my hand. He was in high spirits. Indeed, I found his attitude a little unseemly, considering my circumstances, if not his. His warm charm, however, was impossible to resist.

"My dear Count von Bek. You cannot know the odds against your being here and our meeting like this. Luck, if not the gods, seems on our side. The dice are tossed by a fierce wind, but now at least there is a little hope."

"What is the task? What do you seek to accomplish?"

Lobkowitz looked at Lord Sepiriz in surprise. He seemed to expect the black giant to have told me more. "Why, sir, we seek to save the life and soul of your dear wife, my protégée, Oona, the dreamthief's daughter."

I was horrified. "My wife is in danger? What is happening back there? Is someone attacking the house?"

"In relation to our position in the scheme of things, she is no longer at your house in Canada. She is further inland, deep in the

Rockies, and facing an enemy who draws his strength from every part of the multiverse. Unless we reach her at exactly the right moment, where our story intersects with hers, she will perish."

I could not control the pain I experienced at this news. "How did she come to be where she is? Could you not have helped her?"

Prince Lobkowitz indicated his costume. "I was until lately, sir, in the service of Catherine the Great. Where, I might add, I met your unsavory ancestor Manfred."

For one of such habitual grace, he seemed in poor temper. I apologized. I was a simple man. I had no means of understanding this topsy-turvy tumble of different worlds. It was more than I could normally do to try to imagine the space between the Earth and the Moon. Yet my veins beat with anxious blood at the thought of my beloved wife in danger, and I feared for my children, for everything that had meaning to me. I wanted to turn on this pair and blame them for my circumstances, but it was impossible. Another intelligence lurked within my own.

Gradually his presence was growing stronger. Elric of Melniboné, who believed in the reality of only one world, understood perhaps instinctively the complexity of the multiverse. His experience, if not his intellect, told him how one branch sometimes intersected with another and sometimes did not, how branches grew quickly, took on bizarre shapes, and died as suddenly as they appeared.

Elric understood this science as his own sorcerous wisdom, captured over years of education in the long dreams which gave the Melnibonéan capital its nickname of the Dreamers' City. For Elric's people extended their lives through drug- and sorcery-induced dreams which assumed their own reality, sometimes for thousands of years. By this means, too, did their dragon kin, to whom they were related by blood, sleep and dream and manifest themselves, no doubt, in others' dreams. It was dangerous for anyone but the full adept to attempt such an existence. And dangerous, I knew, to try to change a narrative which gave some kind of uneasy order to our lives. At best we could create a whole new universe or series of universes. At worst we could destroy those which now existed and by some mistake or unlucky turn of the cards consign ourselves and everything we knew to irreversible oblivion.

My twentieth-century European sensibilities were repelled by such ideas, yet Elric's soul was forever blended with my own. And Elric's memory was filled with experiences I would normally dismiss as the fantasies of a tormented madman.

Thus I accepted and refused to accept at the same time. It was a wonder I had the coordination to mount the huge horse. He was at least as large as the famous old warhorses of past legends. I looked for Sepiriz, to ask him a question, but he had gone. The saddle and stirrups were modified for a man of my size, yet the saddle still felt huge, giving me an unfamiliar sense of security.

There was no doubt my horse was pleased to have a rider. He moved impatiently, ready to gallop. At Lobkowitz's suggestion I cantered the stallion around the arena. The Nihrainian steed trod the ground with evident familiarity, tossing his great black mane and snorting with pleasure. I noted the strong, acrid smell he exuded when he moved. It was the smell I normally associated with a wild predator.

Lobkowitz followed me, saying little but clearly noting my handling of the animal. He congratulated me on my horsemanship, which made me laugh. My father and brothers had all despaired of me as the worst rider in the family!

As we rode, I begged him to tell me more about Oona and her whereabouts. He asked that I respect any reticence on his part. Knowledge of a future could change it, and it was our task not to change the future but to ensure that, in one realm at least, it be a future I desired for my loved ones and myself. I must trust him. With some reluctance, I bowed to his judgment. I had no reason, I said, not to trust him, but my head ached with many questions and uncertainties.

Sepiriz returned bearing a scabbarded sword. Was it the sword I knew as Ravenbrand, which Elric called Stormbringer? Or was it the sister sword, Mournblade? Sepiriz did not tell me. "Each sword is of equal power. The power of the other avatars weakens in proportion to their distance from the source. It is as well it happened this way," he said. "The Kakatanawa have already gone home. The circle tightens. Here."

As I reached to accept the sword, I thought its metal voiced a faint moan, but it could have been my imagination. There was, however, a distinct, familiar vibrancy to the hilt as it settled into my right hand. Automatically I hooked the scabbard to the heavy saddle.

"So," I said. "I am prepared to follow a road for which I have no maps, in a quest whose purpose is mysterious, with a companion who seems scarcely more familiar with the territory than I am. You place much faith in me, Sepiriz. I would remind you that I remain suspicious of your motives and your part in my wife's endangerment."

Sepiriz accepted this, but clearly he did not intend to illuminate me further. "Only if you are successful in this adventure will you ever know more of the truth concerning the swords," the black seer told me. "But if you do, indeed, succeed in fulfilling your destiny, of serving Fate's purpose, then I promise, what you hear shall hearten you."

And with that Lobkowitz yelled for us to be off. We must be free of Nihrain before the new eruption, when all here will be destroyed, and Sepiriz and his brothers will ride out into the world to fulfill another part of their complex destiny.

I could do nothing but follow him. The prince bent over his horse's neck and rode with impossible speed out of the huge amphitheater and down corridors of liquid scarlet veined with black and white and tunnels of turquoise, milky opal and rubies. All carved in the same relief. Faces begged and twisted in agony. Their eyes yearned for any kind of mercy. Vast scenes stretched for miles, every figure minutely detailed, all exquisitely individual. Landscapes of the most appalling beauty, of elaborate horror and hideous symmetry, rose and fell around me as I rode. All were given movement by my own speed. Were they designed to be seen thus? A creative style best appreciated from the back of a galloping warhorse?

I began to believe that I inhabited a fantastic dream, a nightmare from which I must inevitably wake. Then I remembered all I had learned from Oona and realized that I might never wake, might never see her or my children again. This infuriated me, firing me with a righteous anger against Fate or whatever less abstract force Sepiriz and his kind served.

I put all that emotion into my riding, into following the expert Lobkowitz through tunnels, chambers, corridors of dazzling diamonds and sapphires and carnelians, down long slopes and up flights of steps, our horses' hooves never quite touching the ground of the paths we traced. I gasped and braced myself to fall the first time the horse galloped across the air separating one part of the mountain from another. By the second experience I had learned to trust its surefooted pace over an invisible landscape.

We galloped through oceans of lava, through foaming rivers of dust, over blue-veined pools of marble, sometimes blinded by a fiery light, sometimes plunging through pitch darkness. The great black horses never tired. When we passed through caverns of ice, their breath erupted like smoke from their nostrils, but they were otherwise undisturbed by any natural obstacle. Now I understood what a valuable animal Sepiriz had loaned me.

In spite of my anxieties, I began to know an old, familiar elation. The sword at my side was already wrapping me in her bloody gyres, sending me a taste of what I would experience if I unsheathed her. I dared not draw the thing from her scabbard, for I knew what she would make of me, what pleasures I would taste and what mental torments I would experience.

I was filled with a dreadful mixture of fear and desire. Knowing my wife was even now in danger, I longed to feel the hilt in my hand again and taste the most terrible drug of all, the very life stuff of my foes. What some called their souls. As the spirit of Elric combined with that of the sword, together they threatened to overwhelm the part of me who was Ulric von Bek. Already far too much of me longed to charge into battle on this magnificent horse, to hack and pierce, to slice and skewer, to lift my arm and let death come wherever it fell.

All this horrified Ulric von Bek, that exemplar of liberal humanism. Yet perhaps here was a time when a rational, modern man was not best suited to deal with the realities around him. I should give myself up wholly to Elric.

Should I do that, I thought, I would in some way be abandoning my wife and children. I had to hang on to the humanistic person I was, even though increasingly Elric lurked just below the surface, threatening to take me over and make me a willing tool of his killing frenzy.

How I yearned never to have known this creature, nor ever to have had to rely on his help. Yet, I thought, if I had not involved myself with Elric and his fate, I should not now be married to his daughter, Oona, whom we both loved in our own ways. At least in this we were united. What was more, the last Emperor of Melniboné had saved me from torture and degrading death in the Nazi concentration camp.

This final thought helped me sustain a balance within myself as the Nihrainian steed carried me higher and higher out of the depths, up into the roaring chasm and then down black shale, rivulets of red lava, a rain of pale ash. The Nihrainian horses continued to follow their own peculiar route parallel to this reality. The stink of sweat and sulphur remained in my nostrils. The neck of the great beast steamed, bulging with straining muscles as it continued down the flanks of the black mountain and out into a world which turned by degrees from night to dawn and from lifeless ash to rolling meadowlands with copses of oak and elm.

I was tiring. The horse's pace slowed to a steady canter as if to enjoy the cool, autumnal air, the scents of sweetly fading summer. The leaves of the trees turned gold and brilliant yellow and russet in the low, comforting light. Lobkowitz, still ahead of me, his greatcoat and tricorn hat covered with light gray ash, turned in his saddle to wave. He seemed jubilant. I guessed we had crossed another barrier. Our luck was holding.

At last we rested beside a pond on which a few white ducks squabbled. There were no signs of human beings, although the whole area had a pleasant, cultivated look. I mentioned this to

Lobkowitz. He said he thought that we were in a part of the multiverse which for some reason had ceased to be inhabited by human beings. Sometimes entire futures vanished, leaving the most unexpected traces. He guessed that this land had once been settled by prosperous peasants. Some action in the multiverse had affected their existence. Their natural world had survived as they left it. Everything they had made had vanished. Every little pact they believed they had with mortality brushed aside.

He gave a small, sad shrug.

Lobkowitz said that he had witnessed the phenomenon too often not to be convinced that he was right. "You might note, Count Ulric, a certain barrenness to those gently rising and falling hills, those old stones and trees. They are a dream without its dreamers." He rose from where he had been washing his face and hands in the pond. He shivered, drying his palms under his arms as he waited for me to drink and wash. "I am afraid of places like this. They are a kind of vacuum. You never know what horrors will choose to fill it. An untrustworthy dream at best."

I followed his reasoning, but did not have his experience. I could only listen and try to understand. I knew I did not have a temperament for the supernatural, and I thus would never be thoroughly comfortable in its presence. Not all my family had a natural affinity with infinite possibility. Some of us preferred to cultivate our own small gardens. I wondered with sudden amusement if I might be the horror who chose to fill this particular vacuum. I could see Oona and our children cultivating a farm, a pleasant house . . .

And then I understood what Lobkowitz feared. There were many traps of many kinds in the multiverse. The harshest climate could hide the greatest beauty, the most attractive shireland could disguise hidden poisons. With this realization, I was glad to remount the big, tireless stallion and follow Lobkowitz through endless meadows until starless, moonless night fell, and I heard the sound of water far below me.

I hardly dared look down. When finally I did, I saw little, but it seemed the big Nihrainian horse was galloping across a lake. We slept in our saddles. By morning we rode over the high, tough grass of a broad steppe. In the distance we saw grazing animals which, as we drew closer, I recognized as North American bison.

With some considerable relief I realized that we were probably upon the same continent as my imperiled wife. Then the bison vanished.

"Is she nearby?" I asked Prince Lobkowitz when we next stopped on a rise overlooking a broad, winding river. All wildlife seemed to have disappeared. The only sound we heard was the remorseless keening of the west wind. We dismounted and ate some rather stale sandwiches Lobkowitz had carried in his knapsack from Moscow.

His reply was not encouraging. "We must hope so," he said. "But we have several dangers to overcome before we can be certain. Many of these worlds are dying—already as good as dead . . ."

"You take much in your stride, sir," I said.

" 'Some polish is gained with one's ruin,' " he said. He quoted Thomas Hardy, but the reference to our circumstances was obscure to me. He threw the remains of his sandwich onto the ground and watched it. It did not move. I was puzzled. Why were we studying a piece of discarded food?

"I see nothing," I told him.

"Exactly," he said. "There is nothing to see, my friend. Everything around it is unaffected. Nothing comes to investigate. This place looks very tranquil, but it is lifelessness. Eh?" He kicked at the stale bread. "Dead."

Lobkowitz stamped back to his horse and mounted.

At that moment I do not believe I had ever seen a more heavily burdened individual.

Thereafter I treated my companion with a different respect.

CHAPTER SEVENTEEN

Against the Flow of Time

Moons and stars saw many passings
Many long suns rose and fell
Many were the women dancing
Many were the warriors singing
Many were the deep drums calling
Calling to the Gods of War!

W. S. HARTE,
"The Shining Trail"

he rolling hills of that ersatz Sylvania behind us, we found ourselves in a grey terrain of shale and old granite. The world had changed again. Ahead was a succession of bleak, shallow valleys with steep, eroded flanks. High in the cloudy skies carrion eaters circled. At least they were a sign of life or, if not, the promise of death. The floors of the silvery limestone valleys were rent with dark fissures, long cracks which ran sometimes for miles. A leaden, sluggish river wound across the depressing landscape. In the distance were low, wide mountains which from time to time gouted out red flames and black smoke. This was not unlike the dead world Miggea of Law had created.

I asked Lobkowitz if anything had caused the withering of these worlds we crossed, and he smiled wryly. "Only the usual righteous wars," he said. "When all sides in the conflict claimed to represent Law! This is characteristically a land which has died of discipline. But that is Chaos's greatest trick, of course. It is how she weakens and confuses her rivals. Law will characteristically push forward in a predictable line and must always have a clear goal. Chaos knows how to circle and come from unexpected angles, take advantage of the moment, often avoiding direct confrontation altogether. It is why she is so attractive to the likes of us."

"You do not want the rule of Law?"

"We could not exist without Chaos. Temperamentally I serve Law. Intellectually, and as a player in the Game of Time, I serve Chaos. It is my soul that serves the Balance."

"And why is that, sir?"

"Because, sir, the Balance serves humanity best."

We were cantering through the shallow dust of a valley. A few hawthorn trees had managed to grow in the hollows, but mostly the scenery was bare rock. Slowing to a walk, Lobkowitz turned in his saddle and offered me a white clay pipe and a tobacco pouch. I declined. As he filled his own bowl, tamping it with his thumb, he sat back in the big wooden saddle and gestured towards the horizon. "We have kept our coordinates, I do believe. At this rate it will not be long before we reach our destination."

"Our destination?"

Almost apologetically Prince Lobkowitz said, "It is safe to tell you now. We travel, with a little luck, to the city of the Kakatanawa."

"Why could we not have gone back with the Kakatanawa when they returned home?"

"Because their path is not our path. If my judgment is accurate, when we find them, they will have long since been back at their positions. Those warriors are the immortal guardians of the Balance."

"Why are we all from different periods of history, Prince Lobkowitz?"

"Not history exactly, my friend, for history is just another comforting tale we tell so that we do not go mad. We are from different parts of the *multiverse*. We are from the multitude of twigs which make up this particular branch—each twig a possible world, yet not growing in time and space as we perceive, but growing in the Field of Time, through many dimensions. In the Time Field all events occur simultaneously. Space is only a dimension of time.

"These branches we call spheres or realms—and these realms are finely separated, usually by scale, so that the nearest scale to them is either too large or too small for them to see, though perhaps the physical differences between the worlds are scarcely noticeable."

Prince Lobkowitz gave me a sideways look to check if I was following his argument. "Yet there are occasions when the winds of limbo breathe through the multiverse, tossing the branches to and fro, tangling some, bringing down others. Those of us who play the Game of Time or otherwise engage with the multiverse attempt to maintain stability by ensuring that when such winds blow, the branches remain strong and healthy and do not crash together or proliferate into a billion different and ultimately dying twigs.

"Nor can we let the branches grow so thick and heavy that the whole bough breaks and dies. So we maintain a balance between the joyous proliferation of Chaos and the disciplined singularities of Law. The multiverse is a tree, the Balance lies within the tree, the tree lies within the house, and the house stands on an island in a lake . . ." He seemed to shake himself from a trance, in which he had been chanting a mantra. He came smartly awake and looked at me with half a smile, as if caught in some private act.

It was all he would tell me. Since I could now anticipate further answers to my questions as it became possible for him to offer them, I grew more optimistic. Was he relaxing because we were getting closer and closer to where Oona was in some mysterious danger? If Lobkowitz was so optimistic, there was every chance we would be there to rescue her.

On we galloped as if we rode on the soft turf of an abandoned shire, although the limestone now was melting and turning to a sickly, sluggish lava beneath the Nihrainian horses' hooves. The stink of the stuff filled my nostrils and threatened to clog my lungs, yet not once did I feel afraid as we crossed a sea of uneasy pewter and reached a shore of glittering ebony far too smooth to accept any mortal steed's hoof. The Nihrainian stallions took the slippery surface with familiar ease. Ducking as large trees came towards us, we found ourselves in a sweet-smelling pine forest through which late-afternoon sunlight fell, casting deep shadows and calling the sap from the wood. Lobkowitz let his horse stop to crop at invisible grass and turned his face upwards to admire what he saw. The sun caught his ruddy features. In the heightened contrast he resembled a perfect statue of himself. Great shafts of sunlight broke through the silhouettes of the trees and created an incredible mixture of forms. For a moment, following Lobkowitz's gaze, I thought I looked into the perfect features of a young girl. Then a breeze disturbed the branches, and the vision was gone.

Lobkowitz turned to me, his smile broadening. "This is one of those realms all too ready to mold itself to our desires and take the form we demand. It is particularly dangerous, and we had best be out of it soon."

We cantered again, across sparsely covered hills and through valleys of sheltered woodlands, and entered a broad plain, with a greying sky hovering over us and a cold breeze tugging at our horses' manes. Lobkowitz had become grave, turning his head this way and that as if expecting an enemy.

The clouds streamed in towards us, thick and black, and lowered the horizon. In the far distance I could make out the peaks of a tall mountain range. I prayed they were the Northern Rockies. Certainly this great, flat plain could be part of the American prairie.

It began to rain. Fat drops fell on my bare head. I was still wearing the clothes Sepiriz had first given me and had no hat. I lifted a gloved hand to hold off the worst of it. Lobkowitz, of course, was now dressed perfectly for the weather and seemed amused by my discomfort. He reached into one of his saddlebags and tugged out a heavy, old dark blue sea-cloak. I accepted it.

I was soon even gladder for the cloak as the wind came whipping in from the northeast and hit us like a giant fist. Doggedly the Nihrainian stallions maintained their pace. As their great muscles strained harder, there was a hint of tiredness now. The endless veldt stretched all around us. Still no obvious signs of beaver, birds or deer. Once, as the wind howled fiercely and caused even my stallion to reduce his speed to a dogged plod, there came a gap in the clouds. Red sunlight brightened the scene for a moment and revealed a herd of deer running for their life before the wind. The first I had seen. They were clearly trying to escape the region. I had the distinct feeling we were not heading in the sensible direction. I remarked on the wind during a lull. Lobkowitz looked concerned as he confirmed my guess that we were heading into a tornado. Knowing little of such things in Europe, I could not recognize one. All I understood was that it was wise to find shelter.

Lobkowitz agreed that, as a general rule, it was usually wise to seek cover.

"But not this time. He would find us, and we would be more vulnerable. We must continue."

"Who would find us?"

"Lord Shoashooan, Lord of Winds. He commands a dangerous alliance."

Then, as if to silence my friend, the wind again became a shouting bully. The rain was a giant's fingers drumming on my back as we cantered on, crossing marshes, rivers and grassland with equal ease. The only thing powerful enough to slow us was that cruel, relentless wind. It seemed to carry hobgoblins with it, tugging at my body and teasing my horse. I could almost hear its hard, cackling laughter.

Lobkowitz rode in close now, stirrup to stirrup, so that we should not lose each other in the weather. Every so often he tried to speak over the wind, but it was impossible. I was sleeping intermittently in my saddle when the horses slowed to a walk. My body ached, yet they were almost tireless. This seemed to be the nearest they came to resting.

Mile by mile the prairie became low hills, rolling towards the mountains, slowly transferring into the range that rose tall and ragged into the soughing sky. The wind seemed to give up once we reached the foothills. Suddenly the clouds parted just as the sun was sinking, and the mountains were a vivid glow of ocher, russet, sienna and deep purple shot through with bands of darker yellows and crimsons. All mountain ranges have their characteristic beauty. I had seen such magnificent color only in the Rockies.

"Now we must be *more* than careful." Prince Lobkowitz dismounted on the slope and was leading his horse up towards a wide cave mouth above. "We'll shelter here tonight and ensure our sleep. We shall need to be alert. Perhaps take watches."

"At least that damned wind has dropped."

"Aye," said Lobkowitz, "but he remains our main enemy here. He is cunning, often seeming to depart, then licking around at you from a fresh point on the compass. He loves to kill. The more he can devour at a sitting the more content he is."

"My dear Lobkowitz, 'he' is an insentient force of nature. 'He' no more plans and schemes than do those rocks over there."

Lobkowitz looked with some mild alarm towards the rocks. Then he shook his head. "They are benign," he said. "They follow the Balance."

I was becoming convinced that my cousin was a little eccentric. While he could lead me to Oona, however, and back to the safety of our home and children, I would continue to humor him. As it was, I could not always tell what he saw or how. I was reminded of visionaries like Blake, who inhabited a world quite as real as that of those who mocked him. Certainly I judged people like Blake with a different and greater respect once I understood that his world had been as vividly real to him as this world was to me. I was still a sufficiently modern gentleman, however, not to relish the social circumstances of meeting and speaking with an angel.

Lobkowitz built a little fire deep inside the cave. The smoke was drawn to a narrow crack at the back which doubtless led into some larger system.

Like all experienced travelers, he was economical with what he carried and yet seemed to want for nothing. With ease he prepared a kind of savory pancake from various dried powders he carried in a small cabinet which fit, with a little forcing, into one of the big gun pockets in his coat.

I asked him why he was so anxious about the wind. True, it was bitter cold, but it had not, after all, turned into a tornado and blown us away. I took my first bite of the food. It was excellent.

"It is because Lord Shoashooan dissipates his power in various strategies. Had he drawn upon his power and concentrated it, we should doubtless be dead by now. But his main strength is elsewhere."

"Who is this entity who commands the wind?"

"He once had a pact with your family, for mutual defense, but that was on another plane altogether. Lord Shoashooan is an elemental who serves neither Law nor Chaos. At this time, he seems to have chosen to ally himself with our enemies, which means inevitably we shall soon be challenging him. Meanwhile the White Buffalo struggles against him on our behalf, which is why he is so weak. Yet for all the White Buffalo is his most powerful enemy, Lord Shoashooan will not be held for much longer. His allies grow strong, both in numbers and in the range of powers they command. Lord Shoashooan tastes his new freedom."

He spoke with such knowing familiarity of this high lord that I wondered for a moment if I should suspect him of being in the creature's service. Meanwhile, it would be wise to take care what I asked him. I then decided he was speaking of a person, or a totem, and asked no more questions.

I was becoming used to this kind of patience. We were situationalists, of sorts, he said, responding to whatever opportunities were presented to us by Fate and making the most of them. That was why, as Pushkin knew, the gambler's instinct was so important.

I had become distracted. The thought that we were only a short distance from Oona made my sleep intermittent. I kept waking and wanting to get back in the saddle, to reach her as soon as possible, but Lobkowitz had already pointed out how ordinary time meant little in this business. It was more a matter of choosing to act when the right coordinates presented themselves. He remarked again that Pushkin would have made a good member of the League of Time, though he was something of an amateur. The best gamblers, like himself, were careful professionals who earned their livings by winning.

I remarked that I could not see Prince Lobkowitz as a cardsharp. He laughed. I would be surprised, he said, at his reputation in the coffeehouses of London, where every kind of game was played. Putting away his cleaned utensils he suggested that I get as much sleep as possible and prepare myself for whatever the coming days would bring.

I was up soon after dawn. I stepped from the cave into the cold autumn morning. The mist had lifted, and I looked out into stunning natural beauty whose wonderful shapes and colors were all touched by the rising sun. I felt like opening my arms to the east and chanting one of those songs with which Indians were said to greet the return of the Sun.

Lobkowitz arose soon after me. With his shirtsleeves rolled up to the elbow, he cooked a piece of bacon and some beans. The fresh dawn air made me hungry, and the smell was delicious. He apologized for what he called his "cowboy breakfast," but I found it excellent and would have eaten another portion had there been one. I asked him if he knew how much longer it would be before we saw Oona. He could not say. First he had some scouting to do.

Only then did I notice that the horses were gone. Our saddlebags and weapons lay just inside the cavern. It was as if a thoughtful thief had led them away in the night.

Lobkowitz reassured me. "They have returned to Nihrain, where they will be needed for another adventure involving your ancestor and alter ego Elric of Melniboné. We cannot ride horses into the territory we now explore. No horses exist there."

"Are you telling me we are in pre-Columbian America?"

"Something like that." He put a friendly hand on my shoulder. "You are an exemplary companion for a man like myself, Count Ulric. I know that you are impatient for more information, but understand how I can only reveal it to you a little at a time, lest we change our future and further weaken the branch. Believe me in this: my affection for your wife is, in its own way, as great as yours. And what is more, her survival depends upon our success quite as much as our survival depends on hers. Many branches are being woven together to make a stronger one, Count Ulric. But the weaving involves considerable skill and good fortune."

"It is taking me a little while," I told him, "to think of myself as a strand."

"Ah, well," he said with the suggestion of a wink, "imagine instead that you are lending the weight of your soul to the souls of a small company who together might save the Cosmic Balance and rescue the multiverse from complete oblivion. Does that make you feel more important?"

I said that it did and, laughing, we picked up our kit and with a spring in our steps, set off along the high mountain trail, admiring the peaks and forests which lay below us and reveling in all the wildlife that now inhabited them. Such scenery eased my soul. I was strengthened by it more, I suspected, than I was strengthened by the sword.

Lobkowitz walked with the aid of a crooked staff. I wore the big blade balanced on my back. It was so beautifully forged that it felt far lighter than it actually was. I must admit I had always thought a Luger or a Walther a more reliable weapon in a pinch, but also I had once seen what happens when someone attempts to fire such a weapon in a realm where it should not exist.

We were comfortable while we walked, but when we stopped, we felt the chill in the wind. Before the end of that first day, a little light snow had touched my face. We were steadily moving towards winter.

The season seemed to be coming upon us rather swiftly, I said.

"Yes," said Lobkowitz. "We are walking against what you would usually conceptualize as the flow of time. We could be said to be walking backwards to Christmas."

I was about to respond to this whimsicality when a pale face some seven feet high blocked the narrow mountain path ahead. A giant peered at us from eye level. When I peered back at the face, I realized it was a realistic carving. What mighty force had placed a great stone head directly in our way, blocking the path? The thing stared at me with a smile which made the Mona Lisa's seem broad, and I found myself charmed by it. Indeed I admired its beauty, running my hand over the smooth granite from which it had been sculpted. "What is it?" I asked Lobkowitz. "And why is it blocking our path?"

"It is a creature called an Onono. A tribe of them used to live in these parts. What you cannot see are the useful legs and arms hidden within what looks like a singularly thick neck. They are extinct in this realm, everywhere but in Africa, where they are a distinct species of their own. You should be pleased this one has petrified. They are formidable and savage enemies. And cannibals to boot." With his crooked staff Lobkowitz levered the thing towards the edge. It began to rock almost at once and then suddenly flew over and down. I watched it tumble into the gorge far below. I expected it to land in the river, but instead, with a snapping crash it went into a stand of dark trees. I found myself hoping it had managed a reasonably soft landing. The way ahead, though a little chipped and eroded, was now clear.

Lobkowitz moved cautiously forward and was wise to do so, for as the path widened and turned we confronted not a stone guardian, but several living versions of the creature we had just sent over the edge. Long, spindly, spiderlike arms and legs were extended from within the shoulder area. Their huge heads, filed teeth and great, round eyes were like something out of Brueghel.

Parleying with the Ononos was not a possibility. Six or seven of them crowded across the pathway. We had to fight them or retreat. I guessed that retreat would sooner or later involve us in fighting them anyway. Lobkowitz unsheathed the monstrous cutlass under his coat, and with a guilty sense of relief, I drew Ravenbrand from her scabbard. Immediately the black blade howled with a mixture of joyous delight and horrible bloodlust. I was dragged towards my foes, Lobkowitz in my wake, as we ran to do battle with these grotesque failures of evolution.

Spindly fingers gripped my legs as I swung my sword full into the face of the first Onono, splitting it like a pumpkin and covering his companions and myself in a gruesome mixture of blood and brains. The things had massive but relatively delicate craniums. Two more of the monsters fell to Ravenbrand, who now shrieked with a disgusting and undisguised love for blood and souls. I heard my voice shouting Elric's Melnibonéan war cry "Blood and souls! Blood and souls for my lord Arioch!" Part of me shuddered, fearing that to invoke that name might be the worst thing I could do in this world.

Yet it was Elric of Melniboné who dominated now. Wading into the hideous Ononos, I drew their crude life stuff into my own. Their coarse blood pulsed through me, giving me a foul, virtually invulnerable energy.

Soon they were all dead. Their twitching hands and feet lay strewn everywhere on the path. Some had sailed down towards the trees. Other parts had landed on the mountainside. The remaining two creatures—who looked like young females—were bounding away on their knuckles and would offer us no further trouble.

I licked my lips and wiped my blade clean on coarse black Onono hair. Nearby Prince Lobkowitz was examining those corpses still more or less in one piece. "These were the last of Chaos in this realm, at least until now. I wonder if they will welcome their cousins." He sighed. He seemed to feel sympathy for our defeated attackers.

"We are all Fate's fools," he said. "Life is not an escape plan. It is an inevitable road. The changes we can make in our stories are not great."

"You are a pessimist?"

"Sometimes the smallest of changes can become significant," said Lobkowitz. "I assure you, Count Ulric, that I am anything but a pessimist. Do not I and my kind challenge the very condition of the multiverse?"

"Which is?"

"Some believe the only power which makes existence in any way choate is the imagination of man."

"We created ourselves?"

"There are stranger paradoxes in the multiverse. Without paradox there is no life."

"You do not believe in God, sir?"

Lobkowitz turned to regard me. He had a strange, pleasant expression on his face. "A question I rarely hear. I believe that if God exists he has given us the power of creativity and has left us with it. If we did not exist, it would be necessary for him to create us. While he neither judges nor plans, he has given us the Balance— or, if you prefer, the *idea* of the Balance. It is the Balance I serve, and in that, perhaps, I am serving God."

I became embarrassed, of course. I had no wish to pry into another man's religious beliefs. But, raised as I was in the Lutheran persuasion, there were certain questions which naturally occurred to me. His was a religion of triumphant moderation, it seemed, whose purpose was clear and whose rules were easily absorbed. The Balance offered creativity and justice, a combination of all human qualities in harmony.

A harmony not mirrored in the busy wind which again began to lick at what little flesh we had exposed. It lashed us with rain and sleet. It blinded us and chilled us to our bones, but we continued to follow the mountain trail. Winding around great cliffs and across narrow ridges, on both sides were drops of a thousand feet or more. The wind seemed to attack us when we were most vulnerable.

In certain parts of the mountains' flanks, high overhead, some snow had begun to settle. I became alarmed. If we had heavy snow, we were finished, I knew. Doing his best to reassure me, Lobkowitz failed to convince himself. He shrugged. "We must hope," he said. " 'Hope ahead and horror behind, tell of the creatures I have in mind.' " He seemed to be quoting from the English again. Only when he made such quotations did I realize that our everyday speech was German.

From somewhere in the distance came the faint, cawing voice of a bird. Lobkowitz became instantly alert.

We rounded a great slab of granite and looked out over a descending cascade of mountain peaks towards a frozen lake. I must have gasped. I remember my own breath in the air. I heard my own heart beating. Was this Oona's prison?

Far out in the lake I could see an island. On the island had been raised some sort of gigantic stepped metal pyramid which dazzled with reflected light.

Leading from shore to island, a pathway, straight and wide, shone like a long strip of silver laid across the ice. What sort of thing was this? A monument? But it seemed too large.

The wind then slashed stinging sleet into my eyes. When they cleared, a rolling mist was covering the lake and the surrounding mountains.

Lobkowitz's face was shining. "Did you see it, Count Ulric? Did you see the great fortress? The City of the Tree!"

"I saw a ziggurat. Of solid gold. What is it? Mayan?"

"This far north?" He laughed. "No, only the Pukawatchi have ventured up here, as far as I know. What you saw was the great communal longhouse of the Kakatanawa, the model for a dozen cultures. Count Ulric, give thanks to your God. Intratemporally we have followed a dozen crooked paths all at the same time. The odds on accomplishing that were small. By chance and experience, we have found resolution. We have found the roads to bring us to the right place. Now we must hope they have brought us to the right time."

Lobkowitz looked up with a broad smile as out of the air a large bird dropped and settled on his extended forearm. It was an albino crow. I looked at it with considerable curiosity.

The crow was clearly its own master. It walked up Lobkowitz's arm, sat on his shoulder and turned a beady eye on me.

Lobkowitz's manner revealed that he had held little hope of our success. I laughed at him. I told him I was not pleased with my fate. He admitted that overall he believed we had been dealt a pretty poor hand in this game. "But we made the best use of the cards and that's the secret, eh? That's the difference, dear count!"

Fondling the proud bird affectionately and murmuring to it, he obviously greeted a pet he had thought lost. I suspect, too, that he was half-mad with disbelief at his own successful quest. Even now I could tell he was torn between greeting the bird and craning for another glimpse of the golden pyramid city. I understood his feelings. I, too, was torn between fascination with this new addition to our party and peering through the swirling clouds for another view of the fortress, but the clouds now made it impossible to see more than a few feet ahead.

It was dark before we decided to stop in a small, natural meadow. We drew the big cloak over a little shelter in the form of tough bushes rooted into the mountainside and were thankfully able to light a small fire. It was the most comfortable we had been for some time. Even Lobkowitz's pet crow, roosting in the upper parts of a bush, seemed content. I, of course, immediately wanted Lobkowitz to tell me whatever new details it was possible for him to reveal. Anything which would not affect the course of our time-paths.

There was very little, he apologized. He did not think we had much further to go. He frowned at his bird, as if he hoped it would provide him with advice, but the creature was apparently asleep on its perch.

Lobkowitz was awkwardly cautious, perhaps fearing that we were now so close to our goal that he dare not risk losing it. A pull or two on one of his numerous clay pipes, however, calmed his spirits, and he looked out with some pleasure at the dark red and deeper blue of the twilight mountains, at the clearing sky and the hard stars glittering there. "I once wandered worlds which were almost entirely the reflection of my own moods," he said. "A kind of Heathcliffian ecstasy, you might say."

He seemed emboldened and continued on more freely. "Our business is with the fundamentals of life itself," he told me. "You already know of the Grey Fees, the 'grey wire' which is the basic stuff of the multiverse and which responds, often in unexpected forms, to the human will. This is the nourishment of the multiverse, which in turn is also nourished by our thoughts and dreams. One kind of life sustains another. Mutuality is the first rule of existence, and mutability is the second."

"I have not the brains, I fear, to grasp everything you tell me."

I was polite, interested. "My attention is elsewhere. Essentially I need to know if we are close to rescuing Oona."

"With considerable luck, more courage and any other advantages we can find, I would say that by tomorrow we shall stand on the Shining Path which crosses to the island of Kakatanawa. Three more have come together. *Three by three and three by three, we shall seek the Skrayling Tree,* ha, ha. This is strong sorcery, Cousin Ulric. All threes and nines. That means that every three must come together and every nine must come together to link and form a force powerful enough to restore the Balance. There is much to overcome before you will see the interior of the Golden City."

Our fire sustained us through the night, and in the morning ours was the only patch of green in a landscape covered by a light snow. We packed our gear with care and secured everything thoroughly, for we knew the dangers of slipping on that uneven trail.

The wind came back before noon and blustered at us from every angle, as if trying to uproot us from our uneasy balance on the mountain face and hurl us into valleys now entirely obscured by thick, pale cloud. We kept our gloved fingers tight in the cracks of the rock face and took no chances, advancing step by careful step.

At last we were climbing down, moving into a long valley which opened onto the lakeside. In contrast to the frozen water, the valley was green, untouched by the snow on the upper flanks. It felt distinctly warmer as we reached the shelter of pleasant autumn trees.

Lobkowitz's face was now a stark mask as he kept his eye upon the gap in the hills through which we could sense the glittering golden pyramid.

Soon enough the clouds parted again, and the sun shone full down on an unimaginably vast fortress. As we neared it I began to realize what an extraordinary creation it was. I had seen the Mayan ziggurats and the pyramids of Egypt, but this massive building was scores of stories tall. Faint streamers of blue smoke rose from it, obviously from the fires of those living in it. An entire, great city encompassed in a single building and constructed in the middle of the pre-Columbian American wilderness! How many brilliant civilizations had risen and fallen leaving virtually no records behind them? Was our own doomed to the same end? Was this some natural process of the multiverse?

These thoughts went through my head as I lay staring at the multitude of stars in the void above me that night. Sleep was almost impossible, but I finally nodded off before dawn.

When I awoke, Prince Lobkowitz was gone. He had taken his cutlass with him. Only his saddlebags were left behind. There was a note pinned to one of the bags:

MY APOLOGIES. I HAVE TO GO BACK TO COM-
PLETE SOME UNFINISHED WORK. WAIT FOR ME
A DAY. THEN CARRY ON TOWARDS THE SHINING
PATH. LET NOTHING DIVERT YOU.
—LOBKOWITZ

I guessed that the albino crow had gone with him, until for an instant I spied it circling above me before disappearing down into a canyon. Perhaps it followed Lobkowitz?

With little to do but nurse my fears, I waited all that day and another night for Lobkowitz. He did not return. Superstitiously I guessed we had celebrated too early.

I mourned for him as I took up his belongings and my own. I wondered where the bird had gone. Had it followed him to his fate or taken another path? Then I began the long climb down towards the frozen lake and the silvery trail which led across it.

I prayed that I would at last find Oona in the great, golden pyramid the Kakatanawa called their longhouse.

CHAPTER EIGHTEEN

The Hawk Wind

Then he told the deed he'd done,
Told of all that endless slaughter,
Red beneath the setting sun.

W. S. HARTE,
"The War Trail"

he trail down to the lakeside was surprisingly easy at first. Then, as usual, the wind came up, and I had to fight it to stay on my feet. It attacked me from every point of the compass. Now I , too, had the strangest feeling that not only was it intelligent, but it actually hated me and wanted to harm me. This made me all the more determined to get down to the valley floor. Gales forced their way through layers of my clothing, sliced me across the throat and drove icy needles into my eyes. My hand felt lacerated from trying to protect my face.

Several times, on a difficult part of the mountain trail, the gusts sprang from nowhere to grab me and more than once almost succeeded in flinging me down into the distant gorge. Sometimes they struck like a fist into the small of my back and other times attacked my legs. I began to think of this wind as a devil, a malignant personality, it seemed so determined to kill me. In one terrible moment I set off an avalanche I barely escaped, but I pressed on with due care, keeping a handhold on every available crack and clump of grass as the full-force gale tore and thrashed at me. Somehow I eventually reached the valley.

I stood at last on the flat, staring up a long, narrow gorge towards the lake. I could see a few dots on the shore, and I hoped one of them might be Lobkowitz awaiting me. I could not believe he had betrayed or abandoned me. He had seemed so elated the night before, anticipating our sighting of the causeway and the golden ziggurat of Kakatanawa.

The ziggurat became more impressive as I approached.

From this distance I could see signs of habitation. It was evidently a huge and complex city to rival any of the great cities of Europe, yet arranged as a single vast building! From various parts of the ziggurat, which was verdant with gardens, hanging vines, even small trees, I saw the blue smoke of small fires rising into a clearing sky. Everywhere was busy movement. The place was thoroughly self-contained and virtually inviolable. It could have withstood a thousand sieges.

A huge wall ran around the whole base. It was extremely high and capable of withstanding most kinds of attack. The tiny specks were people amid large, animal-dragged passenger vehicles and commercial carts. The general sense was of busy activity, casual order, and unvanquishable might. If such a city had ever existed in my world's history, then it survived only as a legend. How could something so magnificent and so enormous be completely forgotten?

In contrast to the order of the city, the activity on the shore was confused. I saw a few figures coming and going. Some sort of dispute seemed to be taking place. I tried to see who was arguing with whom.

Foolishly I had let my attention focus on the distance rather than on my immediate surroundings. The gorge had narrowed. The trail dipped down into a shallow, green meadow blanketed with a light coating of snow. Enclosed by high rocks, the depression might have once been a pond or old riverbed. I was so busy craning my neck to see the group on the shore that I was taken entirely by surprise.

I slipped, losing both my bundle and Lobkowitz's. My feet slid from under me, and I fell headlong.

When I came to rest I found myself surrounded by a large band of Indians. They were silent, menacing. They emerged from among the rocks, glaring in full war paint. Though they had the appearance of Apache or Navajo, their clothing was that of woods Indians, like the Iroquois. They were clearly intent on butchering me. But there was something wrong.

As they drew closer, spears and bows at the ready, I began to realize how small they were.

I tried to tell them I came in peace. I tried to remember the Indian signs I had learned in the Boy Scouts in Germany. But these fellows were not concerned with peace. The tiny men screamed unintelligible insults and orders at me. There was no doubting their belligerence but I hesitated before defending myself. Not one of them reached much above my knee. I had been flung into some children's fairyland, some elfin kingdom!

My first impulse was laughter. I began to make some remark about Gulliver, but the spear that narrowly missed my head was unequivocal. I continued to try to avoid bloodshed.

"I am not your enemy!" I shouted. "I come in peace!"

More miniature arrows zipped past me like bees. They were not deliberately trying to miss me. I was amazed at their bad marksmanship, as I was not, after all, a small target. They were clearly terrified. After one last attempt to persuade them to see reason, I acted without thinking, without any hesitation, and with a growing frisson of relished destruction.

Reaching over my shoulder I sensuously slid the shivering, groaning runeblade from her hard scabbard and felt the black silk mold to my hand, the black steel leap to life as she scented blood and souls. Scarlet runes veined her ebony blade, pulsing and flickering within the steel as she sang her terrible, relentless song. And it seemed I heard names in the humming metal, heard great oaths of revenge being taken. All this bonded me even closer to the weapon. My human self remained horrified, distant. Whatever else inhabited me anticipated a delicious feast. As well as drawing on the experiences of Elric of Melniboné I also became, in some hideous way, *the sword itself.*

I gasped with the joy of it even before the gleaming metal took her first little souls. Strong little souls. They were helpless against me, yet despite their fear they would not run. Not at first. Tough, hardy bodies pressed around my legs, and I had to force a certain delicacy upon the blade in order to slice away their embracing limbs. They behaved like men who had reached their limit and now did not care if they died. As I pressed forward against them, cutting them down like vermin, they fell back around something they were clearly protecting.

I was curious, even as I continued to kill. My sword possessed my will. She would not cease her feasting. She would not stop drinking until she had drunk every shred of every soul and drawn them shrieking into my eager veins. Half of me was disgusted with my actions, but that half did not control my bloodlust nor my sword arm. I stabbed and slashed and chopped with slow, steady strokes, like a man stropping a razor.

They were now entirely fearless, these little men, as if reconciled to their violent deaths. Perhaps even welcoming them. They came at me with tomahawks and knives and spears and arrows. They even used a kind of sling to fling live snakes at me. I let them strike if they chose. There is no venom known which can kill a Melnibonéan noble. We are weaned on venom.

The snakes and arrows were brushed aside by the sword I knew as Ravenbrand. Her speed was a bloody blur. Flint clubs and short, stone swords grazed me but did not cut me. Every pygmy who died wailed in sudden understanding as he gave me fresh life. I laughed aloud in my killing. I let the stolen energy fill me with godlike invulnerability. I lusted to murder and celebrated every stolen soul! Small they might be, but the pygmies were near-immortals and thus rich with supernatural life stuff. After the crude souls of the Ononos, this fairy blood was a delight. It poured into me until I felt my physical form would contain it no longer, that it would all burst out of me.

I fought on, carrying the attack. I laughed at their agony and their fear. Even those who tried to surrender, I killed. I sighed with the sweetness of their slaughter. The majority, however, battled on with enormous courage, preferring to die bravely, because they knew death was their only future.

Up and down, my sword arm rose and fell as, driven by my old berserk blood-craze, I pursued groups of the warriors and continued to slaughter even when most of them had finally lost heart for a fight. At last there was only one band left. With their buffalo-hide shields and quartz-tipped spears, they had formed a ring around a pair of large boulders and clearly intended, like their fallen comrades, to defend their position to the death.

I slipped the blade of my sword between the legs of the nearest warrior and dragged the razor-sharp blade upward to cut him neatly in two. He squealed and wriggled like a tortured cat. Most, however, I simply beheaded. It was hard, precise, mechanical work. The creatures were considerably denser than they looked.

At last all that was left of the pygmies was what they had defended. He lay in a small clearing formed by the boulders. A wizened old man spread over the primitive stretcher like a stain. Everywhere around him were piled the corpses of his warriors. Not one was remotely alive. Small, headless corpses, like so many slaughtered chickens. Spattered with the blood of his people, the man must have been over a hundred years old. His skin was thin as tissue paper, and his fingers were like picked bones. He was an animated corpse, an unwrapped mummy, a husk of a creature, yellowed and fading into nothingness with none to mourn him. But his eyes burned with life, and his lips moved, whispering violently and with considerable pain in a patois I could barely understand. A much corrupted Old French dialect? I had learned that it was often a mistake in the multiverse to try to identify a language too closely.

"Would you loot the last of our honor, Prince Silverskin?" He glared angrily at me and tried to lift a hand weakly shaking a bloody rattle decorated with small animal skulls. All he had left was his mockery. "Your folk have taken everything else from us. You leave us nothing but our shame, and we deserve to die." He was neither strong nor unreconciled to death. There was no need for me to finish him. I had always had a distaste for killing the helpless, which had made me something of a laughingstock as a boy in Melniboné. The old man was already as good as dead, his raspy breath coming with increasing difficulty and slowness. In spite of his afflictions he was able to whisper at me from the rough stretcher on which he lay. "I am Ipkaptam, the Two Tongues."

He was a grey man. The life had been sucked out of him, but not by the sword I now resheathed.

"Are all my people dead?" he asked me.

"All those whom you sent against me," I said. "Why should you wish to have me killed?"

"You are our enemy, Pale Crow, and you know it. You have no soul. You keep it in the body of a bird. You use our own iron against us. You would steal our best-kept treacheries and learn too much about our masters' whims. Does it matter where we are or what we face now? All human aspiration is brought low by human greed and human folly. Now we are tainted by the human curse, and so we fade from this sphere. Is our epic to tell of our self-deception, of our certainty in our own superiority? It is the end of the Pukawatchi. There are only two important realities in this world: starvation and sudden death . . ."

This speech exhausted him. I motioned him gently to silence. But he said:

"You are the man the boy became?"

I could not follow this. I thought he was raving. Then he said clearly, "There are only old people, women and children to weep for the Pukawatchi. Our ancient tribe reconciles itself to the end. We are no more. One day even our name will be forgotten."

My impulse, now that the blood frenzy had passed, was to comfort him, but I did not know how to do so.

I knelt among the raw, red meat I had made of his men and took his withered hand in my gauntleted one. "I meant you no harm and would have gone on my way if you had not attacked me."

"I know," said the old man, "but we also knew that our death time had come. It was written that the black blade would destroy us if we let it go. We have failed in all our ventures. Our oaths lie dry and unfulfilled in dying mouths. It is time for us to die. All our treasures are gone. All our boasts are empty. All our honor has been taken from us. We have nothing to return with save our shame. So we died with honor, trying to take back our black blade. Is it your son, then, who stole it?"

The old man's gaunt features were parchment on bone. His eyes sparked and then faded before I could try to answer.

"Or are you another self altogether?" The shaman rose from his stretcher and reached out, trying to touch me. A soft song whispered on his lips, and I knew that he spoke not to me but to the spirits he believed in. He looked into a world becoming far more real to him than the one he was leaving.

He died upright in an attitude of pride and did not fall back until I laid him down and closed his eyes. His people had died, as they wished, in battle and with honor against an old foe. Their remains looked frail, like children's corpses, and I knew a pang of conscience. Yet these people had been trying hard to kill me. They would be stripping my still-warm body even now, had they won.

In the end I made no attempt to bury them, but rather left them to be cleaned by the carrion-eating birds congregating overhead, drawn in by the stink of a blood-drenched wind.

Soon I could clearly make out what lay before me, but I was no less mystified. I saw a tall black elephant carrying a huge open howdah with what appeared to be a birchbark canoe used as a canopy. Astride the beast was a handsome Indian whose style of costume and decoration resembled the Kakatanawas and was typical of the Indians who had once inhabited the North American woods. A Mohican, perhaps? I guessed him to be some sort of chief. His concentration was not upon the arriving buzzards but on what lay immediately in his field of vision.

The scene was made worse by its absolute silence.

A black, horrible and completely *silent* tornado, thin and vicious at the base, lowering, thick and menacing above, was almost a perfectly reversed pyramid. This edifice of frozen, filthy air blocked the way from shore to island and, with the city as its background, formed a terrifying harmony. The silver trail ended sud-

denly, as if the tornado had somehow eaten it up. The path across
the ice to the city ended as well. I felt I neared the very center of
the world. But compared to this, my journey had been easy until
now.

All the forces who opposed the Balance were gathering to defend against its saviors. We faced not the opposing philosophies of
Law and Chaos, but the Spirit of Limbo—the mindless yet profound creature which yearns for death, which aches for death, but
not merely for itself. It demands that all creation shall know oblivion, for all creation is the only equal to that monstrous ego. If
other persuasions fail, self-murder and the murder of as many others as possible become the only logical option. I knew from Nazi
Germany that from small, mean dreams such egos grow until their
nightmares become the condition of us all.

Against all my usual skepticism I was now in no doubt that
this barely frozen force was a supernatural tornado. There was
also no doubt it intended to block the way of those who confronted it. I knew I looked upon a magical event of some magnitude. From where I had paused, taking what cover I could, I could
feel its vibrant evil. A whole world of evil concentrated into this
unmoving whirlwind. Were I still a believer, I would have thought
myself in the presence of Satan incarnate. I marveled at the
courage of the single warrior facing it.

All around me now was that awful, oppressive stillness.
Progress forward was nearly impossible. I felt as if I waded through
heavy water rather than air.

The great beast was a mammoth, and like the Indian, it was
frozen in motion.

Then I saw a woman's figure in the shadow of the giant pachyderm. An arrow fitted to her bow, she faced the tornado. Over her
slender shoulders was a beautiful white robe, thrown back to
allow her the shot.

Time was standing still here. Even my own actions grew more
sluggish by the moment.

I forced my way forward, hoping that my eyes were not merely trying to console me that the figure I saw was who I thought it was.

A little nearer and I was certain. It was Oona! I tried to move in her direction when suddenly I was overwhelmed by a mighty, deafening noise. It was like the note of a horn, echoing through every dimension of the multiverse. Echoing on and on forever.

The tornado shrieked and sniggered and raged. It had come fully alive now! I saw fiendish faces within it and limbs of sorts.

My hair and clothes were whipped backward. I felt my body sucked at, clutched at, investigated. The wind became even more aggressive. The whole scene was alive now.

Through all this wild bluster came the sweet, clear note of a flute. My wife was nocking her arrow to her bow. I feared to call out and distract her. What did she hope to do? Did she think she could kill a whirlwind—and a supernatural whirlwind at that— with an arrow? Why was Oona walking so calmly towards her death? Did she not sense the thing's power? Was she in a fresh trance? Dreaming within a dream?

And who, or what, had sounded the horn I heard?

Again, instinct took charge of my will, and without a second thought I ran towards the causeway, shouting to Oona to stop, to wait. But she did not hear me above the terrible shriek of the tornado. She walked slowly, with an odd, unnatural gait. Was she entranced?

The tall Indian seemed to know me. He tried to stay me with his hand. "Only she can make the Silver Path across the ice. Wherever she passes, that will give us our way. But she goes against the Winds of the World. They are Winds gone mad. She goes against Lord Shoashooan."

I yelled something back at him, but that, too, was snatched from my mouth by the railing currents.

A sudden cut of cold wind slashed across my face, momentarily blinding me. When I could see again, Oona was gone.

Behind me I sensed a presence.

The Indian was climbing onto the back of the mammoth. Behind him, marching down the beach, came a group of warriors who appeared to have stepped off the set of *Götterdämmerung*. Save for the fact that not all were Scandinavians, I confronted as unwholesome looking a bunch of hardened Vikings as I had ever seen. Immediately I reached for my sword.

The leader stepped forward out of the press. He wore a silvered mirror helm. I had seen it before. I knew him. And something in me, however terrified, knew the satisfaction of confirmed instinct. My instincts had been right. Gaynor the Damned was abroad again.

If I had not recognized him by his helm I would have known him by that low, sardonic laughter.

"Well, well, Cousin. I see our friend heard the sound of my horn. He seems to have inconvenienced you a little." He held up the curling bull's horn, covered in ornate copper and bronze, which hung at his belt. "That was the second blast. The third will bring the end of everything."

And then he drew his own blade. It was black. It howled.

I was desperate. I had to help my wife. Yet if I did so now, I would be attacked from behind by Gaynor and his brutish crew.

Then it was as if Ravenbrand had seized my soul, conscience and common sense, and I found that I'd drawn it again without thought.

I began to advance towards the armored Vikings.

I heard the thin, sweet sound of a bone flute. It echoed like a symphony around the peaks. Gaynor cursed and turned, flinging his hatred towards the Indian, who sat cross-legged upon the neck of the mammoth, his eyes closed, his lips pursed, playing his instrument.

Something was happening to Gaynor's sword. It twisted and shivered in his hand. He screamed at it. He took it in *both* hands and tried to control it, but he could not. Was I right? Did the flute actually control the sword?

Then my own sword almost dragged me towards the causeway and my wife. Behind me I heard the shouts of Gaynor and his men. I prayed they were diverted by the Indian. I had to help my wife, my dearest love, my only sanity.

"Oona!"

My voice was turned to nothing by mocking breezes. Every time I tried to call out, the wind stole my every sound. All I could feel and hear were the vibrations in the sword which had somehow found a common harmony with the whirlwind. Did I carry a traitor weapon? Did this sword bear some loyalty to the howling black tornado in whose depths I now made out a glaring, gleeful face, delighting in what it would do to the lone woman still walking towards it, arrow nocked to bowstring, stance resolute, as if she were about to take a shot at a stag?

Black fog jetted out of the tornado. Long tendrils swam to surround and engulf Oona, who stepped in and out of the tangle like a girl playing hopscotch, her arrow still aimed.

And then she loosed the arrow.

The gigantic, inverted pyramid of air and dust began to shout. Something very much like laughter issued from it, a sound which turned my stomach. I ran all the faster until I was standing on the causeway which now moved like mercury under my feet. It took me several moments to regain my balance and discover that I did not need to sink into it. With an effort of will I could walk along it. With even more effort, I could run.

And run I did as Oona let fly a second arrow and a third, all in a space of seconds. Each arrow formed the points of a V in the thing's face. It raged and foamed, seeking to shake the arrows loose. Its eyes were full of a knowing intelligence, yet one which had lost all control of itself. Lord Shoashooan was still grinning, still laughing, and again his tendrils were curling, tightening, drawing my wife into the depths of his body.

The flute's note rose for a third time.

Oona was violently ejected from the body of the tornado. Clearly the arrows had worked some mysterious magic in conjunction with the flute. She was flung back to the Shining Path and lay, a tiny heap of bones, covered by that bright, white buffalo robe, on the shifting quicksilver.

I yelled to her as I ran past with no time to see if she still lived, so determined was I to take revenge and stop the creature from attacking her again.

I was swallowed by an ear-piercing shriek, inhaling foul air and confronting an even fouler face which leered at me from the depths of the wind. It licked dark blue lips and opened a yellow maw and extended its tongue to receive me.

Instead, the green-brown tongue was cut in two by my Ravenbrand, which yelped its glee like a hound in chase. Another movement of the blade and the tongue was quartered. Intelligence again bloomed in those hideous eyes as it realized it was not dealing with an ordinary mortal but with a demigod, for with that sword bonded to my flesh I knew that I was nothing less. A mortal able to wield the powers of gods and to destroy gods.

Nothing less.

I began to laugh at those widening eyes. I grinned in imitation of its bloody mouth as it swallowed its parts back into its core and re-formed them. And while it used its own energy to restore itself, I struck again, this time at one of the glaring eyes, cutting a slender thread of blood across the pupil. The monster moaned and cursed in painful anger. Oona's arrows had weakened him.

I struck at the smoky tendrils as if they were flesh, and the sword cut through them. But Lord Shoashooan was constantly forming and re-forming himself, constantly spinning himself into new guises within his inverted cone as if he tried to find the best way of destroying me.

But he could not destroy me. I fed off the stolen souls of scores of the recently dead. Fresh souls and, moreover, no demon duke to share them with. I knew that familiar, horrible ecstasy. Once tasted it was always feared, never forgotten, always desired. The vital stuff of all those I had killed filled my human body and turned it into something at once unnatural and supernatural, the conduit of the sword's dark energy. Oona was a forgotten rival. Now I belonged to the sword.

Deep into the being's vitals the sword plunged. Only Ravenbrand knew where to stab, for only she was completely on the same plane as the demon lord whose powers I had once sought to harness myself. Now I had no such fine ambition. I was fighting for my life and soul.

The black energy pouring into me sharpened my senses. I was hideously alive. I was completely alert. I parried every tentacle's attempt to seize me. I laughed wildly. I drove again and again at the head while all around me the thing's whirlwind body shrieked and screamed and thrashed, threatening to destroy the mountains.

Whatever part of me was myself and whatever was Elric of Melniboné, I clung to those identities, and it seemed a thousand other identities were drawn to them. Drawn by the power of the black sword. Could good come out of evil, as evil often came from good? This was no paradox, but a fact of the human condition. I struck two-handed at something which might have been the thing's jugular and was rewarded. The tornado suddenly collapsed into a wide, filthy cloud, and I was covered with what I supposed was its inner core, its blood. A green sticky mess which hampered my every move, for all my extraordinary strength, and seemed to be hardening on my flesh.

I had struck the thing a crucial blow, but now I was helpless, whirling around and around and suddenly flung, as my wife had been flung, out onto the Silver Path. I landed winded, but I still clung to the sword and was able to stumble to my feet just in time to see a monstrous white buffalo charging down on me.

My instinct and my sword's natural bloodlust worked together. I brought the great black battle blade up like a skewer and gored the massive bison in the chest. A second blow and the buffalo went down. A third and her blood was gouting onto the ice.

I turned in triumph, expecting to receive the congratulations of those I had saved.

The face that met mine was that of a second newcomer. It was as bone-white as my own with eyes just as crimson. He could easily have been my son, for I guessed him to be no older than sixteen. There was an expression of disbelieving horror on his face. What was wrong? He was the boy I had seen on the island, of course. Who was he? Neither my son, nor my brother. Yet that grim face had a distinct likeness to the rest of the family.

"So," I said, "the enemy is vanquished, gentlemen. Is there more work to do?" I was met with silence. "Have you no stomach for the adventure?" I was still strutting with egocentric euphoria which came with so much bloodletting.

Then I realized that these men were looking at me with considerable gravity, as if I had committed some error of taste or perhaps even a crime.

Ayanawatta stepped forward. He reached out and wrenched the sword from my hand, flinging it to the path. Then he turned me around and showed me what lay behind me. "She was to lead us across the ice. Only White Buffalo Woman can walk the Shining Path. Now she is dead."

It was Oona. Her white buffalo robe was stained with blood. She had three sword wounds. The wounds were exactly where I had struck the white buffalo.

Slowly the horror of what I had done infused me. I picked up the sword and flung it far out across the ice.

In my battle madness, as she had come to save me, I had killed my own wife!

CHAPTER NINETEEN

The Shining Path

Golden was the city ere Rome were mud,
Philosophies she dream'd ere Greece was form'd,
Senses she explor'd before the rise of Man;
Long was her glory before decline began.

ALBERT AUSTIN,
"Ancient, In Ancient Days Atlantis Dream'd"

 isbelievingly I stumbled towards the frail corpse. Had I really killed my wife? I prayed that this was the illusion and not the bizarre beast I had cut down with my sword.

The wind had fled in defeat and left behind it a deep, triumphant silence. I heard my own footfalls on the silvery path, smelled the sweet salt of fresh blood as I knelt and reached towards the warm, familiar face.

Then I was knocked sprawling. The albino youth I had first seen on the island stooped and swiftly wrapped my wife in the buffalo robe. Without hesitation he began to run towards the great pyramid city. As he ran, the Silver Path extended before him and remained behind him where he passed. I raised myself to follow him, but I was exhausted. I had no sword. All my stolen energy was draining from me.

I stumbled and fell on the unstable causeway. My hands sank into mercury. I tried to crawl. My cry filled worlds with sorrow.

Then Lobkowitz was there, and with the Indian stood over me and helped me to my feet.

"He seeks to save her," said Lobkowitz. "There is a chance. See? Even in death she has the power to make the path."

"Why did you let me—?" I stopped myself. I had never been one to blame others for my own follies, but this was worse than anything I could possibly have imagined. There were terrible resonances within me as Elric's memories confronted mine and came together in common guilt. Only now did I remember who I really was. How had Elric managed to take me over so thoroughly? I looked about me, expecting him to appear as he had first appeared to me in the concentration camp. But our relationship was by now far more profound.

Lobkowitz signed to the Indian. "Ayanawatta, sir. If you would take his other arm . . ."

Ayanawatta responded immediately, and I was hauled bodily up as the two men mounted the massive pachyderm who waited impatiently for us.

Now I could see the reasons for their urgency.

The Vikings were returning. Already they were running towards the pathway, which would be as useful to them as it would be to us. They had reassembled around their leader, who, in his mirror helm, still looked for all the world like my defeated enemy, Gaynor the Damned. I heard their voices echoing across the ice. Were they gaining on us?

I struggled to find my sword, but the two men gripped me tightly, and I was too weary to fight them.

"Do not fear Gunnar and company," said Prince Lobkowitz. "We will reach the safety of the city before they catch up with us."

"Once we are through the gates, he cannot harm us," the other man agreed.

I was relieved to see that at least the youth was safe. His pace dropped to a walk as he passed beneath the gateway and disappeared within. I looked back again. Gunnar—or Gaynor—was still pursuing us. There was something odd about the perspective. They seemed either too far away or too small in relation to the gigantic mammoth. Perhaps all this was an illusion or another dream? Should I trust my own eyes? Could I trust any of my senses? I felt as if I had swelled enormously in size and lost substance at the same time. My skin felt like a balloon about to burst. My head was fuzzy with a kind of fever. All perspective around me seemed to be warping and shifting. The mammoth became smaller, then larger. I felt sick. My eyes ached, and I could hold my head up no longer.

As the pair dragged me towards the city I lost my senses entirely. By the time I recovered we were behind the tall walls of the Kakatanawa city, and an unexpected security filled me. The youth with my wife's corpse was nowhere to be seen. Indeed, to my astonishment, the great courtyard around the gigantic city was completely deserted. And yet I had noted complex activity earlier as I approached the ziggurat. It seemed that everything had become an inchoate illusion, like a dream without rational meaning. How could such a vast city now give the impression of being empty?

Even the mammoth appeared surprised, lifting her huge trunk, her tusks actually making whistling noises in the air as she raised her head, and trumpeting out a greeting which received no response, save from the echoes among the empty tiers and the distant peaks.

Where were the Kakatanawa, the giant Indians who had brought me to the Chasm of Nihrain and ultimately to this world? I tried to free myself from the friendly hands still holding me. I needed to find someone who would give me the answers. I think I was babbling. At some point thereafter I fell into a deep sleep. But it was not a comforting sleep. My dreams were as disturbed as my life had become, and as mysterious.

In those dreams I saw a thousand incarnations of Oona, of the woman I loved, and in those same dreams I killed her a thousand times in a thousand different ways. I knew a thousand different kinds of remorse, of unbearable grief. But out of all this spiritual agony I seemed to find a tiny thread of hope. I saw it as a thin, grey wire which led from tragedy towards joyous resolution, where all fear was driven away, all terror quietened, all gentle dreams made real. And I wondered if Kakatanawa were just another

name for Tanelorn, if here I might rest and have my love and my
life restored.

"This is not Tanelorn." I awoke refreshed. The black giant
Sepiriz was staring down at me. He held a goblet in his hand
which he offered me. Yellow wine. I drank and felt better still. But
then memory came back, and I sprang off the dais on which I had
been lying. I looked around for my sword. Apart from the platform
on which I had slept, the room was entirely empty. I ran into the
next room, out of a door, into a corridor. All empty. No furniture.
No occupants.

"Is this Kakatanawa?"

"It is the city of that people, yes."

"Have they fled? I saw them . . ."

"You saw what travelers have seen for centuries now. You saw
a memory of the city as she was in her prime. Now she dies, and
her people are reduced to those few you have already met."

"And where are they?"

"Returned to their positions."

"My wife?"

"She is not dead."

"Alive? Where?"

Sepiriz tried to comfort me. He offered me more of the wine.
"I told you that she was not dead. I did not say she was alive. The
tree alone no longer has that power. The bowl alone no longer has
that power. The disk itself alone has no power. The staff alone no
longer has the power. The blade alone no longer has that power.
The stone alone no longer has that power. The pivot is gone. Only
if the Balance is restored can she live. Meanwhile, there is some
hope. *Three by three, the unity.*"

"Let me see her!"

"No. It is too soon. There is more to do. And unless you play
your prescribed role, you will never see her."

I could only trust him, though his assurances had hidden aspects to them. He had promised me I would see Oona again, but
he had not told me she might take a different form.

"Do you understand, Count Ulric, that the Lady Oona saved

your life?" asked Sepiriz gently. "While you fought Lord Shoashooan most bravely and weakened him considerably, it was the dreamthief's daughter who dealt him the final, dissipating blow, which sent his elements back to the world's twelve corners."

"She shot those arrows, I remember . . ."

"And then, after you precipitously attacked the demon duke, thinking you saved her, she aided you again. She at last took the shape of the White Buffalo whose destiny was to make our final road across the ice. She had the greatest tradition of resisting Lord Shoashooan. Do you understand? She became the White Buffalo. The Buffalo is the trail-maker. She can lead the way to new realms. In this realm, she is the only force the wind elementals fear, for she carries the spirit of all the spirits."

"There are more elementals?"

"They combined in Lord Shoashooan, who was ever a powerful lord with many alliances among the air elementals. But now he has taken them in thrall. Although the twelve spirits of the wind are conquered by his powers, they can still re-form. All the winds serve him in this realm. It is why he succeeds so well. He commands those elementals who were once the friends of your people."

"Friends no longer?"

"Not while that mad archetype enslaves them. You must know that the elementals serve neither Law nor Chaos, that they have only loyalty to themselves and their friends. Only inadvertently do they serve the Balance. And now, against their will, they serve Lord Shoashooan."

"What is his power over them?"

"He it was who stole the Chaos Shield which should have brought your wife to this place. Lord Shoashooan waylaid her and took the shield. That was all he needed to focus his strength and conquer the winds. Had it not been for Ayanawatta's medicine, she would not have been with us at all! His magic flute has been our greatest friend in this."

"Lord Sepiriz, I undertook to serve your cause because you

promised me the return of my wife. You did not tell me I would kill her."

"I was not sure that you would, this time."

"This time?"

"My dear Count Ulric." Prince Lobkowitz had entered the room. "You seem much recovered and ready to continue with this business!"

"Only if I am told more. Do I understand you rightly, Lord Sepiriz? You knew that I would kill my wife?"

The black giant's expression betrayed him, but I saw the sadness that was there also. Any blame I felt towards him dissipated. I sighed. I tried to remember some words I had heard. Was it from Lobkowitz, long ago? We are all echoes of some larger reality, yet every action we take ultimately decides the nature of truth itself.

"Nothing we do is unique. Nothing we do is without meaning or consequence." Lobkowitz's soft, cultured Austrian accent cut into Sepiriz's silence. The black giant seemed relieved, even grateful. He could not answer my challenge and feared to answer my question.

The ensuing silence was broken by a loud noise from outside. I walked past the dais on which I had been sleeping. I was almost naked, but the room was pleasantly warm. I went to the window. There was a courtyard outside, but we were many stories above it. Old vines, thicker than my legs, climbed up the worn, glittering stonework. Autumn flowers, huge dahlias, vast hydrangeas, roses the span of my shoulders, grew among them, and it was only now I understood how ancient the place must truly be. Now it was a better home to nature than to man. Large, spreading trees grew in the courtyard, and tall, wild grass. Some distance below on another terrace I made out an entire orchard. Elsewhere were fields gone to seed, cattle pens, storehouses. There had been no one here for centuries. I remembered the tales told of the Turks capturing Byzantium. They had believed they brought down an empire, but instead found a shell, with sheep grazing among the ruins of collapsed palaces. Was this the American Byzantium?

In the courtyard the great black mammoth, Bes, was being

washed down by the youth, White Crow, and his older companion, Ayanawatta. The two men seemed good friends, and both
were in the peak of physical fitness, though White Crow could not
have been more than seventeen. His features, of course, were
those of an albino. But it was not my family he resembled. It was
someone else. Someone I knew well. My urge was to call to him,
to ask after Oona, but Sepiriz had already assured me she was no
longer dead. I forced myself to accept his leadership. He did not
simply know the future—he understood all the futures which
might proliferate if any of us strayed too far from the narrative
which, like a complicated spell involving dozens of people in
dozens of different actions, must be strictly adhered to if we
wished to achieve our desire. A game of life or death whose rules
you had to guess.

Looking up, the youth saw me. He became grave. He made a
sign which I took to be one of comradeship and reassurance. The
lad had charm, as had the aristocratic warrior at his side.
Ayanawatta now offered me a faint, respectful bow.

Who were these aristocrats of the prairie? I had seen nothing
like them in any of the wonderful historic documents I had studied about the early history of northern America. I did, however,
recognize them as men of substance. Warriors and superbly fit,
they were expensively dressed. The quality of workmanship in
their beaded clothing, weaponry and ornaments was exquisite.
Both men were clearly prominent among their own people. Their
oiled and shaven heads; their scalp locks their only body hair,
hanging just so at an angle to the glittering eagle feathers; the
complicated tattoos and piercings of the older man; the workmanship of their buckskins and beading—all indicated unosten-
tatious power. I wondered if, like the Kakatanawa, they too were
the last of their tribes.

Again I was struck by the sense that, from within, the city
seemed totally deserted. I looked back at tier upon tier fading into
the clouds which hid the city's upper galleries.

Turning I could see beyond the great walls to the lake of ice
and the ragged peaks of the mountains beyond. The whole world

seemed abandoned of life. What had Sepiriz said about the inhabitants of this city? It must have housed millions of them.

I asked Lobkowitz about this phenomenon. He seemed unwilling to answer, exchanging looks with Lord Sepiriz, who shrugged. "I do not think it unsafe, any longer," he said. "Here we have no control of events at all. Whatever we say, the consequences will not change. It is only our actions which will bring change now, and I fear . . ." He dropped his great chin to his chest and closed his brooding eyes.

I turned from the window. "Where are the Kakatanawa, the people of this city?"

"You have met the only survivors. Do you know the other name for this city—the Kakatanawa name? I see you do not. It is Ikenipwanawa, which roughly means the Mountain of the Tree. Do you know of it? Just the tree itself, perhaps? So many mythologies speak of it."

"I do not know of it, sir. It is mainly my wife who concerns me now. You suggest she might live. Can time be reversed?"

"Oh, easily, but it would do you no good. The action has already taken place. And will take place again. Your memory cannot be changed so readily!"

"What *has* changed within these walls?" I asked him.

"Nothing. At least, not in many hundreds of years. Perhaps thousands. What you saw from the ice was an illusion of an inhabited city. It is one which has been maintained by those who guard the source of life itself. The reflective walls of the city serve more than one purpose."

"Has no one ever come here and discovered the truth?"

"How could they? Until recently the lake was constantly boiling with viscous rock, the very life stuff of the planet. Nothing could cross it, and nothing cared to. But since then cold Law has worked its grim sorcery and made the lake as you see it now. This is what Klosterheim and his friends have been doing. In response the pathway was conjured by Ayanawatta and White Buffalo, but of course, it is now being used by our enemies. We make the paths, but we cannot control who uses them after us. It will not be long, no doubt, before they realize the trick and find a way of entering the city. So we must do all we have to as quickly as possible."

"I understood that time, as we know it, does not exist." I was becoming angry, beginning to think they tricked me. "Therefore there is no urgency."

Prince Lobkowitz allowed himself a small smile. "Some illusions are more powerful than others," he said. He seemed about to leave it at that, then added, "This is the last place in the multiverse you can find this fortress physically. Everywhere else it has transformed itself."

"Transformed? This was a fortress?"

"Transformed by what it contains. By what it must guard. At one stage in the multiversal story, this was a great and noble city, self-contained and yet able to help all who came to it seeking justice. Not unlike the city you call Tanelorn, it brought order and tranquillity to all who dwelled here.

"The human story is what changes so drastically. Passion and greed determine the course of nations, not their ideals. But without change we would die. So simple human emotions, those which have brought down a thousand other empires and destroyed a thousand Golden Ages, worked to bring about the destruction of this stability. It is a story of love and jealousy, but it will be familiar enough to you.

"This fortress—this great metropolis—was built to guard a symbol. First, a symbol was chiefly all that it was. Then, through human faith and creativity, the symbol took on more and more reality. Ultimately the symbol and the thing itself were one. They became the same, and this gave them strength. But it also gave them dangerous vulnerability. For once the symbol took physical shape, human action became far more involved in its destiny. Now symbol and reality are the same. We face the consequences of that marriage. Of what, in essence, we ourselves created."

"Are you speaking of a symbolic tree?" I asked. I could only think of old German tree worship, still recalled in our decorated Yule pines. "Or of the multiverse itself?"

He seemed relieved. "You understand the paradox? The multiverse and the tree are one, and each is encompassed by the other. That is the terrible dilemma of our human lives. We are capable of destroying the raw material of our own existence. Our imaginations can create actuality, and they can destroy it. But they are equally capable of creating illusion. The worst illusion, of course, is self-deception. From that fundamental illusion, all others spring. This is the great flaw which forever holds us back from redemption. It was what brought an end to the Golden Age this place represented."

"Do you say we can never be redeemed?"

Lobkowitz brought his hand to my shoulder. "That is the fate of the Champion of Humanity. It is the fate of us all. Time and space are in perpetual flux. We work to achieve resolution in the multiverse, but we can never know true resolution ourselves. It is the burden we carry. The burden of our kind."

"And this dilemma is repeated throughout countless versions of the same lives, the same stories, the same struggles?"

"Repetition is the confirmation of life. It is what we love in music and in many forms of art and science. Repetition is how we survive. It is, after all, how we reproduce. But when something has been repeated so many times that it has lost all resonance, then something must be done to change the story. New sap must be forced into old wood, eh? That is what we try to do now. But first we must bring all elements together. Do you understand what we are hoping to achieve, Count Ulric?"

I had to admit that I was baffled. Such philosophies were beyond my simple soul to fathom. But I said, "I think so." All I really knew was that if I played out my role in this, I would be reunited with Oona. And nothing else much mattered to me.

"Come," said Sepiriz, almost taking pity on me. "We will eat now."

We walked outside to a wide path curving around the city.

"What is the exact nature of this place?" I asked. "Some center of the multiverse?"

Lobkowitz saw how mystified I was. "The multiverse has no center any more than a tree has a center, but this is where the natural and the supernatural meet, where branches of the multiverse

twine together. These intersections produce unpredictable consequences and threaten everything. Size loses logic. That is why it is
so important to retain the original sequences of events. To make
a path and to stick to it. To choose the right numbers, as it were.
It is how we have learned to order Chaos and navigate the Time
Field. Have you not noticed that many people out there are of different dimensions? That is a sure sign how badly the Balance is
under attack." Lobkowitz paused to look up. Tier after tier, the
vast building disappeared into wisps of white cloud.

"The Kakatanawa built this city over the centuries from the
original mountain," Lobkowitz told me as we continued past deserted homes, shops, stables. "They were a great, civilizing people.
They lived by the rule of Law. All who sought their protection
were accepted on condition that they accepted the Law. All lived
for one thing—for the tree which was their charge. They devoted
themselves to it. Their entire nation lived to serve and nurture
the tree, to protect it and to ensure that it continued to grow.
They were a famous and respected people, renowned across the
multiverse for their wisdom and reason. The great kings and
chiefs of other nations sent their sons to be educated in the ways
of the Kakatanawa. Even from other realms they came to learn
from the wisdom of the People of the Tree. White Crow, of course,
follows his family's long tradition . . ."

I said that I understood Kakatanawa to mean 'People of the
Circle'. Why did he say "tree"?

He smiled. "The tree is in the circle. Time is the circle, and
the tree is the multiverse. The circle is the sphere in which all exists. Space is but a dimension of this sphere."

"Space is a dimension of time?"

"Exactly." Lobkowitz beamed. "It explains so much when you
realize that."

I was saved from any further contemplation of this bewilder-
ing notion by a sharp wailing sound. With sinking heart, I rushed
to the nearest balcony. I saw dark clouds drawing in on the jagged
horizon, gathering around one of the tallest peaks and writhing
and twisting as if in an agonized effort to assume some living form.

The clouds were making one huge figure, drawn by all the winds now in thrall to Lord Shoashooan. A long streamer of cloud sped from the central mass, across the ice, over the walls of the great fortress city, and lashed at our flesh like a whip, then retreated before we could respond.

Even Sepiriz bore a thin welt across his neck where the cloud had caught him. I imagined I saw a flash of fear in his eyes, but when I looked again he was smiling. "Your old friends march against us," Lobkowitz said. "That is the first taste of their power. From this moment on, we shall never know peace. And if Gaynor the Damned is successful, we shall know agony for eternity."

I raised an eyebrow at this. Lobkowitz was serious. "Once the Balance is destroyed, time as we know it is also destroyed. And that means we are frozen, conscious but inanimate, at the very moment before oblivion, living that death forever."

I must admit I had begun to close my ears to Lobkowitz's existential litany. A future without Oona was bleak enough to contemplate.

Food forgotten, we watched the blue-black bruise of cloud forming and re-forming around the peaks of the mountains. A shout from another part of the gallery and we could see over the great gateway to the city, to the half-faded path which Ayanawatta had created with his flute. It now spread like dissipating mercury across the ice with men moving through it, leaping from patch to patch. The figures were tiny. They were not Kakatanawa. I thought at first they were Inuit, bulky in their furs, but then I realized that the leader had no face. Instead the light reflected from a mirrored helmet which was all too familiar to me. Another man strode beside him, one whose gait I recognized, and on the other side of him a smaller man, also familiar. But they were too far away for me to see their faces. They were without doubt his warriors.

The same Vikings who had tried to stop us reaching the fortress.

"Time is malleable," said Lobkowitz, anticipating my question. "Gaynor is now Gunnar the Damned. Merely a fraction of movement sideways through the multiverse. He has gathered himself together, but he dare not live now without that helmet—for all his faces exist at once. Otherwise he is here in your twelfth century, as indeed is this city and much else . . ."

I turned to look at him. "Does Gunnar still seek the Grail?"

Lobkowitz shrugged. "It is Klosterheim who longs for the Grail. In his warped way he seeks reconciliation. Gunnar seeks death the way others seek treasure. But not merely *his* death. He seeks the death of everything. For only by achieving that will he justify his own self-murder."

"He is my first cousin, yet you seem to know him better than I do." I was fighting off a creeping sense of dread. "Did you know him in Budapest or Vienna?"

"He is an eternal, as you are an eternal. As you have alter egos, fellow avatars of the same archetype, so he takes many names and several guises. But the relative you know as Gaynor von Minct will always be the criminal Knight of the Balance, who challenged its power and failed. And who challenges it again and again."

"Lucifer?"

"Oh, all peoples have their particular versions of that fellow, you know."

"And does he always fail in his challenges?"

"I wish that were so," said Lobkowitz. "Sometimes, I must say, he understands his folly and seeks to correct his actions. But there is no such hope here, my dear Count. Come, we must confer. Lord Shoashooan gathers strength again." He paused to glance out of another opening in the great wall winding up the ziggurat. "Gaynor and his friends bring considerable sorcery to this realm."

"How shall we resist them?" I looked around at the little party, the black giant, Prince Lobkowitz, the sachem Ayanawatta and White Crow. "How can we possibly fight so many? We are outnumbered and virtually unarmed. Lord Shoashooan gathers strength while we have nothing to fight him with. Where's my sword?"

Sepiriz looked to Lobkowitz, who looked to Ayanawatta and White Crow. Both men said nothing. Sepiriz shrugged. "The sword was left on the ice. We cannot get the third until . . ."

"Third?" I said.

Ayanawatta pointed behind him. "White Crow left his own blade down there with Bes. His shield is there, too. But again, we lack the necessary third object of power. There is no hope now, I think, of waking the Phoorn guardian. He dies. And with him the tree. And with the tree, the Balance . . ." He sighed hopelessly.

The silence of the city was suddenly cut by a squealing shriek, like metal cutting metal, and something took shape above the ice directly behind where Gaynor and his men were moving cautiously along the dissipating trail.

I was sure we could defeat the warriors alone, but I dreaded whatever it was I saw forming behind them.

It shrieked again.

The sound was full of greedy, anticipatory mockery. Lord Shoashooan, of course, had returned. No doubt, too, Gaynor had helped him increase his strength.

White Crow turned away from the scene. He was deeply troubled. "I sought my father on the island, in my crow form. I thought he would help us. That he would be the third. But Klosterheim was waiting for me and captured me. At first I thought that you were him, my father. If you had not been near . . . The Kakatanawa came to rescue me after Klosterheim went away. They released me and found you. My father is, after all, elsewhere. He followed his dream and was swallowed by a monster. I thought he had returned to the Dragon Throne, but if he did, he has come back for some reason. This must not be." He lowered his voice, troubled. "If that man is who I am sure it is, I must not fight him. I cannot fight my own father."

I frowned. "Elric is your father?"

He laughed. "Of course not. How could that be? Sadric is my father."

Ayanawatta touched his friend's arm. "Sadric is dead. You said so. Swallowed by the *kenabik*."

White Crow was genuinely puzzled. "I said he was swallowed. Not that he was killed."

CHAPTER TWENTY

The Pathfinder

Pour the beer and light the feasting fires,
Bring you in the tall Yule trees,
Without, let Father Frost and Brother Death reside
Let Mother Famine fly to farther fields,
Raise high the trees and high the ale-cup lift,
Let good will rule and to ill will all folk give short shrift.

OLD MOORSDALE SONG

ord Shoashooan did not merely take shape above the fading causeway. He drew strength from the surrounding mountains. Storm clouds boiled in from north, south and west, masses of dark grey and black shot through with points of white, tumbling swiftly towards us.

Shale and rocks began to fly towards his spinning form, and from within that bizarre body his grotesque face laughed and raved in its greedy rage, utterly deranged. He was now more powerful than when either Oona or I had fought him. His size increased by the moment. Pieces of ice flew up from the lake to join the whirlwind's heavy debris. And when I looked deep into it, I saw the twisting bodies of men and beasts, heard their cries mingled with the vicious shriek of the cruel Warlord of Winds.

Realizing suddenly what he faced, White Crow frowned, murmured something to himself, then turned and began to run back down the long, curving roadway between the tiers. Sepiriz and Ayanawatta both cried out to him, but he ignored them. He flung some cryptic remark over his shoulder and then disappeared from

289

sight. Was he deserting us? Where was Oona? Did he go to her? Was she safe? And who did he think his father was? Gaynor? How did White Crow hope to avoid conflict?

Questions were impossible. Even Sepiriz seemed flustered by the speed with which Lord Shoashooan was manifesting himself. The maddened Lord of Winds was already ten times more powerful than when he had sought to block our way across the ice.

Prince Lobkowitz was grim as he hurried up the ramps. Higher and higher we climbed, and the tornado rose to match our height. The causeways grew tighter and narrower as we neared the top of the city, and the wind licked and tasted us, playing with us, to let us know there was no escaping its horrible intelligence, its vast destructive power.

As we neared the top, heavy pieces of earth and stone flew against the walls of Kakatanawa, chipping at surfaces, slashing into foliage. A large rock narrowly missed me, and Sepiriz shook twice as he was hit. Part of an outer wall fell. Through the gap I saw the tiny figures of the Vikings on the ice moving in closer, but we were momentarily safe from any immediate confrontation with them. We had no way to resist the invader even if we could engage him. Lord Sepiriz carried no sword. Save for Ayanawatta's bow and Prince Lobkowitz's cutlass, we had no weapons.

We had reached a broad-based tower with dark red walls and a deep blue ceiling and floor; a central spiral staircase led like a cord of silver up to a platform and what was clearly an experimental laboratory. An alchemical study, perhaps? Certainly Prince Lobkowitz had expected to find it there. He began at once to climb the stairs.

"Let's have a better look at our enemies," he murmured.

We followed him up. Here was an assortment of large, chunky machinery, mostly constructed of stone, like an old mill with huge granite cogwheels and smaller ones of beaten gold and platinum. Apparently this people, too, had no notion of smelting iron. The strange, bulky cogs and levers worked a series of lenses and mirrors. There was something familiar about all this.

Of course. My father had experimented with a smaller version at Bek before the first war. I realized we were looking at a rare form of camera obscura, which, by means of mirrors, could show scenes of the surface around the city. It was not entirely mechanical in nature. There were other forces involved in its construction, more common to Melniboné than Munich. Indeed, when Lord Sepiriz joined the stocky prince, he easily made parts move by a murmured command and a gesture. Gradually the two men brought the scene outside the gates into view.

I had been right. Gaynor the Damned led them. Near him was his turncoat lieutenant Klosterheim. The third man also wore a helmet, which obscured most of his face, but his eyes were shockingly familiar. He had an edgy, wolfish air, as did all the Vikings, but his was of a different quality. There was something fundamentally self-contained about the figure, and I feared him more than the others.

The Vikings did not look as if they had slept or eaten well for some time. Their journey here had clearly not been an easy one. I had rarely seen a hungrier bunch of cutthroats. They watched the Wind Demon with considerable wariness and did not look happy to be of Gaynor's party now. They were almost as nervous of the huge whirlwind as we were! Only the stranger in the black helmet seemed to be in a different mood. His eyes in shadow, his pale lips half-hidden by the upwardly thrusting chin-guard, the man was smiling. Like his eyes, his smile was one I recognized and feared.

Still larger rocks smashed into the walls, leaving deep gashes. Sepiriz was furious, muttering about the age of the place and what it had meant for so many millennia.

I think he had believed us safe, at least temporarily, in the remote fortress city, but these events were proving far more dangerous and whimsical than he had expected. He realized he may have underestimated the danger. The developing situation appeared to have defeated his imagination.

A gritty wind howled into the tall camera and whistled around the complicated confection of copper wires and polished mirrors, the worn granite cogwheels and brass pivots, the pools of mercury. There was a busy humming, a rattling and buzzing as the wind touched the delicate, half-supernatural instruments. Polished glass flashed and blinded me. Thin tubes rattled and hissed and scraped together.

Lord Shoashooan's voice whispered through the tall rooms, finding strange, ugly echoes. "Mortals and immortals both, you face your end without dignity or grace. Accept the fact that the Balance is finished. Its central staff has been lost, its scales discarded. Soon the tree itself will die. The regulator of the multiverse has failed you. Law triumphs. The steady calm of complete stability awaits you. Time is abolished, and you can anticipate, as do I, a new order."

"The order you promise is the stasis of death," Lord Sepiriz replied contemptuously. "You it is, Lord Shoashooan, who dishonors your own name. You it is who lacks both dignity and grace. You are a busy noise surrounding a vacuum. To destroy is your only effect. Otherwise you are less than a bird's dying breath."

A groan of anger. The walls rattled and cracked as the whirlwind's strength increased still more. Outside another great crash as masonry loosened and tumbled.

Lord Sepiriz's hands played over the strange instruments. His shoulders were hunched with the urgency of his actions. His eyes flashed from one point to another as if he sought a weakness somewhere.

He was reading signals within the mirrors, frowning over swirling glasses and tubes.

The chamber shook. It was like a heavy earthquake. My companions looked at one another. Clearly they had never anticipated such a force. Though outwardly artificial, this city had once been a wild mountain. Within she was *still* a living mountain. And Lord Shoashooan had the power to challenge this mountain, to threaten its destruction!

Outside, the entire landscape was filled with the wildly whirling debris. Below, at the apex, stood Gaynor and his men, looking up at the once invulnerable gates of the city as the wind remorselessly battered them to destruction. I could already see the gates beginning to bulge and split. Their iron bands and hinges, which hitherto could withstand any attack, now warped and twisted under the pressure.

We were deafened by the roaring sound, and our hair and clothing lashed violently in every direction. Lord Sepiriz shouted at me. He signaled. I could not understand what he wanted.

The mercury pool that was a mirror swirled again, and I saw a man's face in astonishing detail. It was the stranger who had come with Gaynor and Klosterheim. He stared upwards, presumably at his supernatural ally. His eyes, like mine, were crimson. They contained profound and complex experience. I wondered how any human soul could bear the burden of knowledge revealed in those eyes. Only Elric of Melniboné was sorcerer and warrior powerful enough to consider taking that burden. I doubted if there had ever been a human character equally strong.

The pool's surface flickered to show, full-length, a black-armored, black-helmed warrior. He had a huge round warboard on his arm, canvas covering its blazon. With some surprise I saw that he carried a black sword identical to my own. Then, for the first time, the truth began to dawn on me. It was so enormous it had eluded me. Three of us? Three swords? Three shields? But who carried the shields?

Sepiriz pulled me away from the mirror pool. "It is drawing you in. You'll drown in that if you're not careful. Many others have."

"Drown?" I laughed. "Drown in a reflection of myself?"

Ayanawatta came to join me. "So you understand." He radiated a certain calmness. He represented common sense in all this insanity. "You would not be the first to do that." His smile was quiet, comradely. "Some might say that was your friend Gunnar's fate!"

The more I knew this tall red man, the more I liked and respected him. He was a natural leader. He was unassuming, egalitarian, but acted decisively and with due caution. All the great leaders, like Alexander, could sit at backgammon with common soldiers and still have them believe him a living god.

I wanted to ask Ayanawatta where the rest of his people were. His tribal style was familiar to me, but I was not sufficiently knowledgeable to identify it. This was no time to satisfy such curiosity. Events were moving too swiftly. We had all been thrown together by our different circumstances. I had no idea how Gaynor and company had reached Kakatanawa or why they were here.

The shrieking air was painful. My ears felt as if needles were being inserted and twisted in them. I covered them as best I could and noted that my companions were equally affected. Lord Sepiriz found some wax and handed it out to us. Stuffing the slick, malleable material into my ears relieved the worst of the howling. I could hear Prince Lobkowitz when he approached me. Cupping his hand around my ear, he spoke into it.

"We cannot fight Lord Shoashooan or his allies. We lack the necessary tools to destroy him, so all we can do now is retreat. We must abandon the outer city and seek the deeper reality within. We must fall back to the Skrayling Oak."

That was all he was able to say before the screeching wind grew even louder and fingers of ice wormed their way into my clothing and found the flesh beneath. I knew piercing agony and swore aloud at the fierceness of it just as White Crow reappeared in the doorway. There was something behind him. Something dark and looming. I longed to draw my sword, to run to his assistance, and then I realized it was a beast with him, his trusty pachyderm, Bes. Fearing for her safety, he had returned for her. Her saddle was still on her back, and her burdens were covered by a great white buffalo robe edged with blue and scarlet, which made it seem as if she had a Bactrian hump. Whether she would be better off with us or without us was an open question at that moment.

Bes moved as rapidly as the rest of us as we dashed through the camera obscura and through various other chambers, all of which were clothed in different raw metals, many of them precious. Our feet slipped and slid on the floors of these tunnels. Our reflections were distorted by the curving, polished walls. Twice my own face appeared, enlarged and transformed into something leering and hideous. The others scrambled to get away from the place. I found myself laughing in my grief-madness. How close these people had been to changing the eternal verities! What had destroyed them?

At last we were all crammed into a crystal room scarcely large enough to take the curling tusks of the great mammoth, let alone the rest of us. My hand was on the huge, curved ivory surface of one tusk as she turned her mild, unfrightened eye to regard me. A wall had fallen away behind her, revealing that we were above an unstable lake of rising and falling crystals.

Sepiriz muttered and growled, motioning with his staff over the crystals. They hissed in reply. Sluggishly they formed a rough shape and then fell back into the same amorphous mass. Again Sepiriz spoke to the crystals. This time they swirled rapidly and formed a cone with a black center.

Then we fell!

I shouted out, trying to resist the descent as the entire top of the city was enveloped in a sulphuric cloud. The crystals opened like a mouth threatening to swallow me. I stared in awe into a world of intense green foliage. Every shade of green, so vivid it almost blinded me.

The rest of the world roared into a void and disappeared.

We stood in the swaying top branches of a huge tree. The ground was so far away that I could see nothing below. Only endless leaves. Foliage stretched out and downwards from the canopy. I peered through giant limbs, heavy twigs and myriad leaves, into the complexity of all that grew from a single, vast trunk. For what might have been miles I could see massive branches, themselves supporting other branches which supported still more branches. I was dazed with wonder. The city had contained a mountain that in turn contained this measureless oak!

With a sign, Sepiriz jumped into the foliage. I saw him sink slowly, as if through water; and then I followed, and we were all descending little by little through womb-rich air, salty and thick with life. Everywhere the branches of that great tree stretched into infinity. The trunk of the tree was so large we could not see the whole of one side. It was like a wall stretching on forever. The thickest limbs were equally difficult to accept for what they were.

I was overwhelmed by the scale of it all and wondered if I would ever find my wife again. Impotent fury bubbled in me. Yet I remembered the admonition I had heard more than once since my adventures began so long ago in Nazi Germany: *Every one of us who fights in the battle, fights as an equal. Every action we take has meaning and effect.* My moment was bound to come. This hope sustained me as we drifted like motes of living dust down through the lattice of intersecting realities, of dreams and possibilities. We sank down into the multiverse itself and let it embrace us.

Countless shades of green were dappled by a hidden sun. Sometimes a shaft of golden or silvern light blinded me or illuminated a mysterious, twisting corridor of foliage. Leaves that were not quite leaves, yet which proliferated and reached enormous distances. Branches that were not quite branches became curling, silver roads on which women and men walked, oblivious of the intricacy around them. And these branches turned back and put out further branches, which in turn formed a matrix within a matrix, a billion realities, each one a version of my own.

Oona! I struggled in the hope of glimpsing my wife.

Down we sank in Sepiriz's supernatural wake, down through what was at once concrete reality and abstract conception, passing through countless permutations, each one telling the same human story of conflict without and within: the perpetual conflict, the perpetual quest for balance, the perpetual cycle of life, struggle, resolution and death which made us one with the rest of creation. What put us at odds with creation was, ironically, the very intelligence and imagination which was itself creative. Man and multiverse were one, united in paradox, in love and anger, life, death and transfiguration.

Oona!

Through golden clouds of delicate tracery, through russet, viridian and luminous lavender, through great swathes of crimson and silver, we fell. Looking up I saw only the wide branches of a tree stretching to where the roof of the pyramid would be. It became obvious the area enclosed by the Kakatanawa city was far greater than the city itself. The city could have rested on the topmost branches of the multiversal tree. If it guarded the crown of the tree, who or what guarded the trunk and roots below?

Where was my wife? Was I being led towards her or away from her?

Oona!

Slowly I fell, unable to decrease or otherwise control my descent. Save for my concerns over my wife, I had no real sense of fear. I was not sure if I had died or if I was still alive. The question was unimportant. What seemed solid as we dropped towards it became less dense as we passed through it. And in turn the tenuous grew solid.

I could not imagine the variations in scale involved. Outside the pyramid, I was a speck of dust in the quasi-infinite multiverse. Within, I was the size of galaxies.

I passed through the substance of the tree as through water, for here mass and scale were the means by which the multiverse ordered its constantly proliferating realities, enabling them to co-exist. Perhaps it was *our* mass that changed as we fell and not the tree's. I realized that I felt no ordinary physical sensations, merely occasional electrical pulses from within my body that altered in intensity and rhythm with every breath I took. I had the feeling I was not breathing air at all but sweet ichor, what some might call ectoplasm. It flowed like oil, in and out of my lungs, and if it had any effect on me at all it was only to sharpen my vision.

Where was Oona? I had the peculiar impression that I was not only "seeing" with my eyes, but with all my other senses, including the ordinary ones of touch, smell and hearing. Unfamiliar, dormant senses now wakened in response to some recognizable suprareality, this vision of a living multiverse.

Perhaps a man of more intellectual bent might have understood all this better, but I was helplessly in awe. In my exhilaration I felt I was in the presence of God.

I fell through a field of blue, perhaps a sudden patch of sky, and as I did so my soul filled with a rare sense of peace. I shared a contented tranquillity with all the other human souls who occupied this place. I had passed briefly through heaven.

Once more I floated among green-gold branches and could see my companions above and below me. I tried to call out to Lobkowitz, who was nearest, to ask where Oona was, but my voice made only broad, deep rolling sounds, not recognizable words.

These tones took on shape and a life of their own, curling off into the depths of blossoming scarlet. I tried to move towards the color field, but a gigantic hand seized me and set me back on course. I heard only what seemed to be the words "Catch up cave," and looking back I saw that the hand was Lobkowitz's though he seemed of ordinary size and some distance off. The hand and arm retreated, and I accepted this as a tacit warning that I should not try to stop my descent or change my course. The peculiarities of scale and mass which seemed so odd to me were clearly the natural conditions of this place. But what exactly was the place? The multiverse? If so, it was contained in a single mountain on a single planet of a universe. How could that be?

My emotions seemed to be dissipating. My whole being was evaporating, joining the ectoplasmic atmosphere through which I floated. Terror, anxiety, concern for my loved ones, became abstract. I lost myself to this sense of infinity. I did not expect to stop my fall nor ever know an ending to my adventure. I was mesmerized by the experience. We were all in the embrace of the Tree of Life itself!

I remembered the Celtic notion of the Mother Sea to which the wandering spirit always returned. Its presence became increasingly tangible. Was this what dying felt like? Were my loved ones already dead? Would I join them?

Unconcerned now, I was content to drift down and down through the verdant lattice and not care if I ever reached a bottom. Yet increasingly I began to notice areas I could only describe as desolate. Branches had withered and broken as vitality had been drained from them by Law or by Chaos or by the ordinary, inevitable processes of decay. And slowly it began to dawn upon me that perhaps the entire tree was truly dying.

But if the multiverse were no more than an idea, and this was only then its visualization, how could it possibly be saved by the actions of a few men and women? Were our rituals so powerful that they could change the fundamentals of reality?

Below me now I saw an endless flow of pale green-and-yellow dunes racing and rippling, as if blown by a cosmic wind, crossed by curving rivers of chalky white and jade, dotted with pools which bubbled and gasped. I smelled rich salt. I smelled a million amniotic oceans. Around me a dark cloud gushed rapidly upwards and spread away, forming its own tree shape. Another followed it, dark grey, white, boiling foam. Another. Until there was a forest of gaseous trees. A hissing forest that rose before me and then collapsed into shivering star clusters. More green-gold branches. More peace. Eternal tranquillity . . .

The whispering gases arose again, the darkling turbulence, and a shrill voice yelling into a gorge of bubbling blood. I was losing my own substance. I could feel everything that was myself on the very brink of total dissipation. At any moment I would join the writhing chaos all around me. Whatever identity I had left slipped towards total destruction. Intellectually I felt some urgency, but my body did not respond.

Only when I remembered Oona did any sense of volition return.

Looking about me and down I saw three huge human figures standing on a surface of glittering, rainbow rock. To my horror, I recognized them. How had they arrived here before us? How much more powerful had they become?

Three giants. Klosterheim and Gaynor the Damned I identified at once. The third was the black-armored man I had seen with them earlier. But now I recognized him completely. It was indeed Elric of Melniboné. The canvas cover had been removed from his shield, which displayed the eight-arrowed sign of Chaos. A black runeblade trembled on his hip. There was no doubting his identity. But what of his loyalty?

The three had obviously come here by supernatural means. Now standing to my left on a great limb they were completely unaware of me and were arguing fiercely among themselves. I was apparently too small for them to see just as they were almost too huge for me to contemplate. I looked up at Lobkowitz above me. He was staring at the three figures with open dismay.

A gust of wind raced past us unexpectedly, and we were swept away from the gigantic figures, losing them among the branches.

I saw Sepiriz leaping and rolling towards me in an extraordinary sequence of movements. Thus he negotiated this strange version of space. He spoke, but his words were meaningless to me. Lobkowitz then said something. I saw White Crow and Bes, with the white-skinned youth clinging to the beast's thick fur. Where was Oona? Imitating Lord Sepiriz's strange tumbling method of locomotion, Ayanawatta trailed him as they came rolling towards me.

Is Oona with you?

Their voices were enormous, booming, on the verge of being incoherent. Their bodies were huge. Bigger even than Gaynor and company. But the hands that reached towards me were only as large as my own. Each hanging on to one of my arms, Sepiriz and the Mohican sachem were concentrating on guiding me slowly through our descent.

I stood on spongy material that reminded me, stupidly, of my childhood, when we had played on our feather beds. I saw myself in a field of multicolored flowers. There were millions of varieties and colors, but the petals were all small and tight and gave the picture the quality of a pointillist painting. I half expected to see that my companions were also made up of tiny dots. They did, indeed, have a slightly amorphous quality.

The vivid colors; strong, amniotic scents; the warm, womblike air—all emphasized the total silence around us. When I spoke I communicated with my companions, but not in any familiar way, and it made me economical with words.

A fern as big as the world opened its fronds to embrace me. A million shades of green turned slowly to black as they disappeared into the distance. Endless slender saplings, silver and pale gold, appeared so substantial I expected at any moment to see a woods-man padding through them.

White Crow and the mammoth were nowhere to be seen. Where *was* Oona? I longed for a glimpse of my wife. I wept with guilt at my own hasty folly. I hoped with impotent optimism.

Ayanawatta, Lobkowitz and Sepiriz surrounded me and moved with me, guiding me in long, wading steps. Their outlines were now sharper, and everything had a more tangible quality. Were they taking me at last to Oona? The sweetness of the wild-flowers began to dominate the saltier tastes of the sea. Ahead of us was another blinding mass of varied green. With wonder I looked upon the Skrayling Oak, the object of so many dream-quests.

I was distracted from this vision by a sense of more than one self nearby. It was hard enough for me to cope with the presence of Prince Elric, whose experience was supernaturally mingled with my own and manifested itself always in my dreams if not contin-ually in my conscious mind. It felt as if these other intelligences, these alter egos, were also Elric. Mentally I was in a hall of re-peating mirrors, where the same image is reversed and reflected again and again to infinity. I was one of millions, and the millions were also one.

I was intratemporally infinite and contained by the infinite. Yet that infinity was also my own brain, which contained all oth-ers. The mind of man alone was free to wander the infinity of the multiverse. One contains the other and one is contained in the other . . . Not only were these paradoxes of particular comfort to me, they felt natural. For all my fear of the place, I now knew a re-sounding resurgence of hope. I was returning home. I would soon be reunited with Oona. In this long moment, at least, I knew she was safe, hidden between life and death.

Only if the tree itself died would she die. But whether it was certain she would live again, I could not tell.

The green, gold and silver lattice of the mighty tree filled the horizon. Framed against it I saw three groups of three men. Each of the men had his head bowed, and each had his hands wrapped around a tall, slender spear. At their belts were polished war clubs. They wore their hair in single scalp locks decorated with eagle feathers, and their bodies were tattooed and painted in a way I had seen before. All were pale and distinctly similar, in both physique and face, yet every one was different. I knew who they were. They were the last of the Kakatanawa, the guardians of the prophecy, of the tree. Perhaps they now stood funeral watch for the tree itself. There was something somber about the scene when there should have been joy.

"The tree is sick, you see." Sepiriz's deep voice sounded in my ear. "The roots are being poisoned by the very creature enjoined to protect them. That which regulates the Balance was stolen by Gaynor, then found by another . . ."

"What creature is it that guards the roots?"

"Gunnar's Vikings would probably tell you it was the Worm Oroborous, the great world snake who eats his own tail—the dragon who both defends and gnaws the roots. Most of your world's mythologies contain some version. But Elric would know him as a blood relative. You have heard of the Phoorn?"

Already there were too many echoes. I might have replied that Elric would no doubt recognize the name, but I was not Elric! I refused to be Elric! The Phoorn name, in my present state, had no more significance to me than any other. Yet I did know what he meant. I was simply denying the memories which came un-summoned from my alter ego. Images crept insistently into my consciousness. My being was suffused with a deliciously terrifying sensation. My blood recognized the word even as my brain refused it.

"Why have you brought us to this place, Lord Sepiriz? And why are those three here? Why so gigantic? I thought we had escaped them. I thought we came here for our security. I also thought we came to find my wife! Now you confront me with my worst enemies!"

The ground rose and fell beneath my feet like a breathing beast.

"Elric is not your enemy. He is yourself."

"Then perhaps he is indeed my worst enemy, Lord Sepiriz."

I could see them now, wading towards us in all their martial weight, swords drawn and ready to spill blood. Again I was all too aware that we were virtually unarmed.

Something vibrated forcefully against my feet. I looked down, half expecting the ground to be thoroughly alive. Wildflowers swept like a tide around my legs. There was activity in the depths below. I imagined infinite roots spreading out to mirror the boughs above. I imagined caverns through which even now the dark reversals of ourselves prowled, seeking bones to break and spirits to suck. Was this the route the giants had taken to arrive here now? Had Shoashooan been unable to gain access to this oddly holy place?

Then far away and below I heard a wild, angry howling. I understood Lord Shoashooan had not been left behind.

There was more movement over near the tree's wide trunk. The multiverse was shaken by a long, mournful groan. I breathed in a familiar scent. I could resist the memory no longer.

"I know the Phoorn," I said.

CHAPTER TWENTY-ONE

The Skrayling Tree

Seeking the worm at the heart of the world,
Wild warriors carried carnage with their swords
To Golddune, the glittering gate of Alfheim.
Bold were these bears in their byrnies of brass,
White-maned horses bore them in their boats,
To wild Western shores and rich reiving,
Where three kings ruled in Hel's harsh realm.
Bravely they defied Death's cold Queen,
So came in conquest to the Skrayling Tree.

THE THIRD EDDA,
"Elrik the White" (WHELDRAKE'S TR.)

 was surrounded by the finest flowing copper spreading like a woman's auburn hair, lock after lock, wave after wave into a crowd of people hiding among tall grasses, waiting to join with me. Did they protect my wife? I sought only Oona. I prayed Oona had lived long enough for me to save her. As I came closer to the riders, I saw they were not people. They were instead intricately shaped and colored scales, dimpled by millions of points of light, flashing with a thousand colors, each one of extraordinary beauty. I was aware that I saw only a shadow of an older glory. And where another might have known wonder, I knew sympathy.

I looked on the body of a sickly Phoorn, blood-kin to my ancestors. Some said we were born of the same womb before history began.

The Phoorn were what the people of the Young Kingdoms called dragons. But these were not dragons. These were Phoorn, who flew between the realms, who had no avatars, but made the whole multiverse their flying grounds. The Phoorn had conquered entire universes and witnessed the deaths of galaxies. Blood-kin to the Princes of Melniboné—who drank their venom and formed bonds of flesh and souls with them, creating even more terrible progeny, half-human, half-Phoorn—they had loyalties only to their own kind and the fundamental life stuff of the multiverse.

My blood moved in harmony with this monster's, and I knew at once that it was ill, perhaps dying, its soul suffused with sadness. I understood our kinship. This Phoorn was a brother to my forefathers. The poor creature had known past anguish, but now he was near complete exhaustion. From a half-open mouth his poison dripped into the roots of the tree he was sworn to protect. He was too weak to drag his head clear. Massive quicksilver tears fell from his milky, half-blind eyes.

His condition was obvious. His skefla'a was gone. The membrane which drew sustenance from the multiverse itself and allowed the Phoorn to travel wherever they chose was also the creature's means of feeding. They might take thousands of years in their passing, but ultimately, without a skefla'a, the Phoorn were mortal. There were few of them left now. They were too curious and reckless to survive in large numbers. And this one was the greatest of the Phoorn, chosen to guard the Soul of Creation. It was rare enough for these elders to grow weak, almost unheard-of for one to sicken.

"What supernatural force is capable of stealing a skefla'a from the great world snake?" said Sepiriz from somewhere nearby. "Who would dare? He guards the roots of the multiversal tree and ensures the security of the Cosmic Balance."

"He sickens," I said. "And as he sickens his venom increases its effect . . ."

"Poisoning the roots as the Balance tips too far. Virtue turned to vice. This is a symbol of all our conflicts throughout the multiverse." Lobkowitz joined us. Wildflowers ran around our legs like water, but their nauseating stench was scarcely bearable.

"A symbol only?" I asked.

"There is no such thing as a symbol only," said Sepiriz. "Everything that exists has a multitude of meanings and functions. A symbol in one universe is a living reality in another. Yet one will function as the other. They are at their most powerful when the symbol and that which it symbolizes are combined." Lord Sepiriz shared a glance with Prince Lobkowitz.

Out of nowhere came the high, lovely sound of the flute. I knew Ayanawatta had begun to play.

The Kakatanawa were aroused. They lifted their great heads and stared around them. Their eagle feathers trembled in their flowing scalp locks. They shifted their grip on their war clubs and lances and made their shields more comfortable on their arms. They readied themselves carefully for battle.

Was this to be the final fight? I wondered.

The sound of the flute faded, drowned by a harsher blare. I sought the source.

There above us was Elric of Melniboné, blowing on the heavily ornamented bull's horn Gaynor had brought with them. Elric's black helm glowed with a disturbing radiance as he flung back his swirling cloak and lifted his head, making a long, sharp note which cut through the quasi-air; caused great, dark green clouds to blossom and spread; shook the ground beneath my feet and made it crack. Through the cracks oozed grey snapping paste which licked at my feet with evident relish.

I jumped away from the stuff. Was it some monster's tentacle reaching up from the depths? I heard it grumbling away down below.

Defended by the Kakatanawa, I approached the Phoorn. In relation to this ancient creature I was about the size of a crow compared to Bes, the mammoth. I walked through a forest of tall stalks which might have been oversized grass or saplings of the original tree, and eventually I stood looking up at those huge, fading eyes, feeling a frisson of filial empathy.

What ails thee, Uncle? I asked.

Thin vapor sobbed from the beast's nostrils. His long, beautiful head lay along the base of the tree. Venom bubbled on his lips with every labored breath and soaked into the roots below. His mind found mine.

I am dying too slowly, Nephew. They have stolen my skefla'a and divided it into three parts, scattered through the multiverse. It cannot be recovered. By this means they stop me from finding the strength I need. I know the tree is being poisoned by my dying. You must kill me. That is your fate.

Some cruel intelligence had devised the death of this Phoorn. An intelligence which understood the agony of guilt the Phoorn must feel at betraying his own destiny. An intelligence which appreciated the irony of making the tree's defender its killer and of making the Phoorn's own kin his destroyer.

I have no weapon, Uncle. Wait. I will find one.

I looked over my shoulder to question Lord Sepiriz. He was gone.

Instead, Gaynor the Damned stood behind me, some distance away. His armored body glistened with brilliant, mirrored silver. On his right hand was Johannes Klosterheim in his puritan black. On his left hand was Elric of Melniboné in all his traditional wargear. Gaynor's dark sword hung naked in his mailed hand, and Elric was drawing another black blade which quivered and sang, hungered for blood.

They stepped forward as one, and the effect was startling. As they moved closer towards me, their size decreased until by the time we were face-to-face, we were all of the same proportions.

I peered past them. Something lurked behind them, but I could not determine what it was.

"So good of you to grant the dragon mercy, Cousin Ulric." Gaynor's voice was quiet within his helm. He seemed amused. "He will die in his own time. And you have killed your wife, too, I note. Your quest has scarcely been a success. What, in all the worlds, makes you believe that you will not continue to repeat these tragedies down the ages? You cannot escape destiny, Cousin.

You were ordained to fight forever, as I am ordained to carry the instant of my death with me for eternity. So I have brought us both a blessing. Or at very least a conclusion. You were never fated to know peace with a woman, Champion. At least not for long. Now you have no destiny at all, save death. For I am here to cut the roots of the multiversal tree, to send the Cosmic Balance irredeemably to destruction and take the whole of creation with me to my punishment!"

He spoke softly and with certainty.

I had no reason to listen to him. I refused to let my annoyance with his crazy mockery show in my voice. I was greedy for my lost sword, which I had flung out over the ice. What could I do against such odds?

"So," I said, "the void has a voice. But the void is still a void. You seek to fill up your soulless being with empty fury. The less you are able to fill it, the more furious you become. You are a sad wretch, Cousin, stamping about in all your armor and braggadocio."

Gaynor ignored this. Klosterheim allowed himself a slight glint of amusement. From his bone-white face Elric's crimson eyes stared steadily into mine.

All I thought when I looked at him was *Traitor*. I hated him for the company he kept. How was it that he had been on my side against Gaynor on the Isle of Morn and now stood shoulder to shoulder with the corrupter of universes?

Klosterheim looked worn. He had drained himself with his conjuring and spell casting. I was reminded of the dying pygmy I had encountered on the way to Kakatanawa. Klosterheim, like me, had no natural penchant for sorcery. "You are unarmed, Count Ulric. You have no power at all against us. This evil thing that you call 'uncle' will be witness to the final moments of the Balance as it fades into nonexistence. The tree falls. The very roots are poisoned and can be attacked with steel at last. The multiverse returns to insensate Chaos. God and Satan die and in death are reconciled. And I shall be reconciled."

These supernatural events, like a constant, ongoing nightmare, had clearly affected his sanity rather more than mine. But I had something to focus on. Something more important than life or death, waking or dreaming. I had to find my wife. I needed to know that I had not destroyed her.

Where was White Crow? What had he done with Oona?

Through the dark, gorgeous mist roiling at Gaynor's back, shadows stirred and drew closer.

The Kakatanawa.

Where is my wife? I asked. *Where is Oona?* But they were silent, moving to enclose the three threatening me.

Gaynor seemed unworried. As the Kakatanawa advanced, they reduced in scale, so that by the time they confronted Gaynor and his henchmen, they were equal in size. They remained, however, impressive warriors, handsome in their beautifully designed tattoos which rippled over their bodies and limbs from head to waist, a record of their experience and their wisdom.

"This is blasphemy," intoned one. "You must go." His voice was resonant, very soft, and carried enormous authority.

Gaynor remained unconcerned. He gestured to Elric, who again took up the big horn. Elric placed the instrument to his lips and drew a deep breath.

Even before he began to blow, the noise below my feet increased. Out of the subterranean caverns, an ally was rising, the echoes of his voice whispering and whining through the caverns and crags of the underworld. I imagined all those ethereal inhabitants, the Off-Moo and their kin, seeking shelter from that destructive malice. I feared for friends I had last seen in those endless caves lying between the multiverse and the Grey Fees. Did they perish below as we were to perish above?

But there was also something happening above us. A distant shrieking, almost human. It consumed everything with its sinister aggression.

The growing noise alerted the Kakatanawa. All simultaneously looked skyward in surprise and alarm. Only Gaynor and his friends seemed careless of the commotion.

There came a thrashing and slashing from far above. A metallic chuckling. A muttering, rising voice became a distant howl. Louder and louder it grew, crashing through the branches of the great Skrayling Tree, sending jagged shards of light in all directions. It seemed that entire universes might spin to land and be crushed underfoot. I felt a sickness, a realization of the magnitude of Death accompanying Lord Shoashooan's descent towards us.

It could be nothing else but the Lord of Winds. Summoned by that traitor Elric! What possible promise could Gaynor have made to him?

My cousin intended to destroy the multiverse and destroy himself at the same time.

And Lord Shoashooan was stronger than ever, hurtling at us from above and below!

Gaynor stepped forward, his sword held in his two mailed hands, and swept the dark blade down towards the tree's already dying roots.

NO! I moved without thought and leaped forward. Unarmed I tried to wrestle the pulsing sword from his fists.

Klosterheim advanced with his own blade drawn. But Elric had turned and leaped towards the dragon, using his pulsing sword to climb the glinting peacock scales, a tiny figure on the dragon's side. I heard his crooning song join with that of his sword, and I knew the Phoorn heard it, too. What did Elric want? The creature was too weak to move its head, let alone help him.

Then it came to me that Elric intended to kill it. That was to be his task. To kill his own brother as I had killed my own wife. Was all our ancient family to die in one terrible, unnatural bloodletting?

I hardly knew what to do. I had no sword. I could not stop them all. The Kakatanawa had held their positions. I realized that they were guarding something.

Not the tree any longer, but the same shadowy shape I had glimpsed before.

Lord Shoashooan howled downwards while beneath our feet the other wind was beginning to test at the ground. I was convinced it must soon erupt under us.

Elric reached a point close to the dragon's back. He had his sword in hand, his shield on his arm, the horn at his belt. His cloak swirled around the ivory whiteness of his skin. His crimson eyes flashed wolfishly, triumphantly. I saw him raise the sword.

I forgot Gaynor, who pointlessly continued to hack with compulsive energy at the tree's roots. I left Klosterheim stumbling in my wake. Over that heaving, spongy ground, with one tornado advancing from above and another apparently from below, I ran back towards the dragon. White Crow appeared at my side. He did not pause but reached out towards me. He tore the talisman from his neck and placed it around my own. Why had he given me the miniature of Elric's great shield? How could a trinket possibly protect me?

I will bring her now. It is time . . .

He shouted something else, but I did not hear him. I began to climb in Elric's wake. Even against his own wishes, I had to save the Phoorn, for only he could ever save us. I had no clear idea of what to do next, but since Elric had gone mad and was trying to kill his brother, I had to try to stop him.

Another sound trumpeted over the noise of the winds. Looking back I saw Bes. Her body was covered in dark copper mesh which swayed as she trotted. As she came nearer, I realized her size was almost the equal to the Phoorn. Her great, linen-covered platform swayed on her back, its flaps wild in the wind. Riding on the neck of the beast, spear in his hand, was White Crow in all his paint and finery, his pale scalp lock lying along his left shoulder. His face was prepared for war. Behind him came the buffalo hide–draped platform resembling a circular bier laid out with a body which clutched a sword to its chest. I knew this had to be Oona.

I was torn. Was I to continue on and try to stop Elric, or should I turn back to tend to my wife? This all seemed part of my torment. I wondered how much of it Gaynor had planned.

The unstable ground began to heave like quicksand. Bes had difficulty keeping her footing. White Crow signaled for me to go on. I looked up. Elric was putting the horn to his lips.

And then, from somewhere, sweetly cutting through the raging howl of the wind, I heard the crystalline sound of Ayanawatta's bone flute.

As Elric blew another blast on the horn, the notes immediately blended with the music of the flute. Rather than canceling each other out, they resonated and swelled into a grand harmonic. Urgently I continued to climb up the clattering dazzle of the Phoorn's scales.

The tornado was still tearing its way downwards, and from below, the ground around the tree's roots was beginning to spit and bubble.

I lost sight of Elric above me but noticed the Phoorn's breathing had changed. Did he understand that Elric was trying to kill him, as he had begged me to do?

Lord Shoashooan crashed in upon us. His grinning, whirling heads flashed rending teeth. His wild, swinging arms ended in long claws. His feet had scythes for nails. And everywhere he danced he brought destruction.

I was certain that once Lord Shoashooan joined with his twin elemental, even now dancing just below the surface as Shoashooan danced above it, everything would begin to collapse in a final appalling cataclysm!

From behind me the nine Kakatanawa advanced upon Lord Shoashooan. Ayanawatta's flute rose above the din, sounding delicate and somber now.

Lord Shoashooan blustered and swung wildly about him, but his belligerence had no force. The sound of the flute had some effect on him. Perhaps it calmed that berserk rage?

I thought I glimpsed the outline of White Crow and Bes moving below. They, too, were bound to be destroyed.

Then all at once the nine Kakatanawa surrounded the base of the tornado. Their hair and clothing streaming out from their bodies in that hideous turbulence, they held their ground. Linking arms and shields and with lances thrust outwards, war clubs at their sides, they formed a circle around the whirling base—a ring strong enough to contain Lord Shoashooan as soon as he touched

the exposed roots of the tree at which Gaynor maniacally continued to hack while Klosterheim looked on impassively.

I saw Ayanawatta walk into the circle formed by the
Kakatanawa, still playing his flute. It was clear from the buffeting
that he would not hold Lord Shoashooan for long, but it was incredible that he could hold him at all. I pushed on, climbing those
yielding, pulsing scales, while above me, I was sure, Elric prepared
to deal his brother a death blow.

I willed myself to find more energy. We must all be weakening
before the force of this stupendous supernatural threat. I reminded myself that we almost certainly witnessed the end of
everything. If I did not discover further resolve within me, I
should reach the moment of my death knowing that I had not
done enough.

This spurred me to complete my climb. I danced along the
Phoorn's back while above me the branches of the great multiversal tree stretched out forever, damaged but not yet destroyed.
I saw Elric. His sword had indeed made a cut in the Phoorn's vulnerable spine, where it met the head. Yellow blood oozed from the
long incision.

I climbed on, determined to stop him. But before I could
reach him he took his shield and pressed it down onto the bloody
patch he had made in the beast's hide. The shield fitted the patch
exactly. Blood soaked it through instantly as it was absorbed into
the Phoorn's flesh. What was Elric doing? He stretched out his
hand to me now. It was as if he had expected me, even welcomed
me.

I made my way forward as the Phoorn's back rippled and
stirred under my feet. *What is it? What do you do?*

*Give me what White Crow gave you! Quickly. I have deceived
Gaynor until now. He still controls Lord Shoashooan but is distracted.
This is our moment. Give me the talisman, von Bek!*

Without hesitation I ripped it from my neck and threw it to
him. He caught it in his gloved fist and, kneeling, placed it at the
center of the wound he had made. A plume of bright red fire shot
up like a beacon, higher and higher until it disappeared among

the branches of the Skrayling Oak. Then, burning brilliant white it sank slowly back, spreading out as it turned to pale blue and covered the Phoorn's wound. The Phoorn let out a long, deep sigh which blended with the sound of the flute.

Sensing what was happening, Lord Shoashooan yelled and feinted at the Kakatanawa warriors. But they held their ground. They stabbed at him with their spears. They swung their war clubs against his whirling sides, struggling to control the spin of their weapons as the winds flung them back.

White Crow was immediately below. He had brought Bes to a stop. The patient mammoth paused, kneeling in the midst of all this wild confusion.

Ayanawatta drew another extended breath and continued to play. Above me on the Phoorn's shoulders, Elric raised the horn to his lips again.

At this blast Gaynor ceased his ferocious hacking and glanced up, his mirrored helm catching the green-gold light of the dying tree.

Guided by the horn and the flute in unison, the great round bier began to rise into the air, the white hide falling away beneath it to reveal my own wife, Oona, seemingly dead, lying upon yet another version of the Kakatanawa war-shield. This one was twice the size of the shield Elric had put between the Phoorn's shoulders. Seeing it at last Gaynor let out a frustrated shout and looked around him for his men. There was only Klosterheim. Gaynor beckoned to him. Rather reluctantly the ex-priest came forward to join him, crying out in a peculiar singsong as the Kakatanawa attempted to tighten their circle about the raging Lord of Winds.

Higher rose Oona, lifted on Ayanawatta's and Elric's music. I saw that she lay in the position of old knightly tomb figures, her legs crossed at the ankles, a long black sword clasped between her breasts and a red sandstone bowl on her chest from which rose a willowy plume of smoke.

White Crow dropped down from Bes's neck and ran towards the Phoorn. He slung his lance over his back and began to climb up the breathing scales as Oona's floating platform, buoyed by the notes of the flute, drifted high over the Phoorn's back, paused and then began to descend as Elric and White Crow called out in unison. They were chanting a spell. They guided Oona's flight with their sorcery, bringing the great round shield, the third part of the missing skefla'a, down towards the faintly glowing blue wound. The shield completed the membrane which all dragons must have if they are to fly between the worlds, and which is in so many unknown ways their sustenance.

They had re-created the stolen skefla'a and brought it back to the dying Phoorn! Was it this which sustained my wife between life and death?

At last the great disk covered the dragon's back, and Elric gently lifted Oona from it as I joined him. She seemed unusually at peace in his arms. But was it the peace of death?

I touched her. She was warm. Upon her chest the faintly smoking bowl, one of the great treasures of the Kakatanawa, their Grail, rose and fell with her slow, even breathing.

Instantly now the Phoorn drew in a full breath. It took all our efforts to cling to those swelling quasi-metallic scales and move towards one another.

The wind still shrieked and raged, but the Kakatanawa ring held. The warriors all called out the same strange, high-pitched ululations, their actions and voices completely in unison. The spears ran in and out of the spinning darkness, containing the howling thing but scarcely harming it.

The scales of the Phoorn steadily changed color. They deepened and ran with dozens of different shades, taking on a fire that had not been there before. White Crow clambered towards me. He pointed to Oona, lying half held in the blue-grey membrane where Elric had placed her, still unmoving, as if she lay in a womb. Elric was beside her on his knees. He took the large ring from his finger and reached through the membrane to place it on Oona's forehead. I tried to call out to him but failed. Surely he could not mean her ill. He was her father. Even a Melnibonéan would not be so ruthless as to kill his own child.

I felt a light hand on my shoulder. White Crow had reached me. Clearly exhausted, his eyes gleamed with hope. "You must take up the sword," he said. "Oona has brought it to you." And he pointed to where the black blade still lay, clutched in her hands, but outside the peculiar organic stuff of the Phoorn skefla'a.

"*Take it!*" he commanded.

Crimson eyes locked onto mine as Elric looked up at me. He raised the sword in his fist and all but hurled it at me. "We have no grace!"

"Fear not." White Crow gasped. "He is of our blood and of our party. We three shall do what has to be done."

At that moment it occurred to me again that Elric could be White Crow's father, which meant that the young Indian was Oona's twin. The evident discrepancy in their ages added a further mystery to the conundrum.

Would it ever be explained? None of us was dead yet, but Gaynor, Klosterheim and Lord Shoashooan appeared to have the greater power!

The Lord of Winds still screamed and raged in the Kakatanawa circle. It seemed the disciplined warriors could not hold much longer. Already there were weaknesses showing as the giants used every ounce of mental and physical energy to contain him.

But I was reluctant to accept the sword. Perhaps I feared I would use it to kill Oona again? I shuddered. A coldness filled me. I was consumed by guilty memory.

"Take it!" Elric shouted again. He rose to his feet, his eyes still fixed on his daughter. "Come. We must do this now. Lobkowitz and Sepiriz say it is the only way." He thrust the sword towards me again.

How had Lobkowitz communicated with Elric? Had they been in league all along? Lobkowitz had explained nothing to me, and I might never understand now.

I accepted the sword. I knew I could not deny the inevitable. There was time only for action now.

As my hand closed on the silk-bound hilt I felt a sudden shock of energy. I looked down on my wife. Her face was tranquil. On her breast the red sandstone bowl glowed and smoked. On her forehead the deep blue stone swirled with a life of its own. Somehow I knew it was the bowl that sustained her life.

Elric's face was shadowy. He moved closer to stand with his body pressed against mine. White Crow came nearer from the other side until both men were almost crushing me. I could not resist. The blade demanded it. All three blades were in our hands now. All three were touching. All three were beginning to sigh and murmur, their black fire mingling, their runes leaping back and forth from one to the other. They conferred.

Oona opened her eyes, looked at us calmly and smiled. She sat up, the silvery web of membrane falling away to merge with the Phoorn skefla'a. She took the red sandstone bowl and blew gently into it. White smoke poured upwards and surrounded us. I breathed it in. It was sweet and delicate, the stuff of heaven. With every breath we took in unison, White Crow, Elric and I moved closer together. The swords merged until there was only one massive blade, and I knew, as I grew in both size and strength, wisdom and psychic power, that the swords were reunited with their archetype as we were reunited with ours. Three in one.

"Now!" It was Sepiriz. He, too, was as enormous as the single creature I had become. "Now you must climb. Now you must restore the tree and return the Balance."

I could see Lord Shoashooan whirling wildly below me. The Kakatanawa could no longer hold him. I heard Lobkowitz's voice. "Go! We will do all we can here. But if you do not go, nothing will be worth it. Gaynor will win."

Once again Elric's familiar personality was absorbing my own. I had no sense of White Crow's individuality. For me it was exactly as it had been before when only Elric and I had combined. But now I felt even more powerful. The black sword had become a monstrous and beautiful object, far more ornate and intricate in design than anything I had ever wielded in battle. Her voice was melodic, yet still as cold as justice, and her metal blazed with life. I had no doubt that I held the *first* sword, from which all others had come. I looked up at the flaking bark, the decaying pulp that now blotched the base of the Skrayling Oak. Gaynor's work had been well done.

I flung my arm forward towards the oak, and the sword did the rest, carrying me deep towards the core of the trunk. The closer I came, the larger I grew, until the tree, though tall, was of more familiar size.

I scabbarded the sword and climbed. I knew what this ascent meant. I knew what I had to do. Elric's blood and soul informed my own as mine informed his. While Lobkowitz had given me only hints, he had told Elric everything he needed to know. Since the time they first saw White Buffalo Woman and Kakatanawa city, Elric had schemed against Gaynor while pretending to serve his cause. And now, too, I knew who White Crow was.

On my belt was Elric's horn, and I moved with the agility of White Crow. The outer bark of the supernatural tree was very thick and layered, forming deep fissures and overhangs which afforded me handholds on my route upwards.

I heard a sound below and looked down. Far away the Kakatanawa were being pressed back by the power of the Lord of Winds. Lord Shoashooan had widened their circle until it must surely break. I knew in my bones that unless the Phoorn had more time to heal and recover he would still perish. Oona was doing her best for the great beast, but if Lord Shoashooan were to break free now, the Phoorn would not yet be strong enough to destroy him.

I thought I glimpsed Ayanawatta, Sepiriz and Lobkowitz on the edge of my vision, but then I could not look away any longer. I needed all my faculties to climb the constantly changing organic fissures in the tree.

Noise from the tornado crashed and wailed. Every part of the tree began to shake. I had to exert even more effort to cling to the weird bark. Often pieces crumbled away in my hands. I feared I would soon weaken and lose my grip completely.

An inch at a time I climbed. The air grew thinner and colder and the sounds of the Lord of Winds more shrill. Then something grabbed at my body. It felt as if a giant skeletal hand seized me about the waist. The cold went deep into my guts, and I knew Lord Shoashooan was free.

I fought to keep my grip on the tree. Being held so, I could not climb any further. It was all I could do to hang on.

The Lord of Winds' voice trumpeted a vainglorious note now. Once I thought I glimpsed the Kakatanawa below as they were flung backwards, their ring broken. Lord Shoashooan attacked me and the Phoorn with all his strength.

I heard the pure whistle of Ayanawatta's flute cutting through the roar and bluster. Again I was gripped by the tendrils of wind as Lord Shoashooan tried to pry me loose. Without the strength of my avatars, I should surely have been lost.

But the sound of the flute came clearer and sweeter through all that cacophony and joined with another sound coming from far below, equally high but by no means sweet. This sound writhed around the tree's roots. The sound was the other Lord of Winds. If the Lords succeeded in joining, there would be no overwhelming their combined strength.

With that thought came the energy to force myself up the trunk. At last I stood in the swaying upper branches looking out across a world at night, at the frozen lake, at the rubble to which the great city had been reduced. At my will the sword sprang into my hand. I held the blade high above my head as power flooded into it. I offered myself as a conduit for this huge, supernatural force.

Then I reversed the sword and aimed it at the topmost tip of the tree, plunging it down, down into the soul of all-time, the heart of all-space, down into the center of the Skrayling Tree.

Immediately the sword left my hand and remained in the tree, its point driving deep through the inner wood to the soul of the Skrayling Oak. As it moved down the tree, it did not split but rather expanded the trunk until sword and tree had merged, and a great, black blade lay at the core of the ancient oak.

Then I lurched backwards, grabbing frantically at boughs to stop myself falling towards the faraway ice and the inevitable death of all my avatars. If I fell, we might never know if our sacrifice had been worth anything. Even now I heard the wind rising, higher and higher, ever more vicious. I was losing my grip on the bough. I was surely about to fall, and I had given up my weapon.

A shadow passed fleetingly through the whirlwind's dusty crown. It was Oona, and she was riding the Phoorn.

The great white-gold spread of a Phoorn rising on his wide peacock wings into the air above a storm was a breathtaking sight! On my reptilian relative's broad back, merged with his gleaming iridescent skefla'a but clearly visible, was my wife Oona, vibrantly alive, her head thrown forward in the sheer pleasure of the flight, a bowstave clutched in her right hand and the redstone smoking bowl balanced in her left.

When I fell, the Phoorn fell beside me, almost playfully. His soft breath slowed my descent, and he slid underneath me. I landed gently, painlessly, in his skefla'a. I lay prone just behind my wife. I could see the tree outlined in a golden glare. Within the spreading oak was the deep black of the sword blade, the guard stretching out across the branches, the pommel pulsing like a star. The black blade had completely merged with the oak and become part of the tree's life force.

I was held within the membrane, only able to watch as Oona put down her box, took the redstone pipe bowl and spread her hands in a magical gesture that produced two bowls, one on each palm. I saw her reach out and put a smoking redstone bowl at each end of the black sword's guard. They hung suspended there as she lifted both hands to her head and took something from it. She then placed this object on the sword hilt between the bowls. The ritual was done, and I looked upon the Cosmic Balance.

Oona began to laugh with joy as Shoashooan redoubled his attack. The storm raged on and shot up cold tendrils wrapping around us, still trying to draw us back. Yet she turned towards me, laughed again, and embraced me.

The Balance still swung erratically. It could destroy itself if its movement back and forth became too violent. Nothing seemed to have even the promise of stability as yet.

Below us, seemingly even more powerful, the great plume of

the tornado fanned out, gathering stronger and stronger substance. The limbs of the tree began to thrash uncontrollably again as Lord Shoashooan unleashed a desperate anger.

Once more I heard the clear note of the flute. Oona heard it, too. The Phoorn began to bank through the dirty light, sweeping through the edges of the whirlwind, down through the green-gold haze of the tree, down past the slender black shaft which glowed at the center of the trunk. Down towards the greedy Lord of Winds.

I had done everything I could do. I prepared myself for the death Lord Shoashooan undoubtedly planned for us. If I could have thrown myself into his center and saved Oona I would have done so, but the membrane prevented any dramatic movement.

This was how my ancestors had traveled with the Phoorn, protected by the skefla'a which allowed the monsters to sweep like butterflies so delicately between the realms of reality. Few Melnibonéans had made such flights, though my father Sadric was said to have voyaged longest and furthest of any of us, after my mother had died giving birth to me.

It was only now that the realization came. My shame was coupled with a sudden rush of relief. The Kakatanawa Grail had done its holy work! The wounds I had inflicted upon Oona were thoroughly healed.

With decreasing energy, the Phoorn fought valiantly against the sucking wind drawing us to it. His massive wings beat upon the ether as he strained to escape. Oona became increasingly alarmed. Filling the entire world before us was the spreading bulk of the Skrayling Oak framing the pulsing black sword. Its crosspieces formed the Cosmic Balance, which again began to sway wildly. The conflict was by no means decided.

Looming behind us was the ever-growing presence of Lord Shoashooan. The Kakatanawa warriors were nowhere to be seen. Lord Sepiriz, Ayanawatta and Prince Lobkowitz had disappeared. Neither was there any sign of Gaynor or Klosterheim.

Then I heard the flute's refrain. Ayanawatta's clear, pure tones cut through all the raging turmoil.

The Phoorn lurched this way and that in the force of the tornado. The air grew colder and colder. We were slowly freezing into immobility. I became drowsy with the cold.

Again the flute piped.

The Phoorn's wings could no longer beat against the thinning ether. His breath began to stream like gaseous ivory from his nostrils. Slowly we were losing height, being pulled deeper and deeper into the heart of the whirlwind.

The voice of the Phoorn sounded again in my mind. *We have no strength to escape him . . .*

I prayed that I could die with Oona in my arms. I pushed with all my strength against the clinging membrane, too weak now to reach her. She was holding tight to the scales as the freezing wind sought to dislodge her from the Phoorn.

I was now convinced that Sepiriz, Lobkowitz and the Kakatanawa had all perished. Somehow Ayanawatta continued to play his flute, but I guessed he could not survive for long.

I love you. Father—Ulric—I love you both.

Oona's voice. I saw her turn, seeking me, yearning towards me with her eyes. She could not loose her grip, or she would be torn from the back of the Phoorn. Again I strained against the membrane. It flickered with scarlet and turquoise and a soft pewter brilliance. It did not resist me, but neither did it allow me to break free.

Oona!

From below something roared and spat at us. The whole of the surface erupted, fragmenting into millions of spores which spun away past us into the infinite cosmos. Scarlet and black streamed up at us, as if the whole world exploded. Searing hot air was a sudden wall against the cold. Silence fell.

I heard a distant rumbling. A roaring. I knew what this meant. What shot upwards towards us was magma. Rock as swift and lively as a roaring river and far more deadly. We were directly above an erupting volcano. We would burn to death before the whirlwind destroyed us!

But Oona was pointing excitedly up towards the distant Balance, clearly visible now on the staff that had replaced the black sword. I knew then that this was the original iron which Sepiriz and his people had stolen to make Stormbringer. This was the metal the Kakatanawa had told the Pukawatchi to fashion. She was what whole nations had died to possess. Her magic was the magic of the Cosmic Balance itself. Her power was strong enough to challenge that Balance. Those who mastered her, mastered Fate. Those who did not master her, were mastered by her.

What Oona showed me was not significant at first, but then I realized why she was elated. The bowls that formed the twin weights of the Balance were gradually finding equilibrium.

The boiling air struck hard against Lord Shoashooan's cold turbulence. I saw his face, closer this time, as his teeth snapped at us and his flailing claws grasped and held the Phoorn. The beast beat his wonderful wings helplessly and would surely perish.

But the hot air was consuming Lord Shoashooan. He was col-lapsing in it. Slowly his grip loosened, and he began to wail. I felt my head would burst with the volume. What I had taken for an-other aspect of Lord Shoashooan's strength had been his opposite, conjured from the benign Underworld whose denizens had helped us in the past. A counterforce as powerful as the Lord of Winds, which could only be rising from the core of the Grey Fees.

Shoashooan had weakened himself in his pursuit of us. At last we felt his grip relax, and we were free. And he in turn was now pursued. One great Lord of Winds gave chase to another! We watched the turquoise-and-crimson air, foamy masses of creamy smoke roiling in its wake, as it enclosed and absorbed its filthy op-posite. It purified the Lord of Winds with its grace alone and brought at last, against Lord Shoashooan's will, a kind of uneasy harmony. With the tornado still grumbling from within, the flute's simple tune faded into one single note of resolution.

We stood looking up at the Skrayling Tree, looking up at the great black staff of the Balance, at the cups which must surely be the Grail, which had restored Oona to life. At the central pivot of the Balance Oona had placed the blue jewel of Jerusalem, my ring. The same Templar ring which Elric had carried from

Jerusalem. The ring which resembled our small, ordinary planet, seen from space. The ring which had helped us restore the Balance.

The Kakatanawa resumed their watch, again immobile. The great Phoorn settled near the roots of the tree, and my wife and I dismounted and embraced at last. Almost at once the huge beast curled himself about the base of the tree. He returned peacefully to his stewardship. The roots were already restoring themselves.

At the moment of our embrace, we stood beneath a sharp, blue sky, with a sweet wind blowing surrounded by ruins. The tree grew larger and larger as the Balance grew stronger, until it filled the entire firmament, and the roots were green and fresh again, winding out from the ruined Kakatanawa city, out through the deep, deep ice—

Where the surviving avatars of Gaynor, Klosterheim and their men still moved with weary determination towards us.

The Vikings' eyes stared sightlessly. Their lips moved wordlessly. They held their weapons tightly, the only reality the Vikings could be certain of. It was clear they longed for the release of a slaughtering. They no longer cared how they died.

It was still not over. I looked around for a sword but found nothing. Instead I saw the prone bodies of Elric and White Crow. I saw Prince Lobkowitz, Lord Sepiriz and Ayanawatta, all unarmed, standing together around Bes, the mammoth. The great Phoorn seemed to have immersed himself in the trunk of the tree.

We did not have a weapon among us, and Gaynor and his men were still armed to the teeth. They understood their advantage, because their pace quickened. Like hungry dogs scenting blood, they hurried towards us. Elric and White Crow slowly revived only to become aware of their threatened destruction.

Had I survived so much to see my wife cut down before my eyes? I dug around among the rubble for a sword. There was nothing. Lord Shoashooan had reduced the entire great city to dust.

They were almost on our island. I urged Oona to flee, but she held her ground. Ayanawatta had come to stand with us. His handsome, tattooed features were calm, resolute. He slipped his bone flute from his bag in one fluid movement and placed it to his lips. We watched Gaynor and his men advance across the ice.

As Ayanawatta played, no note issued from the flute itself, but I began to hear a strange, subterranean sound. Groaning, creaking and cracking. A distant rushing. And another eruption of warm air at our feet. Things burst upwards through the shattering ice. They glistened with fresh life.

Gaynor saw them, too. He yelled to his men, instantly understanding the danger, and began to dash towards us, sword drawn. But the fresh, green roots of the Skrayling Oak spread everywhere, smashing up through the ice, overturning great blocks and collapsing back into what was rapidly becoming water once more.

Desperate now, Gaynor persevered. He labored to the edge of the ice, our island shore only a few paces away.

And there he stopped.

Bes the mammoth stood facing him. She shook her tusks, menacing him, all the while her mild eyes regarding him with a terrifying calm.

He turned. Hesitated.

Further up the shore Klosterheim and several of his men leaped to our island as the last of the ice around them melted. Sheets of clear, pale water appeared beneath the winter sky. A great fissure had torn apart the remaining ice sheets and was widening rapidly as Gaynor, trapped between two dangers, still hesitated, not knowing how to avoid defeat. Bes stomped relentlessly towards him, and he was forced back onto the ice. He began to run, slipping and sliding, towards a nearby spur of rock jutting out from the beach.

He almost reached the rock, but his armor and his sword became too heavy for him. He sank as quickly as the ice vanished. He stood up to his waist in black water, raging to survive, roaring out his anger and frustration even as he slipped suddenly beneath the waves and was gone.

Gone. A warm, gentle breeze blew from the south.

I could not believe that angry immortal had simply disappeared. I knew by now that he would never die. Not, at least, until I, too, died.

Oona tugged at my arm. "We must go home now," she said. "Prince Lobkowitz will take us."

Klosterheim and the other survivors looked listlessly at the spot of water where their leader had vanished. Then, turning towards us, the leading Viking shrugged and sheathed his sword. "We have no fight with you. Take our word on it. Let us make our way back to our ship, and we will return to where we belong."

Elric had affection for some of these men. He accepted their offer. "You can sail *The Swan* back to Las Cascadas. And take that disappointed wretch with you." Smiling he indicated a gloomy Klosterheim. "You can tell them what you witnessed here."

One of the tall black warriors laughed aloud. "To spend the rest of our days as reviled madmen? I have seen others cursed with such reminiscences. They die friendless. You'll not come with us, Duke Elric? To captain us?"

Elric shook his head. "I will help you get back to the mainland. Then I have a mind to go with Ayanawatta when he returns to take the Law to his people and fulfill the rest of his destiny. We are old friends, you see. I have some eight hundred years until my dream is ended, and only then shall I know if I had power enough to summon Stormbringer to me in that other world. My curiosity takes me further into this land." He lifted a gloved hand in farewell.

Sepiriz shrugged and spread his hands in gentle acquiescence. "I will find you," he said, "when I need you."

White Crow came close to look directly into Elric's face. "My future does not seem to hold much joy," he said.

"Some," said Elric, staring back. He sighed and looked up at the snowcapped mountains, the silver sky, the few birds which flew in the warm, clean air. "But most of that is in slaughter." He turned away from White Crow as if he could no longer bear to look at him. At that I finally understood that White Crow was neither son nor brother nor nephew nor twin. White Crow was completing his own long dream-journey, part of his apprenticeship, his training as an adept, his preparation for his destiny, to become Sorcerer Emperor of Melniboné. White Crow was Elric himself, in his youth! Each had been moved in his own way by what he saw in the face of the other. Without another word, White Crow returned to stand with Bes. He would be the last Melnibonéan of noble blood to be sent to Kakatanawa for his training. Their city gone, the giants had only one duty, to guard the tree forever.

"It is done at last," said White Crow. "Fate is served. The multiverse will survive. The treasures of the tree have been restored, and the great oak blooms again. I look upon the end of all our histories, I think." He clambered up into the big wooden saddle and goaded Bes towards the lapping water.

None of us tried to stop him as White Crow guided the noble old mammoth into the waves and began to descend until Bes had submerged completely. He turned in the saddle once and raised his bow above his head before he, too, disappeared back into his particular dream, as we all began to return slowly to our own.

"Come," said Lobkowitz. "You'll want to see your children."

nd so another episode in the eternal struggle for the Balance was completed and resolution achieved. How human endeavor has the power to create and make real its most significant symbols I do not know, but I do know that a logical creator might build such a self-sustaining system. In spite of my adventures, my belief in a supreme spirit remains.

Ayanawatta believed strongly in his dream, somehow reinforced rather than contradicted by the Longfellow account, and went on to found the Iroquois Confederacy, a model for the federal system of the United States. Ulric and I worked first for the UN and later for Womankind Worldwide, whose work becomes increasingly important.

Passing without incident from one realm to another, Ulric, Prince Lobkowitz and I returned, traveling chiefly by rail, from Lake Huron to the Nova Scotian coast.

As dreamers, we both experience dreams and we create them. The experience brings us wisdom, which is why such dreams are coveted by dreamthieves. But they place equal value on creative dreams. These can be more volatile and hard to negotiate, let alone control. In the so-called Ghost Worlds, where everything is malleable, one learns to value the power of supernatural logic.

Ulric and I were to know only one more unusual adventure together, but there is no question that our relationship had altered. Our love, our understanding of the value of our public work, was deeper, yet there was an uneasy, rarely mentioned memory. Ulric had, indeed, killed me as I tried to help him in my assumed shape of White Buffalo. And he did almost destroy the Skrayling Tree as a result. These thoughts continue to burden him.

He has other dreams. We do not live in a linear multiverse.

We do not tell a simple history with a beginning, middle and end. We weave instead a tapestry. We depend upon repetition but not upon imitation, which is mere corruption, confirming nothing. Each strand must be new, though the pattern might be familiar.

Gunnar's expedition to America left little to show for itself, unless the destruction of Kakatanawa was an achievement. But a few legends were made and others confirmed. As for Gaynor, we would meet him again in a final adventure.

The strange mathematics of the multiverse, which orders the weft and woof of the great tapestries, is the means by which we order Chaos. But the strict formality of the design demands an adherence to ritual similarly found, for instance, in the Egyptian Book of the Dead. Every word uttered, every step on the destined path must be exact, or that destiny will change. The choreography for such actions is the special skill of Prince Lobkowitz and Lord Sepiriz.

As for Elric of Melniboné, he lived out his dream of a thousand years. How that dream ended and its effect on the von Bek family is the last story still to be told.

Oona, Countess of Bek,
Sporting Club Square,
London, S.W.